THE DRESSMAKER

KATE ALCOTT

sphere

SPHERE

First published in the United States of America in 2012 by Random House, Inc
First published in Great Britain in 2013 by Sphere

All characters and events in this publication, other than those clearly in the public domain, are fictitious and any resemblance to real persons, living or dead, is purely coincidental.

A CIP catalogue record for this book is available from the British Library.

ISBN 978-0-7515-4923-2

Typeset in Sabon by M Rules
Printed and bound in Great Britain by
Clays Ltd, St Ives plc

Papers used by Sphere are from well-managed forests and other responsible sources.

MIX
Paper from
responsible sources
FSC® C104740

Sphere
An imprint of
Little, Brown Book Group
100 Victoria Embankment
London EC4Y 0DY

An Hachette UK Company
www.hachette.co.uk

www.littlebrown.co.uk

Kate Alcott is a journalist who has covered politics in Washington DC, where she currently lives.

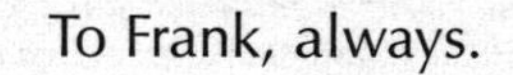
To Frank, always.

Chapter 1

CHERBOURG, FRANCE

APRIL 10, 1912

Tess pulled at the corners of the sheets she had taken straight from the line and tried to tuck them tight under the mattress, stepping back to check her work. Still a bit bunchy and wrinkled. The overseer who ran this house was sure to inspect and sniff and scold, but it didn't matter anymore.

She glanced out the window. A woman was walking by, wearing a splendid hat topped with a rich, deep-green ribbon, twirling a bright-red parasol, her face lively, her demeanor confident and sunny. Tess tried to imagine herself stepping forward so confidently without someone accusing her of behaving above her station. She could almost feel her fingers curling around the smooth, polished handle of that parasol. Where was the woman going?

She gazed back at the half-made bed. No more fantasizing, not one more minute of it.

She walked out into the central hall and stopped, held in place by the sight of her reflection in the full-length gilded mirror at the end of the hall. Her long dark hair, as always, had pulled out of a carelessly pinned bun, even as the upward tilt of her chin, which had so often registered boldness, remained in place. But there was no denying the shameful crux of what she saw: a skinny young girl wearing a black dress and a white apron and carrying a pile of dirty linens, with a servant's cap sitting squarely and stupidly on the top of her head. An image of servitude. She yanked the cap off her head and hurled it at the glass. She was not a servant. She was a seamstress, a good one, and she should be paid for her work. She had been tricked into this job.

Tess dumped the soiled linens down the laundry chute and climbed the stairs to her third-floor room, untying her apron as she went. Today, yes. No further hesitation. There were jobs available, the dockworkers had said, on that huge ship sailing for New York today. She scanned the small room. No valise – the mistress would stop her cold at the door if she knew she was leaving. The picture of her mother, yes. The money. Her sketchbook, with all her designs. She took off her uniform, put on her best dress, and stuffed some undergarments, stockings, and her only other dress into a canvas sack. She stared at the half-finished ball gown draped over the sewing machine, at the tiny bows of crushed white velvet she had so painstakingly stitched onto the ballooning blue silk. Someone else would have to finish it, someone who actually got paid. What else? Nothing.

She took a deep breath, trying to resist the echo of her father's voice in her head: Don't put on airs, he always scolded. You're a farm girl, do your job, keep your head down. You get decent enough pay; mind you don't wreck your life with defiance.

'I won't wreck it,' she whispered out loud. 'I'll make it better.'

But, even as she turned and left her room for the last time, she could almost hear his voice following her, as raspy and angry as ever: 'Watch out, foolish girl.'

The rotting wood planks beneath Lucile's feet were spongy, catching her boot heels as she made her way through the crowd on the Cherbourg dock. She pulled her silver-fox stole snugly around her neck, luxuriating in the plush softness of the thick fur, and lifted her head high, attracting many glances, some triggered by the sight of her brilliantly red hair, others by the knowledge of who she was.

She glanced at her sister walking quickly toward her, humming some new song, twirling a red parasol as she walked. 'You do enjoy playing the blithe spirit, don't you?' she said.

'I try to be an agreeable person,' her sister murmured.

'I have no need to compete; you may have the attention,' Lucile said in her huskiest, haughtiest voice.

'Oh, stop it, Lucy. Neither of us is impoverished on that score. Really, you are cranky lately.'

'If you were presenting a spring collection in New York in a few weeks, you'd be cranky, too. I have too much to worry about with all this talk of women hiking their skirts and flattening their breasts. All you have to do is write another novel about them.'

The two of them started squeezing past the dozens of valises and trunks, brass hinges glowing in the waning light, their skirts of fine wool picking up layers of damp dust turned to grime.

'It's true, the tools of my trade are much more portable than yours,' Elinor said airily.

'They certainly are. I'm forced to make this crossing because I don't have anyone competent enough to be in charge of the show, so I must be there. So please don't be frivolous.'

Elinor closed her parasol with a snap and stared at her sister, one perfect eyebrow arched. 'Lucy, how can you have no sense of humor? I'm only here to wish you bon voyage and cheer you on when the ship departs. Shall I leave now?'

Lucile sighed and took a deep breath, allowing a timed pause. 'No, please,' she said. 'I only wish you were sailing with me. I will miss you.'

'I would like nothing better than to go with you, but my editor wants those corrected galleys back by the end of the week.' Elinor's voice turned sunny again. 'Anyway, you have Cosmo – such a sweetheart, even if he doesn't appreciate poetry.'

'A small defect.'

'He's a dear, and his best gift to you has been a title. Is that too crass? But it is true that he has no literary appreciation.' Elinor sighed. 'And he can be boring.'

'Nonsense.'

'You know it as well as I do. Where is he?'

Lucile was scanning the crowd, searching for the tall, angular figure of Sir Cosmo Duff Gordon. 'This delay is maddening. If anybody can get things operating efficiently and on time, Cosmo can.'

'Of course. That's his job.'

Lucile glanced sharply at Elinor, but she was looking elsewhere, an innocent expression on her face.

Up the hill, away from the shipyard, amid the sprawling brick mansions on the bluffs of the Normandy coast, Tess was marching downstairs to the parlor. Waiting for her was the mistress, a prim Englishwoman with lips so thin they seemed stitched together.

'I want my pay, please,' Tess said, hiding the canvas sack in the folds of her skirt. She could see the envelope waiting for her on the corner table by the door, and began edging toward it.

'You haven't finished my gown for the party, Tess,' the woman said in a more querulous tone than usual. 'And my son could hardly find a towel in the hall closet this morning.'

'He'll find one now.' She was not going back upstairs.

She would never again be backed into that linen closet, fighting off the adolescent son's eager, spidery fingers. That was her envelope; she could see her name written on it, and she wasn't standing around to hear the usual complaints before it was doled out. She moved closer to the table.

'You've said that before, and I'm going upstairs right now to check.' The woman stopped as she saw the girl reaching out for the envelope. 'Tess, I haven't given that to you yet!'

'Perhaps not, but I have earned it,' Tess said carefully.

'Rudeness is not admirable, Tess. You've been very secretive lately. If you pick that up before I give it to you, you have burned your bridges with me.'

Tess took a deep breath and, feeling slightly dizzy, picked up the envelope and held it close, as if it might be snatched away.

'Then I have,' she said. Without waiting for a reply, she opened the heavily ornate front door she would never have to polish again and headed for the docks. After all her dreaming and brooding, the time was now.

The dock was slippery with seaweed. Heart pounding, she pressed into the bustle and chaos around her and sucked into her lungs the sharp, salty air of the sea. But where were the signs advertising jobs? She accosted a man in a uniform with large brass buttons and asked in hesitant French and then urgent English who was in charge of hiring staff for cleaning and cooking on that big new ship.

'You're too late, dear, the servicepeople have all been hired and the passengers will soon be boarding. Bad luck for you, I'm afraid.' He turned away.

It didn't matter how brightly she smiled; her plan was falling apart. Idiot – she should have come down earlier. What now? She gulped back the hollow feeling of not knowing what came next and tried to think. Find families; look for young children. She would be a good nanny. Didn't having seven younger brothers and sisters count as experience? She was ready to go, no trouble at all; all she had to do was find the right person and say the right things and she could get away. She would not, she would *not* be trapped; she would get out.

But no one paid her any heed. An elderly English couple shrank back when she asked if they needed a companion for the trip. When she approached a family with children, offering her services, they looked at her askance, politely shook their heads, and edged away. What could she expect? She must look desperate, tangled hair and all.

'Lucy, look at that girl over there.' Elinor pointed a delicate, polished finger at the frantic Tess. 'My goodness, she's a beauty. Gorgeous, big eyes. Look at her running around talking to people. I think she's trying to get on the ship. Do you think she's running away from something? Maybe the police? A man?'

'I wouldn't know, but I'm sure you'll weave a good story out of it,' Lucy said, waving to Cosmo's approaching figure. He looked, as usual, somewhat detached from his surroundings. Cool eyes, a calm demeanor; always in charge. Following him, at his heels, was a timid-looking messenger.

'Lucile, there is a problem—' Cosmo began.

'I knew it,' Lucile said, her jaw tightening. 'It's Hetty, isn't it?'

'She says she is unable to come. Her mother is ill,' the messenger said. He bent forward almost in nervous homage – as well he might, because Lucile was furious now.

'Tell that girl she can't back out just before we sail. Who does she think she is? If she doesn't board with us, she's fired. Have you told her that?' She glared at the man.

'I have, Madame,' he ventured.

Tess heard the commotion and stopped, arrested by the sight of the two women. Could it be? Yes, one of them wore the same grand hat with the gorgeous green ribbon she had spied from the window; she was right here, idly tapping the ground with that same red parasol.

The other woman's sharp voice jolted her attention away.

'A miserable excuse!' she snapped.

Someone hadn't shown up for the trip, some kind of servant, and this small person with the bright-red hair and crimson lipstick was furious. How formidable she looked. Her strong-boned, immobile face admitted no compromise, and her wide-set eyes looked as if they could change from soft to hard in seconds. There was no softness in them now.

'Who is she?' Tess demanded of a young man attached to the clustered group. Her voice was trembling. Nothing was working out.

'You don't *know*?'

She looked again at the woman, noting how people slowed as they passed, whispering, casting admiring glances. Yes, there was something familiar.

'Oh, my goodness,' she gasped. 'That's Lucile Duff Gordon.'

'Of course. *Couture,* you know. And the other woman is her sister, Elinor Glyn. She's from Hollywood, writes novels. Some quite scandalous, actually.'

Tess barely heard him.This personage bristling with anger was the most famous designer in the world, someone whose beautiful gowns she had seen in the papers, and she was standing only a few feet away. Her chance – this was her chance.

'Lady Duff Gordon, I can't believe I'm actually seeing you,' she burst out, pushing forward. 'I admire you so much – you are so talented. I've seen pictures of your gowns that set me dreaming.' She was babbling, but she didn't care. All she wanted was Lucile's attention.

The designer ignored her.

'I would love to work for you,' she pleaded. 'I know goods. I am a dressmaker, I do very good work; I could be a great help to you.' She thought wildly – what to say next? 'I'm very good at buttonholes – anything you need done. Please—'

'She's desperate, I told you so,' murmured Elinor with a giggle as she straightened her elaborately fashionable hat.

Lucile turned toward Tess. 'Do you know what the job *is*?' she demanded.

Tess hesitated.

'It is as my personal maid. *Now* are you interested?'

'I can do that.' Anything, anything to get on that ship. To be working for Lady Lucile would be an unbelievable opportunity.

'Where do you work now? What do you do?'

'I – work in a home in Cherbourg. And I do dress-making. I have very satisfied clients.'

'A servant of some sort – not a surprise,' Elinor murmured.

Lucile ignored her. 'Your name?'

'Tess Collins.'

'Tessie. Ah, I see.'

'No. *Tess*.'

'As you wish. Can you read and write?'

'Of course!' Tess was indignant.

Lady Duff Gordon's eyes turned appraising at this flash of temper. 'References?'

'I'll have them mailed. Anything you need.'

'From the middle of the Atlantic?'

'There's always a marconigram.' Tess had read about them and hoped she was saying the right thing.

Lucile suddenly tired of the back-and-forth. 'I'm sorry, I know nothing about you,' she said. 'It won't do.' She turned away to talk to Cosmo.

Desperate, Tess had an idea. 'Look, please look,' she

said, pulling open the collar of her dress. 'I made this. I tried to copy the collar of one of your dresses that I clipped out of the newspaper. It's a poor copy, of course, but—'

'Not bad,' murmured Elinor, peering at the collar. It was deftly turned – a crisp linen designed to be worn open or closed, requiring careful stitching. 'Very intricate. Unusual for a servant girl.'

Lucile cast another look in Tess's direction, then fingered the proffered collar. It was one of her best designs. The girl had cut it in perfect proportion to her dress and stitched it by hand; there was not a wrinkle in the fabric. 'You are saying you made this?' she demanded.

'Yes, I did.'

'Who taught you to sew?'

'My mother, who is very skilled.' Tess drew herself up proudly. 'I'm known throughout the county. And I cut my own patterns.'

'Everyone *cuts,* my dear. That just requires a pair of scissors. You mean *design,* I presume.' Lucile reached out without a by-your-leave and lifted the sleeve of Tess's dress, noting the skill of the girl's inset work.

'Yes. I design and I sew. I do everything.'

'Does your employer pay you?'

'Not for dressmaking. But I am good, and I deserve to be paid.' Maybe this was too boastful. She drew in a deep breath and gave it her all. 'I want to work for you. You are the best designer in the world, and I can't believe my good fortune in meeting you. Your gowns are an inspiration – who can design like you? Please give me a chance. You won't be sorry.'

Lucile stared at the girl, her expression unreadable. Something stirred in her eyes as the aides around her fell silent, waiting for what would come next.

'She's probably a bit too independent for you,' Elinor said quietly in an aside. 'You never know. She might not be quite what she purports to be.'

Lucile's expression didn't change, even as a small smile curved her lips. 'Perhaps. But then I could keep my jewellery locked in the ship's safe, couldn't I?' She turned back and addressed herself to Tess. 'You are content with being a maid? I'm offering nothing else.'

'I will do whatever you wish – I just want a chance to prove myself, and work for you.' Yes, yes, she would do anything. She wouldn't daydream or bunch up the sheet corners; she would work and learn and change everything. Tess was having trouble breathing. She felt the hinges of fate creaking, a door opening – or was it closing? Let her like me, she prayed.

'Anything?'

Tess pulled herself straight. 'Anything respectable, none other,' she said.

Lucile's appraising eye traveled the length of the girl's figure, taking in her dark tousled hair, her high, flushed cheekbones and upturned chin, her shabby boots with one broken lace.

'They're going to board us soon. Are you prepared to leave in the next hour or so?' she demanded.

'Yes, I can go immediately.' Tess cut her words sharp and tight. Only one chance, she thought, don't squander it.

The little group around Lucile seemed to be holding its

collective breath. Lucy hesitated one last second. 'All right, you're hired,' she said. 'As a *maid,* you understand.'

Elinor shot her a surprised glance. 'Isn't that a bit impulsive, Lucy?'

Her sister didn't answer, just kept gazing at Tess as if she were peering, unfocused, into the middle distance.

'Thank you – you will never regret it,' Tess said shakily, trying not to wither under Lucile's steady gaze.

'You will need to be dressed for the job, whether you are educated or not.' Lucile was on firm ground again. 'You are to call me Madame. And you'll need a cap.' She nodded toward Cosmo. 'My husband, Sir Cosmo, will take care of the details.'

Tess smiled warily at the tall, thin man with the large, well-tended mustache who stepped forward to talk to her. After asking Tess a few questions, he held a murmured conversation with a White Star Line official. This was, of course, passage only for a servant, so no passport was required. Surely no problem there? They completed their chat with a firm handshake. Tess exhaled so deeply she was dizzy. Yes, the door was opening.

She held on to the rail, following Lady Duff Gordon down slippery steps to a tender that looked grubby and a bit frail. An officious man in a White Star uniform had told them all that the ship was too large for the shallow Cherbourg harbor, so into the tender they were to go. How big was it, that it had caused another vessel to snap its mooring lines on the way from Southampton? Tess peered into the thin gray fog, eager for her first look.

The fog lifted. And there it was, looming so high, so proud and separate, it seemed to rule the sea, not the other way around. Four huge smokestacks reaching gracefully toward the sky. Nine decks, and Tess felt her neck aching from the effort as she counted them. No wonder it was called *Titanic*. The people scrambling to hook the tender to the ship were all out of proportion, like busy ants.

A sailor reached out a hand to Tess, coaxing her onto the gangplank. She stepped up, concentrating now on putting one foot in front of the other. It was happening – no going back now. Goodbye to Sussex, goodbye to the prune-faced mistress and her randy son, goodbye to all. Even to home, to mother, to the brothers and sisters she might never see again. Her heart quivered; she firmly took the next step.

She was at the top. A couple up ahead, a man with a beautifully sculpted chin and a woman wrapped in a white fur cape, took one step onto the ship and paused to embrace. How nice, how spontaneous. The man – his veined hands showing that he wasn't as young as he had at first appeared – suddenly twirled the woman in a deft movement that ended in her swooning, laughing, into his arms. The two skipped lightly away to scattered applause. Were they entertainers?

Right in front of her was a man with a handsome, restless face dominated by a strong, molded chin and a slender aquiline nose. His hands were jammed into the pockets of an immaculate tan cashmere coat. His eyes seemed clouded. By unhappiness? His hair was graying at the temples; probably in his forties, she guessed. A man of business, constantly checking his watch. He seemed enveloped in fog, and did not react to the small performance in front of him, just stood a moment watching the happy pair with what she imagined was a certain wistfulness.

'Hurry along, miss.' The man behind her had a hard, impatient voice. A quick glance back; he looked very important.

'Welcome, Mr. Ismay,' said an officer, reaching past her to shake the man's hand. 'It's an honor to have the chairman of White Star on board. I can promise you a speedy trip to New York.'

Ismay mumbled something; Tess thought he looked like nothing so much as a tall, bony crane. She quickened her step to get out of his way.

Still on the tender, Lucile and Elinor watched the girl ascend. 'I don't think you have servant material there, Lucy,' said Elinor with a chuckle. 'She didn't even wait for the great Lady Duff Gordon to precede her. I love that.'

'I'll put her to work on hems and buttons. If she doesn't do a proper job, she'll be gone the minute we get to New York.'

'You've got some ulterior motive – I know you,' Elinor said, giving her sister a brief hug. 'Keeps things interesting. I'll keep writing about illicit passion and you keep designing the clothes a kept woman would wear.'

'Elinor—'

'Oh, I know, they're for dignified women and stars of all

sorts. Wasn't I good to come out to the ship to see you off?'

'You just wanted to see the *Titanic* up close.' Lucile smiled, returning the hug. She frowned. 'You're much too thin – I can count the bones in your rib cage. You haven't had any surgically removed, have you?'

'Such nonsense. You know as well as I do that only a few crazy women have done that, and I'm not among them.'

'You aren't wearing a corset.'

'Well, there you are. I've given up whalebone. Good luck in New York, and hurry back.' Elinor's voice went from gentle to teasing. 'Madame.'

'It gives me the proper respect,' Lucile retorted.

'Just don't start believing it.'

'I suppose.' Slightly abstracted, Lucile gazed up at the hurrying figure of the young housemaid, who was now at the top of the gangplank.

'You're focusing on that girl, dear. Say goodbye to your loving sister.'

'Oh, hush.' Lucile laughed and planted a bright-red kiss on Elinor's cheek, then turned to go.

Tess resisted staring too closely at the array of important people moving to their cabins in first class; Mother would be mortified. She had been taught manners, after all. Don't gape. But oh, what a fantasy this was. Peek sideways at the gloriously attired women – how she wished she could stroke some of the crunchy silks, examine the design of the intricately woven shawls – and at the men in high collars who looked like rulers of the world. Act like this was all nothing new, just life as usual. Pretend to belong.

'Most of the first-class passengers have no reason to be on this particular crossing, other than to be able to boast that they were on the *Titanic*'s maiden voyage,' Madame said as Tess helped her unpack. 'But it gives them a lovely little tidbit to drop at a New York dinner. It hints at a flexible, even adventurous spirit.' She smiled. 'As long as the faucets are gold-plated, which they are.'

Tess started to reply, but Lucile's finger had flown to her lips. 'Listen,' she commanded.

And Tess heard for the first time the slow rumble, the vibration, of a great ship's engines gathering momentum far below where she stood. Could they watch the departure? she asked timidly.

'There's nothing special about it, I'm afraid.' But Lucile led Tess back outside, where they watched the land recede. One more stop in Ireland, and the *Titanic*'s first voyage out onto the vast sea would truly begin. Madame pointed out a young woman with careful, tiny curls framing her pale skin and a strikingly handsome man attached to her side, the two of them in a seemingly joyful bubble. A couple due soon to be married; a very important society wedding was planned in Newport Beach, she said.

'But then you have people like that,' she said, pointing a delicate finger at a cheerful, round woman waving heartily toward the shore. 'Mrs. Brown. Her money comes from a place called Leadville, in Colorado. Gold-mining interests. No breeding.' She peered downward at the sound of shouts and cheers from steerage. 'Poor uneducated souls – they've sold everything and are heading for what they think are new lives in America. Not likely, unless they learn to wash up.'

Later, when Tess took her satchel down into steerage, hunting for the cot that had been assigned to her, she paused, hunching down under the low ceiling, looking around the crowded room. The air was close – a mixture of smells pungent with garlic, sliced tongue, smoke, and even urine. A man in gray pants was shaving, two children watching him. An old woman with thinning hair sat rocking back and forth, moaning about her stomach. Two boys, tossing a ball to each other. Women gossiping, babies crying. The girl on the cot next to hers gave a friendly smile and offered an apple. All this life, and few would see the upper decks. Nor would those on the upper decks ever see them. But they *were* headed for new lives, just as she was.

She made her way back upstairs as quickly as she could. If she could, she'd take them all with her, but this was her time now. She would stay down here only to sleep, not one minute more. Only when the voices and sounds of crying children faded into murmurs curling up through the decks and polished brass of this amazing ship did she pause and breathe.

Everything was dazzling. Warming to Tess's eagerness, Lucile continued the next day to point out quite casually the stellar passengers: here, an owner of a railway; there, an aide to the United States' President Taft; oh, and there, a famous theatrical producer – she knew them all. Together they strolled among the huge reception rooms, with their elaborately carved chairs, rich mahogany tables, and gilded mirrors, until Lucile announced that she was bored and ready for a nap. No need, then, to iron or clean or run errands? Tess asked quickly if she might wander about a little on her own.

'Go ahead, I'll be on deck at teatime. Good luck with your exploring; even the ship's stewards don't seem to know where everything is.'

Alone now, Tess peeked in the doorway of a large room with mahogany walls and strange machines that looked like mechanical horses. She had heard of them; they were exercise animals, run by electricity. She glanced back and forth. There was no one around. She shouldn't venture in, but this was all so intriguing. She tiptoed inside, wandering the room, touching the horses sheathed in steel plate, debating whether she had the nerve to pull herself up onto one of them. They looked so shiny and cold. What would it be like? She saw the switches. She could even turn one on if no one was here to see.

Then she saw the camel. A camel! She had always wondered what it would be like to ride one. Cautiously, she hoisted one foot into a stirrup, grabbed her skirt, and pulled herself onto the machine. She reached for the switch, then froze.

'Well, I see you are ready for a little exercise.' It was a man's voice. 'Women are far too shy about using athletic equipment, which is such nonsense.' She looked up and saw the handsome man with graying hair she had observed on the gangplank. He seemed more energetic now. He was wearing a blue turtleneck sweater, and although he looked less somber, she suspected that the shadows she saw beneath his eyes never disappeared entirely.

'I hope I'm not doing any harm, but I've not seen machines like this,' she said, flustered as she realised what a sight she presented. Her legs straddled the contraption like those of a simple trollop. Good Lord, what if Madame wandered in here right now. But she wouldn't, surely. And the man didn't seem shocked enough to order her out.

'Nor have most of us,' he said. 'Now, take this electric camel you've become so fond of. What does it need humps for to store water, with the wonders of electricity? Shall I turn it on?'

Tess stared down at him, saw the amused light in his eyes, and tightened her grip. 'All right,' she said a bit breathlessly.

He flicked the switch. Suddenly she was moving back and forth, then up and down, and she couldn't help laughing at the absurdity of it all as she tightened her legs against the camel's sleek flanks of polished oak.

'Is it like riding a real horse?'

'Oh no, nothing like it. I love riding at home.'

'That kind of saddle?'

'Bareback. It makes me feel free.' A sudden flash of galloping along the back roads at home made this venture suddenly seem silly. 'How is this exercise?'

'Your heart and lungs benefit from the movement – that's the theory, anyway.'

Someone was sure to come in soon. 'Turn it off now,' she said.

'It can go faster. Do you want to go faster?'

'No, no.' She glanced at his face, a little alarmed. 'Don't tease me, please.'

He smiled and turned off the camel, then reached out his arms. 'May I help you down?' he asked.

'No, thank you, I can do it myself.' Quickly, before he could say anything more, she slid off the machine, smoothing her skirts.

'You're totally proper now, don't worry,' he said. 'Would you like a little tour?' He offered his arm quite naturally, as if it were a perfectly ordinary thing to do. His mood had lightened, and it was infectious. How good it felt to laugh. Here was the squash court; do you play? And here the Turkish baths, and over there – he pointed – the fanciest of swimming pools. 'A necessity when surrounded by water, wouldn't you say? Nothing too good for the upper classes.'

'I'll get there someday,' she burst out.

'Are you sure you want to?' he asked with what seemed a hint of true curiosity.

She felt brave enough to give a true answer. 'I'll work hard – it's easy in America.' Embarrassed now, she glanced at him and then away. 'Thank you for this,' she said.

'You've done me the courtesy of being here, and I am delighted to be your guide.'

The men she knew never talked that way. 'You know I'm not supposed to be here, don't you?'

'I've seen you with Lady Duff Gordon,' he said gently. 'I'm an American, from the very brash city of Chicago, and not as respectful of British social niceties as I should be. I enjoyed it.'

'So did I,' she said.

'I hope you have a pleasant trip.'

She glanced quickly at a clock. She was late. 'I've got to go,' she said and hurried out, scrambling by the machines, almost tripping. The tea, the tea. She mustn't forget the cream. As she rushed to the ship's kitchen, she found herself thinking about the man's strong hands and wished she had let him lift her down. She would have liked to feel them. Idiot, what a thought to have. One of these days, she decided, she would find out what squash was – and learn to play it. Lord, what was his name? How could she not have asked?

Lucile watched as the girl moved quickly toward her across the deck, precariously balancing on a silver tray a Limoges teapot, a delicate porcelain cup, a small pitcher of cream, and a white sugar bowl.

'It's a miracle you made it,' Lucile said as Tess deposited the tray in front of her. 'These are the thinnest china cups, as I asked?'

'Yes, Madame. I made sure.' In truth, she had almost forgotten in the busy ship's kitchen.

'Tea tastes like dishwater in anything else.'

Tess poured a cup and handed it to her, still a bit flushed.

'How were your explorations?'

'Oh, very nice. I saw so much. There's an exercise room.'

'So I heard. No self-respecting woman would indulge in such nonsense.'

Tess flushed deeper.

'Take all this.' Lucile waved at the tea service. 'I've had enough. I want you to return to the cabin and iron the blue gown I left out for dinner tonight. Be back in a quarter of an hour, and we'll walk the promenade again.'

Tess nodded eagerly, gathering the silver and loading the tray. Strolling the promenade with Lady Duff Gordon was as close as she could get to the designer's rarefied world, and to see such people as John Jacob Astor – the richest man on board, a multimillionare – smiling and chatting with Lucile was a not-to-be-missed experience. She must hurry. She began making her way across the deck, slightly distracted by the sight of two polished men in knickers pushing wood tiles across a painted board. A game of some sort – what was it? Was it squash?

A child's ball rolled in her path. She tripped, tried to right herself, and went crashing, cream flying from the silver pitcher, small cubes of sugar skittering across the deck, still-hot tea burning her fingers. Women seated nearby jumped up, pulling back their skirts from the mess.

'I'm so sorry,' she said, appalled. Somebody tittered.

Madame was standing now, looking down at her coldly. 'Get this cleaned up and get back to my cabin. Immediately.' She turned and walked away.

Tess took the linen napkins on the tray and started mopping up the cream. She'd done it now.

'Nasty piece, that woman. Never mind, if you'll let me, I'll take care of it.'

She looked up and saw a sailor frowning down at her. He was about her age, with a strong, tanned face and sturdy arms. He was gripping a mop. His eyes were kind, and as blue as the sea.

She put everything back on the tray, stood and brushed herself off. 'That's very kind of you,' she said, holding her head high. She wouldn't be humiliated – no more of that. She would stop those titters, and none would see tears from her.

'That's the girl, show them who you are,' the sailor said gently.

And who might that be, Tess thought. The way out of this was to put on her mask, achieve some semblance of invisibility. She wanted to glance back at the sailor, to thank him silently, but she resisted the impulse. Yet she felt his respect as she walked away.

'Your clumsiness was inexcusable.' Lucile's voice was like a hammer hitting iron.

'I know it was, Madame, and I am sorry. I picked it all up – nothing was broken, though there was a chip in the cup—'

'If we were on land, I'd fire you on the spot.'

'It will never happen again, I promise.'

'You promised competence, and I'm not seeing any. But I can't just throw you overboard, can I?'

'I hope not.'

The side of Lucile's mouth twitched.

'The truth is, I would've done anything to sail with you,' Tess said. 'I've admired you for a long time, and you've done things I only dream about. If you had needed a chimney sweep, I would've found a way to be one.'

'I wanted a maid.'

'I'm not a good maid; I don't want to be a maid.' Oh God, she could hear her father telling her to shut her mouth, be obedient. But she might as well get on with it and share the plain truth. 'I went out to service early and I hated it, and all I wanted to do was sew. I'm sorry, I admire you enormously. I just don't know how—'

'To do your job properly,' Lucile finished sharply. She stared at Tess. 'Isn't that right?'

'With all proper respect, it depends on the job.' Tess prayed that her words didn't come across as insolent.

Another twitch of the mouth. 'You don't want to be a maid? Here—' Lucile beckoned Tess over to the desk, where she had laid out the cut pieces for a wool jacket. It wasn't an important piece; if the girl messed it up, it would not be a significant loss. 'Prove yourself. Assemble these without a pattern. The stitching must be hand-done. I will be back in an hour to see how you are doing.'

'Yes, Madame.' Tess picked up a piece of the wool as Lucile left the room. It was loosely woven, a delicate plaid of copper and green – quite fine material, better than she had ever worked with. She must be careful. No, she *would* be careful; this was no stupid teacup. Her head bent forward; her fingers began their precision work. She was breathing better now.

Lucile picked up the completed jacket and held it at arm's length, a frown on her face. She studied it carefully as Tess nervously bit her lip.

'Well, you're obviously determined to prove yourself,' she said finally, fingering the jacket. Tess had tucked the darts perfectly, which wasn't easy to do on a patterned fabric. 'This is a reasonably good job. Meticulous stitching.' She cast a studying glance at Tess, then folded the jacket and tucked it into her trunk. 'Perhaps you have the makings of a seamstress. You might not be dusting bureaus all your life.'

Just the hint of a promise, that's all. But it sent a shiver of relief down deep in her heart. Lord, thank you. If there had been any more talk of dumping her over the side of the ship, she would have jumped on her own.

Lucile glanced at a small jeweled clock on her dressing table. 'That's enough talk about sewing for the moment. Get my dress out, will you, dear? It's almost time for dinner.'

Tess flew to obey as Lucile began rummaging in her jewellery box. 'Did I not bring them?' she murmured fretfully to herself. 'Where are they?'

'Can I help, Madame?' Tess asked.

'Ah, here they are.' Lucile pulled out a small bag of

midnight-blue velvet, opened it, and shook its contents onto the dressing table. Earrings. She picked up one and held it to her ear, facing Tess. 'Beautiful, aren't they?'

'Yes, they are.' Tess was fascinated. She had never seen anything quite like these. Three pale-blue stones, one below the other, all shimmering with inner light, separated by tiny diamonds and what she thought were sapphires. 'What are they?' Tess asked shyly.

'Moonstones from Ceylon, very fashionable.' Lucile fastened the earring in her ear and gently moved her head. The stones danced and glowed. 'They call this the traveler's stone,' she said. 'It's supposed to protect against the dangers of travel, which is total nonsense, of course. But it sells jewellery, I suppose.' She fastened the second earring, then reached for her ever-present lipstick.

This was her cue to go. 'Good night, Madame, I hope you have a nice dinner,' Tess said as she turned to leave, pulling the door closed behind her.

That night, back down in the claustrophobic quarters of steerage, amid the whimpers of children and the snores of their parents, she slipped into restless sleep, the kind where memory flowed like water through her dreams.

The gravel was crunching under the landlord's heavy step as he circled her.

'How old?'

'Twelve,' her father said, twisting his cap in field-

weathered hands. The cow had died yesterday. Diseased. No milk now for the younger children.

'Her teeth?'

'They're good.'

'I can chew with no problem, sir.'

'Don't speak unless spoken to, girl.'

'Yes, sir.'

'You'll do housework. Hard work. Ready for that?'

'Yes, sir.'

Her dream was getting foggy, but her mother's crying from inside the house had become louder. Her father's hands were almost tearing the cap apart.

'She'll do.'

Then her mother was there, grabbing her by the arm, pulling her back into the house. 'She's not a horse,' she shouted.

They were together now, in the bedroom. Her mother grabbed a threaded needle by the bedside and folded it into her hand.

'You see this? Maybe you have to go out to service right now, but I have taught you to sew. It will be your way out of here. Stand straight, be proud.'

Tess awoke with a start. In reality, there had been no fog. And how different the messages from her mother and father.

'I hear your little maid took a tumble on the deck today,' Cosmo said as he and Lucile prepared for bed after dinner.

'Caused a dreadful mess. Some sailor came to her rescue?'

Lucile shrugged. 'Yes, ridiculous. But I rather like her.'

'May I ask why?'

'I don't know if you would understand.'

'Try me.'

'It isn't important. Maybe there's something there, maybe nothing.'

'You haven't pushed her wearing a cap.'

'She's terrible as a maid. I don't know why I should bother.'

'So you're applying that famous costuming eye of yours to a new blank canvas?'

'My dear Cosmo, she jumps to do my bidding, whatever it is. If the cost of that is forgetting a servant's cap, that's fine with me.'

'Something's going on in your head. To be continued, I presume.' He yawned, hoisting himself into bed, his silk pajamas making a swooshing sound as he slid between silk sheets. 'When you're ready, of course.'

Lucile said nothing, leaning closer to the mirror above the vanity, dabbing cold cream onto her lips, removing her crimson lipstick with a steady hand.

'Tess, find my gold silk in that jumble and press it for dinner, please.' Lucile pointed to one of her larger trunks when Tess reported for duty the next morning. 'You can do that without scorching it, I trust?'

'I would never harm your gowns, Madame,' Tess

answered, flushing. She opened the lid of the trunk and gently began pulling out the clothes – the shimmering, beautiful fabrics that filled the massive trunk in Stateroom A-20. She plunged her hands in deeper, shivering at the light silky touch of the fabrics. How could she describe it? They were the consistency of foaming cream. Fabrics she had never seen – delicate as cobwebs, silvery, gold, some as blue as the deepest water, all artfully twisted and looped and draped. This was heaven!

'You seem a bit overcome,' Lucile said, amused.

'They look so floaty and simple. But the structure is wonderful.'

'I make them to mold to a moving body. You can see that, can you?'

'Oh, yes.'

'So your mother taught you to sew?'

Tess nodded, and spoke proudly. 'We worked hard together, cutting, piecing, sewing.'

'What did you make?'

'A shirt for a landowner, a dress for a wedding. A child's christening gown. All things.'

'Quite admirable. But it didn't free her, did it?'

'There were many babies.'

'Ah, the universal trap. And how did you avoid it?'

'We were excited about a seamstress job in Cherbourg; we had friends there. Mother wanted me to escape the village boys.' And her father had known all along it was a servant job; she was sure of it.

Lucile smiled, and, tentatively, Tess smiled back.

'A smart woman, your mother.'

'I promised her when I got my chance I would make the best of it.' She was setting up the iron now, testing it. Not too hot; this was familiar work. The gold gown caressed her fingers, slipping gently onto the board.

'And that's what you're doing now.'

'Yes, ma'am.'

'Madame.'

'Yes, Madame.' Remember this, she warned herself silently. Truly, if Lady Duff Gordon wanted to be called Your Highness, she would happily do so.

Lucile gazed at her thoughtfully. 'My dear, here is lesson number one for using opportunity: waste no time on false humility. Tell the world about your achievements; don't wait for someone else to do it. Did you know I was the first designer to use live models for fashion shows?'

'No, Madame,' Tess replied. The gown was done. Carefully, she hung it on a silk-covered hanger, a bit dazzled by Lucile's relaxed, almost confiding tone.

'Well, now you do,' Lucile said. 'You gain confidence by doing what no one else has done. Or what no one else wants to do.'

Tess couldn't help it; the words slipped out. 'Like dropping teapots?'

Lucile laughed. 'I think you and I will get along fine. Now I'd like you to write a letter for me so I can check out your penmanship.'

'It's very good,' Tess said with a cautious smile.

'Good girl. You've absorbed today's lesson.'

By noon, Tess was free to seek out the fresh air of the deck. A fine morning all around. She found herself making a mental report to her Mother: I got past yesterday's disaster, Mother, and Madame and I are actually *talking*. Surely that's a positive sign. Her reverie was interrupted by shouts from the boys playing tag on the deck and the girls giggling nearby, jumping rope.

'Miss?'

Startled, she realised that a sad-faced man in a rumpled black suit was addressing her. Holding each of his hands was a small, wiggling boy.

'My son, here' – he pushed forward one child – 'has something to say to you. Edmond, speak up.'

The child looked at Tess with imploring eyes. *'Je suis désolé,'* he whispered.

'My sons don't speak English,' the man said apologetically. 'But Edmond knows his ball was what made you stumble yesterday, and he is sorry. His favorite toy, his spinning top, was lost over the side of the ship and he was trying something new. You do speak French, I hope?'

Tess nodded, touched by his courteous formality. This was Mr. Hoffman, someone had said. A widower with two small boys. He kept to himself but was devoted to his children.

'Ce n'est pas grave,' she said to the child, and saw the look of relief in his eyes. Edmond smiled at her as his brother wrapped himself around his father's pants leg, peeking at her. Mr. Hoffman nodded approvingly, and seemed at a loss for what to say next. 'Edmond and

Michel, they are usually good boys,' he said. 'Again, please, we are sorry.' And then he turned on his heel, the children hurrying at his side, vanishing into the ship.

Teatime, again.

'The tea isn't quite hot enough, Tess.' Madame's voice held a touch of testiness. 'And the cake is dry.'

Tess instantly reached for the cup. 'I'll get that fixed right now,' she said.

'Also, tell the kitchen crew to send out some fresh cakes.'

'Yes, Madame.'

'And if there aren't any, what will you do?'

Tess hardly missed a beat. 'Bake them myself,' she said.

Lucile smiled. 'That's the spirit. Forget the tea. Let's walk the promenade.'

'I see you watching me, Tess,' she said casually as they strolled. 'What do you see?'

Tess flushed. 'You seem regal sometimes.'

Lucile laughed and started to respond, but abruptly stopped walking. Advancing toward them was a small group of chattering men and women, all focused on a small, slender brunette in their midst, a striking young woman wearing a casually cut shirtwaist of white linen and a bright-red jersey skirt that swung briskly back and forth. On her head was a small cloche hat. People turned and stared, some whispering.

'What is *she* doing on this ship?' Lucile muttered.

'Who is she?' Tess asked as they walked by. She did not miss the frozen smiles the two women exchanged.

'Another one of those milliners who design ridiculous costumes and think they know couture. She's trying to get attention for something she calls sportswear, which is just slapping together mismatched outfits like the one she was wearing.' Lucile was walking more rapidly now, heading back to her stateroom. Tess rushed to keep up.

Lucile pushed open the stateroom door, letting it slam against the wall, startling Cosmo, who had been sitting peacefully in a chair, smoking his pipe.

'That woman upstart from Manchester who steals my ideas is on the ship,' she said.

'No need to get upset,' Cosmo replied. 'She hasn't even a crown at her disposal to open a shop. She's no competition—'

'No competition? She's working this crowd for all the attention and contacts she can get. Just like that other upstart, the one they call Chanel.' Lucile pulled off her bracelet and threw it onto the dressing table, barely missing the mirror. The diamonds hit with a clatter that made Tess wince.

Cosmo remained calm. He took a long puff on his pipe. 'Lucy, you are top quality,' he said. 'You are *the* Lady Duff Gordon, and everyone on this ship knows no other designer can touch you. Now calm down.'

Only then did Lucile seem to remember Tess's presence.

'Sorry for this peek behind the veil, my dear,' she said. 'Even the regal can get blindsided. There are always people out to get you in my business, something you might as well learn now as later. I've fought for what I have—' She glanced at Cosmo. 'With the support of my dear husband, of course.'

'My wife, as usual, is being a bit flamboyant,' he said evenly. 'Really, dear, you are much too agitated.'

It was as if they were exchanging familiar lines, like actors in a play, and Tess was their audience.

'Of course. I'm a successful woman, with everything I've ever wanted. And I intend it to stay that way.'

'Nicely said.' Cosmo put his pipe down in the ashtray. 'Now I'm going to check and see if we are at the captain's table tonight. That would please you, I'm sure.'

Lucile gave him a bright smile. 'Lovely, dear.'

The tense atmosphere in the room was easing, and Tess felt that she could breathe again. She stood silently as Cosmo smiled in that serene, detached way of his, pecked his wife on the cheek, picked up his glasses, and left the room.

'You have to humor them, you know.' Lucile sighed lightly as the door closed. 'Men can be boring, but they are necessary. One needs to learn to work around them. Don't you think so?'

There was no casual answer, not with the gap between their stations. Tess stayed quiet.

Lucile walked over to the dressing table, picked up her bracelet, and casually tossed it into her jewellery box. 'You didn't answer me,' she said.

'I wouldn't know, Madame,' Tess finally said.

'Why not? Are you saying you've had no experience with men?'

'Not much.'

'Oh, come now, Tess. What about those village boys your mother warned you away from?' Lucile was opening a gold compact filled with powder, and Tess could see her hand shaking slightly.

'I'm sorry about the other designer,' she said. 'Surely she's no threat to you.'

'Everybody, at some point or another, is a threat,' Lucile said, patting powder lightly across her nose and cheekbones. 'That's why I must keep them all on their toes. It's an act, Tess. And it has worked so far.' She looked up, her eyes suddenly almost watery. 'I know what you want, and I'm going to try to help you get there. But it takes more than talent.'

'Thank you,' Tess said.

'So when will I get those references you promised?' Lucile asked abruptly, turning back to her dressing table, reaching now for a bottle of crimson nail polish.

'References?' Tess could only imagine the anger of the mistress of the house she had fled in Cherbourg, who would certainly have nothing good to say about her. References? There were none. Surely Madame had sensed that.

Lucile looked up from dabbing lacquer onto her nails and laughed. 'You should see your face, Tess. Don't worry, I'm not interested in references – I was just playing with you. Tell me more about your life. I'm curious – not many a young woman would have jumped to leave her country on a minute's notice as fast as you did. Why?'

'I actually planned it. For a long time.'

'Were you running away from something?' Lucile asked lightly.

'Just cleaning closets and toilets. And not getting paid for my real work.'

'Any regrets?'

'Absolutely none.' Tess said this with such fervor that Lucile laughed again.

'Well, that's good, because my brain is busy cutting you into pattern pieces. What do you think of that? We're going to stitch a new Tess Collins together. Maybe we'll find a way to hone those sewing skills of yours.'

'I will do my best, truly.'

'I'm quite sure you will.' Lucile covered a yawn with her hand. 'Now if you don't mind, as soon as this polish dries I'm going to take a short nap.'

Tess couldn't stop thinking about their exchange afterward, examining her memory for holes. Had she read Madame correctly? It seemed a promise had been made; surely she hadn't let her own hopes read too much into Lucile's words. But she felt it; it was there, a benevolent mood. And when Madame informed the purser that she wanted Tess's room moved up from the E deck to the A deck? It was to keep her available for longer hours, of course, but what a thrill it was to hear the news. She ran down the stairs to steerage, to the narrow bunk – only one of many crammed together – where she had tucked her few possessions under the mattress. She squeezed past a man coughing thickly into a dirty handkerchief and shut her ears to the high-pitched bickering of two women fighting over a blanket. She inhaled deeply, defiantly. She was breathing in the rank odors of this dark, windowless place for the last time.

'You're leaving us?' the girl in the next cot said, a hint of disappointment in her tone. 'Didn't see much of you, but you're my age and I thought we could talk every now and then. I'm going to my uncle's in a place called the Bowery. Know anything about it? I'll work in his saloon, but he says it's respectable in America. I've still got some apples. Share one?'

Tess shook her head and smiled. 'I can't now, but maybe later.'

'Oh, I don't think once you go upstairs you'll ever come back down here.'

It was true, of course. Tess felt warm colour in her cheeks. 'Goodbye,' she said. 'Maybe we'll meet in New York.'

APRIL 14, 1912

The day was glorious. Madame was napping again in the late afternoon, and Tess luxuriated in her new access to the first-class deck. She was allowed to sit on Madame's deck chair and watch the promenade of privileged people as they strolled by, laughing and chatting, people whose names she should learn. She had never been in a place where everyone seemed on holiday, and if she wanted to stay in their world she had to educate herself.

And then, strolling toward her, she saw John Jacob Astor and his wife. Such an elegant pair! The long, tapered fingers of Mrs. Astor's left hand rested gently in the crook of her husband's arm and her face was tipped toward the lowering sun, as if basking in its light. Tess couldn't take her eyes off them, mesmerised by this first look at what shipboard clothing was for the very, very rich. He wore immaculately creased trousers and a mohair cardigan over a crisp shirt and tie. She, on the other hand, gave little quarter to such casualness – her pale-green gown of cord silk, so perfect with her glowing skin and soft chocolate-brown hair, drew envious glances from other women strollers. The men passing by nodded greetings, some casting equally envious glances at Mr. Astor. 'He bagged quite a trophy out of that messy divorce scandal,' one murmured to another.

Some time later, in the first glow of what was clearly going to be a spectacular sunset, she copied their stroll across the deck, trying to imitate Mrs. Astor's swanlike glide. The other passengers had all disappeared back into their staterooms to prepare for the evening. How had that lucky woman floated so effortlessly? Tess tried, but couldn't quite rein in her own hurried stride.

She heard a chuckle and glanced over her shoulder. A sailor was watching. And, yes, he was the same one who had quietly mopped up when she spilled the tea. Tall, about her own age, somewhat thin, even with those sturdy shoulders. His hair was unruly, but swept aside with careless confidence. And his eyes were just as warm and alert as she remembered – the kind of eyes that didn't miss much. They were indeed as blue as the sea.

'Not bad, but you'd do best walking your own way,' he said. 'Don't want to fall on your nose, do you?'

Tess lifted her chin high. 'No chance of that,' she said, adding, 'I do thank you for cleaning up the mess I made the other day.'

'You handled it well. Walked away quite proper, and no giggles in your wake.'

'My mother's advice was always to hold my head up.'

He nodded. 'First time you let it hang, somebody hammers it down further. Don't be fooled by these people; they're just rich show-offs.'

'Mrs. Astor has true grace,' Tess countered.

'Maybe she does, but so do you,' he said gently, studying her face. 'You just don't know it.' He stepped forward and crooked his arm. 'Shall we stroll?' he asked, half teasingly.

With only an instant of hesitation, she accepted the invitation. They walked a few paces, alone on that deck as the brilliant sky turned orange and gold, and then, laughing, he coaxed her into a skip. A bubble of pleasure filled her throat. She could release herself for this, for just a few seconds, couldn't she?

Only a moment, a quick moment. When they stopped, he put a finger to his lips. 'Good day, ma'am,' he said, his voice lively with humor. 'See? You can play, too. And I'll never tell.' He headed back to work, whistling as he bent to pick up a heavy coil of rope, then throwing it over his shoulder.

He's a village boy, Tess told herself as she leaned against the railing and watched the dance of light on the water. A seagoing version, with a more jaunty spirit than most. And quite beautiful eyes.

She stood there for a long time, mesmerised by the expanse of limitless water reaching to a fiery red horizon. She was filled with yearning – for what, she wasn't sure. But if she listened she could still hear the seductive, melancholy whistle of the trains that had wound their way out of the valley and off to the larger world when she was a child. She had always wanted to be on one of them. Most people had pursed their lips, either disapprovingly or angrily, when she talked about going away. Thank goodness she realised early, somehow, that they were mostly afraid. And never, never was she going to let herself be afraid.

Tess ate dinner alone in her cabin, listening to the faint music of the ship's orchestra as the musicians played in the first-class dining saloon. Around ten, she went out on deck for a stroll under the stars, enjoying the solitude, although unable to resist peeking into the dining room. How huge it was, the width of the entire ship, she had been told. The walls and the graceful pillars were a creamy white; the dining chairs covered in a sumptuous emerald-green velvet. Wineglasses sparkled in the glow of the slender white lamps on each table, their light reflected back again through the tall, arched windows that opened onto D deck. How beautiful it was. All those confident, wealthy men and women, most of them in evening dress, laughing, lifting glasses filled with brandy. She found herself trying to piece together their stories.

There was that couple that had boarded ahead of her, sitting by themselves, heads close, murmuring. They were dancers, Madame had told her – Jean and Jordan Darling – yes, lithe, beautiful, coming home to New York for a Broadway play and, everyone said, genuinely in love. 'A little past their prime,' Madame declared matter-of-factly. 'I've dressed her for several shows, but I suspect she can't afford me anymore.' And there was that handsome man in the tan coat she had met in the gymnasium. In evening dress, he was just leaving the captain's table, which meant that he, too, must be important. His name, Madame had told her when describing the more important personages on board, was Jack Bremerton. 'A Chicago millionaire. No one quite knows how he made his fortune,' she said. 'In banking, or something equally shady. Several wives; rumor is, he's leaving the current one.'

A dining-room steward carrying a tray of glasses suddenly shoved past Tess, pushing her off balance. He stumbled, the tray falling from his hands with a tremendous clatter. At that moment the chairman of the White Star Line strode around the deck corner, head turned to talk to one of the ship's officers. In evening dress, he looked more like a bony crane than ever. The tray crashed to the floor, splattering brandy onto Bruce Ismay's clothes as the glasses smashed into fragments on the deck.

'It was her fault, sir,' the steward said, thinking fast,

pointing to Tess. 'She splatted a whole tea service on deck the other day.'

'That was clumsy of you, young woman,' snapped the officer. 'Good Lord, you *are* the one who made that mess. Why weren't you looking where you were going?'

'I'm sorry,' Tess said in surprise.

'You need to apologise to Mr. Ismay, who is, in case you don't know, the chairman of this shipping company,' the officer said. 'You're Lady Duff Gordon's maid, aren't you? Surely you've been trained better than that.'

'I'm not apologizing, sir, for I've done nothing wrong. I'm sorry the accident happened, but I wasn't the cause.'

'You're not getting away with this, young woman. I'm going to have to talk to the Duff Gordons about your manners.'

'I did nothing,' Tess said, growing dismayed.

A voice cut through from the dark near the rail. 'Actually, her manners are far better than yours, and I suspect her sense of balance is, too. I believe the apology is due to *her,* Officer. Are you in the habit of berating young women – or just those in service?'

Flustered, the officer turned on the steward. 'Go get a towel and clean this up,' he ordered. As the steward scurried away, the officer and Ismay walked on, and Tess heard him say, 'These last-minute hires, you know ... '

'That was a nice scene, wasn't it?'

Tess looked behind her and saw the mysterious Mr. Bremerton. He had left the captain's table and was standing by the teak railing, polished and handsome in his evening clothes.

'Officious little men with power – one of the plagues of the world.' He shook his head. 'Good lesson, though – position doesn't make a gentleman. Or evening clothes, for that matter. But you know that, I hope.'

She did, but it might not be wise to say that right now. 'I really don't want any trouble,' she said.

'You didn't cringe. That took some backbone.'

'I needed to defend myself.'

'Or what?' He looked at her keenly.

'Or it would just happen again.' And again and again. No use trying to explain.

He bowed slightly. 'Very wise. I'm glad to see you – I kept wishing after our time in the exercise room that I had asked your name. May I now?'

She couldn't help smiling. He must think she had been undone by riding that camel. 'My name is Tess Collins.'

He peered closely. 'Of course. Since we seem to keep meeting, let me introduce myself. I'm Jack Bremerton, and I have no business judging others, to tell the truth. What do you think of your voyage so far?'

'I've loved it, Mr. Bremerton,' she said, walking over to the rail where he stood. 'It's a feast for the eyes and the hands.'

'The hands?'

'I love touching the draperies and the silk tablecloths and all the beautiful fabrics, and thinking about where I would put them, how I would cut and tuck them.'

'You sound like you want to be a designer yourself.'

'I'm going to be, someday.' Just the fact of saying it to this stranger made her move up a notch in believing it.

'A lady who is willing to stand up for herself has a dignity that will take her a long way. By the way, please call me Jack.'

'I don't feel comfortable doing that, Mr. Bremerton.' She tried the word out in her mind. *Jack*.

'I accept that, Miss Collins.' He smiled. 'Hope you change your mind at some point. Isn't it a great night? Just look at those stars.'

'They are splendid.' They were standing so close, she could smell the faint musk of his shaving lotion. Was this really happening? Was this impressive, powerful man actually talking to her?

'It's a pleasure to be watching them with you.' He glanced back in the direction of the dining room. 'It's all very stuffy in there, you know. I left after the duck breasts; don't like figs. Or oyster martinis. It looks beautiful from out here, but nothing glitters quite as much when you get close up.'

'You know I can't go in there, don't you?'

'So they say.' He seemed to be thinking it over. 'Do we agree?'

'What do you mean?'

'That a coterie of snobs can deny you entry into this stiff-backed saloon?'

'They can make the rules they want to make; it's not for me to decide.'

'Well, I disagree.'

She shivered. Was there a way to tell him that in her heart, tucked away quite privately, she had the same rebellious thought?

He held out his arm, his eyes watchful but revealing

nothing. Before she knew it, he was guiding her through the glass doors and right into the magical dining room. With one careless hand, he swept the room. 'Here you are, Miss Collins. Shall I signal a waiter for two glasses of champagne?'

Oh, the carpet was soft. And now she could reach out and actually touch one of the velvet chairs. She could inhale the aroma of many perfumes, see the gold-crusted dining plates filled with exotic food, hear the light talk and laughter that rippled across the well-behaved room, laughter as sparkling as the sea. So much, all at once. White-clad waiters moving solicitously among the tables; diamond rings flashing each time a glass was hoisted; men hovering close to women in low-cut gowns. She didn't recognise the music the orchestra was playing, but she loved it and knew she would never forget it.

And then she spied Cosmo and Madame. *What if they saw her?*

She turned quickly and walked back toward the door. 'I can't stay here,' she said, a flush burning deep into her cheeks.

Bremerton made no objection, just followed her back out to the deck. 'I'm a betting man, Miss Collins,' he said quietly as they stood again beneath the stars. 'After watching you stand up to that oaf tonight, may I make a prediction? Once you get to America, you won't be closed out of any dining rooms again. And you won't be carrying a serving tray for very long.'

'Maybe I'll be busy learning how to play squash,' she said, suddenly encouraged.

He laughed. 'Well, it's not so popular in my country. I'm certainly glad to be going back. No offense, but I get tired of Europe. Too stodgy. Moves too slow.'

'What sort of work do you do?' she ventured tentatively.

'Right now I'm setting up branches to sell the Model T.'

He saw her puzzlement. A motor car, he explained. But, more than that, it was *the* automobile in America. A masterpiece for the masses, actually, and Henry Ford, the man who thought of it, was a genius. He had plans for an assembly line, and soon he would be producing an automobile every ninety minutes.

'Amazing.' She knew she should leave soon, but she didn't want to go.

'You've got me talking tonight,' he said reflectively, looking into the black sea. 'Maybe it's the stars. Is there a young man waiting for you in New York?'

She shook her head. 'No, I don't need that. Madame will help me get work.'

'My money is on you. By the way, I don't play squash, either. Have a nice evening, and I think we should find the opportunity to chat again.' He reached out a hand and touched hers lightly, briefly. Then he gave her a salute and walked off.

She headed back to her cabin, stopping, turning, looking back. Jack had also stopped.

'Good night again,' he said.

'Good night.' She could think of nothing else to say. Taking one more deep breath of the crisp night air, she headed for her cabin. She had actually carried off a conversation with a gentleman who wasn't snapping his fingers for service or groping up her skirts. Someone with polish and manners who treated her as if she were an equal. Surely rich. What would it be like to be rich? Oh yes, she hoped they would talk again. He was obviously cultured; he would know so much more than she about books and music and plays. Still, she would have been tempted to linger longer with him just now if it hadn't felt faintly improper. And why did she have the excited thought that he felt the same?

She hurried down the stairs, consoling herself with the anticipation of a singular pleasure ahead – for in her cabin was one of the most beautiful gowns she had ever imagined, let alone owned.

Just before leaving for dinner, Lady Duff Gordon had lifted a beautiful silk dressing gown wrapped carefully in tissue paper from her trunk and handed it to Tess. It was made of fabric as billowy as smoke, an artful weaving of one deepening colour, starting from a bodice of palest lavender to a skirt of regal purple. 'Here, dear, something elegant and pretty for you,' she had said.

Tess was stunned. 'For me?'

Lady Duff Gordon, looking pleased with herself, was already heading out the door, leaving behind a rich aura of perfume. 'Why not?' she sang out over her shoulder.

Tess took the gown to the light, examining its workmanship with awe. Such artful seaming. Then she wrapped herself in her fairy tale. She put on her lovely gown and twirled to the music, pretending that she, too, was on the dance floor, with Jack Bremerton, wishing only that her mother could see her now, this minute, here on the cusp of a new life filled with immense possibility. She must write home as soon as they arrived in New York. She had scribbled down her family address at the Cherbourg dock for one of Madame's employees, asking him to tell her parents where she was going, but his attitude had been slightly disdainful and Tess, drifting off into sleep shortly before midnight, wondered if the message had ever been sent ... Her eyes closed. Time enough to think about that in the morning.

Chapter 2

It wasn't much of a jolt. More like a slight bump, that was all. Nothing alarming. At first, the hum of the ship's engines continued. Then a sudden silence; they had stopped.

Tess lifted herself up on one elbow, instantly drawn out of a deep sleep. Strange, when you knew something was wrong. Her skin tingled; her muscles tensed. Once before, the night her mother's last baby died, she had awakened like this, already fully sick at heart. Then it had been a thin, tired wail that warned her; tonight, a bump. She jumped from bed, fully awake, and dressed quickly. Whatever was happening, she had better be ready for it.

A few cabins away, Bruce Ismay stiffened at the sound. He knew the rhythms of most ships, and there was something not quite right about that bump. It was nothing, probably, but he didn't like it. He checked the time on his pocket watch. They certainly didn't need any delays, not at this point. He decided to go on deck and hunt up Captain Smith, just to make sure all was in order.

Jean Darling shook her husband awake. She had been cold, shivering in a terrible dream where she was running somewhere and slipping, and something was chasing her, and then came that jolt, as if the ship were shivering, too. Jordan put his arm around her and tried to draw her down with him into the warm pillows, but she pulled back.

'Jordan, let's get up,' she whispered.

'Why?'

'I want to be dressed properly if something is happening.'

He laughed. 'Now that's a novel way of telling me you're intimidated by the presence of Lucile Duff Gordon on this ship.'

Jack Bremerton felt it and didn't care. He sat at the desk in his cabin, poring over the pile of business documents he had brought with him, already impatient for the crossing to be over. He wanted nothing more than to immerse himself in the Ford Company's details and get to California, away from the sticky mess of his personal life, which probably proved the truth of his soon to be ex-wife's accusation that he was always running away. He was giving her plenty of money with his apologies, which was more than the pompous ass who scolded that young maid tonight had managed to muster. Interesting woman – hard to forget the abundance of soft hair framing her lively eyes and luminous skin. And such determined ways. Probably worth more than most of the pretenders on this ship, though she didn't know it. So fresh and young. She made him uncomfortably aware of his own advancing middle age.

Lucile felt it as she leaned across her dressing table to remove her moonstone earrings after returning from dinner. She saw the liquid in her perfume decanter shiver and then calm. She would have pointed it out to Cosmo, but he was already in bed. How did he fall asleep so quickly? She so hated his snoring. She hesitated, fingering her earrings, waiting to see if there would be another bump. All seemed fine. Not knowing herself why she did it, she slipped the earrings into their velvet drawstring bag and tucked them into her shoe.

First, a discreet knock at the Duff Gordons' door.

'Ma'am, we've had a small accident,' the steward outside said quickly to Lucile. 'Nothing to worry about. We bumped into an iceberg, but all is well. However, you might want to come on deck.'

Lucile was not fooled for a minute. The steward knew nothing – he was just prattling a reassuring line.

'Get dressed, Cosmo,' she said, shaking her husband's shoulder. 'And put your life belt on. I'm going to wake Tess.'

She was lacing up her life belt, muttering about its clumsy design, when Tess knocked urgently on the door. 'We should hurry,' Tess said as the door opened. She made no attempt to smooth away the troubled frown on her face. It wasn't fitting for her to be urging speed on the Duff

Gordons, but social conventions seemed not to matter right now.

'It's Cosmo who is taking his sweet time,' Lucile snapped.

The hallway was filling fast with people in nightcaps and pajamas, looking comically like stuffed teddy bears in their life belts; there wasn't a silver cigarette holder in sight. Stripped of their grand clothes, they looked quite ordinary, Tess thought fleetingly.

Cosmo finally appeared, stuffing his shirttails into his trousers.

'This way,' Tess said, beckoning them to the stairs. Cosmo and Lucile followed her without objection, joining a good-naturedly grumbling crowd making its slow way to the upper deck. Most of the chatter was relaxed, if a little fretful. Some passengers were complaining they'd never get back to sleep after this silly drill, or whatever it was. Such a bother. When an English surgeon asked Lucile politely if she had watched that smashing poker game in the drawing room after dinner – so exciting – she murmured something pleasant. He turned to his companion, a man still in full evening dress: 'Say, are we on for the gymnasium after breakfast? Hope they serve those pancakes again – the children loved them.'

Just behind Lucile was the woman she had disapprovingly called the 'coarse Mrs. Brown,' the one who had turned a place named Leadville into a fortune in gold. She was laughing at the sight of her fellow passengers in various stages of dress. 'Can't tell a viscount from a duke in this crowd!' she boomed. 'Everybody's britches look the same!'

Nobody else laughed, although there were a few titters. Much of it, it seemed to Tess, at Mrs. Brown's expense.

They were at the top of the stairs.

At first, things seemed calm. People were clustering on the deck, shivering and chatting nervously. 'We hit an iceberg,' a boy said to no one in particular, holding out a large chunk of ice in his hand, as if making an offering. 'See? I grabbed a piece as we passed by. We all did, down below. We were playing.'

As the minutes passed, with no one seeming to know what to do, Tess realised that crew members were struggling to untangle ropes and canvas covers, slipping on the deck, shouting to one another.

Lifeboats. They were launching lifeboats.

As if by signal, people began bumping one another and scrambling toward the railing, shouting as they looked down into the sea. Suddenly there was an acrid, sweaty smell of human fear in the salt air.

Minutes passed. A shiver worked its way through Tess's slender body – this was no drill, no joke. This was real. Her heart beat painfully fast as she tried to think. Sailors, jackets open, eyes wild, red in the face – a couple of them aimlessly waving guns – began shouting orders at the growing crowd of passengers. Tess heard a shot, which started people screaming. Children were wailing as mothers began lifting them into the lifeboats, flimsy contraptions swaying high above the water. One by one, the lifeboats were disappearing over the side for their descent, crowded with passengers.

Tess looked into the distance and saw, drifting far

astern, retreating into the darkness, a tower of jagged ice, sullen and cold. If there had been in her mind any doubt before, it was gone now; they had to get into a lifeboat. She glanced around wildly, realizing with a sinking heart that the lifeboats on this part of the ship were already gone.

'I'll check the bow,' she said to Lucile and Cosmo, both of whom looked stunned. Lucile screamed some instruction over the noise of the crowd, but Tess paid no attention, running as fast as she could, sliding on the deck, stumbling and dodging people in her way.

If anything, the chaos was worse at the bow. The unlaunched boats she saw there were full. A woman struggling for a place began screaming as the boat swung out and began descending without her.

'She's crazy, I'm not getting in that rickety-looking thing,' exclaimed another woman, pulling her coat tight around an evening gown of emerald silk. 'This ship is unsinkable; my husband told me so. He knows all about this kind of thing.' It was too hard to look into her eyes.

Tess watched in horror as the scene grew worse. Jean and Jordan Darling, holding on to each other, were arguing with one of the seamen loading a lifeboat. 'Only women allowed!' he bawled, pushing Jordan away. There was panic now; there were no rules. Somehow everyone seemed to realise at the same time that the ship was tipping alarmingly and there weren't enough lifeboats for the milling crowd on the deck. People were running from stern to bow and back again, desperate to find a place. Tess saw Bruce Ismay calmly stepping into a lifeboat, keeping his head down, ignoring the stares of those who had been denied the last seats. But no one challenged his exercise of privilege. And then she saw Jack Bremerton passing a flailing, crying child into the eager hands of a woman in one of the lifeboats. He did so carefully, almost tenderly; his demeanor calm, his eyes somber.

'Mr. Bremerton!' she screamed.

He turned and saw her, his eyes widening. 'Get in a boat now!' he yelled. 'Go starboard!' The crowd surged, and she lost sight of him.

'Calm down, there are rescue ships on the way!' yelled a seaman.

'I told you,' said a woman eagerly to her husband as she shivered in the cold. 'They'll come for us, we're safer here than in those boats. That's right, isn't it?' He wrapped his arms around her, not answering as, one by one, the lifeboats started down to the water.

Tess turned around and ran back; if there was any chance now of getting off the ship, it had to be from the stern.

By the time she got back up the slanting deck, Lucile had taken action. She had grabbed a rope holding what looked like a huge, ragged piece of collapsed canvas. It seemed dangerous and fragile, but it was the only thing resembling a lifeboat that had not yet been launched. Tess ran to help her hold it steady.

'Here's a boat – why aren't you launching this one?' Lucile yelled at the officer nearest to her.

He didn't answer. Lucile looked furious. There was no order now. Everyone was running and screaming, families were being separated, and the harried seamen shouting to one another did not seem to know what they should be doing.

'Officer, do you hear us? You're the one in charge here, aren't you?'

The officer, whose name was Murdoch, jerked around and saw her. 'Yes, ma'am,' he said. His forehead was glistening with sweat and his eyes were almost popping from his head.

'You've got a perfectly good boat here and I want to get in it,' she declared. Even here, in this chaos, she was an imposing figure.

'Lifeboat One? It's a collapsible, a weak one at that,' he said.

'Nonsense, it will float, won't it? Isn't that the *point* here?'

He hesitated. Then, 'Sullivan, get that boat ready for Lady Duff Gordon!' he yelled to a tall sailor with pockmarked skin. 'I'm putting you in charge of the damn boat!'

Lucile climbed in first, motioning Tess and Cosmo to follow. Tess hoisted herself up onto the deck rail and looked around. Two women were hurrying toward them, one draped in a floor-length shawl.

'Get in, you two,' Murdoch said. They crawled aboard, and only when the smaller of the two looked up did Tess see that it was Jean Darling, the dancer. 'Any more women?' yelled Murdoch.

There was a hesitation, and then a sudden, unruly scramble of seamen jumped into the boat.

'You bastards, can any of you row?' yelled the exasperated officer. 'Bonney, you can row, get in there!'

'I've got work to do here, send somebody else!' the man named Bonney shouted as he untied the lifeboat's ropes.

Tess caught a quick glimpse of him – it was the sailor who had promenaded her across the deck only hours before.

'Do as I tell you, that's an order!'

Bonney hesitated.

'I said *move!*'

Bonney jumped. Landing on all fours, he straightened, saw Tess teetering on the deck rail, and reached out his hand. 'For God's sake, quick—' he said.

The ship was settling more rapidly, tipping downward, bow first.

'Will you get on with it?' Lucile gasped angrily. 'Launch this thing – I'm feeling quite ill!' She clutched her stomach as the boat rocked back and forth, her face pale.

'Yes, ma'am,' said the officer. 'Launch the damn boat,' he yelled. *'Now!'*

'Wait, miss!'

Tess, about to jump in, turned and saw Mr. Hoffman stumbling toward her with his two sons, their legs flailing, one under each arm. 'Take my children – save them, please.' His hair was damp, glued by the sea spray across his forehead. His eyes were imploring.

She reached for the children. Michel clung to his father, crying. With great effort, Hoffman broke the child's grip and handed him to Tess. She had both boys now and turned to jump into the boat.

Too late. She looked down at Lifeboat One as it plunged seaward, almost empty, lurching violently back and forth. All was unfolding like a dream. Below her, the sailor named Bonney was yelling at her, his arms outstretched.

'Jump! Jump!'

She teetered, now holding two frightened boys; it was too late. The lifeboat had already descended some fifty feet. She looked down into Lucile's upturned, shocked face. It was over, wasn't it? It was over . . .

'Don't stand there staring, get in that one.' Murdoch shoved her in the direction of a boat already partially launched, but with its ropes tangled. 'You've got a few seconds before they get it going again.'

Tess slid and stumbled across the deck, managing to hold on to the boys. The boat was crammed with women and children.

'No room, no room!' shouted a sailor.

'Of course, there is.' The buxom Mrs. Brown pushed him out of her way and reached up to Tess. 'Pass the children to me and jump!' she commanded.

Tess obeyed. Two wild tosses; one jump, eyes closed. The boat began its seventy-foot descent from the listing ship, swinging and shuddering as they passed the crowded second- and third-class decks. People stared at them blankly, their faces white with shock, as if survival were part of another world far away.

But as the boat swayed and lurched past them, they began shouting.

'Take my little girl, take her!' yelled a man holding a small child in his arms.

'You are leaving us!' screamed a woman, pointing an accusing finger.

Tess could have touched some of them as the boat lurched back and forth. *Why wasn't she with them?* She saw a flash of hope in the eyes of the man holding the child. Their gaze caught. He was young, worn-looking, maybe a farmer. Blue eyes, an unkempt beard. The child had a sloppy yellow ribbon in her hair, hanging lopsided now over one eye; she kept pushing it back. Her eyes were big with fright.

'For the love of God, take her!' the father screamed, holding the girl up, still looking at Tess.

Tess told the boys to hug each other, then leaned forward and stretched her arms out as far as she could. The child's hands were like small, plump peaches, soft and round.

'Watch out,' yelled Murdoch above, peering over the side. 'Push away, don't let any of them grab you or you'll buckle!'

A sailor thrust his fist hard against the side of the ship, sending the lifeboat swinging. The chance was gone. Tess covered her face as they descended into the black waters below.

She expected a jolt. But the lifeboat hit a surprisingly calm sea, settling in gently, and began drifting slowly away from the ship. Music was still rising into the cold, still air from the A deck. Tess had glimpsed the musicians – somber, playing steadily, braced against deck chairs to keep their balance – during the boat's turbulent descent.

'Praise God, we made it,' cried one of the seamen.

It took a few moments for them all to realise that no one was rowing, a few moments more before the crew members began shouting at one another.

'Who's taking the oars?' yelled one.

'I'm not an oarsman, and who put you in charge anyway?' said another.

'Someone has to row, you bloody fool,' a hoarse voice responded. 'The officer on deck put me in charge, so get to the oars.'

'Never done it,' the other yelled back. 'Jesus, are we going to sink?'

'I can't row – nobody ever showed me how,' said a third seaman. Even here on the water his clothes reeked of tobacco and sweat.

'Oh, for God's sake.' Scrambling forward, Mrs. Brown grabbed an oar and pointed Tess to the one on the other side. 'Let's show these cowards what it means to do your job!'

Tess grabbed the oar and heaved it forward. She had rowed enough times across the pond below the manor house; she could do this. 'Get the back oars!' she yelled at the seamen.

One of the crewmen fumbled with the back set of oars, swearing softly. 'Damn things weigh a ton,' he mumbled. 'But we've gotta get out of here or the ship will suck us under.'

Tess looked back at the *Titanic*. The huge ship was tipping upward, its stern slowly rising into the air – a sight beyond belief. Tess could see human forms, not faces now, rushing back and forth on the decks and bodies jumping into the sea.

'Row!' she gasped. She wielded her oar, pulling as hard as she could, sure the muscles of her back were shredding apart. Suddenly, a tug – she looked down at the sea and into a human face.

A woman, skirts ballooning around her, was holding on to the oar with one hand, clutching what looked like a bundle of rags with the other. 'We've got to help her!' Tess screamed, dropping the oar and throwing herself flat, grabbing the woman as the boat began rocking violently.

'Hang on, I've got her!' It was Mrs. Brown, reaching out into the water with surprisingly strong arms. Together they hauled the woman in, the added weight forcing the boat deeper into the water. They were overfull as it was, dear Lord, would this sink them? But the boat stabilised and Tess grabbed her oar again.

The ship was now almost perpendicular to the starlit night sky, a straight vertical slash, hovering like a dancer on point. The electric lights in the cabins and on the decks were still blazing, and a strange green glow from the still lit lights of the submerged part of the ship illuminated the black sea. It was, oddly, an incredibly beautiful sight.

'It's going down – move, move, or it'll take us with it,' yelled a voice from the stern of the lifeboat. The seamen scrambled for the back oars, no complaints now.

'Oh, God!' screamed a matronly woman with white hair, a spiraling wail that spoke for them all. The ship, bow first, was slowly sinking into the water. People began tumbling like broken dolls from the decks, flopping, flailing into the sea. There was a huge cracking sound – and then the *Titanic* disappeared, swallowed in one huge gulp by the sea, taking with it all light, leaving the survivors in total blackness relieved only by the cold twinkling of the stars.

No sucking whirlpool – how had they escaped that? The lifeboats floated on still waters. The sea was so smooth, it reflected the stars above.

'It is two-twenty in the morning,' a sailor said hoarsely. 'April fifteenth.' Strange, that someone would at that moment have the foresight to check his watch.

Then, rising from the water, an unforgettable, keening sound. It resembled the wail of a bitter wind curving around a snug house, the eerie sound that makes one shiver in bed, grateful to be inside.

'Not this,' wailed the woman with white hair. 'My husband is out there, he must be.'

'Not just yours,' said another voice quietly.

Helpless, no one spoke. They barely dared to move for fear of sinking themselves.

Tess turned her attention to the still form of the woman in the bottom of the boat. Since being pulled from the sea, had she moved? Gently trying to turn her over, Tess saw that she held not a bundle of rags but a baby in a blanket – one that had perhaps been safely asleep in a cradle only an hour before. The child must be freezing. She took off her jacket to use as a wrap, even as the truth seeped into her brain. The baby was dead.

Tess stared at the small face, with its crown of silky hair.

A boy or a girl, she didn't know. She looked now to the mother, realizing that she wasn't stirring, and felt a sense of relief when she saw that the woman, too, was dead, and would be spared the pain of mourning for her baby. Tess wrapped the baby in her jacket, put it in its mother's arms, and tried to weep, but no tears would come.

Chapter 3

CITY ROOM, *NEW YORK TIMES*

NEW YORK CITY

APRIL 15

1:20 A.M. EST

A late-night quiet had descended over the newsroom. All the yelling and running and staccato typing that swelled to its usual climax before deadline was over. Carr Van Anda, a gruff, paunchy man with no peer in his ability to pull a story together on deadline, was not one to waste time on stray observations. But now, surveying his domain, the *New York Times* editor was struck with the thought that this grubby place looked as exhausted as he felt.

Cigarette butts on the floor. Papers crumpled, tossed in the general direction of wastebaskets, scattered like dirty snowballs everywhere. Only a few deskmen left hunched over the city desk. He had a fondness for the night crew; they tended to keep bottles of bourbon in their half-open file drawers at which they nipped leisurely through the night. He hadn't been averse to the offer of a nip or two himself on some of these long night shifts. The bourbon had vanished in the stepped-up pace of the past twenty-four hours, at least among the veterans. No one could afford to lose his edge on a primary night. Now the returns were in, and the morning edition was locked up. It was going to be a great fight. So Roosevelt won Pennsylvania tonight. But Taft had plenty of tricks up his sleeve and the two men hated each other. They were going to split the Republican vote, which meant a great opportunity for the Democrats, no question. Lots of good stories ahead.

He eyed a bottle propped discreetly in the desk drawer of his city editor, leaned back in his chair, and savoured the anticipation of lighting up a fresh cigar. His job was done. He could relax.

'Mr. Van Anda, this just came in.' The night copyboy, his face a shade paler than usual, thrust a wireless bulletin into the editor's hand. Van Anda scanned it rapidly, noting that it was from the Marconi station in Newfoundland.

'You read this?' he asked.

'Yes, sir,' the copyboy said, speaking tentatively. 'It's the biggest ship in the world, sir. How could the *Titanic* hit an iceberg?'

'Son, anything can happen at any time.' Some of these green kids never quite seemed to understand that was *why* there was a news business. 'Now get me everything we've got in the archives on that ship. And' – he stopped him with a raised hand – 'bring me anything we've got on iceberg collisions.'

The bulletins in their metal cylinders began tumbling down the chute from the wire room above, clattering one after another into the *New York Times* city room, each one adding details to the escalating crisis. The front page of the early edition was opened; reporters were writing fast and the Linotype operators were back in business, waiting for orders.

Van Anda lifted his head after reading one report and listened. The chute was silent.

'Is that all?' he asked.

Nobody answered.

He stared down at the report in his hands: a scrambled transmission from the *Titanic* had come in at 12:27, asking for help, but it cut off abruptly in midsentence.

'Almost an hour ago,' he muttered as he read through the morgue files, listening for the clatter of a cylinder. He paid special attention to the specifications for the *Titanic*, counting and recounting the official number of required lifeboats. No matter what scenario might unfold, he realised, there weren't enough. Stupid bastards – a fancy ship without enough lifeboats.

Van Anda paced. How could there be total silence for a full hour from the *Titanic*? He strode over to the reporter writing the original story. 'We're changing the lead,' he said. 'Forget the "worrisome reports" angle. Say the ship has sunk.'

'Are we sure?' asked the reporter, mouth agape.

Van Anda sighed. He had been in the business a long time, and he not only trusted his instincts; he saw no need to defend them.

'I am,' he said, and started to trudge back to his desk. It was time for that cigar. He turned back with another thought. 'Call Pinky Wade. If there are any survivors, I want her on this story. Full-time.'

'She won't like that,' the reporter said.

She would be furious, Van Anda knew that. But she was the best human-interest reporter he had, even if it meant taking her off the mental-asylum story.

'I know, not enough danger for her. Call her anyway.'

ATLANTIC OCEAN

APRIL 15

2:45 A.M. EST

Time had disappeared, floating away on the currents. It was cold, so cold; biting deep into her bones, leaving fragments of ice under the skin of her fingertips and ears. The cold was so impossible, it hurt to breathe. The lifeboat felt as if it bobbed on a bubble of air, as if they were somehow in the sky, not on the black water. Where was the horizon? No one bothered to row anymore. With great effort, Tess tried to bail the frigid water seeping through the floor of the half-sunken boat, even as the pleas for help from the water grew fainter and fainter. She looked at Mrs. Brown, and they shared with their eyes a somber reality. They were low in the water, precariously balanced. Any sudden shifting of weight and they would sink. She stopped bailing as the last cries ended; now the lifeboat moved lazily in circles. A crewman started whistling a mournful tune. She pulled Edmond and Michel close to her, massaging their arms in an effort to impart warmth.

'Merci,' Edmond whispered.

'Maybe it'll help a little,' she replied. Their clothing had frozen to their bodies.

All across the black sea she could see blurs of white. What was she seeing? The faces of the dead, she realised. Faces above the water. They hadn't drowned; they had frozen. It was a graveyard; their faces were the tombstones.

One by one, the bodies began to vanish, sinking down. Those that still floated stared at the sky with sightless eyes. Finally, nothing. The sea was totally calm, a virtual mirror, reflecting the brilliant stars above. The lifeboat floated on the reflected stars, creating an almost magical suspension, as if plucked from a child's dream.

She could not erase from her mind the face of the man holding out the child with the yellow ribbon in her hair. Another few seconds and she could have done it. She had strong arms and hands; she would have lifted the baby up, held her tight, and brought her into the boat. The child would have held on, arms around her neck, and she and the father would have looked at each other; there would have been relief on his face and she would have promised him, without words, to protect and endure ... She replayed this scenario, over and over, through the long night. Was that child now, with sightless eyes, looking up at the stars?

WASHINGTON, D.C.

APRIL 15

7 A.M. EST

The rising sun filled the eastern sky of Washington with hues of orange and gold, thrusting into silhouette the graceful lines of the U.S. Capitol. Had the founding fathers understood precisely how beautiful this sight would be on a soft spring morning? William Alden Smith, a Michigan man of small stature, whose kinder colleagues considered him a rough-edged, somewhat naïve product of the Midwest, asked himself that as he stood staring out the window of his fourth-floor office in the Senate Office Building. Soon enough, he would be back to the legal problems of building railroads in Alaska. He liked giving specific attention to detail, something many of his colleagues could not abide. But it was the sight of the Capitol just past sunrise that stirred his soul. Strolling past the guards, wishing them good morning, getting attention back from them – no competition, this time of day – it gave him confidence that he held a niche in this place of power.

A hurried, sharp knock; his door opened before he gave permission. 'Senator, did you hear the news?' It was an aide, holding up a copy of the *New York Times* as if it were a shield. 'The *Titanic* is supposed to have sunk.'

Smith grabbed the paper, scanning the headline.

'The White Star Line is denying the *Times* story,' the aide said, glancing quickly down at his scrawled notes. 'They're saying everybody is safe and the ship is being towed to port. The *Syracuse Herald* is going with that, and most of the other papers are jeering at the *Times*. But there hasn't been a word from the ship since twelve-thirty last night.'

'They're fools,' Smith said sharply. He knew the reputation of Van Anda – if the managing editor of the *New York Times* said the ship had sunk, the ship had sunk. His eyes traveled down the passenger list, riveted by the famous names. Astor, Guggenheim – my God, even Archie Butt, Taft's White House aide. Who survived? 'Bring me every bulletin,' he ordered.

The aide disappeared and Smith walked to the window, catching his own reflection in the glass. Maybe he wasn't the most imposing legislator in this town, certainly not the most glamorous, but he knew damn well the country would want something more than speeches out of Washington after this catastrophe. There would be a scramble now – everybody in Congress would be grandstanding and orating and introducing addled legislation that would do nothing. The usual harebrained response.

He stared out his window at the Capitol, drawn as usual to the bronze Statue of Freedom crowning the glistening white dome. He felt his indignation rising. This was a disaster, a moral outrage; it should not be happening. Hearings. There had to be hearings, where the tragedy could be dissected and understood. If he moved fast, he was the man to lead them.

ATLANTIC OCEAN

SUNRISE, APRIL 15

Lord, the cold. Tess could not feel her feet or her fingers now. There was nothing, nothing, not even a groan or a complaint from the others; they floated between sea and sky.

Then a hoarse cry – a sailor, the darkness lifting, had spied a ship. Tess peered in the breaking dawn and saw other lifeboats for the first time. People began to shout to one another, women shrieking names of husbands and children. Are you there? Please answer, please be there! One voice, over and over: 'Is my Amy in your boat? Amy, Amy, answer your mother.' Tess waited to hear a child's answering shout, but there was none.

And then, yes, there was a ship emerging from the dark, coming directly toward them. Tess squinted, barely making out the name on the ship's hull – *Carpathia.* It wasn't a fantasy. 'We've made it,' Mrs. Brown said quietly. Tears of relief fell, then froze on her cheeks.

They were the second load of survivors brought on board. Canvas bags were lowered into the jammed first lifeboat, and mothers began stuffing struggling, frightened children inside them, trying to console them, then trusting them to the sailors above. Tess put Michel and Edmond in one bag at their insistence, wishing she could comfort them with her halting French. The exhausted women were next. They hung limply, dangling from ropes looped around their waists, as they were slowly hauled upward.

When it was Tess's turn, she fastened the loop around her waist, tightened the rope, and turned to the sailor who had first helped row. She nodded in the direction of the still figures at the bottom of the boat. 'Help me, please,' she said. 'Don't let them be dumped over the side of the lifeboat.'

'Bring them up only to be buried at sea?' he said, surprised.

'Yes.'

'That's a bit balmy. I'm not doing it.'

'Yes, you are,' she said calmly, not flinching. 'I don't want either of them abandoned. You'll make sure that doesn't happen, won't you?'

He hesitated. 'I'll send them up last,' he promised.

Tess began rising in the air, swinging a few times against the hull of the ship, looking up to see dozens of people watching her progress, many with mouths gaping. How good it felt to look at them, to see their faces, their quick movements, their *aliveness*. Then, swinging free, up and onto the deck. When her numbed legs began to buckle, a woman in a moleskin coat grabbed her.

'There, dear,' she murmured. 'You'll be all right – we're so happy our captain got here in time. These are your children? But they speak no English, just French.' She nodded at Edmond and Michel, clinging to her skirts.

'They aren't mine, and I fear their father didn't make it.'

'I'm French – I'll take care of them, dear.' She looked

past Tess and pointed curiously at the next boat now bumping against the ship's hull. 'The other boats were terribly crowded, but that one is almost empty. Odd, isn't it? How did that happen?'

Tess glanced down at the sea, and felt her heart leap. There it was, the lifeboat holding the Duff Gordons – they were safe. A sailor was helping Lucile into one of the slings, and soon she would be on board. Tess trembled with relief.

And there was the sailor, the one named Bonney; he was safe, too. He glanced upward, and their gazes caught. She waved, and he broke into a grin. She saw Jean Darling; was that her husband with her? Cosmo was holding on to a sailor's shoulder, trying to steady himself. Lucile was on her way up, swaying back and forth in the sling. They were all saved; Madame was saved. Tess waved again, still dizzy with relief. As Lucile stepped onto the *Carpathia*, Tess rushed forward, hugging her impulsively.

'Oh, my dear,' gasped Lucile, patting her lightly on the back and quickly stepping away.

More lifeboats were unloading – more people were swung up high in the slings, then deposited onto the deck of the ship. Tess looked in vain for some sign of Jack Bremerton. Nothing. Just sad, stunned strangers who huddled together or stood apart. There was a stillness to them all, a loss of purpose.

Suddenly Lucile began clapping her hands, almost as if a particularly dramatic performance had just come to an end. 'We've made it to safety, and we're going to celebrate,' she announced to the small band from Lifeboat

One. She called to the captain of the *Carpathia* and issued a blithe order. 'Captain, I'm sure you will do me this *essential* favor, won't you? This is something I must have. Will one of your men take a photograph of those of us who were in my lifeboat? You have a camera, don't you?'

Taken by surprise, the startled captain nodded, beckoning to another officer. 'The ship's surgeon will help you, Madame,' he said.

Cosmo, looking gaunt and weary, murmured to Tess. 'Lucile wants a little ceremony to celebrate our survival, and she wants you in the picture, too,' he said. 'Put your life belt back on, will you?'

Tess stared at Cosmo and then at the sodden vest she still held in her hand. Put it on again? She looked over his shoulder and saw Madame beckoning, her eyes bright and smiling. But there was also something else. What? A tinge of panic? No, not Madame.

'I know it's a shivery old thing, but put it on – it will be a wonderful picture,' she said. 'Come, dear, this will be for the history books. Our stalwart little crew deserves remembrance.'

Lining up next to Lucile were the crewmen who had been in her boat, all of them standing stiffly in their life vests. The tall, wiry one with bad skin, the one named Sullivan, who was in charge of Lifeboat One, was boasting of his own bravery, but none of the others were listening.

Tess glanced at the seaman named Bonney. He was standing to the side, observing the scene with a stony, unreadable expression. Deliberately, watching Lucile, he undid the ties of his vest and tossed it into a refuse bin.

'I'll not be a party to this vain celebration, not when so many died,' he said in a strong voice that carried across the deck.

Lucile's smile faded. 'Your rudeness is surpassed only by your arrogance,' she snapped.

'No, that's your territory.'

'How dare you say that to me?'

'You know what I'm talking about.'

Lucile turned away, her eyes glittering now with hard determination. 'Tess?' She beckoned to the girl to join the huddled, wary-faced crew, some of whom were looking uncomfortably sheepish about Lucile's mandate.

'Go ahead,' Tess said quickly. 'I wasn't in your boat, after all.'

'Very well.' Lucile turned away, taking her place at the center of the group. The surgeon of the *Carpathia*, with some diffidence, but out of respect for the famous Lady Duff Gordon, stood now, holding a camera. A silence fell over those on the deck as they watched.

'Now, everybody – smile,' Lucile ordered.

The camera clicked – a harsh, loud sound. His job done, the ship's surgeon quickly hurried away.

Sir Cosmo spoke then with each crewman in turn, murmuring, walking down the line, a slap on a shoulder here, a handshake there. Gratitude, solidarity, of course. Small murmurings to each man.

'He thinks it's his personal rowing team,' muttered a man from the watching crowd. 'Gentry, managed to snare a private boat.' Tess turned in the direction of the voice, but it had merged into the crowd's murmuring sighs.

Lifeboats were still arriving, and the crowd on the deck was growing, a potpourri of survivors. The shabby and bedraggled, the famous and glamorous, and somehow they all looked alike to Tess right now. Their faces were as pasty and blank as hers, she was sure of that. She looked for Jack Bremerton. A man as confident as he would have found a way to get off that ship. And then again, perhaps not.

Peering over the side, she saw Mrs. Astor, looking faint and ill, her hair loose and snarled, swinging back and forth in a boatswain chair. Sailors were cutting life belts off some of the almost comatose passengers, and stewards were passing out mugs of hot coffee and brandy. The *Carpathia*'s passengers looked at them all in some horror, but mostly with pity, as mothers clung to the side of the ship, crying, hoping with each unloaded lifeboat that a missing child or husband would emerge.

One woman stood very still, without tears, her face strong and hard. She was the wife of one of the *Titanic*'s cooks, someone whispered. 'There is another lifeboat,' she said calmly to whoever was listening. 'My children are on it.' Refusing warm clothes, refusing a hot drink, refusing food, she stood rigid, watching the horizon.

Tess slumped down on the deck, exhausted. She did not want to talk with anyone. The world she inhabited yesterday was gone. There were no beautiful clothes to unpack or iron. No silver tea service, no strolling on the promenade – none of the vanities that had seemed to matter so much. Was it only yesterday?

A shadow fell between her and the light.

'I don't even know your name,' Bonney said quietly.

Startled, she glanced up and, for the first time, really looked at this man who had shared the last carefree moment of her life. A rough, dark stubble covered his face, deepening every line and crevice, making him look much older than the village boy she had met on deck yesterday. He wore a dry flannel shirt but no sweater, as if scorning the cold, and he was smoking, drawing on a cigarette with concentrated ferocity. She was struck by the uncompromising, hard set of his chin. How different he looked. There was no lighthearted grin, no easy set of the shoulders, but then they were both different people from the pair who had met on the *Titanic*'s promenade.

'Tess Collins. And yours?'

He flicked a long ash off the cigarette in his right hand and gazed down at her a bit uneasily. 'Jim. Jim Bonney. I was afraid you weren't going to make it off the ship last night.'

'Me, too,' she said, smiling bleakly.

'Something I have to ask—'

'Yes?'

'A sailor from your lifeboat says he hauled up a couple of dead bodies for you. You want to speak over them, is that it?'

'I just want to see them.'

'All right, come with me.'

She scrambled to her feet, too stiff and cold to stand straight.

A room had been set aside for the dead. Across the floor were the shrouded forms of a dozen people, all waiting now for a few quick words from the captain, then a quiet sliding into the sea. Bonney pointed at one figure. 'I put the baby back in her arms,' he said.

'Good. That's where it should be.'

'I can't help you pray or anything. I'm not a religious man.'

'You cared enough to come get me for this.'

'Are you going to pray? If you are, I'll leave.'

'I just want to say goodbye. I've helped bury a sister; I know how to do this.' Her lip trembled. She was so cold, so tired, so close to tears.

'I'll help with that,' he said more gently.

'It's just that no one who loves them will ever be able to.'

'I'll start if you want.'

She nodded.

He cleared his throat. 'We wish you well and would give you life if we could. But at least you're both together for whatever journey lies ahead.'

'That's close to a prayer,' she said, looking gratefully at his set face.

'Your turn.'

'I turn my face to the rising sun,' Tess whispered, the words coming from somewhere in the recesses of memory. 'O Lord, have mercy.'

The room was dark; more bodies from the lifeboats would be brought in soon. Bonney turned to go.

'Wait.' Tess knelt down by the woman's body, folding

back the towel draped over her face. Plain, strong features, long, dark eyelashes.

'We should—'

'I want to remember her face.'

They stood together for a quiet moment more, then turned and left the room, closing the door tightly behind them. Bonney's hand, in a gesture of awkward tenderness, briefly cradled her shoulder.

A muddled, drifting order was settling over the survivors on deck. They were breaking into clusters, like tribes, all adhering to their own. Voices muttering, sobbing – recounting close calls and instant decisions.

A hoarse chuckle from Jim Bonney. 'Now the accounting begins,' he said.

'What do you mean?'

'We'll see how it plays out. Nothing to do about it. I'm glad we met again, though not like this.' And then he strode away as Lucile approached, casting him a malevolent glance.

Uncertain, Tess stood watching, then moved to Lucile's side.

Jean and Jordan Darling had drawn away from the cluster of survivors, huddling together by themselves, all lighthearted gaiety stripped away. Jean reached out as Lucile passed by. 'Lucile, please,' she said, putting a hand lightly on her arm. 'What would you have done?'

Lucile gave her a hard-edged smile. 'I certainly wouldn't

have tossed a tablecloth over my husband to disguise him as a woman. You are a cheat, and your husband is a coward.'

Jean Darling covered her face with her hands as heads began to turn. Tess was first shocked, then flooded with pity at the sight of her suffering.

'And yours was not?' Jean managed.

Lucile was giving no quarter. 'There was no pretense. Don't you understand the difference?' she demanded.

Jean Darling lowered her hands and looked directly at Lucile. 'He would be dead and I couldn't bear losing him,' she said.

'Really, your behavior is pathetic.' Lucile turned away.

'And what about your actions?' Jean Darling challenged.

'And what *about* me, my dear Jean?' Lucile said calmly. 'Are you criticizing the fact that you and that husband of yours are both alive because of me? You are, you know.' She turned to Tess, who couldn't take her eyes off Mrs. Darling's stricken face. 'Tess, I'm sure you can roust up some crew member to get us a little tea. You'll do that now, won't you?'

The rules still applied. 'Yes, Madame,' Tess said. She was being sent away so as not to hear the rest of this. But something had happened on that lifeboat, the shape and truth of which she might never know. And this made her uneasy.

The cook's wife took her eyes off the horizon long enough to grab at Tess's clothes as she passed. 'My daughter is ten,' she said. 'She's very spirited and well able to take care of her brother. He's five. They're coming soon. I'm very happy about that.'

Tess squeezed the woman's hand, but knew there was no solace she could give. She kept walking.

The day grew warmer as the sun rose higher in the sky. Tess served a makeshift tea with two forlorn teacups and a shabby pot of tepid water to Madame, but there were no complaints. Afterward, she slipped behind a smokestack and curled herself tight, hoping not to be noticed, hungry to be alone with the sun. Her thoughts flashed back to Jack Bremerton, remembering his calm demeanor as he handed that child into a lifeboat, looking up at her, clearly caring that she was still in peril. How could he be gone?

'I hear you were good with the oars.'

She looked up and saw Jim Bonney. 'I learned, living on a lake,' she said.

'You worked them hard, I'm told. I'm not surprised.'

'Why not?'

He glanced down at her. 'Your hands. They've seen plenty of sun. Have you worked on a farm?'

Instinctively, Tess tugged the sleeves of her sweater down over her fingers.

He spoke quickly. 'Nothing to be ashamed of. May I join you?'

Tess nodded, and he sat down beside her. 'If you're not a seaman, what are you?' she said.

'A coal miner – at least, I was,' he said, taking a long drag on his cigarette. 'Until three years ago. We went on strike – the big one, remember?' He looked at her expectantly.

She did remember, though somewhat hazily. It was all politics, her father used to say at the dinner table. Malcontents trying to get money out of the government. They should be grateful for their jobs and not make trouble. He would slam his spoon against his plate, repeating this, staring at Tess. The message was aimed at her; she was the troublemaker, the one who wanted to get away.

'I remember,' she said.

'I was an organiser,' he said. 'Management gave in and we got better wages for the men. Organizing – that's what I want to do.'

'Why in America?'

'Because it works. And people care about it.' Bonney kicked at a piece of debris blowing across the deck, then – with a quick, expert movement – flipped his cigarette over the side. 'There's a lot to be done with the unions in the States, especially in the West. Also' – he looked at her with a sudden smile – 'a man can do what he wants, live the life he makes for himself. There's no bloody class system holding you down.'

'Are you one of these – what are they called – Bolsheviks?'

'No,' he said. 'But I don't dismiss them. There's this

bloke, Vladimir Lenin.' He looked at her hopefully. 'Russian. Have you heard of him?'

Tess shook her head, annoyed with herself. There was way too much she should know that she didn't.

'So what about you? Why were you leaving?'

'I hate feeding cows and pigs and I hate doing rich people's laundry, and I never want to do any of it again.'

He let go with a laugh. 'So we share that. What will you do?'

'I don't know yet,' she said. 'It depends on Madame.'

'Why do you call her that?'

Tess hesitated. Because she was told to, that was the answer. But she wasn't about to say so.

'It's just for the trip.'

'What happens then?'

'I don't know,' she admitted. 'But I think she'll give me work in her showroom. I love to sketch and sew.'

'You're good at it?'

'I'm very good,' she said, scorning modesty.

'Good luck. She's an arrogant one.' His voice stayed even.

'She's been good to me.'

'She's what's wrong with the English class system.' His voice was suddenly sharp and angry.

'Why would you say that? She made it on her own, working hard.'

'Marrying into the titled class. That helped. Gave her license to be cold about other people's lives.'

'I know how arrogant she can be, but there is more to her than that.' She pushed aside the memory of Jean

Darling's face, just for the moment. She would think about that later.

Bonney studied her for a moment, then glanced down to light another cigarette, cupping the flame against the wind. 'Why did you stay out of the picture she wanted?'

'It felt wrong,' she said slowly.

'She'll not let you get away with independent thinking.'

'It's the only kind that comes easy to me.' Brave words; she wanted them to be true.

'Don't fool yourself.'

Tess felt suddenly very tired, not quite ready for his determined opinions. 'I'm trying to do my job, whether you think that is worthwhile or not. I don't want to argue with you.'

'I'm not trying to undermine you. I'm mad at myself.'

'Why?'

'For what happened in that lifeboat. I should have fought harder against her.'

'What did she do?'

'Did you notice how empty our boat was? Do you know why? She wouldn't let us pick up survivors.'

'Oh, my goodness.' This time Tess was the one covering her face with her hands.

'Pretty despicable, right? We could've easily saved people.'

'Maybe you were in danger of being swamped; we almost were.'

'You pulled that mother and her baby into the boat, didn't you? That's more than she would've done.'

'But—' She thought of how fearsome the dark water

had been, how that had frightened everybody. Surely Madame wasn't excluded? 'There must have been good reason – are you sure? The officer on the ship said, I remember, he said the boat was unstable before it was launched. Couldn't that be why?' She felt herself pleading. 'I can't believe what you're saying.'

He gave her a hard look. 'Are you so gone you defend her? I could tell you things.'

'Well, you haven't – nothing that condemns Madame for anything. Everybody did the best they could.'

'There it is, "Madame" again. All right, I see where this is going.' He spat out across the railing into the sea.

She hated it when men spat. 'Well? What did you see?'

'Nothing I can talk about.'

'Then you're making an ignorant denunciation.' Her heart was beating too fast.

His jaw stiffened, his mouth tightening. 'Could be,' he said. 'I see where you are. She's your meal ticket.'

'What a dreadful thing to say,' she blurted angrily. Tears began to trickle down her cheeks, the first she had shed since boarding the *Carpathia*.

He crushed his cigarette out on the deck and slapped one fist into the other. 'I'm angry and too blunt. I don't—'

'Look!' Someone was yelling and pointing from the bow. 'We're going by the damn thing! That's where we went down!'

'Oh, my goodness,' a passenger from the *Carpathia* said, almost gaily. 'I've always wanted to see an iceberg!'

Without a word, Tess and Jim scrambled up and hurried

to the railing. Why am I drawn to this, Tess thought fleetingly. I don't want to see it, but I can't resist.

And there was the iceberg – huge, towering much higher than the ship. A beautifully shaped, evil thing formed by nature. Truly a ghastly work of art, with the sun's rays pierced deep into its shimmering green core.

'Look over there,' someone shouted.

To the right of the iceberg was a wide circular stain of muddy brown water, so distinct it almost looked painted over the blue of the sea. It took a moment to realise what it was.

The wreckage of the *Titanic* lay before them, densely packed, a compost of intimate pieces of lost lives. A baby's bonnet intertwined with a long white woman's glove. Pieces and bits of unrecognizable matter curled and wound together. Chairs floating upright, stools and elaborately carved tables on their sides and upside down, boxes, stray articles of clothing, including a bright-red silk scarf coiled over the surface of the water like some sea serpent – all manner of floatable debris that had formed a tight field, torn free of the *Titanic*. Please, God, no yellow ribbon.

'I'm sorry for what I said about you,' Jim muttered. 'Please forgive me.'

With hardly a thought, Tess cupped her hand over his on the rail. He made no move away, then turned his hand and curled his fingers into hers. Neither spoke as the ship moved on by.

'What can you tell me about them?'

The Frenchwoman nodded toward the two boys asleep under a blanket near the captain's quarters.

'Their father is a widower, Mr. Hoffman.'

'He didn't make it, I'm afraid. Somebody said they saw him handing the boys to you – that they heard him shout, "Tell my wife I love her."'

'But he's a widower.'

'Well, then, they are orphans now,' the woman said sadly. 'We'll have to wait until we reach land to try and find their family. But thank you – at least we know their names.'

'I saw them playing with tops,' Tess said, touching Michel's face. 'Are there any toys for the children?'

'I don't think anything like that survived.'

'I'll find something,' Tess said. Here was a task worth doing.

The long day dragged on. Tess searched the decks, peering at every face, wanting Jack Bremerton to be alive. Finally she mustered the nerve to go to the wheelhouse and ask to see the official survivors list. She scanned it quickly, then more carefully. His name was not on the list. Jack Bremerton had not survived; that's how it was. He was gone. Without even closing her eyes, she could see his handsome profile, hear the warmth in his voice, as they talked that last evening on the *Titanic.* She could almost feel his closeness now. Could he truly be dead?

She handed the list back, turned, and walked out of the wheelhouse.

'You'd do best to come in, Tess. I think my wife wants to talk to you,' Cosmo said. His look had turned almost pitying as he gave a slight bow, opening the door to the room the captain had given to the Duff Gordons.

Madame's stare was alarmingly baleful as Tess walked in.

'So, what do you have to say for yourself?' she demanded.

'Pardon me?'

'Don't feign innocence. I wanted you in that photograph. Why did you so rudely refuse me?'

'I didn't mean to be rude. It wasn't my place to be there.'

'Nonsense. You work for me. If I say you belong there, then you do.'

'It seemed a bit out of place – maybe too soon.' It was precisely the wrong thing to say; she could see it immediately in Lucile's eyes.

'You're questioning my judgment?' Lucile's voice lashed out, sharp and hard. 'Just who do you think you are? You're a little servant girl from a farm until I make you something more, and don't you forget it. You do as I tell you, do you hear?'

'Yes, Madame. I didn't know how important it was to you.' She could hardly stammer the words out.

'It's not for you to know, it's your job to *obey*. That is, if you want employment with me.'

She mustn't say the wrong thing again. 'I want that very much,' she said. 'And I will work hard.'

Lucile gave a sharp laugh. 'Your refusing me in front of all those people was intolerable, Tess. Do you understand that?'

'I'm sorry,' Tess said again.

Lucile's shrewd eyes surveyed the girl's stiff figure, something flickering across her face. 'So you're not telling me you will disobey at will?'

'No, Madame. Never.'

'And who defines your duties?'

'You do.' Tess held her breath. She hated the shiver of needed subservience sweeping over her; at home she would be genuflecting. No more of that. But her own inner pride quavered, mixed with shame.

'What did you hear about our boat? Something you didn't like? Is that why you refused to put on a life vest for the picture?'

'No, of course not. I didn't know what happened, I wasn't there.'

Lucile's voice curled around her like a whip. 'I saw you talking with that sailor. He was no friend of ours in the lifeboat, Tess. And don't you forget it. He's a liar out to make a fortune on a lurid story.'

Then, stunningly, the clouds parted as fast as they had formed. Lucile dismissed her with a quick wave of her hand. 'I'm exhausted. Will you bring me some tea? Hot, this time? The captain, I think, knows now who I am.'

'Yes, of course,' Tess said, both astonished and relieved.

'Yes, *Madame*.' Lucile gave her a brilliant smile. 'Go, go, my dear. And stop looking as if I'm biting your head off. And I hope you'll be less cranky tomorrow.'

The hours, the days, ticked by. When Lucile allowed her free time, Tess began teaching the other women how to stitch together shirts and coats from tarps for the children. Too many of them were still huddled in shirts and jackets scratchy with dried seawater. Some of the children who had been rushed from their beds and into the lifeboats were without shoes. 'I can't feel my toes,' one whimpered to Tess. She kneeled down and massaged his small feet, trying to warm them, hoping to see them turn pink again.

And yet, somehow, there was some laughter, some play.

On the second day, Tess found Jim on deck, surrounded by a cluster of the younger children, carving small figures for them from discarded pieces of wood.

'You're good,' she said, leaning down to inspect his work. What long, deft fingers he had. Not the fingers of a coal miner, surely.

'Thanks. Got my instructions from an uncle who was a wood-carver, but I couldn't make enough money at the work.' He smiled up at her. 'Want to join us?' His manner was easy and gentle, which was clearly why the children were gravitating to him.

Impulsively, Tess sat down with them. He was taking orders from the children. Who wants a giraffe? An elephant? 'Ah, the giraffe wins,' he said to a small girl with a sad, pinched face. The child brightened, and his audience watched in silence as a small giraffe almost magically began to emerge from the smooth wood under his fingers. 'What do you think?' he said to the child. 'Is this a worthy giraffe?'

She said nothing, just grinned, her eyes round and dark, as he deposited it carefully in her hand.

'It's now your good-luck charm,' he said quietly. Then, to Tess after a pause, 'Did she come after you?'

'Yes, she was furious. You were right.'

'She's building her defense.'

'Why?'

'Because she has to.'

For more than an hour they sat there. Each time a small figure was completed for a child, Tess reached out and touched the smooth, newly carved wood. 'You're adding the magic,' Jim said with a grin. And she laughed, loath to leave this sunny little island of pleasure he had created amid so much grief.

'Can you carve a spinning top?' she asked eagerly.

'Sure. For you?' His eyes danced.

'For two small boys who need to play.'

He asked no more. 'Give me a few hours,' he said.

All were chilled now by the sight of the cook's wife. Time after time, someone would gently guide her to a cabin, but she would get restless and distraught, drifting soon back to the railing, fastening her gaze again on the horizon. 'They're coming soon,' she said softly. 'My children are in a boat. They are rowing a bit slowly.' Her face was almost radiant now. Her eyes glittered in a strange way.

'That woman obviously has a weak character,' Lucile said at one point as Jean Darling trudged past them on the deck, carrying a basket of bread for her husband. 'She's certainly burned her bridges with *me,* not that the same thing won't happen with everybody else when her husband's deception becomes public.' Lucile brushed a few shriveled raisins from the biscuit crumbs on her plate onto the deck.

Automatically, Tess bent to pick them up and throw them over the railing, watching them loft into the air and then down to the sea. She was getting better, she hoped, at keeping her thoughts to herself. But she had always done that, and why had this servile gesture come so automatically? Perhaps to hide those thoughts. She wondered at the vigor of Lucile's contempt for the Darlings.

Too many dreams – dark ones filled with wailing. It was late when she knocked at Lucile's door the last night. Cosmo was up with the radio operator, sending telegrams, including one that she had given him for her mother, so Lucile would be alone. 'I've brought you an extra blanket in case you're cold,' she said as the door opened.

'That's not necessary,' Lucile said crossly. 'I'm tired, and I don't want any more blankets or anything else right now.' She was wearing a battered old sweater over a flannel gown that had been donated, a combination that made her look strangely vulnerable. 'Go to bed. Why aren't you asleep?'

'I can't,' Tess said.

'Why is that?'

'I keep dreaming about the ship going down.'

'It's over, and we survived. That's all best put behind us,' Lucile said firmly. But her gaze flickered. 'Oh, come in, then,' she said, opening the door wider.

Tess stepped in. The tiny room, so stark and bare. Something more than luxury had been stripped away.

'Aren't you still a little – afraid?' she whispered.

Lucile went still. Her face seemed to break, then quickly reconfigure itself. 'I'm always afraid,' she said.

'You are?'

'Of water,' Lucile quickly amended. She sat down, clasping her hands in front of her. 'I almost drowned when I was ten,' she said abruptly. 'People were on the shore, watching. None of them tried to rescue me. I screamed, I cried. No one came.' She could have been reciting a grocery list, her voice was so matter-of-fact.

'What happened?'

'A boy had the common sense to climb out on a rock and throw me a line. I managed to hang on and he pulled me in. I don't talk about this. I do hope you know I don't want it repeated.'

'That must have terrified you,' Tess said quietly, imagining the fear of a drowning child.

'No, I wouldn't allow it. Sit down.' Lucile patted the lumpy, narrow bed.

Tess lowered herself next to Lucile. They were sitting so close, she could smell vestiges of Lucile's favorite jasmine perfume, now at the bottom of the sea.

'You will learn to move on,' Lucile said, almost gently. 'You will, Tess. I've learned not to show fear, to take charge, to stand up and be strong. Isn't that what you want, too?'

'Yes.'

Lucile reached out and took Tess's hand, squeezing it so tightly Tess almost jumped. 'Don't allow anyone to make you suffer, dear. We need to be thinking about what comes next, not about the past.' She hesitated for a second, and then said, 'I have something for you.'

She reached into the pocket of her baggy sweater and pulled out the velvet drawstring bag. 'Take these,' she said. 'My gift for your future.'

Tess opened the bag and gasped as Lucile's moonstone earrings – sparkling with light even in this dense, windowless space – tumbled into her hand. 'I can't take these,' she stammered.

'Think of them as salvage, my dear. They've already saved my life, and I have plenty more at home. Jewellery can be soothing, you know.'

It was so oddly offhanded, Tess was at a loss. She gently put them back on Lucile's lap. 'I don't need these – I just wanted to tell you I feel altered somehow,' she said. 'I just needed to know you understand – that maybe you have nightmares, too. And you have comforted me. That's all I want.' She searched Lucile's face in confusion. Was she insulting her?

'Are you afraid I'll change my mind and demand them back?'

'No, not at all.'

'Well, then, perhaps for another time.' Lucile slipped the earrings back in their velvet pouch and then into her pocket. 'And, as for how we deal with fear, we are who we are. I think that's enough for tonight.'

Tess didn't want to leave. She didn't want their short moment of intimacy to slip away. 'When did you decide that you wanted to sew, to be a designer?' she asked impulsively.

Lucile blinked, as if startled at the question. 'I sewed clothes for my dolls,' she said after a pause.

'My mother made me a rag doll and I sewed for her, too.'

But Lucile wasn't interested in any more shared experiences. 'Really, dear, we were all children once. Now go to bed and come back early. We have work to do.'

Tess sat down at Lucile's desk the next morning, looking as efficient as possible as she opened a drawer and pulled forth a notebook and a pen. If she had expected the intimacy of the night before, it was certainly not there now.

Lucile was pacing, talking about the messages being sent and received from her various showrooms in London, Paris, and New York. There were showings of her spring line scheduled *everywhere,* she said with satisfaction. So much needed to be coordinated, and remaking the gowns lost on the *Titanic* would take time. Nothing must cast a pall over the New York opening. She talked rapidly, firing off instructions as Tess scribbled them down on notepaper. Clients had to be notified, courted, rounded up. Was Mrs.

Wharton still planning to purchase the coral tea gown she adored in London? What about the models? Were they all assembled and ready to go or not? And if not, why not?

'Actually, I believe the publicity from this disaster might help,' she said, her voice trailing off as she looked at Tess writing silently. She began to drum her lacquered nails against the table.

'My dear, I've noticed you spending a fair amount of time with that odious seaman. Since your mother isn't here, I just want to warn you – you can do better.'

Tess's cheeks began to burn. She opened her mouth to answer, but Lucile cut her off.

'Second, we might as well get to this. We need to talk about your future. I don't need a maid in New York; I have two.'

Her voice had hardened, businesslike, and Tess, shocked, braced herself. Now came the dreaded repercussions of her disobedience.

'But, I thought—'

'Yes, I know, I mentioned something about working in my shop. And I know you're good with buttonholes.' Lucile sighed again, paced the room for a few moments.

'I can do much more than that,' Tess said with a rush. 'I'm good, I can be a true help to you, I—'

'Oh, Tess, you should see your face. Don't worry, I'm just teasing. I'll find a place for you. You're quick and intelligent. I will try you out in the shop – we'll start from there. Why are you looking at me that way?'

'I'm bewildered. It's as if, sometimes, a game is being played.'

'Game? *Game?* Oh, for heaven's sake.' Lucile's light laughter bounced through the air. 'Now sit down for a moment – I want to give you an idea of what we're going to face when we dock tonight. We are all celebrities now, you know.'

Tess wasn't quite sure what that would mean. Only gradually had she realised that the fate of the 'unsinkable' *Titanic* had drawn worldwide attention, that newspapers were clamoring for details, that inquiries were being planned, that the U.S. Congress would be involved. Radio messages had been flying back and forth between the *Carpathia* and the shore. Somehow it had seemed to her to be the private tragedy of the survivors, which she saw now was absurd.

'It's going to be a circus,' Lucile warned her. Tess should try to avoid the reporters; they were jackals and would crawl all over anybody unfamiliar with their deceits. She and Sir Cosmo would do the talking. There would be drivers from her New York office with cars at the dock to whisk them off to the Waldorf-Astoria hotel, so she was to stay close and not wander off. On second thought, they might stop at her salon; Madame was quite sure all the models would be there. 'And wait until you see this hotel, dear,' she said cheerfully. 'You will *die.*'

Tess winced at that. 'I'll make sure everything is ready,' she said, preparing to leave the room.

Lucile must have caught the shadow that flitted across her face.

'By the way, I've forgotten the name of the family you were working for in Cherbourg,' she said. 'Who were they, dear?'

'We haven't talked about them.' They both knew she had never named them.

'Perhaps not.' Madame surveyed her thoughtfully. 'But then . . .'

Why this cat-and-mouse game? She could say nothing. No, she would take a chance. 'Thank you for your kindness last night,' she said. 'You comforted me, and I am grateful for that.'

Once again, that sudden shift of expression on Lucile's face. 'It isn't what I do,' she said after a pause. 'But you brought it out of me.'

A short silence. And then it ended.

'Oh well, I know about made-up worlds. Do be sure you understand about the one we are entering – and that's the last time I'll ever remind you.' Madame smiled, her eyes dancing. 'So prepare yourself. We're about to go through Alice's looking glass.'

PENNSYLVANIA STATION

NEW YORK CITY

APRIL 18

7:00 A.M.

Pinky Wade sat hunched in her seat, staring out a grimy window as her train pulled slowly into the tunnel below the new Penn Station, that vast edifice of soaring arches and splendid skylights held up by magnificent pink granite columns. She jumped slightly as the conductor strode into the railcar and bawled out, 'New York City, end of the line!' Quickly she gathered her belongings, which consisted of a small satchel with an extra shirtwaist and toiletries. Pinky Wade was proud that she always traveled light.

She stepped from the train and started to mount the stairs, looking up toward the skylights expectantly. Yes, the light was bursting through, dancing off the heads of hurrying passengers and shimmering over every polished surface. Usually she loved this elegant passage from the train to the waiting room, loved stepping onto the gleaming travertine marble floors, imagining that she was in some kind of grand palace. She had no heart for it today, though. Weary and cranky, she was still smoldering over the *Times*'s demand for her presence. She made a half-hearted attempt to straighten out the mess of stringy hair pinned carelessly on top of her head, then glanced down at her shoes. Van Anda would probably make a few cracks about the length of her skirt, which now skimmed a few more inches above the top of her ankles. What did he expect her to wear when she was working?

She walked past a huge, gold-framed mirror and stopped, staring at her reflection. Well, surprise, she looked as cross as she felt. How could Van Anda have pulled her off the mental-hospital investigation to stick her with survivor interviews? It made her uneasy. He was a good boss, backed her up on most of her assignments. But in the end he was just like any other man in the newspaper business: when you've got something pathetically sentimental, bring in a woman reporter; that's what they're good for. If she had been booked on the *Titanic* – now that's a story that would have been worthwhile. Now she was stuck with the too-easy job of wringing human-interest accounts out of survivors.

She walked on, indignation rising. Sometimes she wondered why she kept reporting. Would her father ever admit to being proud of her? She had grown up hearing from him how smart she was, but then there were the little sharp-edged asides: most women are married by your age; what about a family? Pinky stopped again, scrambling in her bag for taxi money. She had more freedom to do what she wanted to do than most women, and maybe he hadn't liked sharing with her the guilty joy of the job. When she was exposing abuse at an orphanage or forcing reform in a mental hospital, she felt powerful. The truth was, she could still be yanked off an important story as quickly as a child being pulled away from a candy box.

She sighed as she hurried out of Pennsylvania Station and joined a line of people waiting for taxis. At least they didn't have to put up with horse-drawn hansoms anymore.

CITY ROOM, *NEW YORK TIMES*

NEW YORK CITY

APRIL 18

10:00 A.M.

Van Anda had hardly slept in three days, not that it mattered. Every other paper in the country was eating humble pie. Only the *Times* had had the nerve to print the story of the *Titanic*'s sinking before the White Star people finally stopped lying and confirmed it. This was the coup of his life, and there was no way he was going to lose that lead now. The *Carpathia* was due this evening, and he was almost ready. A whole floor at a local hotel had been reserved for his reporters, and they were ready to go. A dozen phones had been installed, with direct access to the rewrite desk. 'We were first, and we're going to stay first,' he crowed to the excited reporters in the city room.

'Hello, Carr.'

He looked up to see Pinky Wade standing in front of him, her arms crossed, a frown on her face. He smiled, noting that her skirts had inched up again. She was pretty enough – rosy skin, bright eyes, and a laugh that always had a bounce to it. Also something of a chameleon, which helped on undercover assignments. Plenty of courage and strong opinions. If it weren't for her smart mouth, she might even get away with pouring tea in one of those mansions on Fifth Avenue. She always gave the impression that she held enormous amounts of energy bottled inside her ready to burst out at any moment. No one loved a good story more than Pinky.

'You're to be down on the dock when the ship pulls in,' he said without preamble. 'Get steerage as well as first class. Quick takes – we'll piece it together. Did they see the iceberg, when did they realise what was going on. The more detail the better; get some near-miss stories. Get me—'

'Hello, Carr.'

Van Anda could see that she was really angry this time.

'Hello, Pinky.'

‘Why me?’ she asked.

‘Because you’re the best human-interest reporter I know. And I’m sorry you don’t have to risk your life for the story. I’ll try to rectify that later.’

She couldn’t help but smile. He did have a sense of humor.

‘I want to get on the ship before it docks,’ she said.

‘Great. You find a way; I’m happy.’

WASHINGTON, D.C.

APRIL 18

3:30 P.M.

Senator Smith barely made the train pulling out of Union Station, swinging himself up on the lower step as it began to move, a briefcase stuffed with papers tucked precariously under one arm, two aides scrambling up after him.

‘You’re impressing those reporters,’ one of them said, pointing at a swarm of men holding cameras and notebooks, now rapidly being left behind on the platform.

Smith was secretly pleased to hear his aide’s somewhat awed, breathless report. He’d shown them audacity all right, and it hadn’t taken long. His position on the Commerce Committee had helped, of course. His resolution to set up an investigation, with himself chairing, had gone through the Senate like a hot knife through butter; now, there was a good old midwestern expression. And he was going to start the hearings in New York instead of

Washington – right there in midtown at the Waldorf hotel. He'd snag more witnesses there, and get to them faster. Tomorrow morning, the show would begin.

The senator settled himself into a seat and checked his watch for the twentieth time. 'We've got to get on the *Carpathia* before it docks,' he said to the aides. 'Those White Star people will vanish if we don't slap subpoenas on them right away. Especially that slippery Ismay.'

'You think they planted those phony messages saying the ship hadn't sunk?' asked one.

'Absolutely.' It made him angry, thinking of all the people who had set off for Halifax to greet friends and family members after being reassured that the *Titanic* was safe. A brutal, cowardly lie, and for what? To gain more time for White Star officials to save their hides?

He frowned and leaned back in his seat. Yes, he had played his cards right. No one in Congress had thought faster than he. This, he told himself, staring out at the passing landscape, would crown his career as a public servant. If he made it in time.

Slowly the *Carpathia* inched forward, steaming ever closer to New York Harbor. By five o'clock people had begun lining the railings, straining for a glimpse of land. The evening would be brisk, and Tess pulled her sweater close. She watched the cook's wife, who had now taken to wandering the deck, grabbing at people's arms. 'Have you seen my children? Are they eating dinner?' she kept repeating.

'Please tell them I'm waiting. If they don't come soon, I have to go find them.'

Jim was standing by himself, smoking a cigarette, staring ahead where land would soon appear.

Tess looked around swiftly; Lucile was nowhere near. 'Will you be met?' she asked shyly, joining him at the rail, feeling awkward. Most likely, reaching land would make them strangers to each other again.

'Nobody here for me.' He said it with a light shrug. 'White Star says they're bunking us down somewhere for the inquiry. We'll see; Ismay has other ideas.' He looked down at her, seeming to search her face for something. 'I heard some U.S. senator is coming aboard soon to start interviewing the officers and crew,' he said.

'The captain says the government hearings begin tomorrow.'

Jim let out a short laugh. 'That means the politicians take over. Sorry, but I figure it will be one more dance of greedy businessmen finding excuses for their mistakes. No one gets blamed – that's what usually happens. None of them care about all the poor blighters in steerage or the men down in the boiler room. The stokers – they never had a chance.'

'You knew someone down there?' she guessed.

'A friend. A good man. We were going West together. He was stoking the boilers when we hit the iceberg. Sometimes I think I should've been down there shoveling coal with him, but I was sick of coal; told him nothing was going to get me within a mile of the stuff again.'

'I'm sorry.'

It was inadequate, but he didn't seem to mind.

'None of those men stood a chance, you know. The rest of us, we get to live and find out things. Nobody on that shore will care about them or remember them. I should've been with them, gone down with the ship.'

'They needed you on that lifeboat – you were the only one who knew how to row and what to do,' Tess said quickly. 'You were just doing your job. I know it feels wrong to be alive when all those people died. I feel that, too.'

He smiled slowly. 'It's all right, Tess. I guess there's enough pain and sadness on this ship without wishing for more of it.'

'And your carvings comforted the children,' she said quietly. 'I admire you for that.'

'I didn't do much,' he said. 'The girl I made the giraffe for? Both parents lost; she hasn't spoken a word since she told someone in the lifeboat her name. She followed me around all the time. Watched me carve for hours.'

Tess breathed deeply, wishing she could expel the anguish. Who would understand, other than those who were there?

'The children made this whole bloody time bearable. And so did you.' He seemed embarrassed, hesitated, and then reached into his pocket, pulling out something that he put in her hand, gently closing her fingers over it.

'This is for you – maybe not a memento you want, but it's what I found myself making. It's just whittling.' He smiled. 'Welcome to America, Tess. I hope we see each other again. Goodbye.'

'Jim—' It was the first time she had spoken his name.

But he put his finger to his lips, the gesture she remembered from their promenade on the deck of the *Titanic,* and walked away.

Tess opened her hand. She was holding a carefully carved wooden lifeboat. Peering at it in the waning light, she saw two tiny figures inside – each holding what looked like an oar. When she looked up to thank him, he was gone.

And so was the cook's wife. What happened? One moment there she was, standing on the deck. And now gone in search of her children; slipped into the sea.

Chapter 4

THE *CARPATHIA*

THURSDAY, APRIL 18

9 P.M.

It wasn't as difficult as Pinky had anticipated. It took just a little chatting-up of a friendly dockworker to discover that a tugboat was set to go out to the *Carpathia* before the ship docked – an important senator from Washington wanted to get on and talk to people. That had to be William Smith, the senator from Michigan, who was slated to chair a congressional investigation. Starting tomorrow morning. What a show *this* would be.

Then it was a matter of being in the right place at the right time, wearing a pair of pants cajoled from a copyboy, her hair tucked under a cap, looking like a dockworker, when Senator Smith came hurrying up, sweat on his brow from the race from the train station. A little bustle, some hellos, some 'welcome, sir's, some shouts to crew members, all in a flurry, and Smith and a couple of officious-looking aides stepped into the tugboat. The important thing always, Pinky knew, was to act like you belonged where you were forbidden to go. Hesitation was the mark of an amateur.

Whistling, she jumped onto the tugboat in the dark. Maybe this would be worthwhile after all.

The tugboat captain cut his engine and slowly approached the *Carpathia*. Pinky looked up and saw clusters of people huddled in sodden knots at the rail, hunched forward like mourners on a funeral ship. Not even a child's shout or wail broke the silence from the deck above; for a moment, the soft lapping of waves against the tugboat stern was the only sound. Then, unexpectedly, thunder began to roll and lightning crackled in the sky.

She considered trying to sneak closer to the aides surrounding Smith for a better idea of what they were about, but she couldn't take her eyes off those still figures on the ship. The tugboat inched forward; they were almost touching the hull.

Suddenly there was an explosion of flashing lights, revealing the presence of several more tugboats approaching the *Carpathia*. Flashpowder. Shouts.

'Hello, up there!' bellowed a voice through a megaphone. 'Are you the survivors? Any of you want to talk? Jump in, we'll take care of you!'

Pinky smiled. She knew who that was, holding the megaphone – a *World* reporter, full of strut and swagger and few brains. How could he think making all that noise would persuade anyone on *this* ship to jump into the sea?

Had it not occurred to him to sneak on and scoop everybody else? This would make her job easier.

Within minutes, as her rivals kept shouting up to the silent watchers on the deck, she was climbing a rope ladder behind Smith and his entourage, slipping onto the deck and stepping back into the dark. She was sure no one saw her.

Tess was watching the newcomers climb aboard when she saw a shadowy figure break from the group and dodge behind a smokestack. She made her way across the deck for a closer view, wondering why someone was trying to hide. She saw a woman in dungarees, mumbling to herself as she tried to shove long, thick hair under the cap on her head.

'Could you help me with this? My hair won't stay in place,' she said impatiently as Tess approached.

'Who are you?' Tess asked.

'An impostor, obviously. Please?'

Maybe it was the casual cheerfulness of her request. For whatever reason, Tess found herself lifting the back of the cap and tucking in Pinky's wayward locks, resisting an impulse to laugh. 'You look silly,' she said.

'Well, so would you if you were disguised as a man. I should've cut this whole mess off.'

'So who are you?' Tess asked again.

'I guess I'm stuck with explaining, aren't I? I'm Sarah Wade, but everybody calls me Pinky.'

'Why are you hiding in the shadows?' Tess stepped backward to get a better look at this rather bizarre creature, and stumbled over a coiled rope. Jim's carving flew from her pocket, hit the deck, and skittered toward the edge. With a sharp cry she reached for it.

Pinky was faster. She dived and caught the piece of wood just before it went over the edge and into the sea. Silently she stood and handed it back to Tess, squinting at it through the meager light.

'A boat?' she said, curious.

'Yes. Thank you.' Tess's hand was much quicker this time as she took the carving and shoved it back into her pocket.

'Okay, to answer your question, I'm a reporter. I want to talk to *Titanic* survivors, and this outfit made it easier to get on the ship. Did I alarm you?'

'Hardly, sorry.'

Pinky looked almost comically crestfallen. 'Oh, right. You think I look silly.'

'A little. How did you keep from being found out on the boat that brought you out here?'

'Men aren't too observant, in my experience.'

'Unless you're wearing a skirt,' Tess said.

'Oh, right. Then they just want to get their hands underneath.'

Tess laughed. She liked this cocky little person. 'Are pants more comfortable than a skirt?' she asked.

'Of course, kind of freeing – like bloomers but better,' Pinky said. She peered at Tess's sloppy, worn sweater, something obviously out of a ragbag. 'I'm guessing you were on the *Titanic*. Am I right?'

'Yes,' Tess said, her smile vanishing. The question was coming from another world – a safe world, one she hadn't inhabited for days.

'It must have been dreadful.'

'Yes,' Tess repeated. She felt itchy now. Unwilling to stand still.

'Will you tell me about it?'

'Tell me about you first.'

'I work for the *New York Times*. It's one of the good papers, not a scandal sheet. Everybody says so.' She quickly amended her words. 'Well, almost everybody.'

'I don't think I can take your word for that,' Tess said, thinking of the newspapers she had seen in Europe.

'You would be a bit naïve if you did. Lots of people say we're obnoxious and deceitful, and sometimes it's true. Look, I just want to hear your story. I don't know who you are, but I'm glad you survived. I assure you, that is not a deceitful statement. What's your name?'

'Tess Collins, and please don't call me Tessie.'

Someone that immediately touchy was probably a servant. 'How did you end up on the *Titanic*?' Pinky asked. She tried not to make her voice hurried, but she couldn't waste time if she was going to get more interviews before Smith and his crowd caught her.

'I was hired as a maid for the trip, and I was lucky.'

'Why were you lucky?'

'Because I had a cabin in first class, where the lifeboats were.'

Pinky waited again. She got her best information that way.

'People died because they weren't able to get on the boats,' Tess said.

'There weren't enough, right? That's what we're hearing.' Pinky pulled a notebook and pencil from her pocket and began scribbling. 'How did you escape?'

'I made it into one of the last lifeboats, with two children; their father asked me to take them.'

'Did he make it?'

'No.'

This would be good colour. 'Whose maid are you?'

Tess stiffened. 'I'm only that for the journey.'

'Sorry.' It took time to be adroit, time she didn't have. 'So who—'

'I work for Lady Lucile Duff Gordon.'

'The designer?'

'Yes.'

'Was she in your boat?'

'No. Look, you can get better stories from other people.' It suddenly occurred to Tess that she was disobeying Lucile, getting herself into more peril. She didn't want to talk about anything more. She just wanted this reporter to go away.

'I'm sorry, it must be brutal to get questions fired at you so fast.' But Pinky wasn't through. 'If all the lifeboats were on the upper deck, then mostly first-class passengers survived?'

Tess saw again the faces from steerage. 'I think so,' she said. 'Most of the others couldn't get to the boats in time.'

'Then you were doubly lucky.' Pinky scribbled faster. Here it was, that whole rotten class-division thing again.

This was going to be one more story, she was sure of it, of the rich getting preferential treatment over the poor. She didn't have the count yet, but she was certain many more first-class than steerage passengers survived. What a corrupt world it was. She stopped, pencil poised. 'Why weren't you in the boat with Lady Duff Gordon?'

'It was launched before I could get in.'

'Why? Was it full?'

Tess hesitated. 'No. I don't know why.'

'How many people in it?'

'About twelve or so.'

The pieces were fitting together amazingly fast – on her first try. The imperious Lucile Duff Gordon, the not-too-nice doyenne of the fashion world – this world-famous rich woman saved herself in an almost empty boat. Pinky closed her notebook. She wanted to ask more questions, but she had to catch other passengers before Senator Smith finished handing out his subpoenas. If she didn't go back on that tender with him, she'd get stuck in the crowd at the disembarking.

'Thanks, you've been helpful,' Pinky said, shoving notebook and pencil into her pocket. 'It was nice to meet you.' She turned to go, then stopped. 'Good luck,' she said, reaching out a hand. 'Maybe we'll meet again on shore.'

'Thank you for saving my carving,' Tess said suddenly.

'Sure,' said Pinky. 'Maybe you'll tell me the story behind it next time.'

'Story?'

'There's always a story,' Pinky said as she turned away,

dodged behind a smokestack, and disappeared into the crowd.

The ship moved on slowly, and soon those on board found themselves staring at what looked like thousands of people on the pier who, in their silence, seemed almost a mirror image of themselves. Bundled in heavy, dark coats and bowler hats with rain dripping onto their collars, the families waiting on the dock stood in lines arranged alaphabetically under large posters. It was a forlorn effort to somehow organise the reunion of survivors and families without chaos, doomed to failure.

Hoarse voices began crying out names, hoping to hear answering shouts. Women began to cry. People pushed forward as the gangplanks were hoisted into place, many groaning in frustration when they realised that first-class passengers would be first to disembark. Doctors in white coats and nurses in starched caps moved among the waiting men and women, armed with smelling salts and cold compresses for those who might faint or suffer heart attacks when they learned the worst. It was coming for many of them, a snaking live wire of dread traveling through the crowd.

Senator Smith stood on the bridge of the *Carpathia*, looking out past the black sea at the crowd on the dock, his stomach roiling. He hated ships, hated the sea. His hands felt sticky with salt water. He had a strong urge to wash them, but perhaps that urge was primarily to wash away the memory of the frozen-faced Brit he had just interviewed. How could the man be so stiff in the face of what had happened? All Ismay was worried about was saving his own hide. Smith grabbed the railing as the ship suddenly rocked sideways, pushing down the bile in his throat. He had to get off this thing. But his instinct had been right. He was glad he had come on board and caught Ismay before the wily fellow had a chance to hop a returning ship, escaping any accounting to the people of the United States. His resolve to see this through, to pursue every angle, was strengthening. It wasn't just about making a name for himself in Washington anymore. Didn't those people down below him, watching the ship come closer, knowing their lives were forever altered – didn't they deserve to know the truth of *why* that bloody ship went down? They were close enough now – he could see their faces: a woman with hands clasped in front of her mouth as if in prayer; the man next to her peering upward in obvious anguish, hoping to catch a glimpse of a familiar face. A wife? A child? He swallowed hard. He could do this. He *would* do this, follow every lead, no matter what, for if he was anything he was a righteous man.

And that Brit, with his flat, expressionless eyes, would be the first witness, whether he liked it or not.

Lucile hesitated at the top of the gangplank as she looked down on the faces turned in her direction, jolted by the sheer nakedness of emotion they displayed. She shuddered, clutching at Cosmo's arm.

'Walk quickly, dear,' Cosmo said. 'These people don't want to see us.' He held on to her firmly as dockworkers began clearing a route for the first-class passengers through the crowd and to their waiting automobiles. With Tess following close behind, the Duff Gordons made their way to the parking area and their Packard Victoria. And standing there, talking to the driver, a long coat hiding her pants, was Pinky Wade.

'Welcome back to New York, Madame Lucile,' she said cheerfully, not looking at Tess. 'I'm Pinky Wade of the *New York Times*.'

'No interviews now,' Cosmo said gruffly.

Lucile paused as she started to enter the car, scanning Pinky's face. 'Any relation to Prescott Wade?' she asked.

'My father,' Pinky said shortly.

Lucile's eyes widened slightly. 'I knew your father. Long after he became famous covering the Beecher trial, of course. A very gallant adventurer, as I recall. Climbed mountains, and other things.'

'Well, he did get around.' As usual, Pinky looked down when her father's name was dropped into a conversation.

'We must go,' Cosmo said. 'No interview, please.' He opened the front door and nodded to Tess to climb in next to the driver.

'Of course not, you've all been through a terrible experience.' Pinky shut her open notebook with a snap. 'But life goes on, and I'd like to talk to you later – about the ship and, well, I'm not much into fashion, but I'd be interested in how you're planning to market your spring collection.'

Lucile nodded. 'That can be arranged,' she said, getting into the car.

'I know this sounds terribly inappropriate, but it's always a bounce for the social set here when you arrive,' Pinky said with a grin, thinking fast. Anything to keep this woman's attention. 'And I hear your sister is ready to shock Hollywood again with her latest novel – can we talk about that, too?'

This time Lucile laughed. 'I'm having a dinner tonight at our hotel – why don't you join us?'

'No, that's not a good idea,' objected a startled Cosmo.

'Oh, for heaven's sake, I knew her father,' Lucile said impatiently. 'Well?'

'I'd be delighted,' Pinky said. Even she was a little shocked. With pain and sadness wrecking the lives of the people still on the dock behind them, this woman was planning a fancy dinner? She had better get back to the newsroom and write fast. This was too good to miss.

'I know what you're thinking,' Lucile said before vanishing into the car. 'But you put it well, Miss Wade. Life must go on. Dinner is in an hour.'

Tess glanced back at the figure of Pinky Wade standing on the curb as the car drove off, wondering if she should mention their encounter on the ship. But Lucile and Cosmo had launched immediately into an argument.

'You're too careless with your invitations,' Cosmo began.

'Nonsense,' Lucile said. Cosmo was entirely too cautious. That girl's father had been a delightful man, very responsible, not just a grubby reporter; surely this Pinky woman knew she had a legacy to live up to. There were so many more important things to think about! There were dozens of things to do in preparation for the New York spring show; thank goodness they were staying at the Waldorf. Tonight would be lovely: no more terrible shipboard food; good friends, gracious dining ... How could he want to spoil her fun?

'Tess, you're invited too, dear,' she said.

Slumped in her seat, Tess dozed, letting herself enjoy the feel of the soft leather cushion caressing her head. She had never been in so luxurious an automobile. Outside, scraps of a new, busy city slipped by, too quickly for her brain to absorb. She would face its demands and energy tomorrow. Right now, all she wanted was a room alone, with clean sheets and a soft pillow. She closed her eyes and, with a sting of melancholy, her thoughts drifted to Jack Bremerton. He was gone, and with him her silly fantasies about seeing him again. A brave man, gone. Her thoughts turned to Jim, reliving their moments of goodbye on the *Carpathia* – his blue eyes, his kindness, his serious intensity. She could no longer dismiss him as just a village boy. Not that it mattered, because she would probably never see him again, which deepened her melancholy. By the time the sleek black Packard in which they rode pulled up at the Waldorf, she was in a hazy, deep sleep.

Stepping into the private upstairs dining room of the Waldorf later that night was like stepping into a red velvet–lined jewel box. It was the most elegant room Tess had ever seen. Her feet – shod now in borrowed shoes – immediately sank deep into the carpet. Waiters hovered. Tentatively, Tess pulled a chair up to the table, inspecting the ironing job on the elegant white linen tablecloth with a practiced eye. She knew the difficulties of ironing linen and lace, and this was meticulous work.

'Does it meet your standards, Tess?' Lucile said, apparently amused at the girl's inspection. 'We are on land now, no rolling deck beneath our feet. Tonight, I intend to enjoy myself. The ordeal is over. Isn't that right, dear?'

Tess was spared an answer as several friends of the Duff Gordons came bursting through the door, all descending with lavish cries and hugs and kisses. She fingered the wispy chiffon gown Lady Duff Gordon had pronounced that she should wear, feeling oddly naked. What was she doing here under these glittering chandeliers, watching waiters pour champagne into thin-stemmed crystal glasses? Back in Cherbourg, she would be waiting on this table, not sitting at it.

'I feel we are welcoming you back to the land of the living,' said one woman in a low, tremulous voice as she planted a moist lipstick kiss on her friend's cheek. 'Dearest

Lucile, we are so grateful you were saved. Look—' She reached back with her hand and pulled forward a dignified-looking gentleman with a very dark mustache. 'We brought Jim Matthews to celebrate with us!'

Lucile had already taken a few sips of champagne, enough to bring a hovering waiter to refill her glass, and her colour was high. She reached out her hand. This was one of her favorite, most sycophantic fashion writers – a man who always touted her designs. 'My dear friend, I'm delighted to have you here, even though you refuse to take my advice and leave that awful newspaper business.'

'But then where would New York be able to read the best coverage of the latest Lucile designs?' the man asked with a smile, bending to clasp her hand.

Everyone laughed, though Tess noted Sir Cosmo's eyes narrowing. He became intent on lighting his pipe when he saw her looking at him. With the match lit and the pipe in place, Cosmo was staring disapprovingly at the door. Tess followed his eye.

Pinky Wade was standing there, surveying the scene with interest. She obviously wasn't intimidated by her surroundings. She wore a nondescript dress that was much too short and stained on the bodice, and her boots were shabby. She had a huge, floppy bag tossed over her shoulder.

'Welcome, my dear, are you staying for dinner?' Lady Duff Gordon swept her with a critical eye. 'The girl is a walking clothes disaster,' she murmured to a nearby friend. 'Why do women do this to themselves?'

Pinky seemed oblivious. 'Absolutely. It's free, isn't it?'

She smiled brightly at the gathered crowd and plunked down in an empty seat. Spotting Tess across the table, she waved.

'You know her?' Cosmo said, lookly sharply at Tess.

'I met her on the *Carpathia*.'

'That wasn't a good idea.' His voice was cool.

'We spoke only briefly,' Tess said quickly.

'I understand. But Lucile *did* advise you not to talk with reporters.'

'Quite a dinner you're having,' Pinky said, cutting in. She beckoned to one of the waiters holding a cheese plate, scooped up a silver spoon, and began helping herself, pleased with the way things were going. Van Anda had been deliriously happy with the material she had picked up on the ship. Her stock was so high in the *Times* newsroom that he told her she could follow the *Titanic* story from any angle she wanted. Which was exactly what she was doing tonight. She glanced at Tess, and felt even more confident of her decision to keep collecting string on Lifeboat One rather than dumping it into her first story. There was more to learn, she was sure of it, and getting this invitation had been a major stroke of luck. She spread a healthy scoop of Camembert onto a small roll, appreciatively munching away as she looked around the room, not wanting to seem too focused on Lady Duff Gordon. This stuff was good – salty and buttery. She'd try the Fourme d'Ambert next.

Why, Pinky asked herself, was there such a mystique around this flashy woman with the pretentious last name? For someone who loomed so large in the gilded world of the New York rich, she looked very small with her flaming, almost defiantly red, hair. A curious package altogether.

'My dear, I do hope you like the cheese, but we must save room for the delicious filet mignon the chef is preparing for us right now,' Lucile sang out across the table. Her laughter rippled through the dining room – lighter, more girlish than Pinky had expected.

Pinky reached for the Fourme d'Ambert, cutting herself a thick slice. 'I certainly will,' she said cheerfully. 'So are you going to tell us all about your experience, Lady Duff Gordon?'

'Yes, what happened, Lucy?' implored a woman with a boa wrapped around her shoulders. 'Oh, Lucy, tell us from start to finish! How did you survive?'

Lucile cleared her throat, casting a triumphant glance at Cosmo. 'My dears, looking down from the deck, hearing the screams of the poor souls below, I won't deny that I feared those black waters,' she said, her naturally husky voice descending an octave. 'It was the most incredible adventure of my life, and it took every ounce of resolve to cheat fate.'

'Just how did you do that?' Pinky asked quietly.

'By keeping my head when others lost theirs,' Lucile replied coolly.

For the next five minutes, she held her audience enthralled. She lamented the incompetence of the ship's crew, the flimsiness of the canvas lifeboat, the coldness, the fear. She described how, even with the ice water of the sea seeping up through her toes to her ankles, she managed to hold off the hysterics of the other survivors ... and then, in a broken, almost breathless whisper, told of the awful moment when the *Titanic* plunged to the bottom of the sea. 'Women and men were clinging to bits of wreckage in the icy water, and it was at least an hour before the awful chorus of shrieks ceased,' she said.

Cosmo cleared his throat, putting a cautionary hand on his wife's arm. She shook him off.

'I remember the very last cry, a man's voice calling loudly, "My God, my God –"' Lucile's voice broke off. Her hands, quickly hidden, had begun to shake.

By now the small roomful of people had been reduced to tears. Even the waiters were riveted in place, listening, eyes wide, holding plates in midair. Swept away by her own account, Lucile lifted her face to the shimmering light from the crystal chandelier, not even attempting to wipe away the tears trickling down her cheeks.

Tess looked down at her own clenched hands beneath the tablecloth. She could almost taste the salt, the anguish; almost grab on again to the rough, wet sides of her own boat, the telling was so vivid. She glanced up at the faces of the well-dressed men and women leaning forward under the glittering chandeliers, oohing and aahing, tossing in questions at Lucile's dramatic pauses.

'Oh Lucy, how fortunate that you had the intelligence to devise your escape,' murmured one of the guests. 'How brave you were.'

'People were deluded, scoffing that the ship couldn't possibly sink.' She seemed briefly to be somewhere else, dreaming. The room went quiet. There was palpable relief when she regained her normal authoritative tone. 'I saw them pull back from the lifeboats, refusing to board. I hate to say this, but they were idiots. They didn't use their heads. Those who stayed calm had the best chance to survive.'

'How many in your boat, Lady Duff Gordon?' Pinky asked abruptly.

'We were in the captain's boat, and we might have been able to take a few more if the crew hadn't been so disorganised,' Lucile replied.

'Who gave the order to launch prematurely?'

'It wasn't premature – the ship was sinking, for heaven's sake.'

'We weren't the only half-full boat, Miss Wade,' Cosmo cut in, his words clipped tight. 'We've heard that the loading of passengers was botched across the ship.'

'But yours was the emptiest – makes one wonder,' Pinky said. Her tone was non-accusatory, and her eyes lit up as waiters began serving thick cuts of filet mignon on pink china rimmed in silver. 'Wonderful meal,' she said with a nod to Lucile. 'Thank you for inviting me.' She began cutting into her meat, as rosy and tender as any she had ever eaten, chewing happily as the others shifted uneasily and played with their forks.

'Are you criticizing me after what I endured?' Lucile demanded.

Pinky wiped her mouth with an impatient sweep of her white linen napkin. 'I'm not criticizing you, I'm stating a fact,' she said. 'If I understand correctly, you even called the shots in the lifeboat.'

'That's quite enough on this tragic event,' Cosmo said, cutting quickly into their exchange. 'My wife remains distraught, as do I. We hoped you were joining us tonight to share our celebration of life, not to attack.'

With hardly a sound in the room, Pinky put her fork down on the edge of her plate and looked up, gazing steadily first at Lucile and then at Cosmo.

'It's not enough to celebrate survival,' she said calmly. 'There are people downstairs in the hotel lobby, down at the docks, in the tenements on the East Side, who lost husbands and wives and sisters and children, and they have nothing to celebrate. People like you always survive. You owe more.'

Again, silence.

'This isn't the usual rich-versus-poor story you like to tell,' Jim Matthews said, glaring at Pinky. 'Lucy, you've told an incredible story, and your behavior was heroic, that's my opinion. I know Mr. Hearst will want your account for the *Sunday American*. Can we use it? With your signature?'

'I think not—' Sir Cosmo started to say, but Lucile interrupted him with a decisive shake of her head. She would not be cowed by this rude girl.

'Of course you may,' she said.

Pinky pushed her chair back from the table and rose. Somehow she had managed to clean her plate. 'That's definitely brave of you,' she said. 'I hope you'll fill out more details about what went on in your lifeboat. I'm hearing some tales. Good night, all.'

She glanced at Tess, silently answering her surprised

look. Yes, she had been talking to others about Lifeboat One.

Tess's eyes followed Pinky as she threw her bag over her shoulder and marched out the door. No one else here seemed to be paying attention. Lady Duff Gordon was already in animated conversation with one of her friends, and a thin vein of laughter had begun to ripple around the table, clearly at Pinky's expense. It was as if they were behind glass, safe from the anger of others. Overdressed, caked in makeup. Lipsticked cigarettes in crystal ashtrays, smelling sour. Tess slipped out of her seat and hurried after Pinky.

'Wait,' she said.

Pinky paused at the opening elevator doors. 'What are you doing, trying to get your head chopped off? You shouldn't be following me. She'll fire you in an instant.'

'You're right about it not being enough to survive. I wanted to tell you that.'

'Be careful, those are dangerous words. You work for pompous, privileged people who never learn anything. I still don't know why you're risking your job. Go back and eat the fancy desserts she's providing.'

'I'm not hungry.' It was true. The meal tonight might as well have been sawdust.

'What's taking away your appetite?'

'It's too soon. And it's too much.' She could say it – she had to say it, whether it was disloyal to Lucile or not.

'Of course, these people don't change. Did you think it would be different?'

Tess drew a deep breath. 'Yes,' she said simply.

Pinky peered curiously at Tess. For someone who had been a servant in America for no more than a few hours, she was taking some big chances. But her own anger was turning to chagrin: She was an idiot. She could have learned more about what happened on Lifeboat One instead of taking an easy shot at a puffed-up designer who could see a major disaster only through the prism of her own experience. She should have kept her wits and listened, asking questions, not making stupid speeches.

'I'm not angry at you, I'm the one who made a mess of things. I should have shut my mouth and listened.'

'But you spoke up.'

'So, okay, will you talk to me?' Pinky challenged.

'What is it I can tell you? Everybody did the best they could.' She had said this before, somewhere.

'Oh, I see. Back in the employ of the fabulous Lady Duff. Okay, see you later.'

Pinky stepped into the elevator, letting the doors close behind her.

Flushing, Tess turned to go back to the dining room. She had been dismissed, just dismissed, as if she wasn't worth anything. She stopped. Lucile, arms folded in front of her chest, was standing at the end of the hall.

'If you do not like my food, I can make other arrangements,' she said in an icy tone. 'Is that what you want?'

'I wasn't hungry,' Tess managed.

'That woman insulted me. Blatantly. And you apparently admired that. That's why you followed her out here.'

'No, not like that . . . ' Tess tried to say more, but no words came out. Lucile stared at her, an impenetrable gaze. But Tess saw again something elusive flitting back and forth in Madame's eyes. And then it disappeared.

'You may – let me put it differently – you are *ordered* to return to your room.' Lucile turned on her heel, pausing to add, 'Get some sleep, in a decent bed, finally.' She marched back to the dining room, not waiting for Tess's response.

Pinky stared at her image in the gilt-framed mirror at the back of the elevator as it descended. Women preened and primped in front of this thing every night, pinching their cheeks for a rosy glow, adjusting their hair, stroking their diamonds. But right now she was looking at herself, and she looked grubby. Sharp-eyed, sharp-tongued, and grubby.

She shouldn't have turned her back on Tess; she could have said something more. Why did she always feel that it was up to her to correct the unfairness of the world? Her father scolded her often enough. Lose your coolness and you'll lose your journalist eye; that's what he said.

The elevator doors parted and she stepped out into the Waldorf's lobby, where preparations were already under way for the beginning of the U.S. Senate's *Titanic* inquiry. It was a smart decision to move fast, before the survivors became restive to go home. More people were gathering, probably afraid they wouldn't get seats in the morning. Even she was nonplussed at the increased intensity of the scene. Women in shabby clothes sat unheedingly on the rich brocade chairs, some of them crying and wiping their eyes. Men in tweed caps, eyes haunted, milled about, talking to one another, holding themselves apart from this alien environment. Pinky glanced down at her notebook: 706 survivors out of some 2,223 people. Sixty percent of the first-class passengers survived, most of them women. No surprise there. And only twenty-five percent of those in steerage.

Young men in stiff collars carrying boxes into the hotel were hurrying back and forth through the lobby, vanishing into a huge ballroom lit with crystal. Pinky's gaze traveled back to the center of the room, where the action seemed concentrated around a slight man in a black coat. His mustache was so big it almost swallowed his face.

So now she could meet William Alden Smith legitimately. No use keeping out of his way; he surely knew she had sneaked onto the *Carpathia* – that is, if he and his aides had read her survivor interviews in the late edition. But maybe not. Notebook out, Pinky wedged her way closer, scribbling down everything she could hear. 'Hello, Senator Smith,' she said with a big smile. 'I'm Pinky Wade, from the *New York Times*. What—'

'Yes, Miss Wade, I think we've traveled together. Am I right?' His eyes were quick, more intelligent than she had expected.

'Yes, sir.'

'Were you the one in the cap, whistling?'

Pinky felt a slight blush creep up her neck. She nodded.

'I thought so. It's a good song, "Good Night, Ladies." But it isn't a sailor's tune.'

'Next time I'll choose a better one,' she said. 'Can I ask a question now?'

He smiled and nodded. He had thrown her off balance for a second or two; that felt good.

'Who's your first witness tomorrow?'

'Bruce Ismay.' No reason not to tell her. He knew her reputation; this was a reporter to cultivate.

'Is it true he was trying to set a speed record?'

Smith blinked, startled. 'Who told you that?'

'I've got my sources, Senator. You can read all about it in the night edition of the *Times*.'

'I have no comment,' he said stiffly.

'Okay, but it sounds like the focus of your inquiry is on White Star's culpability, right?'

'*Alleged* culpability. We will cover everything, Miss Wade. Including the fact that there weren't enough lifeboats.'

'My editor figured that out first. Be sure to ask Ismay how many people were in his. There were a lot of places in those lifeboats that went begging. Especially in Lifeboat One.'

'I know that,' he said, annoyed. This woman was getting on his nerves.

Pinky grinned. 'Thanks, Senator. See you tomorrow morning.'

She turned, satisfied; at least she had a fresh top for the earliest morning edition. She headed for the door, then stopped. Sitting in a corner of the lobby, half hidden by a monster elephant-tree plant, was one of the sailors she had talked with on the *Carpathia*. He looked depressed, almost as if he was deliberately hiding himself.

Pinky edged through the crowd toward the man. 'Hello again,' she said, pushing back the huge leaves of the plant. 'It's me, Pinky Wade. What's wrong?'

Startled, he looked up at her. 'What are you doing here?'

'Oh, just a little more reporting. We didn't talk too long on the ship. Anything else you want to tell me?'

'No.' He slumped back down in his seat.

'Are you going to have to testify?' she asked.

'I hope not.'

'I would sure like to know what happened in that lifeboat.'

He looked up at her again, more thoughtfully this time. Assessing her usefulness to him, she figured. 'Maybe you will,' he said.

'Now?'

'Now.'

Pinky pulled up a chair.

It must have been long past midnight, but Tess couldn't sleep. The first night of her life in a bed with a thick, luxurious mattress that felt heavenly, covered in the smooth crispness of fine percale sheets, and she could not close her eyes. The Duff Gordons were arguing with each other, their voices rising and falling in the next room, gaining energy as the hours passed. Only when they shouted could she hear the words. 'I'll say what I want to say, and no one will stop me, not even you,' Madame railed at one point.

Tess threw an arm across her brow. She knew enough about marital fights – she had certainly lived through many of these late-night sessions between her parents.

She rose, moving silently across the room, wary of making any noise. She stopped before a handsome mahogany dresser and poured herself a glass of water from a fragile porcelain pitcher, staring into the mirror. Only a few days ago, she wanted nothing more than to *be* the fabulous Lucile. All that she had dreamed about and hoped for had been delivered to her. She had moved into the orbit of the woman she most admired.

But things were tipping, turning sideways. That one warm moment on the ship – Lucile understanding the pain, sharing this awful experience – what a wonderful thing. To know that she cared, that she understood what it was like to try and break free and move upward – overwhelming. Yet those flashes of – say it plain, no one was listening – *cruelty* . . . What was there to say about them? Sometimes the fabulous Lucile didn't seem quite so fabulous anymore. But at other times she seemed to be reaching out, in need. How could Tess not offer solace?

And yet she couldn't shake the feeling that there was something else going on that she didn't understand.

Pinky was right – it wasn't enough just to survive. And maybe Jim was, too: maybe she was trying too hard to hold on to her meal ticket in this new country.

She bowed her head, weary at being faced once again with conflicting emotions. Stand up, challenge, do what you want. Yes. That's what had got her off the farm, got her fleeing Cherbourg, got her on the *Titanic*. No. Be careful, be loyal, challenge nothing. Why had she survived? Why not all those poor souls praying and pleading in the water? Why not Jack Bremerton? She owed a debt, but it wasn't clear to whom – or how it was to be paid.

She fingered the carving of the lifeboat she had placed in front of the mirror, moving her finger gently around its curves and crevices. Impulsively, she dipped a finger into a jar of cold cream and drew the outline of her face on the mirror, then stepped back. Odd – the size of the image didn't change even as she retreated. Shouldn't it be shrinking? She moved forward; it stayed the same. She was no larger, no smaller.

She drained the glass, grateful for the cool water, then returned to bed. She fell into a restless sleep with one last conscious thought: whatever was to come next would not be the glamour of strolling the deck of the *Titanic*. That was gone forever, if it had ever existed.

Chapter 5

WALDORF-ASTORIA

APRIL 19

Tess knocked lightly on the Duff Gordons' door the next morning, not sure what to expect. Lucile answered almost immediately, looking wan and listless. There was no sign of her husband. Silently, she pointed to a copy of the *American* on her bed.

Tess picked up the paper. 'MY HARROWING EXPERIENCE ESCAPING THE TITANIC' was the headline, followed by a first-person account of Lucile's near-death adventure, enhanced with lurid prose. So melodramatic, it took her breath away.

'Did I say all that last night?' Lucile asked. Her voice was subdued.

'Some of it. But it's been embellished; it's not fair.'

'I feel terrible. Cosmo is furious.'

Lucile looked so fragile, her face crumpled and tired, that Tess, impulsively, took her hand. 'It's just someone's idea of a way of selling newspapers,' she said. 'The same way it's done in England.'

'But not with me as the victim.' The older woman sank down on the silk-covered sofa next to the window. 'Cosmo says I've put myself front and center of this disaster and we will pay dearly for it. That everybody will go after us now, making up all sorts of stories. Why are they mocking me?' She snatched the paper and threw it to the floor. 'Did you read some of those sentences?' She quoted, in a mincing voice: "I said to my husband, we may as well get into the boat, although the trip will be only a little pleasure excursion until the morning.' I never said that! Did I?'

'No, you didn't – you weren't at all flippant.' There was no use reminding Lucile of how much she *had* said last night. 'You were just telling your story.'

'Thank you, dear. You understand.' Lucile seemed genuinely comforted. 'There's nothing about me in the *New York Times*, fortunately,' she said. 'The Wade girl wrote about the failings of the ship's captain and the muddled response of White Star, and threw in a few narrow-escape stories – the full front page. She didn't write about my dinner. Probably realised she owed us something for that good meal she gobbled down.' Lucile glanced sideways at Tess, her only acknowledgment of their confrontation the night before.

'What a scruffy lot, these reporters,' she continued.

'Now help me get ready, dear. I have to get to my shop. Thank goodness I shipped most of the dresses for the show ahead of time. It would have been truly dreadful if they had all gone down. The—'

'What about the inquiry?' Tess asked, surprised.

Lucile looked at her sharply. 'After this story? Tess, if I go down there I will be inundated with reporters. You know what the bellman who brought up the papers this morning said? He said people downstairs were talking about the "millionaires" boat.' How can I go down and be subjected to that mockery?' She waved her hand dismissively, looking less wan and more determined. 'You go and find out what happens. You had your dress sent to the hotel laundress last night, didn't you? I'm going to my salon.'

Tess had her hand on the doorknob when she turned back. She had to ask. 'Did anything terrible happen in your lifeboat?' she asked softly.

'Are you trying to condemn me, too?' Lucile's voice was suddenly fierce.

'No, of course not. But—'

'Nothing happened, for heaven's sake. Absolutely nothing. And all this talk about our boat being huge is ridiculous. It was quite small. Aside from the Darlings' deception, there was nothing happening. Now do you feel better?'

'Yes.' But she didn't. Lucile's smile was too hard at the edges.

At nine o'clock, Tess made her way to the hotel's already crowded East Room. She could hardly breathe as she pushed her way in. The room simmered under the full voltage of five huge crystal chandeliers, made all the more stifling by the hundreds of people pushing their way in, many of them – especially the ones in shabby dress – jammed up against the walls. She felt sweat building under her arms and wished she had something lighter to wear. Cosmo had slipped an envelope with her pay in American dollars for the first week under her door last night, but she could not imagine spending it on anything as frivolous as clothes. It was all she had.

A large woman slipped her ample girth into one of the last remaining seats behind Tess and leaned forward to chat. It was Margaret Brown.

'Well, hello again, my fellow oarsman, I do declare.' Her face was so round and motherly. 'Your lady certainly made the news this morning, didn't she?'

'Unfairly,' Tess said quickly.

'She didn't give the interview?'

'Well, she did, yes.'

'Ah, too bad. Though it's not quite fair to call their raft the "millionaires' boat," I'd say. There were plenty of millionaires on all the boats. But getting singled out isn't good. There might be a hard time ahead for the Duff Gordons.'

'She was just trying to tell her story.'

Mrs. Brown looked kindly at Tess. 'You are a loyal young woman, I see. If she's lucky, Lady Duff Gordon will be spared any further attention. This very proper Senator

Smith doesn't plan to call any women to testify. He says we're too delicate to be put through such a public trauma. Isn't that ridiculous? Here's what I think. These men don't want to hear anything critical *about* us or *from* us.'

'Do you think—' Tess began. But her attention was suddenly caught by a woman in a shabby coat shouting from the back of the room. 'Why do you all hate me? What did I do except save my own life?' the woman yelled.

A moan swept the room, an almost inaudible wash of sound.

'Ah, there we are,' murmured Mrs. Brown. 'Some man in first class probably gave her his lifeboat seat. Everything's still raw.'

'These hearing are beginning too soon.'

Mrs. Brown leaned close. 'Honey, Neptune was exceedingly good to us,' she whispered, her eyes warm and kind. 'We made it out of those waters, and now we bear witness.'

Indeed. That gave Tess momentum. She stood, pointing to the woman being elbowed against the wall. 'Someone give that woman a place to sit down,' she shouted as loudly as she could. 'Don't you see, she's one of us. Shame!'

Silence fell across the room. Tess made no move to sit down. Let the merely curious onlookers laugh or disapprove, she didn't care; she could feel the fear and pain around her.

There was movement at the doorway. A chair was offered and the woman sat down. A sigh rolled through the room, releasing the tension. Tess took her seat again, stunned at her own fury, and now fully conscious of the stares directed her way.

'Good for you, honey,' Mrs. Brown said heartily, patting her on the back. 'You stood up and hit them between the eyes.'

'I may get in trouble.'

Mrs. Brown's eyes widened in astonishment. 'Trouble? Everybody gets into trouble in America – that's what it's about. People don't like being scolded with the truth, and they damn well need to be sometimes. You stood up for someone. What's wrong with that? I'd rather hear truth being defended than all the gossip and rumors people are passing around. I'm not even sure the rumor about that amnesiac being dumped in the hold is true.'

Tess straightened up. 'What amnesiac?' she asked.

'Some poor soul from steerage whose brain got addled somehow. Nobody's claimed him, they say.'

'Are you sure he was from steerage?'

Mrs. Brown looked at her curiously. 'I don't know who you were hoping it would be, dear, but no first-class passenger would be unidentified by now.'

Tess lowered her head, knowing this to be true.

'Now, here's a story for you – you know those small boys you saved?' Mrs. Brown said, changing the subject.

'Are they all right?' Tess said quickly, her heart skipping a beat. It had been hard to say goodbye to Michel and Edmond. 'Have the authorities located any family?'

'You might say so.' Mrs. Brown's face turned sorrowful. 'It turns out Mr. Hoffman's real name was Michel

Navratil. He was kidnapping his sons. Their mother is very much alive and frantic to claim them.'

'Oh, my goodness.' If that sad-faced man on the *Titanic*, who clearly loved his boys, had been stealing them, was anybody who he appeared to be?

'So many stories.' Mrs. Brown nodded in the direction of a coolly beautiful woman dressed in black sitting nearby, fanning herself with vigor. Her hair was luxuriously abundant, her face pale as a porcelain teacup.

'Now there's Mrs. Bremerton, one of the wealthier widows. She's undoubtedly here to figure out whom to sue. Turned me down when I asked for a donation for the Survivors Committee. Some people just want their money for themselves. Take the stuff too seriously, in my opinion.'

Tess stared at the woman Mrs. Brown had pointed out, mesmerised by her calmness. She could hardly believe it; this was Jack Bremerton's wife. 'She must be devastated,' she whispered.

'Given the fact that everybody knew he was going to divorce her, probably not.' Tess gasped, and Mrs. Brown shot her a curious glance. 'Was he a friend of yours, dear?'

She was trying to think of an answer when there was a sudden stir at the door. Grateful for the diversion, she turned to watch. The senator who had stalked the decks of the *Carpathia* was making his way down a narrow aisle. He was about in his late fifties, she guessed, with a huge mustache on a face so strongly sculpted it could grace a monument. Striding past Tess and Mrs. Brown, he made his way to the head of a table positioned against the back wall, which was already filled with members of the investigating committee. He wore a black coat with a velvet collar, which he threw off the moment he claimed his chair.

Senator Smith banged his gavel for silence in the room. 'Order, please!' The hearing was about to begin.

Pinky nodded to her photographer to move closer as she stared at Bruce Ismay, wondering why it was that rich, important men never seemed to know that it was a big mistake to look *too* rich at a public inquiry. The elusive manager of the White Star Line wore a dark-blue suit with a navy silk scarf threaded through his high collar, and everything – down to the linen handkerchief in his breast pocket – oozed privilege.

'You should've taken off that diamond ring, Ismay,' she murmured to herself. She signaled the photographer to shoot just as Ismay put his hand up, the huge diamond glittering in the light from the chandeliers. The flash went off with a sharp explosion.

'Get those photographers out of here!' Senator Smith roared. 'You have a statement, Mr. Ismay?'

A seemingly rattled Ismay cleared his throat and tugged at his cuffs. 'I would like to express my sincere grief at this terrible catastrophe,' he began. 'We welcome this inquiry by the U.S. Senate and we have nothing to hide. Absolutely no money was spared in the construction of the *Titanic*.'

'So why were you urging the captain to go fast through that ice field?' shouted a man by the door.

Smith banged his gavel, repeatedly this time. Would he be able to keep this crowd under control? Perhaps the hearing should have waited a few days. No, Ismay would have escaped the witness chair. Smith banged again, more urgently.

'What were the circumstances of your departure from the ship?' asked Smith when the room quieted down.

'The boat was there,' Ismay replied. 'There were a certain number of men in the boat, and the officer called out asking if there were any more women, and there was no response, and there were no passengers left on the deck.'

A few people moved restlessly, looking at one another. No passengers left on the deck? Nonsense.

'What was the full complement of lifeboats for a ship of this size?' Smith asked.

'All I can tell you is, she had sufficient boats to obtain her passenger certificate,' Ismay said firmly. 'She was fully boated, according to the requirements of the British Board of Trade.'

Smith leaned back in his chair. Fully boated? What did that mean? Ismay knew there weren't enough boats. And he knew they weren't filled properly, but he was never going to admit it.

The questions kept coming from Smith, and the other members of the board of inquiry, for the next two hours. The air in the room became so stifling, even Senator Smith was wiping his face with a large white handkerchief. Finally he banged his gavel to announce a recess, accepting the fact that Ismay had managed to artfully dodge every question that would impugn the White Star Line.

But what Ismay hadn't done was clear himself of the stain of his cold behavior. That cheered Smith up. The next witness, he declared to the room, would be Arthur Rostron, the captain of the *Carpathia*. An honorable man; a good contrast.

Tess made her way through the crowd to the lobby, eager for some fresh air. People began pushing one another with urgency, jostling to get out, and she suddenly felt a stab of the same panic that had gripped them all on the *Titanic*. She started to push, to squeeze through, then forced herself to take a deep breath. This was not the deck of that doomed ship; this was a room, that was all – a crowded room. She took another deep breath; she was almost to the door. It would be a long time before she felt comfortable in a crush like this.

She spied Pinky by the elevators, looking directly at her, a small, inquiring smile on her lips as she approached, the same large bag she had carried last night slung over her shoulder. The strap was extra long, causing the bag to flop about below her waist, hitting against other people exiting the room. A few irritated glances were shot in her direction, but she seemed impervious to them. 'Oops,' she said once, after stepping on a fragile toe.

'You're getting people mad at you,' Tess said.

'Nothing new about that,' Pinky said with a shrug. She hesitated. 'I'm sorry I turned my back on you last night. I made a mess of the evening.'

'No, you didn't. You said what you had to say, and I admire that.'

'I mean, I didn't stick around to get enough information. Will you answer a few questions now?'

Tess nodded. 'If I can help, but I don't know if I can.'

'I'm hearing Lady Duff Gordon refused to let the crew go back for survivors when it would have been easy to bring more into the boat. What do you think?'

'How could I know? I wasn't there.'

'Nice dodge. Well, that's what I hear from a sailor on the lifeboat.' Pinky abruptly changed course. 'I also hear from a Mrs. Brown that it was the women who took over the rowing in your boat, and that you were one of them.'

Tess nodded, then laughed. 'The sailors were impossible. I don't think the ones in our boat ever had an oar in their hands in their lives.'

'That's a good quote,' Pinky said, scrambling in her bag for her paper and pencil. 'Think of how many times women have to step up when men turn cowardly. And the pompous cretins won't even let us have the vote—'

'You're a suffragist?'

'Of course.' Pinky was amused at the instant curiosity on Tess's face. 'And you will be, too, if you stay here.' Then, in one of her abrupt transitions, 'Which sailor gave you the carving of a boat?'

'That doesn't matter – it was just a carving.' Why this seemed to be information she didn't want to give, she didn't know. Maybe because Pinky seemed to want to know everything and could spring surprises too easily.

'Oh.' Pinky allowed herself a disappointed look, but she had her answer. Maybe a romance on board? That would make a nice sidebar. Or, perhaps – oh, forget it. She folded the retrieved notebook and stuffed it back into her bag. She liked Tess. No need to peel any more layers. At least, not now.

The chandelier began to blink, signaling the resumption of the hearings. 'It's time to go back to the hearing room,' Tess said, bracing her shoulders.

Pinky caught the movement. 'They're morons, to hold these hearings so soon,' she said quickly. 'You must think we're ghouls.'

'I see ghouls everywhere today,' Tess said. 'Nobody looks real.'

'It's kind of a dance, you know? It's not to be taken personally. At least, not all the time.'

'You know it can hurt,' Tess replied.

'I do. And I'm not out to hurt you.' They exchanged swift, unguarded glances. For just a second, Tess let herself believe that Pinky understood the conflicts between head and heart.

Captain Rostron was an unusually tall man, something Tess had noticed from the first moment she saw him on the deck of the *Carpathia*. She remembered how his bald head had shone under the morning sun.

The room fell quiet as he began his testimony. There was a daunting distance of fifty-eight miles between the

Carpathia and the *Titanic,* and if he hadn't moved fast when he got the distress call time would have run out. He posted extra lookouts and ordered emergency gear brought on deck and bedding prepared for the survivors. He ordered all hot water on the ship to be turned off so that every drop of water could be converted into steam. And, icebergs or not, the ship would travel at full speed.

'Captain, could you describe the *Titanic* lifeboats that carried the survivors?' Senator Smith asked at one point. 'How many can they hold?'

Tess closed her eyes, waiting for the answer.

'The collapsible boats could hold sixty to seventy-five comfortably,' he replied.

The next witness was Charles Lightoller, the second officer of the *Titanic,* the highest-ranking officer to survive. It was clear immediately that Lightoller realised that Senator Smith was no expert in maritime affairs. Smith's first questions about technical matters were clumsy, obviously uninformed. Each time Lightoller patiently explained some detail, as if to a child, he would give a little smile and tilt his head, as if to let others in on the joke. He seemed almost cocky as he slumped back in the witness chair, fielding questions about the proximity of icebergs, the speed of the ship, the absence of warnings.

Then, unexpectedly, a direct question. 'You were in charge of loading the lifeboats, sir. Why were so many not filled to capacity?'

'I was afraid that fully loaded boats might collapse on the way down to the water,' Lightoller said smoothly.

'But weren't people clamoring to get on?'

'Some were, some weren't.'

Tess thought of the chaos, of people being shoved into boats or pushed away from them, of the shouts and screams and total confusion of those last hours.

'Would you do it differently if you could?'

'No, I handled it the best way possible.'

Glances were exchanged in the room: indignant ones accompanied by exclamations; furtive ones darting back and forth with lips sealed. Tess stared at the man in the witness chair. She had seen smooth liars before. Just say something calmly and convincingly and there will be those who believe you.

'They're going to close ranks,' a man behind her muttered. 'Nobody gets the blame.'

Tess was left to sit and stare and wonder at her own naïveté.

Lightoller's testimony – without a breath of criticism for his employer – continued for hours but was finally over, and a clearly weary Senator Smith adjourned the hearing for the day. Some in the audience went up to shake his hand, with polite murmurs of praise. But many just filed out, talking among themselves.

Smith collected his papers. Ismay, Lightoller – their testimony came as no surprise. They knew damn well they were in trouble if there was a ruling of negligence. They knew Americans could sue them, even if they were British. And they knew they would face a British inquiry when this one was over.

Shoulder on, he told himself. One thing he had accomplished: none of the Britons were going anywhere for a long time.

Pinky pushed herself back from her desk at the *New York Times*, the broken wheel of her chair catching once again on the pine boards of the newsroom floor. Tonight, she didn't care. Today's testimony would be in everybody's stories tomorrow. Not hers. Her story was juicier – written fast, headlining the early night edition – and it was more than a good story; it dug into the world of the entitled rich. What idiots they were. So the Duff Gordons hadn't done anything worse than anyone else? She didn't believe it. They deserved to be brought down. They were foils for the real story: mostly poor people died, and mostly rich people were saved; that was the fact of it.

She wadded up her discarded copy sheets into tight little balls and threw them, one after another, into a box mounted against the far wall. It was a good way to let off steam after a deadline, and she was one of the best shots in the newsroom. And oh, it felt good to have won an argument with Van Anda. How could she name the man who had given her the information? He would immediately be fired or deported; that's what they did with those sailors. 'Okay,' he had finally said. 'You're opening up things here, so be ready for what comes next.' Tomorrow she'd talk to some suffragists who felt that it was a scandal to save women and children first. *That* would raise some hackles.

Van Anda's amused voice cut through her concentration. 'Good job, Pinky,' he said. 'Smith will be mad as hell that you got this on your own instead of waiting for testimony. Do you have to keep showing up your fellow reporters? Go home, you've got those hearings tomorrow.'

'In a minute.'

'Yeah, I know.'

A slow rumble began beneath their feet. The presses were running.

'You can go now,' he said gently. Where did she go? he wondered. Not for the first time, he marveled at his star reporter's single-mindedness; her refusal to share anything about a private life that he suspected centered around a hot plate in a lonely rooming house. The women in this business were a strange lot.

Pinky sent one more wadded ball sailing across the room and leaned over, heaving her canvas bag up over her shoulder. She gave Van Anda a mock salute and strode out of the newsroom, kicking at an orange peel on the floor. Why was this place always so filthy? Somebody should write the shocking story of poor housekeeping at the *New York Times*. She smiled to herself as she took the stairs, two at a time. She could have tap-danced down tonight. Once again, that lovely feeling of twirling under the stars, beholden to no one, standing clear and tall on a bold byline that thousands would see, and if that wasn't enough, then nothing was.

Tess stepped outside the revolving doors of the Waldorf-Astoria, breathing in the sharp, cold air. It felt wonderful. She wondered if Lady Duff Gordon was back yet from her shop. Surely she was, it was already sunset, and the street before her – filled with a noisy mix of horse-drawn clattering carts and automobiles – was bathed in a rosy glow.

But she didn't want to go upstairs to find out. Not yet. There was a park nearby, a hotel doorman told her, quite a nice park, right here in the middle of the city. He was astonished that she hadn't heard of it.

'Tess.' It was a calm, familiar voice.

Jim Bonney stood on the sidewalk, hands shoved into the pockets of baggy pants held up with a knotted belt missing a buckle. If anything, he looked shabbier than before. She saw the disdain in the eyes of the doorman, who was dressed in a navy-blue uniform with glittering brass buttons. She had seen that look today in the eyes of many of the Waldorf's bellboys and waiters as steerage survivors crowded past them.

'Jim,' she said, astonished at her own rush of pleasure. 'I was afraid I wouldn't see you again.'

'I wanted to check up on you. I figured, well, she's over in that fancy hotel and my two feet can get me there – find out how we do on stable ground.'

'Well, nothing is moving beneath us.'

'No waves, no dipping horizon, no creaking decks.'

'No water.' She shivered slightly. 'Going for a walk feels like – freedom.'

'Can I keep you company?'

She felt wary. 'Did you read about Lady Duff Gordon?'

'Yes.' His smile came quickly, then vanished. 'It's amazing what she manages to do to herself.'

'I am still working for her, you know.'

'Yes, I know. We could walk and talk at the same time, couldn't we?'

The light in his eye was too engaging to resist.

'Yes, we can,' she said. She cast a glance at the doorman, whose eyes traveled the length of Jim's unprepossessing figure in obvious disapproval.

Jim's eye followed her glance. 'Don't let him bother you,' he said with a shrug. 'He's probably only months or a year removed from wearing clothes like mine. That's too close for comfort. I'll be the guy saving his job one of these days. And you'll be sweeping by him in ostrich feathers.' Jim spoke with such good-humored confidence, she couldn't help laughing as they walked away from the hotel.

'Were you there for the testimony today?' she said.

He nodded.

'What did you think?'

'I was proud of the girl who spoke up.'

Tess coloured, pleased. 'Thank you, but the testimony?'

'We're lucky we had a man like Rostron bent on saving us,' he said soberly. 'He's brave. Lightoller? Just another corporate man, being careful to use a whitewash brush, that's what I think.' He paused. 'I saw you talking with that woman reporter, or I would have come over at the recess.'

'Have you met her?' Tess was surprised.

'Sure. She was on the *Carpathia* running in every direction, collaring sailors to get them to talk,' he said. 'Full of bounce and energy. Not a bad sort. Just doing her job, the way we all are.'

'Did you talk to her?'

He shrugged. 'For a few minutes, like the others.'

'I like her,' Tess said hesitantly. 'But she still makes me uneasy.'

'She's got her facts straight, Tess.'

'But she wants villains. Every detail has to lead to something darker.'

He sighed, running his fingers through his hair. It was brown, with flecks of gold, something she hadn't noticed before. It kept falling in his eyes, and he kept flipping it back; she had a sudden impulse to smooth it back for him. 'Well, you know how I feel about that,' he said.

'I do. But the newspapers made a mockery of Lucile this morning; it wasn't fair.'

He gave her a startled look. 'Fairness has nothing to do with it. She was no heroine in that boat. And if I'm called to testify I have to tell the truth.'

'You would drag her through the mud?'

'That's not how I see it.'

'I know she orders everybody around and wants things done her way – oh Jim, we're not going to spoil our walk with another argument, are we?'

'You think I'm too judgmental.'

'Stubborn. I like that word better.'

'That's kind of you. "Harsh" is more like it.'

'Yes, I guess it is.'

'Look, I haven't told you everything.'

Tess pulled her coat closer against the evening chill, but also as a shield. She didn't want to talk about this anymore; there was no way of explaining Lucile. She was still piecing it together herself. But those small glimpses of someone different underneath – they were real, she was sure of that. She wasn't being dutiful; this was standing up for someone who needed loyalty. She pressed her lips together, resisting a sudden throbbing in her head. She wouldn't dwell on it, not now. 'I see more to her than you do,' she said.

'Okay.' He took a deep breath. 'Maybe at some point you might have to choose who you believe.'

'I don't want to have to do that.'

'I'll not put you in that position,' he said slowly.

The tension eased. He took her arm. 'No, Miss Collins, I am not going to spoil our walk. Your escort' – he bowed elaborately – 'may be a stubborn, clumsy sailor, but he isn't about to wreck his few precious moments with you.'

She laughed, relieved. He might be only a sailor, but she felt pleasure in his company, and she wanted no quarrels. How good it felt to hear his words dancing teasingly in the air now, not like blunt instruments.

They walked slowly up Fifth Avenue, inhaling the sights and sounds of the largest city Tess had ever seen. A street market was closing down, and they stopped to watch two grizzled puppeteers dismantle a cardboard stage and pack up their puppets, ignoring a group of children clamoring for more performances. A woman in a wrinkled apron offered Tess an apple, and she realised suddenly how hungry she was. But at that moment a street vendor's pushcart pulled up next to her.

'Hot dog?' Jim said, pointing to the basket of steaming sausages in the man's cart.

'Dog?' Tess asked, puzzled.

'Frankfurter,' he said, rolling his eyes. She reddened, then nodded. She remembered what they were now, but such a strange name.

Hot dogs in hand, they continued their walk, drinking in the wonders of New York. They passed a splendid hotel that looked like a French château, and stopped to watch all the elegant carriages pulling up to its doors, depositing and picking up men and women in resplendent evening garb. Silk top hats on the men; lush, low-cut gowns on the women. Some even wore diamond tiaras that sparkled in the light. Which ones might be clients of Lady Duff Gordon? Probably several, Tess thought, feeling a twinge of pride.

The park loomed ahead, a leafy enclave of winding paths and grassy lawns. Together they crossed the street and entered, choosing a path flanked by towering elm trees, watching as the golden light filtering through their leaves began to fade. She lifted her face, comforted by the soft glow of twilight. There were only a few people scattered across the rolling lawns, mainly children – getting in one last toss of the ball before going home for dinner. Jim did most of the talking, at first somberly, telling her about his friend who had died in the ship's boiler room. Then about the American West, especially California, which he described as a paradise with such fervor that Tess found herself growing interested. All she had ever thought of was getting to this country, not how large and diverse it was. New York alone was overwhelming.

'Think you'd ever want to go there?' he asked.

'Maybe, someday. But not now.'

'You'll do well in this city,' he said, surveying the lush terrain of Central Park. 'I can see it offers what you want.'

'I hope so,' she said. 'I can learn design from Lucile – that's the best part. Meeting her is the biggest stroke of luck I've ever had.'

'I might say that about meeting you,' he said quietly.

She felt a second shiver of surprised pleasure.

'I mean,' he continued, flushing slightly, 'maybe you can teach her a few things, too.' He looked down at her with such a warm, open expression, she almost believed what he said next. 'Our worlds aren't that different, you know.'

Oh, but they were. An astonishing thought – already? Only days ago it would have been true. And somehow, because of that, perhaps, she felt suddenly free to act on impulse. She took his arm.

'Shall we?' she asked. 'Just to prove we can still do it?'

'Why not?' he said, breaking into a grin.

And for just a moment, for a few, brief skips, they were back on the deck of the *Titanic* in the glow of that golden setting sun, before everything changed forever.

They walked slowly back to the Waldorf, walking close, not touching, Tess listening to his droll commentary on their surroundings. He wasn't intimidated by the gathering theater crowds, the furs, the marvelous black carriages, brass fittings glittering, clattering by. The gas lamps were lit now, their glow rivaling that of the vanished sun. Even the horses in Central Park had their noses in the air, he said. She laughed, deciding on his dare to stroke a lush mahogany beauty, and was delighted when the mare nuzzled at her jacket.

'She wants a treat,' Jim said playfully. 'Or maybe she wants you to "turn" her collar. Isn't that what you do?'

'Well, I've never worked in leather – we'd both have to be patient.'

He acknowledged her small joke with a generous laugh. They moved on, Tess acutely aware that his tall, muscular figure and strong features – in spite of his shabby clothes – were drawing attention as they walked.

'I've never thanked you for my carving.' They were in sight of the hotel. He would be gone soon.

'I wanted to make something for you that marked what happened, what we shared,' he said, slowing his step.

'I wish we had been in the same lifeboat.'

He took a deep breath, answering in a low, suddenly impassioned tone. 'When I saw you teetering on the edge of the rail, holding those children, I knew you wouldn't abandon them. And I knew you couldn't make it into the boat – you wouldn't have time to jump. I wanted to climb back up the ropes and grab you. It would've been impossible, but the sight of you standing there, doomed, never left my thoughts that night.'

They both fell silent. They were almost at the hotel. 'So, once more, goodbye,' Jim said. He stopped, then tipped her chin up gently with his hand. His face was so close. Was he going to kiss her? No. But she felt his breath as he said, 'Next time, I'm taking you for a ride throught the park in one of those carriages. If you'll let me.'

'Yes,' she murmured, pushing all thoughts of his being a village boy out of her mind for the moment. Then quite quickly he was gone, whistling striding west.

Slowly she walked toward the hotel, enveloped in a pleasant haze. She would heed her mother's warnings later, not now.

Ahead of her, a crowd had formed around the hotel. Did this city ever get sleepy? The streets were even more of a scramble here, almost a duel between the cars and the carriages, with drivers shouting at one another, the horses, the people dodging them as they zigzagged, crossing the street.

She saw the center of attention. A newsboy at the door of the Waldorf, clusters of people around him, stood waving the early edition of the next morning's *New York Times*. Tess hurried past, not ready. But a bellboy who recognised her at the elevators thrust a copy of the paper into her hands. 'You'll want to see this,' he said.

Tess took a deep breath and stared at the headline.

DID COWARDLY BARONET AND HIS WIFE

BRIBE SAILORS NOT TO GO BACK FOR DROWNING?

EYEWITNESS SAYS YES AND HINTS AT MORE

Underneath, the byline: Sarah Wade.

The elevator doors opened and she stepped in, head down. No one else entered with her. The doors closed. For just one fleeting moment, she would be enclosed in a protective box of steel and cable that was impenetrable. How wrong she had been to trust Pinky. Who told her those things? Somebody who hated the Duff Gordons, of course. Was it Jim?

All she knew right now was that when she emerged she would be faced with the ordeal of trying to comfort the woman who only days before was the most invulnerable woman she had ever met. She longed for a slow ascent.

Chapter 6

Lucile threw a towel over the lit lamp, ignoring Cosmo's complaint about the danger of fire. Right now, she declared, she couldn't stand any more light than necessary. She couldn't stand to have anyone see how swollen from crying her eyes were, and the ugly blotchiness of her skin.

'I was right, wasn't I? Cosmo, tell me I was right.'

'Lucy, you took charge and made a sensible decision to save the lives of the people in our lifeboat. No one can fault you on that.'

'Well, they have. I've never been attacked like this.' She flung herself into the sofa's abundance of silk pillows, her hair matted and disheveled.

Cosmo picked up their copy of the *Times* and threw it into a wicker basket. He sat heavily on the sofa next to his wife. 'It'll be all right,' he said.

'Those men turned on us.'

'All it took was one.'

Simultaneously, they turned toward Tess.

'What decision are you talking about—' she began.

Lucile leaped to her feet, her swollen eyes blazing. 'Who talked to this woman?' she demanded, kicking at the wastebasket, knocking it over and sending newspaper pages skittering across the room.

'She spoke to many people,' Tess said.

'I see. And did that "many people" include *you*?'

'Yes.'

'What did you say?'

'I told her people in steerage couldn't get to the boats in time.'

'What else did you prattle on about?'

'She asked why your boat was almost empty and I said I didn't know.'

'Ah, yes. That started it. Then there's that sailor friend of yours. He's the one out to get us, that's who; he's the one filled with all the innuendos and lies. Not much of a mystery, is it?'

'Jim isn't a vindictive man,' Tess said quickly.

'Oh, now it's "*Jim.*"' Lucile was furious. 'Not vindictive? Whose side are you on? He managed to disappear when I gathered people for the photograph. Is he why you didn't join us? And where was he when Cosmo so generously thanked the crew for keeping us safe? Not vindictive? Oh, for God's sake, he's obviously an ignorant product of his class and has no judgment. He's self-righteous, through and through. You had better tell me everything, right now.'

'Lucy, calm down,' Cosmo interjected. 'Our accuser is anonymous. This isn't testimony, it's just malicious gossip.'

'Who else would have called us cowards?' she said, staring at Tess. 'And *bribery*? For paying those poor men a little money to get them started again? Who else?'

'Lucy, I said calm down!' Cosmo snapped.

'Maybe it was Jean Darling. No, she wouldn't dare.'

'Perhaps.' He pulled a cigarette from a silver cup on his dressing table and lit it, a slight tremor in his hand prolonging the task.

'The newspapers are trying to ruin me,' his wife said, ignoring Tess's pale, set face.

'I'm the one described as a "cowardly baronet," you might recall.'

Lucile sank down on the sofa. 'At this moment, I need all the support you can give me. How can you be thinking of yourself? I know I shouldn't have talked for that article; I knew that the moment I walked into the shop and heard the fabric cutters whispering. Oh, they all said the interview was wonderful, that they were so happy I had survived. But the tone was dutiful, not like last night in the dining room when my friends hung on my every word.'

'You did keep them enthralled,' Cosmo said dryly.

'All right, I put myself in the spotlight at just the time when the newspapers were clamoring for scapegoats. So too many rich people survived, and all that – why do *I* have to pay a price?'

She glanced at Tess. 'What are you standing there for?' she demanded.

'I'm waiting for your permission to leave.'

'Well, I haven't given it.'

'I would like to go, please.' No, at this moment she would like to run. So they *had* paid money to the sailors.

'You disobeyed me. You talked to that reporter. I should fire you.'

No begging, Tess told herself. She was beyond that.

A silence. Then, in a calmer tone, Lucile said, 'You look ridiculously bedraggled. Dear Tess, we must get you some decent clothes.'

Tess blinked. Another sudden shift from anger to – to what?

'I can go, then?' she asked.

'Go, go, for heaven's sake. But I want you to come with me to the shop tomorrow morning. Someone else can report back on the inquiry. Now please go tell the hotel switchboard we will be taking no calls from reporters anymore, no exceptions, and I will meet you downstairs at eight-thirty. My driver will be waiting; his name is Farley. And, Tess?'

'Yes?' Tess stepped back, away – anything to get away from this volatile woman. She wanted out of here. Oh, how she wanted out of here.

Lucile suddenly stood and cupped both of Tess's hands in her own. 'Now don't get upset,' she said. 'I know you wouldn't betray me. I have a terrible temper, and surely you won't take this too personally.' She leaned closer and kissed Tess's cheek, the sweet scent of her floral perfume wafting into the air. 'I'll make up for this, dear.'

Tess nodded, slightly dazed. She opened the door, murmured good night, and left the room. Lucile had apologised – sort of – to *her*. This thing about the money would be straightened out; it wouldn't be bribery. Lavish tips were part of their way of life. It had to be Jim who gave Pinky that story. Who else cared? Not the sailors who lined up for pictures, she was sure of that. He must have known it was coming, or guessed it, or something. And he hadn't said a word on their walk, just let it hit her full in the face. Don't jump to conclusions, you don't know, she told herself. Her hands were shaking; she couldn't stop them.

And she couldn't quite forget the word *prattle.*

'You really whipped into her, Lucy. For God's sake, what are you trying to do?' Cosmo said as the door closed behind Tess. 'Be your mother?'

'That awful woman? For heaven's sake, no.'

'You seem to be treating this girl as if you were, my dear.'

'I don't want her to—'

'To what? Take control, defy you?'

'I don't care what she does, Cosmo, for heaven's sake. There's no use scolding her for her friendship with that sailor; she looked sufficiently stricken as it was. In fact, she looked *too* stricken.'

'Perhaps she's going to be a constant reminder of that terrible crossing.'

Lucile paused, absorbing this. 'She didn't call me Madame. Have you noticed?'

'Yes,' Cosmo replied.

'That's required for her job.'

'It's too late,' Cosmo said simply.

'She doesn't give you proper deference, either.'

'I rather like not being *Sir* Cosmo.'

'You are impossible. Please don't make me sad.' Lucile swept a hand over her eyes and fell back into the comforting folds of the sofa cushions. 'I'm much too tired, and none of this is worth an argument. Tomorrow I'll do battle.'

'My dear, we have to face facts. That story will stir an outcry on both sides of the Atlantic, and we are in deeper than I thought we would be. This diligent Senator Smith will soon focus on us, I'm afraid.'

'They wouldn't dare. And if they do I won't allow it.'

Cosmo walked over to the lamp and flicked the overheated towel to the floor. The edges were already singed.

WALDORF-ASTORIA

SATURDAY MORNING, APRIL 20

'So you're the new fetch-and-carry girl? All the way from England or France or somewhere? Kind of silly – Lady Duff's got her pickings here. Well, pile in. She'll be issuing me orders the second she comes out the door.'

The man gesturing Tess into the waiting black car outside the Waldorf the next morning had large, full lips and a sardonic grin that annoyed her. He had no higher status than she did, other than that conferred by a driver's license.

'I'm not a fetch-and-carry girl,' she retorted.

'My dear, you are whatever she wants you to be,' he said affably. 'You're joining her crew of minions – the slavering, trembling minions that work for the mighty Madame. I'm one of them – I'm Farley.'

Tess had barely settled herself in her seat when Farley jumped to attention, opening the door for Lady Duff Gordon, slamming it quickly in the faces of a handful of reporters who rushed up to the automobile. He shoved the car into gear and roared into the Fifth Avenue traffic. Tess slumped, glancing cautiously at Lucile, whose face was more heavily powdered than usual. No mention of their encounter last night; there would certainly be none from her.

The workrooms for Lucile Ltd. were in a dingy building just below the Flatiron Building, on Twenty-third Street. 'It's the pride of New York,' Farley said to Tess, pointing to the Flatiron. 'Does look like an iron, don't you think?'

Maybe it was her general sense of apprehension, but it didn't look like an iron to Tess; it looked ominous, more like the prow of a ship.

A cluster of people waiting for an elevator scattered like sparrows as Lady Duff Gordon entered the building. 'Nobody's allowed to take the elevator when Madame is here; she won't share it,' Farley whispered to Tess.

'Don't whisper around me, Farley,' said Lucile. She stepped into the elevator and beckoned Tess to follow. Her loft, on the top floor of this building, was her sanctuary – the kingdom she had created and ruled. No one went there without her permission.

The elevator doors opened onto a vast workroom that took Tess's breath away. Everywhere there were worktables heaped with sumptuous brocades, richly hued woolens, and fragile laces. Seamstresses were bending over dressmaker's dummies, their mouths filled with pins, shaping, draping, pinning, while slender-figured women in gray crêpe kimonos lounged against the wall, waiting to be called for fittings. The place bristled with activity and excitement.

'Wonderful, isn't it?' Lucile called out over the hum of sewing machines and chatter.

Tess nodded vigorously, looking around, openmouthed. She followed Lucile as she threaded her way past the tables, alternately smiling and frowning as she inspected a seamstress's work, picked up a bolt of fabric here, another there, testing their heft and crushability while calling out to various employees – here, finally, was the woman she had been so in awe of on the *Titanic*.

At the back of the vast workroom was Lucile's glass-walled office. The room was bursting with an abundance of flowers – roses, peonies, daffodils – every kind imaginable, perched on every available surface, including the floor, all adorned with what must be congratulatory notes.

'All my clients and friends were happy I survived,' Lucile said wryly as she stepped into the room. 'We'll soon see if they still are.'

Waiting just inside the door, clustered together as if for

comfort, a group of men and women with dutiful expressions jumped to attention.

'Good morning, Madame,' said one.

Lady Duff Gordon plucked a pair of horn-rimmed spectacles from her handbag, put them on, and stared at each person in turn.

'The runway must be put in place today,' she said. 'And the draperies closing it off from the workroom must be hung. I don't see anyone working on that out there.'

'We need the workroom space for another few days,' said a woman in what looked like a white baker's coat. 'All the last-minute—'

'There is always last-minute work to do,' Lucile said, cutting her off. 'Move the work benches closer together. We have to get that runway up early. If there are problems with it, we don't have time to correct them and we have a full house of clients coming. Do I make myself clear?'

'Yes, Madame.'

Lucile turned her attention to a young man with thinning hair. 'James, where are we on the wedding gown? I don't see my beaders working out there.'

'They'll be in this afternoon,' he replied hastily.

Lucile began pacing, her voice rising. 'Why aren't we further along?' she demanded. 'Why aren't the gowns being shaped on the models yet? They're standing out there with nothing to do, and time is running out! The wedding gown is the centerpiece of the show – the beading must be perfectly done, and it needs to be started *immediately*. I said all this yesterday – why isn't it happening?'

'Everyone is working at top pace—' began James, looking nervous.

'I've been alone in the ocean, struggling to survive, and nobody here is making sure the gowns for the show are ready?' Lucile waved her hand, taking in the lush array of flowers filling the room. 'My friends are my clients, and my clients are my friends. They cannot be subjected to incompetence.'

Tess saw a couple of people in the room exchange glances. One arched an eyebrow and rolled her eyes. This, then, was standard bchavior; obviously Lady Duff Gordon knew showmanship.

Unexpectedly, the designer pointed at Tess. 'Now here's someone who knows something about competence,' she declared. 'May I introduce Tess Collins, my fellow lifeboat survivor?' She grabbed a silk dress from the arms of one of the seamstresses, shook it out, and held it up. 'Tess, what do you think? Should this have been cut on the bias or not?'

All eyes were on Tess. She studied the dress, wondering what she was expected to say. No matter, the weight of the heavy silk gave her the correct answer. After all those years sewing with her mother, she knew something about fabric. She could do this.

'No,' she said firmly. 'The draping will sag with one wearing.'

Lady Duff Gordon triumphantly tossed the dress back into the arms of the seamstress and turned to the balding young man who had spoken first. 'James, if you're not careful, I will replace you,' she warned. 'Take Tess to the drawing table – let's see her draw this design the way it should be cut.'

Tess wasn't sure of her drawing abilities; she had always done rough sketches, holding the patterns in her mind, not on paper. She told James this the minute they moved out of the room, which was obviously a great relief to James, who then more kindly began to initiate her into the eccentricities of Lady Lucile.

'She likes to throw out little challenges that make people scramble, which is usually fine. But we'll do anything to keep her diverted this morning.' He sighed. 'Everyone showed up with a copy of the morning *Times* today, and it was hard to get them to work. I told them to be sure they stuffed them into the waste bins before she came. Nobody's talking about anything else around here. That's why things started slow today.' He glanced at Tess soberly. 'Haven't told her yet we've had some orders canceled. Important ones. She'll be furious.'

'I don't know what I'm supposed to do here,' Tess confessed.

'Madame likes to keep new hires off balance,' he said. 'I'll start you on the presser.'

The shop was magical. When she wasn't ironing gowns, Tess wandered among the tables, fingering the wonderful fabrics, watching the skilled seamstresses sew. At one table an elderly man sat painstakingly sewing buttonholes, separately knotting each stitch and pulling each one exactly as tight as the last. She was riveted when the fittings began. Watching as the pinning and tucking of one of Lady Duff Gordon's floating creations on a human body brought it to life. And staring at the feet of the seamstresses on the pedals of their Singer sewing machines was like watching an intricate dance. She wished her mother could see this. The memory of her – those nights beside the fire, sewing aprons and shirts for her children, the needle flashing in and out of the goods – gave Tess a fleeting stab of pain. She was totally, hopelessly, in love with this place and all that was in it – every sound, every smell, every morsel of light and movement.

Through the glass walls of her office, Lucile watched Tess carefully, allowing herself a measure of satisfaction. The girl's eyes were round as melons. So she was swept up in the glamour of it all, which was precisely what should happen when all was fresh and new. It had been wise to pull Tess away from the censorious carnival taking place back at the Waldorf.

At that moment Tess glanced up. For an instant their gazes locked. And Tess saw the triumph in Lucile's eyes.

This is what you want, and I have it to give.

Tess felt a sudden chill. She turned away first.

WALDORF-ASTORIA

SATURDAY MORNING, APRIL 20

It was only nine in the morning, but Pinky could feel the sweat turning her hands sticky as she waited for the second day of hearings to begin. Chairs were jammed into every corner of the room, and the air was thick and sour with the smoke of dozens of cigars. Every newspaper had extra editions out on the street now, all filled with stories of bravery and cowardice and death, but the hysteria of the reporters was getting funny.

The room was filling rapidly. She half expected the Duff Gordons to send somebody to launch a counterattack, maybe get their friends to freeze her out. But everyone was picking the story up. Just put together the words *bribery* and *millionaires' boat* and there were stories for a week of good sales. She didn't see Tess, either, but that was no surprise. Lady Duff would have made sure to steer her away from today's hearing. She took her handkerchief and pressed it against her forehead, gratified by the glances of envy from her colleagues. It wasn't just getting a good story – all the free-floating anger over who lived and who died on that ship now had one more big focal point. A coup, of course, but she knew how things worked in this business. Today Lady Duff was the villain; tomorrow someone else would be. Already the men who survived were apologizing, cringing almost. How good could it get?

'Well, young lady, what are you grinning about this morning?' Senator Smith had walked into the room and paused by her chair.

'Being here, Senator,' she said, recovering quickly from her surprise. 'You know it's the only place in town.'

Smith smiled and let his starchy demeanor drop for just a second. He rather liked this feisty woman. 'Of course, it is.'

'Did you read my story about the Duff Gordons bribing sailors not to go back? Any comment?'

His smile faded. 'I would prefer you had waited for the testimony.'

'Does that mean you're going to call the Duff Gordons to testify?'

'I'm not on a witch hunt.'

'Well, are you going to subpoena them?'

'That hasn't been decided.' Smith turned away and took his seat at the witness table, quickly gaveling the hearing to order.

The first witness was the only surviving telegraph operator, Harold Bride. Deathly pale and surprisingly young-looking, Bride was in a wheelchair, wincing as he maneuvered his left foot – heavily bandaged – through the crowd.

Smith started his questions gently, and Bride's responses grew stronger as he talked. He and the second wireless operator had tried to raise help from other ships. At one point, he said, he had advised the other operator to use SOS instead of CQD. 'It's the new call, and it may be your last chance to send it,' he joked. The two men had laughed; he remembered that.

The room grew still when Bride was asked to describe how he managed to survive. 'I fell overboard, holding on to one of the collapsible boats, and then I slipped under it, into some kind of air pocket,' he said. 'I freed myself from it and cleared out of it. There was a big crowd on top when I got on. I was the last man they invited on board.'

A tremor swept the room. *Invited?*

'Were there others struggling to get on?'

'Yes, sir.'

'How many?'

'Dozens,' Bride said. The word seemed not only to wrench the last shred of energy from his testimony but to strip the official proceedings of their detachment. There was a restless moving, the sound of sniffling and nose-blowing. The anguish in the young man's voice was seeping through the room.

'Dozens,' Smith repeated. 'In the water? With life preservers on?'

'Yes.'

'The word *invited* seems somewhat unrealistic,' a panel member interjected.

'That's the way I put it. And that's all I have to say on that.'

'What about the boats with room for more? Were people afraid of being sucked under with the ship?'

Bride stayed steady. 'I estimate I was within a hundred and fifty feet of the *Titanic,*' he said. 'I was swimming when she went down. And I felt practically no suction at all. Some of the boats should have come back and helped.'

So much for *that* excuse for not going back. Pinky scribbled furiously, thoroughly satisfied. Her pencil hovered at one point as a sudden, surprising thought stopped her hand. Was she angry at the whole bloody lot of them?

During a break in the late afternoon, Pinky spotted a familiar figure breaking away from a group of sullen-looking *Titanic* crewmen and walking toward her.

'You really took on the Duff Gordons this morning,' said Jim Bonney.

'So I did good?'

But his gaze had shifted; he was looking around, eyes darting from one spot to another, a worried frown on his face.

'You're probably not the best person to ask, but I'm looking for someone; she works for the Duff Gordon woman.'

'You mean Tess Collins?'

'Yes,' he said, a little startled.

'I haven't seen her today.'

'I have to see her,' he said. 'Talk to her.'

'My guess is Lady Duff took her down to her studio. Sorry, I may be a reporter but I don't know everything.'

He seemed to be trying to decide how much to say. 'Look, the whole crew is being shipped out to Washington tonight. I have to see her before we go.'

She knew that Senator Smith was preparing to move the hearings to his home base, but she hadn't thought it would happen this quickly. 'When?' she asked.

'Late, but I guess you knew.' Distracted, he shoved his hands into his back pockets, still scanning the room.

No, she hadn't, but she wasn't about to say so or be closed out of the story. Maybe that's why Smith had been so affable. He thought he was going to shake her and the New York tabloid reporters off his back. 'Lady Duff has a reputation as a hard taskmaster,' she said cheerfully. 'You probably won't see Tess around here until evening. So much for romance.' It was a shot over the bow, but it was always fun to see what happened when she took a chance.

He hardly seemed to hear. 'Can you reach her?'

'Sounds like something important.'

'Look, you seem like a decent sort. If you see her, tell her I'm leaving, will you?'

'Sure. If you'll talk to me again,' she added quickly.

'Okay, but not now. Later.'

Maybe he even meant it. 'You're very talented, by the way. I liked that lifeboat you carved.' Another shot over the bow.

'She showed you?' His eyes lit up.

'Something like that.'

'Thank you,' he said, and turned to go.

'Aren't you going to say goodbye?' He was good-looking; it was hard not to tease.

He wasn't unaware, casting her an amused look. 'Well, I'll be seeing you, I suspect. You're the one covering this show, right? See you in Washington.' He turned away and strode off, leaving Pinky feeling quite pleased as she stared after him. She had confirmed not only who made Tess's carving of a lifeboat but why it mattered. That was good. It was always delicious to know more about people than they thought you knew.

Lucile calmly surveyed her workroom as her cutters, seamstresses, and pattern-makers packed up their things and began making their way home. The fading light outside cast a wash of gold over the tables and the sewing machines, even reaching the almost finished runway at the far end.

'Tell me now. How many order cancellations?'

James glanced down at the sheet of scribbled notes in his hand. 'About ten, Madame,' he said.

'Did anyone have the courage to say why?'

'Other obligations,' James replied weakly.

'What about reservations for the show?' She stared out at the racks of folding chairs stacked at the end of the room, ready for placement.

'A few cancellations, not many.'

'Mrs. Wharton?'

'She sends her regrets; she is unable to come.'

'James, I am aware of how many copies of the *Times* were stuffed into the trash bins. I'm sure it was on your orders.'

James, his face gray, gave a funny little bow. 'Yes.'

'Thank you. Good night.'

James glanced at Tess, who stood at the door of the office. 'Miss Collins will do well here,' he said unexpectedly. Then, 'Good night.'

His footsteps echoed through the empty loft as he walked away, and now it was only Lucile and Tess.

'We should have a delicious meal waiting at the hotel,' Lucile said, pulling on her gloves. She held her head high. 'Their chef is absolutely the best, and the three of us will dine in our suite.'

Tess followed Lucile to the elevator, trying to hold down

the euphoria this wonderful place had aroused in her. How could she ever have envisioned something as good as this? Just holding the fabric, watching the meticulous work of elegant stitching and beading – it had been a day unlike any other. She didn't know how she would fit in here, but she knew that she could. She knew, more than anything, that she wanted to.

The cables pulling up the elevator groaned, louder because of the emptiness of the building. It seemed to take forever to reach the top floor. Tess and Lucile stepped in and the elevator creaked downward with a slight swaying motion that made Tess nervous. When the doors opened on the first floor, they were instantly confronted by a mob of reporters.

'Did you bribe the sailors?' shouted one.

'Why was your boat so empty?' screamed another.

'How do you defend rowing away from the dying?' bellowed a third.

'Where is Farley?' Lucile said under her breath, ignoring the shouts, the many other questions, pushing her way to the street with Tess close behind.

And then there he was, muscling reporters out of the way, guiding them with a steady hand into the car – the blessed, safe automobile. Tess jumped in, and Farley tried to close the door.

A face poked in – the blotchy face of a man with stale tobacco breath that made Tess cringe. 'We've got reports that a man was in your boat masquerading as a woman,' he shouted. 'Can you confirm that?'

'I won't deny it,' Lucile said.

'Was it the dancer Jordan Darling?'

The door was swinging closed. Lucile held it briefly and leaned forward with a wintry smile. 'I won't deny that, either,' she said.

The door slammed, Farley jumped behind the wheel, and they shot out into the street, heading uptown through the streets of New York, passing vegetable stands and churches with needle-shaped spires and polished carriages pulled by proud prancing horses, while all the while, beneath the concrete, in the dark depths of the subway, the trains rumbled and roared, hurtling their invisible occupants forward to unseen destinations.

Cosmo stood at the front desk in the Waldorf's lobby, frowning over the stack of mail the clerk had just handed him. 'Is this all?' he asked.

'Yes – sir,' the clerk said, hesitating. Obviously he was an American who wasn't sure how to address British nobility, which made Cosmo impatient. He turned to go.

'Oh, sir, there is a message for a member of your party,' the clerk said quickly. 'Do you want to take it up?'

'Yes, of course.' Cosmo reached out for the proffered slip of wrinkled paper, glancing at it as he headed for the elevator. A message for Tess? What was this about? Just one line, scrawled hastily in pencil:

Will you meet me at the south entrance to Central Park tonight? Please.

No signature. Cosmo stared at the message for a long moment, then, slowly, he crumpled it in his fist, throwing it into a trash receptacle by the elevator. Now fully annoyed, he punched the elevator button. Obviously that infernal reporter was out to pump Tess for more information. No use telling Lucy about it – she'd just throw another fit. Just a bit of luck he had stopped and managed to intercept it in time. There was enough turmoil in their lives right now; they didn't need more.

NEW YORK TIMES

SATURDAY NIGHT, APRIL 20

Pinky didn't dance down the stairs of the *Times* building tonight; she was too tired. She had to get some groceries, pick up her father's medicine – and have another go-around with Mrs. Dotson, that fleshy, constantly disapproving nurse's aide who had never forgiven her for not melting into the role of a surrogate daughter. Mrs. Dotson wanted more money. Every night she complained of how hard it had become to care for Prescott Wade – his incontinence, his anger – all in a long-suffering, resigned tone as Pinky sat at the table, trapped in a narrow corner of reality that she escaped as often as she could. But it wouldn't work tonight.

She hated asking herself the kind of blunt, direct questions that had shaped her reputation as a reporter. She had no answers for the ones that affected her own life. How long would he live? How much could she afford to pay for his care?

The streets, as usual, were deserted as she made her way home under the flickering streetlights. Whenever she saw a figure in the shadows, she straightened her shoulders and strode forward, determined to show as much confidence as a man. She would not shrink from facing the streets of this city. The first time she did, she would end up in a puddle, a failure; of that she was sure.

It would help if her father smiled once in a while. She never knew for sure if he refused to do so out of stubbornness or because he simply couldn't. After all, he was Prescott Wade, revered, lionised – and he must know that no one came around anymore. Most people thought, like Lady Duff Gordon, that he had died – not that they remembered taking note of such finality. It was easier to assume a kind of hazy, comfortable slide into nonexistence – painless, of course – so that when actual death came they could cluck and reminisce but shed no tears. That's what a life of celebrity brought. Who would remember her? What would she be? A package of bylines, mouldering in a folder in the *New York Times* morgue. She tossed *that* thought into a bin of rotting tomatoes as she headed for the meat counter of the neighbourhood delicatessen.

Mrs. Dotson had her coat on already when Pinky turned her key in the lock. 'He didn't have a good day,' she announced as the door opened.

'He never does, Mrs. Dotson.'

'Well, it's hard on me, with you traveling and all.'

'This is what I do, Mrs. Dotson. This is how I pay the bills.' She pulled packages of beans and chicken from her canvas bag and put them on the countertop, wishing this woman would go home now, without the usual complaints.

'I know you work hard, dear.' The older woman's tone had turned ingratiating. 'But, you know, he's slipping more every day. I hope you won't be traveling much. What a shame if you weren't here when his time comes. If I have to stay overnight more, I'm going to need some extra money; it's only fair. You've been gone a lot. Not that you shouldn't be for your work, of course.'

It wasn't unreasonable. What would she do without Mrs. Dotson? Put her father in one of those hellish institutions she had been investigating? 'We'll work it out,' Pinky said.

'Five dollars more for night work.'

'Three.'

'Four – and a half.' Mrs. Dotson had become braver.

'Four – that's all I can afford.'

'All right.'

They stared at each other. The negotiations were actually complete.

'I liked your write-up today, dear. I read it to your father, though he didn't seem to care much.'

What a hurtful thing to say, and Pinky didn't believe it for a moment. Mrs. Dotson, she wanted to say, we are not friends. We don't like each other. Let's not pretend otherwise – just take care of my father, go home when you're done, and don't be chatty. I hate chatty.

Instead, she said, 'Thank you.' She shoved her hand into her bag and came up with a fistful of bills. She peeled off several and handed them silently to Mrs. Dotson, who grabbed them and left quickly, with the usual promise of being back early tomorrow morning.

Pinky pulled out a knife and started cleaning the chicken, then paused. She should check on her father first.

The room was dark, not that it mattered. She flicked on the light.

'Well, it's about time you got home.' His eyes were closed, and his voice seemed more raspy than usual. She could see stubble on his chin, which meant that Mrs. Dotson hadn't found the time to shave him today.

'I have deadlines, you know that.'

'Out to knock the pins from under the gentry, right?'

'Just like you did.'

'Right. Past tense.'

'Can I get you anything?'

'My life, maybe. And, if you're not too busy, my dinner.'

She had long ago vowed not to let him make her cry. This towering figure of a man she had adored and emulated lay like a lump of sodden clay on the bed, and she couldn't help him. There was nothing to investigate or fight for here – all there could be was endurance. She turned to leave the room.

'Baked chicken?' he said.

'Yes.'

'You make good baked chicken.'

She walked back to the kitchen, feeling better. She knew an apology when she heard it.

The park had receded into the gloom of night. Still Jim stood by the 59th Street entrance, as late as he dared, peering down the street for some sign of Tess. Each time he saw a slim woman approaching with a brisk stride, his hopes went up. And each time he was wrong.

'Not your lady, huh?' A carriage driver, a jovial-looking man with drooping wattles and a badly faded cap, smiled sympathetically. 'Well, there's always next time.'

Jim tried to smile back. He rubbed the nose of the sleepy mahogany mare hitched to the carriage, remembering the sight of Tess's graceful hand stroking her mane. Only yesterday?

Finally he gave up. 'Thanks for your company,' he said to the driver, then strode away, his pace quickening with every step.

Chapter 7

A weary Senator Smith leaned back against the coarse weave of his seat as the train south to Washington gained momentum. Finally, a respite from the hysteria. His own bed tonight; a civilised hearing on Monday, surely.

'Senator, you wanted me to take some notes?' An aide had approached, his voice gently prodding.

Smith straightened in his seat. Dictating his thoughts helped him sort things out. 'My primary job, of course, is to find out *why* that ship went down. Are you writing?'

'Yes, sir.'

'It could have been a series of small mistakes fatally aligned, but people don't want to hear that; they want one reason, not many reasons. They don't want to examine the moral and practical decisions we're contending with.' He sighed. Was it too overwhelming for them all – himself included – in this age of progress to see a product of the best minds and the most modern equipment so spectacularly punish its creators?

'You've seen the papers, Senator?'

'Indeed. They are clamoring for villains.'

'Especially this British couple. Are you going to bring the Duff Gordons to the witness stand?'

'Why are you asking me? I'm tired of being hammered about that.'

The aide was clearly taken aback. 'Sorry, Senator. I just thought—'

'To answer your question, I'd rather not; it would anger the British too much.' He slumped back in his seat. 'And they're already mad at me. Did you see this?' He pointed to a story in the *American*. 'Henry Adams – you know who he is?'

'Yes, sir.'

'The man's an admirable historian. He says we're running on our own iceberg, that we're a society cracking apart. He says the entire fabric of the nineteenth century is foundering, do you hear? And all of us, friend or foe, will go with it.'

'Maybe we should do this later?'

'Yes, I think that would be better.' Ah, home. He could impose order better there. That damn fellow Ismay was furious that he had to stay, and well he should be. This thought gave Smith a moment of satisfaction. He felt a righteous yearning for justice. He would follow this investigation wherever it might lead. And at least now he wouldn't have the New York tabloids on his back every moment. Reason enough to postpone wading into the sticky business of interrogating British nobility.

NEW YORK CITY

SUNDAY MORNING, APRIL 21

This was usually the most restful day of the week. Jean Darling sat with the Sunday-morning paper in her much loved breakfast room, with its bay of encircling windows that diffused the golden light. She was wearing her favorite dressing gown, the one with fox cuffs and collar bleached to a pure white; Jordan liked to see her in this on Sundays. The most restful day.

Usually she sipped her coffee, enjoying the lush panorama of Central Park spread out before her, across the street and three stories below. How exciting it had been when she and Jordan, swept up in a wave of glory after their first Broadway play, were able to walk through these elegant rooms and know that they, two minor English vaudeville players, could hold up their heads and say, 'Yes, we will take this.' How long ago? Years.

But she didn't lift her cup to her lips. She simply held herself still, staring at the translucent, fragile china filled halfway. She could perhaps have been a statue, almost carved from stone. But a statue would feel no pain.

Next to the cup was her morning copy of the *New York Herald*. And there was the story she had feared would find its way into the caterwauling agony of mistakes and suffering sweeping the country since the sinking of the

Titanic. 'Dancer's Shameful Disguise,' read the headline. 'Dressed as a Woman to Save Self in Millionaires' Boat.' Directly beneath was a photograph of Jordan, looking into the camera, a half smile on his lips. So vulnerable.

She skimmed the story. It was what she expected, a mocking screed on the man 'who abandoned women' to save himself. Her eye stopped only on one sentence. 'Asked to confirm this new information on the despicable happenings in the Millionairès' Boat, Lady Duff Gordon said, "I won't deny it."'

Such cruelty. Her dear husband, a man of courage and integrity, ruined. Their professional lives were over, of course. By tomorrow morning, all their bookings would be canceled.

What would she change? If she hadn't insisted, Jordan wouldn't have pulled that cloth close around his shoulders and head and run with her to the lifeboat; if the boat hadn't been almost empty, he would have refused to board. She knew it to be true. He wasn't a coward, he was simply trying to live. Was that wrong? Had anyone died for Jordan to live? No.

She stared now through the window out onto the winding paths and foliage below, which had imbued her on so many peaceful mornings with a sense of well-being. All she wished for now was an absence of pain.

Jean heard Jordan's footsteps approaching from the hall. Carefully she folded the newspaper and tucked it inside a bottom cabinet of the lovely old hutch they had bought on their honeymoon. That wonderful honeymoon. The trip to Morocco when they first danced as partners.

They were in step from the very beginning, flowing through routines of magical grace, embracing the cheers of their audiences, and going home to each other. She smiled, looking up, waiting for his cheerful face to light up the room. How many women had such a precious gift of love? Why, why should she have given him up to death?

Jordan walked into the room, giving her his usual funny little bow of greeting. 'And how is my lovely wife this morning?' he asked. 'How is our world today?'

She lifted two fingers to her lips and blew him a kiss. 'Wonderful,' she said. She stood and walked over to him, curving one arm around his shoulder, reaching with the other for his hand. She would shed no tears. A barely discernible web of fine lines appeared around her eyes as she smiled again. 'It should start with a dance, don't you think? This is, after all, the most restful day.'

Lucile paced the length of her empty loft, frustrated by the silent sewing machines. Things should be humming and buzzing, but she didn't dare insist on Sunday work in New York anymore, not since the Ladies' Garment Workers' Union began bullying shops like hers. It was outrageously unfair. She didn't operate some sweatshop like the Triangle people had, for heaven's sake. She paid her workers well, and none were under fourteen years old; she could have fattened their purses if they had worked today. She sighed, trying to relax. She was always nervous just before a show. But seeing her name smeared once again all through those stories about Jordan Darling posing as a woman was unnerving. All she did was answer a question, and she wasn't sorry to see Jordan Darling exposed. But attaching *her* name to the story so prominently was ridiculous. She hadn't confirmed *anything,* and that reporter who wrote the story knew it. But Cosmo wouldn't listen. He had thrown the paper into a trash basket and walked out of the room this morning, saying nothing.

Lucile slowed her pace, studying the newly constructed models' runway at the end of the long room. It looked fully presentable, sleek and polished, and her mood lifted. It was such a thrill just before a show – the anticipation, the excitement. She loved it all. She stepped up onto the runway, pulled herself straight and began strolling, head high, in the manner she had taught her models every season here, in London, and in Paris. She turned with a practiced grace and walked back, impatient now for Monday. This was her domain, and she wanted it busy with life. She wanted what she knew, and she wanted to forget the *Titanic.* Surely all this would blow over soon; surely there would be no more cancellations. The elegant women of New York loved her designs. They wouldn't take flight. She wanted to feel safe again.

She suddenly became aware of movement in the shadows at the far end of the loft. It must be Farley, with a message. She stepped off the runway and walked toward the figure, partly alarmed, but mostly indignant. No one had permission to be up here without her consent. No one.

'Who is there? And what do you want?' she demanded.

'You always were the bossy one,' a woman's voice said with a giggle. 'Don't you recognise your own sister?'

Lucile gasped. 'Elinor?'

'And why are you so surprised? I booked myself on the first ship out after we heard of the sinking, and got your telegraph from the *Carpathia*. Did you think I wouldn't come?'

'Oh—' Lucile could hardly speak as her sister stepped out of the shadows, that silly red parasol on her arm. Had she thought that? Had she wondered if Elinor would twirl past even the worst of happenings in her usual manner, never quite connecting?

'I should have known you would come – you always were the impulsive one.'

'That trait has paid off splendidly.' Elinor's voice was brisk. 'I needed a new screenplay anyway. This time Hollywood will have to wait.'

'Thank you. You don't know how much I need you.' Something was bursting inside.

Elinor tossed her parasol onto a cutting table and extended her arms. 'From what I've seen in the papers, I have a fair idea,' she murmured.

Their embrace lasted only a moment, but in that fraction of time Lucile felt the first true comfort she had experienced since the sinking of the *Titanic*.

Sunday morning. Tess lay in bed in her hotel room, staring at the intricate molding that joined the walls and ceiling. She stretched out her toes, at the same time winding her fingers through the bars of the brass headboard, pulling tired muscles straight. She had stood for so long yesterday, her back still ached, and it felt good to lie here in leisure, even though she couldn't erase her troubled thoughts. She didn't want to be thinking of Jim, turning over reason after reason why she hadn't heard from him. Surely he would have some explanation; she *wanted* him to, but his silence seemed to say it all. Had he been reluctant to tell her what was coming, and then ashamed to admit his role in it?

She pushed him firmly from her mind. Today was hers. Lady Duff Gordon had announced quite magnanimously last night that she would not be required to work on Sunday. Courtesy of the union rules in New York, she was free to enjoy the Sunday street markets. And Tess had seen the look of pleasure on her employer's face when she, Tess, was actually disappointed by the news. Yes, Lucile, she said to herself. I love that magical place. Your seduction is working.

Pinky slung the market basket over her shoulder and began to tiptoe out of the apartment, ignoring the unwashed dishes. Nothing was noisier than the clatter of dishes being washed. He was asleep, and she wanted to get out before he woke again. She didn't want any more demands this morning. She had shaved him earlier, a routine he usually enjoyed, but not today. So okay, some days were better than others. She was getting tired of telling herself that.

'Where the hell are you going?' he yelled from the bedroom.

'Out to the market. It's Sunday, remember? I'll get some fruit, some bananas? You like those. I'll get the papers, too.'

'Come here, Pinky.'

Damn. Pinky put down the basket and walked into her father's bedroom. She felt a thud in her heart. He looked so ashen.

'They don't pay you much, do they.' It wasn't a question.

'Oh, it's all right.'

'You can't kid me – I heard you bargaining over money with that fat excuse for a nurse last night.'

She smiled in spite of herself. 'Maybe you can talk her into losing weight, then she won't need so much money.'

'Very funny.' His voice was raspy but gentle. 'When are they going to give you a raise?'

Her own question, of course. 'I'm getting some good stories, and next week I'm covering the suffragist parade. I'll get one soon. They need me.'

'Don't believe your own press notices. Big mistake.'

There it was again, more advice on how to do her job. Pinky shifted her weight, edging back toward the door. 'Look, I've got to go or all the best stuff will be picked over. Okay?'

He nodded. 'Sarah—'

She stopped. He never called her Sarah.

'I'm sorry, kid.'

She almost went back to kiss him on the forehead. But she couldn't trust the stinging in her eyes.

Tess saw Pinky first. Chatting with a vendor, her hair blowing across her face, looking as totally comfortable in this market, with its colourful awnings and boxes of lettuce and peaches and children playing around the skirts of their mothers, as she did at the hearings. Looking benign and cheery, as if she weren't out to destroy lives and reputations. Tess started to turn away.

Too late. 'Tess?' Pinky was approaching. 'So Lady Duff gave you a day off? You've come to a great Sunday market.' Her voice was relaxed but tentative. She was braced.

'Why did you do it?' Tess hadn't known what she would say the next time they met, but there it was.

Pinky started. 'What?' she said.

'*Cowardly* baronet? *Bribing* the sailors to go back? It's not true.'

'I didn't make it up,' Pinky said quickly, taken aback.

'But you took somebody's word for it. Somebody who didn't have the character to put his name behind his charges. Who was it?'

'Look, Tess, I don't like being attacked. I had sources from the ship—'

'A sailor?' Tess said, dismayed.

'Yes, if you have to know.'

'Not Jim Bonney.' Please, not Jim Bonney.

'You mean the sailor who's sweet on you? The one who carved that lifeboat of yours you weren't hanging on to too tightly?'

It was Tess's turn to be taken aback. 'Yes,' she said.

'Well, you're some friend. And I don't have to tell you anything.' It was her day off. She needed fruit and vegetables for dinner; maybe she would make a stew for her father. He loved onions; she hated them. She didn't have to stand here and be attacked.

'All you want to do is get a good story. You don't care about ruining lives.'

Pinky slammed her basket down on the ground, ignoring the glances from shoppers around her. She was too tired for diplomacy. 'All *you* want to do is be like those self-involved, self-satisfied people you work for, looking down their noses at everyone else. So I'm wrong? What's your story? Do you know what happened in that boat?'

'You're not pulling me into that. No, I wasn't there, but Lucile swears that nothing bad happened.' She was having trouble catching her breath. 'Why do you hate them? You've got a privileged life yourself. Look at the freedom you have! You have so much power. Why don't you use it more kindly?'

'What do you think America is?' Pinky said with mystification. 'Some Nirvana where everybody is as rich as the Duff Gordons? So you come here and eat off a table filled with crystal and china the very first night and you think that's what it's all about? And that people should be free to ignore or harm other people if they can get away with it? And then you get mad at me, when I'm just trying to tell the truth?'

'You throw out one self-righteous pronouncement after another. And I don't think you care about the truth.'

'Look, I work hard to find out things and I try to be a good reporter. You're the one who's self-righteous. Are you absolutely positive the Duff Gordons *weren't* trying to bribe the sailors not to go back?'

Tess responded as slowly and calmly as she could. 'They gave the crewmen money, but not as a bribe – it was to *thank* and *help* them. Why is that so hard for you to believe? Why does this make them bad people?'

'Tess, loyalty can make you blind.'

'So can running after headlines.'

'Could you be wrong?'

'Could you?'

They stared at each other. Pinky took charge of what came next.

'So I'm privileged – want to see where I live?' She reached out and grabbed Tess's hand. Market forgotten, Tess allowed herself to be marched down the street, turning finally onto a narrow, twisted road lined with shabby walk-ups. Pungent smells wafted from the windows, cabbage and stew meat and onions; children cried and dogs barked. Lines of laundry between the buildings flapped in a gentle wind. Pinky pointed upward.

'Fourth floor. With my father. He's sick. No pension. Not that anybody else should care. How's that for a self-righteous pronouncement?'

Tess stood silent for a moment.

'Are you saying you're poor? Is that it?'

'I'm saying I have a great job that doesn't pay a lot of money, and it gets frustrating. Especially' – Pinky took a deep breath and tried to speak calmly – 'when I'm told I am both privileged and self-righteous.'

'From my perspective, you are' – Tess took a deep breath of her own. 'Some of both.'

'Maybe I am. I see people shoved into institutions and left to die by the rich people who attend balls and don't give a fig for anybody other than themselves.'

There was no use ramming her head against such absolutes. 'Can't you look at the good things, too? Lady Duff Gordon employs people and pays them decently and . . . treats them well.' She blushed at her own exaggeration. 'Doesn't that count for something with you?'

'You Brits, with your titles,' Pinky retorted. 'She's doing what works for her.'

'She isn't a terrible person, Pinky.'

'Okay, but I know what I believe. I think you're trying too hard to please that woman, and her kind can't be pleased.'

'She could have left me on my own after we got here, but she didn't. Do you know how important that is to someone like me?'

'You don't have to bow too deeply, Tess.'

The words stung. 'I don't understand why you use your power the way you do.'

'I try to fight a few battles that get attention. And I try to change things a little. But I get riled, because I can't change things a lot.'

They stood again in silence for a few moments.

'I might as well tell you,' Pinky said reluctantly. 'I got my story about what happened in your lifeboat from a sailor named Tom Sullivan. Creepy guy, but he was there.'

Tess felt a wash of relief. It wasn't Jim. 'How can you trust him?'

'He didn't get the amount of money he thought he would get from Lady Duff, so he's mad. They got stingy on the payout. Works for me.'

'Can you possibly admit that you might be wrong?'

'Only if she denies it under oath. Even then, I'm not so sure. Why did you think Bonney was my source?'

At that moment, a boy in a green cap weaved past on a wobbly bicycle, forcing them both to step aside. Tess was grateful for the time to frame her reply. 'I didn't think it. I feared it,' she said slowly. 'Do you understand?'

'Oh, sure.' Pinky mentally scored one for her instincts yesterday, but it didn't give much satisfaction. 'What do you say we go back to the outdoor market? I can introduce you to the best apples you'll ever taste,' she said, a touch of cheer back in her voice.

Tess started to shake her head.

'I'm not a bad sort,' Pinky said quickly. 'I like you. You'll do all right here, Tess.'

It was the same thing Jim had said. 'I'm not sure how to think of you. Whether I should be wary of you or think of you as a friend.'

A friend. Pinky liked that. 'I do my job. Nobody likes reporters.'

'You are too sure of yourselves.'

'Unlike Lady Duff?'

Tess was silent.

Pinky sighed. 'Okay, would it help if I told you that my father thinks I'm a raging harpy sometimes?'

Tess couldn't help smiling. 'I guess it does. For now, anyway.'

Silently, in mutual consent, they walked back the way they had come. Soon the brilliant awnings and overflowing carts of the outdoor market came into view. Tess shaded her face from the sun, comforted by its warmth, thinking of Jim. She felt her spirit relax. For one day, surely, it was all right.

The sun was high when Tess made her way back from the outdoor market to the Waldorf, a small basket of apples under her arm. Pinky had done much of the talking as they wandered the stalls together, chattering away about New York, offering advice on where to buy cheap shirtwaists and the best places to buy decent tea. There was going to be a suffrage march starting from Washington Square in a few days, she said, a big one, the biggest yet, and it was the kind of story she loved covering, because it was about oppression and women's rights. The leader would be a woman mounted on a white horse. A splendid, huge white horse. There would be banners and babies and even men – a few, anyway. What kind of existence did women lead anyhow, all trussed up in corsets and suffering through childbirth while their husbands spent nights in brothels? Marriage was a trap.

It all flowed out so passionately. There were suffragists in England; Tess had read about them, even seen them marching once, carrying banners they waved back and forth. But it was always something that happened far away. Suffragists? Women declaring independence? They were strangers, from some privileged planet. Women with the time and the energy to do something besides change bed linens and clean toilets.

'Well, they won you the vote, didn't they?' Pinky said.

'It did me no good. It took enough energy to fight off the son of my employer in Cherbourg. He figured he had license to grope.'

'You see? You had no power to stop him.'

'I don't see how my being able to vote could have kept his hands where they belonged.'

Pinky looked at her with the impatience of a schoolteacher facing the slowest of pupils. 'It might have meant you had a voice and could influence the politicians who want to stay in power enough so maybe someday there would be a law sending gropers like that to jail.'

'I would love to see that day.'

'Then come to the march. I'll tell you a secret,' Pinky said.

'A secret?'

'It's just the most exciting thing. I'm covering the march, and they've agreed to let me ride the white horse before the march begins. I can't tell you how much that means to me.' Pinky spoke with the reverence of an acolyte.

'You can ride?'

'Of course.' She laughed. 'You know one of the best

things? Women gathering, marching, doing anything together makes a lot of men go crazy. They yell and scream and taunt and shake their fists. You know why? They're scared. They're scared we'll actually gain power and force them to change.' Her eyes brightened with the mischievousness of a child. 'That's fun to watch.'

'I know men like that,' Tess said. It hadn't taken much for the officer on the *Titanic* to blame her for a man's clumsiness. And she was used to it – would that horrify Pinky? Probably. It felt good to be walking along, talking about women and voting and power and white horses. And oh, the sun felt so good on her skin. Pinky was chattering away about her next *Titanic* story as Tess only half listened. It was all quite peaceful.

'We've got reports that there were a few survivors who didn't get counted, probably because they were steerage and didn't speak English,' Pinky said. 'The funny thing is, one rich guy was missed because he was unconscious at first and wearing a ragged jacket.'

Tess stopped dead. 'Do you know who it was?'

'A Chicago guy named Jack Bremerton.'

'He's alive? He's all right?'

'Yes.' Pinky shot her a quick glance. 'You know him?'

'We met on the ship.'

'He's quite the important person, I'm told. The very famous Henry Ford came to see him, and he's already back in his office and working again. Sounds to me like he's still delirious.' She giggled. 'By the way, I've talked my editor into sending me to Washington tonight for tomorrow's hearing.'

'Washington?'

'Smith decided to continue in his home territory. The whole crew was sent down there yesterday. Any message you want to give your sailor?'

'He's not my sailor.' It flustered her to hear the tease in Pinky's voice. And now she couldn't ask any more about Mr. Bremerton.

'Well, I've talked to you both, and each of you lights up at the mention of the other. Doesn't mean a thing, of course.'

Tess was only half listening, remembering the handsome, smiling man with gray hair on the *Titanic.* He was here. Here in this city, now, and as far away as the moon. She wished she could see him. Oh, this was ridiculous – she was harboring a schoolgirl's crush. In the real world, what she fantasised was impossible. And Jim – Jim was gone, without a word to her.

'Tess? I'm leaving. Any message for Jim?' Pinky raised an eyebrow, waiting.

'No, no message.'

Chapter 8

WALDORF-ASTORIA

SUNDAY EVENING, APRIL 21

Lucile was chattering away, looking very happy as Cosmo buttoned up the back of her beautiful tea gown. 'Come in, come in,' she called gaily as Tess entered the suite. 'We're going to have a lovely evening because the most wonderful thing has happened. My sister is here!'

'That's the first time you've ever called me wonderful,' an amused voice called out from the other room. And then there she was, the handsome woman Tess remembered twirling a parasol on the dock in Cherbourg, stretching out her hand. 'Hello, Tess,' she said with a smile. 'I'm Elinor Glyn – I don't think we managed a proper introduction before. I hear you turned out to be anything but a proper maid – thank goodness for that.'

'How did you get here so quickly?' Tess asked, surprised.

'Well, dear, my ship didn't sink.'

She said it with such light casualness. So there was still, after all, an ordinary world where jokes could be made. Tess liked her immediately.

'Elinor says we're eating dinner in the Palm Room tonight, no more taking meals up here, like people guilty of something,' Lucile said, pulling away from Cosmo's hands and twirling around. 'It's the Darlings that need to keep their heads down now. Did you see the story about his shameful masquerade?' She pulled on white kid gloves and twirled in her long, slender gown of raspberry silk. 'Isn't this the loveliest dress? Maybe I will model it myself at the spring show. Wouldn't that be different?'

'You are the best model for all your gowns, dear,' said Cosmo promptly, almost automatically. He glanced at his watch and urged his wife to hurry. Their reservation downstairs was in ten minutes.

'Tess, you must join us,' Lucile said. 'I have a gown ready for you in the next room.'

It wasn't really an invitation, of course, more like an order. But Elinor's arrival had improved Lucile's mood with astonishing speed. Tess caught her breath when she saw the gown hanging on a closet door. It looked amazingly similar to the one Lucile had given her before the *Titanic* went down. The same colours, the same cut. Had she chosen it on purpose? It slid off the hanger, floating on her fingertips, as flimsy and ethereal as passing time.

The Palm Room – cupped under a magnificent domed ceiling – was filled with the easy formality and discreet murmurings of well-dressed diners. The maître d' lifted the red velvet rope to admit their party, giving all a deferential bow, including Tess. No gaping, she told herself. Don't act like a servant girl. All around her, mirrored walls reflected a mixed glow of crystal, amber marble, and candlelight that created an almost bewildering swirl of dancing images. Beautiful.

'Head up, Tess,' murmured Elinor. 'You're dressed like a queen. Enjoy the fact that everyone is looking at us.'

'I don't feel like one.'

'Pretend, for heaven's sake.'

Patrons were indeed taking note of their arrival, whispering as they walked past. But there was an edge, a sharpness to their voices, like the sound of a knife swiftly cutting through air.

'They don't wish us well,' Tess said.

'A mix of envy and malice – the usual thing. Look at my sister; that's how to do it.'

Lucile, her hand resting in Cosmo's crooked elbow, was not simply walking but sweeping into the room, as if any moment applause would break out and she would take a triumphant bow. Her face was flushed. To Tess, she looked like a sunflower reaching for light.

'Now, Tess, I have to know. Are you staying or ready to run?'

Seated now, Elinor asked the question in a relaxed, quiet voice, but her eyes were cool. A bottle of champagne was being uncorked by the sommelier, and waiters were hovering, one behind each chair.

'I have no plans to leave,' Tess said, startled.

'Lucy seems to think you may have talent. You've got an opportunity to prove yourself, a bigger one than you realise. But things aren't going to go well here for a while.'

'I know.'

'My sister keeps putting her foot in her mouth. This latest jab at the Darlings was idiotic.'

Tess stirred uncomfortably, not sure if she was expected to agree or simply to wait in silence.

'I'm not trying to test you; I put no value on discretion. On the contrary, I've found that strutting one's stuff gets a woman ahead – at least in the movie business.'

'It's not quite the same in the servant business,' Tess murmured.

Elinor laughed. 'You're not in it anymore,' she said. 'Look, I can't stay here very long. Much as I want to support my sister, I have to get to Los Angeles.' She tapped an ash from the end of her cigarette into an ashtray, the silver of her delicately slender cigarette holder catching the light. 'So let me put it to you plainly. Lucile needs eyes and ears at the shop right now. And you're the obvious person at the moment. Cosmo found an apartment for you today down near the Flatiron Building, not far from Lucile's loft. You can't stay here – the hotel wants your room. This won't last too long, but Lucy can't go home until she gets through her spring show and knows for sure that she won't have to testify at the inquiry. Then you can do whatever you want. You'll have references.'

'What does that mean, to be her eyes and ears?'

Elinor shrugged and smiled. 'Oh, you'll know.' Her smile faded as she looked at Lucile chattering away to a silent Cosmo. He was sipping his champagne, his face a study in blankness. 'Lucy had better watch out,' she said softly.

'For what?'

'A great many unpleasant things could happen.'

Carefully, Tess picked up a silver fork to eat the salad now before her. Delicate greens, white asparagus, and ham cut into small pieces – but the stuffed olives were most tempting. A quick glance at Elinor assured her that she had chosen the right fork. 'Do you think she'll have to testify? Senator Smith isn't calling women before the commission.'

'I know; any female who went through that experience is too delicate to speak of it. Such hooey. But Smith might feel forced to. Lucy is deluged with criticism, and it's her own fault. His, too, for that matter.' She rolled her eyes, glancing at Cosmo. '*Bribing* the crew not to go back? My goodness.'

The maître d' approached. 'A message for Lady Duff Gordon,' he murmured.

'Later, not now,' Lucile said, waving him away.

The maître d' leaned closer, whispering something in Cosmo's ear, then handed him the note. Cosmo scanned it quickly, his expression frozen.

'You aren't listening to me,' Lucile said impatiently. 'Must you be reading while I'm talking to you?'

Cosmo pushed his chair away from the table and stood. 'I think we'll finish our meal upstairs,' he said pleasantly to the maître d'. 'Send the menus and a waiter up to our suite as quickly as possible.'

'For heaven's sake—'

'Be quiet, Lucy. Let's go.'

'But—'

'Hush,' Elinor murmured. She grabbed her sister's arm. Asking no questions, Tess followed them out of the restaurant, feeling the eyes of the other diners on them once again. She kept her head up, this time with effort.

Cosmo shut the door of the suite and faced them, lips tight and drained of colour. 'Jordan Darling has hanged himself,' he said, keeping his eyes on Lucile. 'His wife found him a few hours ago.'

A shiver – where did it begin, her stomach, her legs? – spread, cold and uncontrollable, through Tess's body. Her hands began to shake.

'Who is the note from?' Elinor asked.

Cosmo stared at the paper in his hand as if it might explode at any moment. 'His wife. It's for Lucile.'

'I don't want to see it,' Lucile said. The flesh beneath her chin was trembling.

'You will have to hear it, then.' Cosmo passed the note

to Elinor, who read aloud one scrawled sentence at the end of the message, the letters in wavery purple ink.

Why were you so cruel?

Lucile sank into a chair with a moan, covering her face with her hands.

'She's distraught – you didn't do this,' Elinor said quickly.

The shiver had subsided, but Lucile's denunciation of Darling on the *Carpathia* scratched at Tess's brain. No, no, Lucile didn't kill him – no, that was horrible.

'But I did play a part,' Lucile said slowly.

Only then was Tess able to release her pity and desire to comfort by speaking up. 'I'm so sorry,' she whispered.

Lucile looked up, her eyes grateful. 'Thank you,' she said.

'Don't leave this suite tomorrow, Lucy,' Cosmo said. 'Pull back. I will tell everyone you are in mourning. Do you hear me? And, for God's sake, do not talk to any reporters.'

WALDORF-ASTORIA

NEW YORK CITY

MONDAY, APRIL 22

The sun was barely up when Tess left the hotel, glancing anxiously around as she made her way out to Farley in the waiting car. Good, no reporters yet. What a dark night it had been, haunted with dreams of throwing herself onto railroad ties, trying to protect Lucile from an oncoming train; walking into a room and seeing Jordan Darling's body hanging from a silk drapery sash – from what had her fevered brain created *that*?

The reality of today would be even more frightening. It was now her job to hold things together at the shop, Elinor had said late last night, after an almost catatonic Lucile finally fell asleep. She didn't have to know everything; she just needed to be there as a calming influence. There was no way Lucile's presence outside this room wouldn't result in more terrible stories. She could do it.

With her stomach turning cartwheels? Impossible. 'I've only been in the shop once,' Tess protested, trying not to panic. 'I don't know anything about how the place is run.'

'You're going to learn some quick lessons tomorrow, but remember, you have James to help you. He knows a lot,' Elinor said soothingly. 'This is just for a couple of days. Life is an act – most of it, anyway. Get out there today and pretend you're in charge, for goodness' sake. Do you hear me? Lift up your head and *pretend*.' A flicker of a smile passed over her face. 'It's the secret to everything.'

As she left to go to her own room, Cosmo handed her a set of keys on a small steel key ring, folding the cold metal into her hand with a scribbled address on a piece of paper. 'For your flat, Tess,' he said quietly. 'It will be ready on Tuesday. The bed will be made, towels there. Some food. Let me know what you need.' His face had been pinched tight as a withered plum – her first realisation that he, too, was suffering. He looked not at all like the polished, calm man she had first met on the dock at Cherbourg. That, surely, had fed the turbulence of her dreams.

There was no grin on Farley's face this morning, but, rather, something of a watchful, wary look. 'So no Lady Duff today?' he asked, opening the door for her.

'No, she's resting.'

He pulled the car out into the street and did not speak for the duration of the trip. Tess stared down at the notes she had taken from Elinor: Check the runway, inventory the gowns for the show. Make sure the embroideries and the finishing details were being done properly. Check the final fittings on the models.

This was crazy, impossible.

'I'm not the person to put in charge of this. Why don't you go?' she had protested.

'The press would love that,' Elinor said, rolling her eyes. 'They'll have Lucy's name smeared all over their stories on Darling's suicide. No, I'm keeping my head down, too; I don't need that sort of attention. You're the one to do this, Tess. Nobody's after you.'

The sound of buzzing sewing machines reassured Tess as she stepped off the elevator and walked into the loft. A few glances came her way as she walked back to Lucile's office, but no questions. It took her a moment to realise that there were fewer people than there had been on Saturday.

James was waiting in the office, looking nervous. 'Where is Madame?' he said.

'She's been working too hard and is taking a rest today.' Tess looked around at the many bouquets of wilting flowers, her nose wrinkling slightly at the sickish smell of decaying blossoms, and hoped she sounded matter-of-fact enough.

'We know what that's about, don't we?' he said. 'Nobody wants a death on their hands. On top of everything else that's toppled her reputation.'

'I think it's up to us to get done today what needs to be done,' Tess said, hoping her voice held a shred or two of confidence.

James turned his back to the glass wall, and Tess realised that he didn't want the seamstresses to see his face. 'I've got bad news,' he said. He walked over to a long table and pointed. A creamy gown covered with intricate beading lay on the table – the wedding dress, the centerpiece of the show.

'It's beautiful,' Tess said, reaching out to lift it up. To her horror, the skirt slipped away from her fingers. It had been slashed open and only half of it remained attached to the bodice.

'What happened?' She could not believe it. All this beautiful work, destroyed.

'Somebody hates Madame,' he said. 'It's monstrous. Nothing like this ever happened before.' He didn't look at Tess, just stared down at the gown as if at a dead body. 'Nobody liked what they were reading in the papers; she wasn't sounding too nice, but still—'

'We have to remake it.'

He shook his head. 'There's no time for that. And there's no way to mend it – it's too fragile.'

'Who knows about it?'

'The beader – she left in tears. She said she couldn't work here anymore. Everybody out there knows what happened now.'

Tess fingered the ruined silk and the broken bead strings, remembering a stitch her mother had taught her for mending torn curtains: two loops and a twist; the trick was in the twist. If that wasn't enough, she could try gathering the fabric in with tiny bits of elastic.

'James, could you bring in a seamstress, someone you trust?'

'Yes, ma'am.'

'I think I can fix this, but I need your help with everything else. I can't run this shop. I don't know how.'

'Nobody can, except Madame. It's a lot of smoke and mirrors, you know. But you can count on me to help.'

Tess gave him a shaky smile of gratitude. 'Maybe we should tell everybody that the dress will be repaired and the show will take place as scheduled, and not pretend that nothing happened.'

'Sounds good to me.' He looked relieved. He started out the door and stopped when she spoke again. 'What else?'

'Choosing which model wears which dress?' she asked uncertainly.

'Sounds good.'

'And maybe somebody could clear out all the wilted flowers; they look too sad.'

'Will do.'

It was a few minutes before she realised, bending over the torn dress, that James had called her 'ma'am.'

SENATE OFFICE BUILDING
WASHINGTON, D.C.
MONDAY, APRIL 22
5 A.M.

Pinky sat on the steps of the Senate Office Building, watching the early glow of sunrise and feeling a bit stupid for being there so early. The hearing wasn't scheduled to start until 10 A.M., but where else could she wait? Van Anda wasn't about to pay for any more nights in a hotel than he had to, so that had meant a midnight train, which put Mrs. Dotson in a tizzy. Only an extra fifty dollars had bought her benevolent services. She'd just have to tell Van Anda she could come down only on day trips after this. Pinky rubbed her aching forehead. She debated going to the Continental Hotel, where White Star was putting up the crew, and waking a few of them; maybe they'd tell her their complaints about being cooped up without any money in a strange city. But it seemed like too much effort.

She pulled her coat closer against the chill. Maybe she should have stayed in New York and followed up on the Jordan Darling suicide. Truly, though, she had no appetite for going after Lady Duff Gordon again, even though the silly woman had brought the latest round of criticism on herself. Tess was too loyal – more than Pinky would have been, job or not. On the other hand, Darling was the one who hopped on the boat wrapped in a tablecloth; he did it to himself. She rubbed her forehead again. Sometimes this *Titanic* story made her weary. Couldn't someone come along and open the blasted building? She wished she had worn a heavier coat.

'Hello there, young lady. I recognise you!'

A woman's voice, hearty and full, coming from a long, sleek black car that had pulled up in front of the building. Pinky stepped closer and peered through the window. Peering back at her was the beaming face of the woman from Colorado who had rowed one of the lifeboats. Margaret Brown – that was her name. Very quotable.

'Come on in, honey, and get warm. We're here for the same reason, that's pretty obvious. You're working, but I'm just curious to see how the esteemed senator handles this on his home ground.' Mrs. Brown opened the door and beckoned Pinky in, immediately offering her a cup of steaming hot coffee from a thermos passed back by her chauffeur. Gratefully, Pinky jumped in and curled her cold fingers around the cup. She'd get an interview out of this, for sure.

'You're the girl with the funny name who works for the *Times,* right? Brash, like me – that's what I hear. So how do you like Washington at sunrise?'

'It's quiet,' Pinky said.

'Not for long. What's the latest news from the city?'

'A suicide. One of the people in Lifeboat One.'

'Ah, poor Jordan Darling. Yes, I heard that back at the

hotel. A fatal masquerade. The humiliation must have been too great,' Mrs. Brown murmured. 'Any good news?'

'The French-speaking orphans – their mother is coming for them.'

'Ah, yes. I heard that, too – poor little things. At least the father did his best to save them. Preparing to die has a way of clarifying the mind.'

'What did it clarify for you?' Pinky asked.

Mrs. Brown laughed. 'Told me to keep doing and saying what I damn well please, and not be bamboozled by anyone. Life is short – no mulling things over for a dozen years or so. What about you?'

'I wasn't on the ship.'

'A nice reporter dodge, dear. You'll have your choices to make, too, in due time.' She smiled, big and comfortable. 'This Senator Smith – I'd like to shake the stuffing out of him. He won't call me to testify, and I want things to go on the record. Especially how the women had to take over from the male cowards.'

'Tell them to me,' Pinky said quickly. 'My paper is the paper of record, you know.'

'Yes, I read your masthead.' Mrs. Brown's eyes were sparkling. 'You know I ran for the U.S. Senate a few years ago? I'm going to do it again first chance I get.'

Pinky was fumbling in her bag for her notebook. 'Can I write that?'

Mrs. Brown folded ample white arms across an equally ample stomach. 'Honey, you can write down anything I say. After being brined, salted, and pickled in mid-ocean, I am now high and dry.'

'What about the Duff Gordons? Should they testify?'

'I think that's what you're hoping for, isn't it?'

'I'm just a reporter.'

'No, you're not. I read your story, and I think you care about what happened in that boat.'

A second of hesitation. 'Well, you caught it,' Pinky said.

'Poor old Smith doesn't want to, but he'll get himself in trouble either way. We'll see. He won't call me because I won't be polite and do it his way. He's afraid if he brings in the British upper class they'll figure out how to run the show. Good chance they will, too.' She peered out the window and up at the Senate Office Building. 'Everything swishing about, to and fro – do you feel it? It's like we're all in a seltzer bottle that's ready to blow. Or maybe it already has and we don't know it yet.'

'Who's complaining *now*?' Senator Smith glared at the aide standing in the doorway of his office in the Senate Office Building.

'Daughters of the American Revolution, sir. They're worried about national morale.'

'Why? We didn't build the damn ship, and we certainly didn't sink it!'

'No, sir. It's just – everybody seems so whipped up. The dancer's suicide – he was quite a favorite.'

'I know, I know.' Smith shoved the mountain of mail before him to the edge of his desk, not caring that several dozen letters fell to the floor. He had been up most of the night, poring over maritime books, reading up on the dangers of ice. To find out that all his plans for the day might be upended by more scandal was too much.

Smith strode out of his office, walking toward the Caucus Room, spirits glum. Charges, countercharges – whom to believe? That sailor who claimed that the lookout had been asleep in the crow's nest – any credibility to that? Not likely; the man was suspect. Smith had the crew, and he had Ismay for a while longer. But survivors were scattering already; they would have to be subpoenaed quickly or their testimony would be lost. And that meant he was going to have to go back to New York, which did not improve his mood.

The guards pushed open the doors to the Caucus Room with effort, and Smith saw to his chagrin that hundreds of people had jammed into the huge room, including – right up front – that irritating woman from the *Times*. And right next to her was that clamorous Mrs. Brown. This most definitely would not be an easy day.

'Quiet, please!' Smith banged his gavel repeatedly, exasperated at how difficult it was proving even to get the hearing under way. He was already hoarse. 'Our first witness will be Fourth Officer Joseph Boxhall, a principal navigator on the *Titanic*,' he announced.

A small man with black hair and a mouth that worked nervously was guided to the witness chair. Pinky glanced over at the door he had come through. With no official witness list, did Smith have all the crew members waiting back there? Getting interviews with them might be hard.

Smith began the questioning. Boxhall took obvious pride in his navigational abilities. He had also been in charge of collecting all warnings of icebergs from other ships, and then charting the *Titanic*'s course. And who gave those warnings to him? The captain of the ship, of course. Had he gotten any warning of ice in the *Titanic*'s path? No. What was the weather like? Clear and calm.

Another member of the panel cleared his throat. 'How do you account for the fact that you could not see the icebergs, if the night was so clear?'

Boxhall screwed up his face and shook his head. He couldn't – sorry.

'Are they more difficult to see at night?'

'Not always. But the water that night was in an oily calm. One little ripple on the water, we would've had a very good chance of seeing that iceberg in time to miss it.'

An 'oily calm': strange expression. But a time-waster to explore. Instead, Smith decided to show off some of his new knowledge, pointing out – with Boxhall nodding eagerly – the differences between the smaller chunks of low-lying ice known as growlers and large expanses of surface ice known as field ice.

'These formations are more frequent in the latitude of the Grand Banks, I understand. And is it customary to be particularly careful in that vicinity?'

'Oh yes, sir.'

'Well,' pressed Smith, 'how did it happen that in that identical vicinity it was not thought necessary to increase the lookout?'

Boxhall paused. 'I do not know.'

Enough. Smith banged his gavel and declared a recess.

Speed and stupidity, that's what did it, Pinky told herself as she elbowed her way through the crowd to the door. Same old story – she'd heard it dozens of times. It was all politics in the end. She was hungry for fresh air.

She escaped the crowd – no one seemed to want to stray too far from the vicinity out of fear of losing a place – and made her way down the marble corridor to the entrance hall. And there, on a corner bench, she spied Mrs. Brown, talking with great enthusiasm to a sailor. Pinky moved closer and saw that it was Jim Bonney.

'Pinky, come over here,' Mrs. Brown called. 'Look at this man's work!'

Jim looked up, his face breaking into a slow grin when he recognised her. He looked tired and rumpled but somehow at ease. He was holding a small, curved knife and a piece of wood in his hands – large hands, Pinky noted for the first time, with strong, slender fingers.

Mrs. Brown scooped the wood from him and held it aloft. 'Look at the detail,' she marveled. It was a carving of the U.S. Capitol, done with impressive intricacy and skill.

'I've seen your work,' Pinky said to Jim with a smile. 'You're good.'

Jim reached for the carving. 'I'm not done, actually. Nothing much else to do around here until they call me to testify.' His eyes flickered up to Pinky's with a question. What could she say? Tess had sent no message.

'Well, I'm enormously impressed,' Mrs. Brown said. She

looked at Jim shrewdly. 'I've got a job for you if you want it, young man. Can you make a replica of that unfortunate ship we were on?'

'The *Titanic*? Sure, I can.'

'With all the details on it – you know, ladders, ropings, crow's nest, that sort of thing?'

He paused, his brow furrowing. 'I'd do better with a set of the plans,' he said. 'And I don't know if I have the time.'

'I can get the plans for you,' Mrs. Brown said with a wave of her hand. 'You aren't planning on sitting around like a vegetable after you've testified, are you?'

A smile pulled at the corners of Jim's mouth. 'No, ma'am, I'll find a job.'

'You have one,' she said with elaborate patience. 'I am commissioning this carving of the ship. Which means I will pay you very generously. You, sir, are very talented, and now you are in my hands. I'll bring you business; I'm good at that. And, in case you don't know it, I'm very rich.' She sighed. 'Mines in Colorado – that sort of thing.'

Pinky watched Jim's face change. He seemed stunned at first. Then he looked down at his hands, as if seeing them for the first time.

'It's a deal,' he said.

NEW YORK CITY

MONDAY NIGHT, APRIL 22

Tess wandered aimlessly around her hotel room, giddy with the knowledge that tomorrow she would be freed of the glances of curiosity from hotel staff and guests; the whispers in the wake of moving through the grand lobby to this small cubicle of privacy. Tomorrow she would be in her own place.

She sat down on the bed, enjoying the silence at first. Then a twist of loneliness. What was happening in Washington? Pinky would have a story tomorrow, surely. Had she seen Jim, talked to him? Was he all right?

Slowly she prepared for bed. There was no use pretending to herself that she didn't miss him. She closed her eyes, conjuring up his face, the easy lope of his walk as they had made their way back to the hotel from the magical Central Park. Only two days ago.

She pulled back the covers and sank into the silky percale sheets. This was no time for foolish meanderings. She had managed to repair the dress, but tomorrow would be a hard and challenging day.

She drifted off to sleep, fingers curled tight around the comforting presence of the metal keys clutched in her fist.

Chapter 9

WALDORF-ASTORIA

NEW YORK CITY

TUESDAY MORNING, APRIL 23

'Did you see the funeral notice in the paper?' Elinor said as she pulled back the heavy drapes, letting in the morning light.

'Yes, of course I did.' A hovering dust, exposed by the light, hung in the air. Lucile coughed, then moaned, clutching a handkerchief to her face.

'Oh stop it, Lucy,' Elinor said impatiently. 'You've played the victim long enough.'

'How can you talk to me that way?'

'Because I know you, and you're too good at indignation and self-pity – that's why. What's done is done, and the sooner we can get you out of here and back to England the better.'

'My note to Jean Darling had no self-pity in it, grant me that.'

'It was fine. The best you could do under the circumstances.' Elinor reached for her cigarette holder and began to insert a cigarette.

'Must you? I'm so tired of the smell of your cigarettes.'

'Worse than the tea and the tarts?' Elinor lit the cigarette and inhaled, staring out the open window. 'You called them "abominable" last night.'

'Please, I'm trying.'

Her sister's expression softened. 'All right.' She pinched the cigarette out and dropped it into an ashtray.

'I know you're cross with me, and clearly Cosmo is. Jordan Darling's suicide was dreadful, and I wish I had never opened my mouth to those reporters. But it is grossly unfair to blame me for what he did. He survived, why couldn't he leave it at that? What is wrong with being a survivor?'

'Quite a lot, perhaps.'

Lucile compressed her lips, annoyed. 'You're going to say something deep and complicated, and I'm going to want to run out of this room.'

'Well, this time I've got you cornered.' Elinor's voice was casual. 'Aren't we the pair?'

'What's that supposed to mean?'

'Look at the two of us. I've been writing stories since I was fifteen. You, my dear sister, put your head down to the needle and sewed your way out of a miserable marriage. Then you came up with the idea of draping clothes over live models and voilà! Success. Helped along, of course, by marrying a title. Now, don't you agree that we're quite the pair?'

'You're setting the scene for something more, I know you.'

'Of course. Maybe we're too used to making our own rules.'

'And what does that have to do with being a survivor?'

'We're not particularly nice people, Lucy. We're both a bit careless, wouldn't you agree?'

'I'm not interested in playing your games.' She didn't have to listen to this – it was just the same old teasing that Elinor enjoyed so much.

'And self-absorbed?'

'That's what Cosmo says.'

'Well, putting your dear husband aside for the moment – and, by the way, he was quite clumsy with his generosity on that lifeboat of yours. Well, you've got your answer.'

Lucile lifted an eyebrow. 'What is it, dear sister?'

'It's simple. The careless and self-absorbed manage to survive. Aren't we lucky?'

A silence fell over them both. Only after a long moment spent staring at the teapot on its silver tray sitting before her did Lucile respond.

'I thought you came here to comfort me.'

'And to wake you up, Lucy.' Elinor's voice was calm. 'We're self-made women; there aren't many like us, wouldn't you say? But we can't afford to believe the fantasies we build about ourselves. Now a question – I hear that sailor who claims you stopped him from rescuing survivors is testifying. What are you doing about it?'

'I don't know what we can do. Deny it, of course.'

'I can imagine how that will go.'

'It will go fine, I'm sure. And as far as believing in my own "fantasies," as you put it, all I have ever wanted is to be successful at what I do best, which is designing. I have done that, and I intend to enjoy it.'

'It can evaporate in a minute, you know.'

'Well, if either of us had stayed focused on that we'd never have got anywhere.'

'Probably not even out of childhood.'

'Mother was impossible.'

'Oh say it, Lucy. She was mean as dirt.'

They sat in silence for a moment.

'We managed,' Lucile said in a different voice. 'Together.'

'Dear Lucy, you took the brunt of it.'

'But I mastered the skill of throwing a phenomenally good tantrum.'

'Which you continue to perfect,' murmured Elinor, eyes dancing.

'Well, of course.'

Again, silence between them – a more comfortable one this time. Lucile nibbled at a tart and sipped her tea. 'Surely these terrible newspaper stories will soon wind down. I can't stand another day of hiding out in this place,' she said finally. 'I'm their scapegoat, but they'll get bored with me; they always do. They'll hunt for fresh ones, don't you think? I've heard of some awful behavior, particularly by the more excitable people in steerage.'

'Don't count on it. You have too good a career and too high a reputation for them to leave you alone.'

Lucile leaned back and closed her eyes. 'I have to get back to my shop. It's my life and I don't want anyone else in charge, and certainly not Tess, who has no competence for business.' Her eyes flew open; she frowned. 'She was a bit vague on how things went yesterday. Did you talk to her? Is she holding something back?'

Elinor watched her sister closely. 'If I tell you she was, you must promise not to get hysterical.'

'Oh, dear Lord.'

'Promise? If you don't, I will walk out of here and get on a train for Los Angeles right now.'

Reluctantly, Lucile agreed. She sat in horrified silence as Elinor told her about the slashed wedding gown. How Tess had set about to repair it; how it had worked.

'Who would do such a thing?'

'She doesn't know. But the absence of your general manager's assistant was suspicious.'

'She didn't tinker with my design, did she?'

'She did what she had to do.'

'That means she did. And she was afraid to admit it.'

'I said, she did what she had to do. And you seem prepared to berate her. Why did you send her in your place, then?'

'I had no choice.'

'What does Cosmo say?'

'He actually thinks I'm feeling maternal. Which is nonsense.'

'Trying *not* to feel maternal is more like it,' Elinor said

The weight of an old, unspoken hurt descended between them.

'I'm not asking anything.'

Lucile turned her head away before answering. 'Mind you don't,' she said.

The muted sounds of the city – horses clattering along the street, the chugging of motorcars and children calling to one another – floated through the open window, the only sounds in the silence that followed.

Elinor sighed, reaching over to pat her sister's hand. 'Well, back to your spring show. I've struck a bargain with a young woman who is going to be a star in the movies, but right now she needs money.'

'What kind of a bargain?'

'We give her one of your gowns and she promises to wear it here and in Hollywood, extolling your virtues as a designer.'

'What is the bargain?'

'We pay her a thousand dollars.'

'My Lord, that's insane! *She* should be paying *me*!'

'Lucy, she'll be a big customer very soon. Haven't you heard of Mary Pickford?'

'I've read about her. I don't need such cheap advertising. No, I won't hear of it.'

Elinor settled back in her seat and reached once again for her cigarette holder, taking time to again light a cigarette. 'My dear sister, you can't afford to pass this one up,' she said.

On Tuesday morning Tess slipped out of the hotel with a small valise, avoiding Lucile's suite. It was a relief, knowing she would no longer be a pretender to these lavish surroundings. Cosmo and Elinor surely had no inkling of how much having a place of her own meant to her. She brushed her hair away from her face, hoping she didn't look as tired as she felt.

The night had been filled with more dreams, the Darlings entwined through them all. She couldn't get them out of her mind. That affable, happy man, he and his wife the embodiment of fantasy – gone, vanished. Yesterday she had pushed her thoughts into a tight corner, knowing they would be waiting for her later. And now they were hammering to be heard. *Cruelty.* The word Jean Darling had used. But Lucile didn't kill her husband – no one could say that. How ironic that a man could be cowardly and then muster the courage – or did it take only shame? – to take his own life. She skimmed the *Times* in the hotel's lobby, reading Pinky's story about yesterday's testimony. No mention of Jim; nothing about the Duff Gordons. A picture of Jordan Darling and one of his weeping wife.

And no way to offer them comfort. None, certainly not from anyone working for Lady Duff Gordon. Jim must know what happened by now. What did he think?

She climbed into the waiting car, her heart heavy. She must pull herself together. Today, just one step at a time. The shop would be frantic; the show – how could it matter in the face of such tragedy – was only days away. Last night James had ticked off all the things that needed to be done, and she felt enormous gratitude that he had so quickly rallied to her side. He was ordering the canapés and the wine. He had even arranged for reminder cards to be hand-delivered to Lucile's patrons today. What else? She tried to focus on her concern about the models. Yesterday one of them had seemed restless and bored, unwilling to stand for final pinnings – and she was the one slated to wear the centerpiece wedding gown.

Tess rubbed her eyes; oh, she was tired, and the day had barely begun. 'Lucile, come back soon,' she whispered quietly. 'This is more your world than it is mine.' She pulled her purse close, comforted once again by the weight of the keys inside.

'There's a problem,' James said as she came in the door of Lucile's office. His bald head glistened with sweat. 'The tucks in the wedding gown made it too tight for the model.'

'I can fix that with a piecing of silk, I think,' Tess said, trying to appear confident.

He shook his head wearily. 'She pulled it off and tore it again. Said she'd never seen such a mess before a show. Then stomped out, probably with a job offer from this woman Chanel already in her back pocket.'

'Bring me the dress. And another model – I don't care who.'

James nodded and hurried from the room.

Her hands trembled as he handed her the gown and she saw the tear. She would have to change the line of the bodice, and that meant the skirt would need to be reconfigured.

Lucile would be upset, but there was no choice. As Tess pulled out the seams and retucked the material – why did it need that underskirt? – she felt something totally unexpected and startling: a sense of euphoria. She could do this. She could salvage Lucile's creation.

The model, a tall, slender girl of about eighteen, stared straight ahead as Tess worked, not seeming to care about or to question anything. Engrossed in the cutting and refitting, Tess worked in silence. The underskirt had bunched under the torn material; it had to go. Scissors poised, she hesitated. Would it be too sheer, or would it just give a hint of the wearer's legs? Anything else would be disastrous. She knew it would work, she was sure of it; the beading would soften the transparency and the entire gown would float much better. Sharp and sure, her scissors began cutting away the underskirt.

Just as she finished, James came bursting in, his eyes alight. 'Miss Glyn called,' he said. 'Isadora Duncan says she will attend the show. That helps make up for Mrs. Wharton backing out, I'd say.'

Tess lifted her eyes from the fabric, her breath catching. 'My goodness!' she said.

'Madame has made her some beautiful clothes,' James said, anticipating her question. 'And she doesn't have to buy anything. She just has to *be* here. Come quick, see the carpet – they're laying it now.'

Tess peered through the door and caught her breath again. From the entrance near the shabby elevator to the back of the loft, a sweep of rich, thick purple carpet was being unrolled and hammered down. The seamstresses and fitters were watching and giggling. This factory they labored in every day, crammed with sewing machines and billowing reams of silk and soft wools, was being transformed. Chiffon curtains were being arranged around the stage, creating a silvery cloudlike setting; a workman was fiddling with the lights, dimming them to a soft glow. The effect was magical.

'Lucile knows how to do this, doesn't she?' James murmured. 'Such a sense of drama. Amazing woman, as maddening as she is.'

'Yes,' Tess said. Could she, too, do all this someday? Maybe, she thought, letting herself slip back to the night on the *Titanic* and Jack Bremerton's unexpected vote of confidence in her. She would probably never see him again, and his faith in her that night had been unearned at the time. But what she knew for certain was how much she wanted to try.

TERRITORIES CONFERENCE ROOM

WASHINGTON, D.C.

TUESDAY, APRIL 23

Pinky had trouble dragging herself to the new hearing room on Tuesday morning. That cheap Van Anda had put her up in a hotel filled with boisterous late-night partygoers, and no amount of banging on the walls or shouting down the corridor had stopped the noise. She had tried to talk with Bonney yesterday, but Smith's people spotted him in the entrance hall and hustled him away with the rest of the crew. Too many witnesses and contradictions; that had left her cranky. A leather-goods man said crew members shot pistols in the air to keep panicked men from filling the boats, while a Brooklyn cleric insisted that there was complete decorum on the ship, no panic at all. She had worked until her early-edition deadline, distracted by anxiety about her father. There was a neighbour 'looking in' on Mrs. Dotson, hopefully with some delicacy, so the woman wouldn't guess that Pinky didn't completely trust her. She probably knew it anyway.

She slipped into a seat near the front, glad she had again come early. She missed the presence of Mrs. Brown – the eminently quotable Mrs. Brown – but that ebullient lady had returned to New York, making lavish predictions for Jim's future as an artist – all a bit over the top, in Pinky's view. But then rich people always made making money look easy.

People were clamoring outside, angry that the hearing had been moved to a room with better acoustics. They didn't care about acoustics; they just wanted to be there and hear all the sad, enraging stories that patch together any disaster, making it tasty and satisfying. God, what an awful thing to think, she told herself. How cynical am I, anyway?

The first witness to take the stand was the lookout in the *Titanic*'s crow's nest – Frederick Fleet, a shabbily dressed man fumbling with a ragged cap. His eyes kept darting nervously in the direction of Bruce Ismay, which was no surprise. How could Smith expect to get complete candor from men whose livelihood depended on White Star?

'Mr. Fleet, your job was to report any danger ahead, is that correct?' asked Smith.

'Yes, sir. They told us to keep a sharp lookout for small ice. And, well, I reported an iceberg right ahead – a black mass.'

'How long before the collision, or accident, did you report ice ahead?'

'I have no idea.' Again, a nervous glance in Ismay's direction.

'About how long?' Smith pressed.

'I reported it soon as ever I seen it.'

'You are accustomed to judging distances, are you not, from the crow's nest? You are there to look ahead and sight objects, are you not?'

'We are only up there to report anything we see,' Fleet responded. 'I'm not so good at judging distance.'

A titter spread through the room. The lookout for the largest, grandest ship in the world couldn't judge time or distance.

'Were you given glasses of any kind?' Smith asked.

'We had nothing at all, only our own eyes, to look out. We asked for them in Southhampton, and they said there was none for us.'

'On this ship, the largest in the world, there was not one set of binoculars?'

'That's right.'

Pinky wrote out the two words in block letters in her notebook: 'NO BINOCULARS.' This would lead her story.

'So how do you think it's going?' she asked Smith at the lunch break.

'You again,' he said shortly, walking away.

She followed him. 'Senator, all I'm asking is, how is this testimony affecting you? I know how it's affecting me.'

'And how is that?' he said, coming to a stop.

'It's worse than sad. It's a mess of inept people and bumbled jobs and selfishness – that's what it seems to me.'

Smith allowed himself a small smile. 'We're trying to put together a puzzle, Miss Wade. There are a lot of pieces not yet in place. I think we may come across more honorable stories than you expect. But remember, human nature is not necessarily courageous.'

Impulsively, Pinky threw in another question. 'It's as much about what some of the survivors did as what White Star did, right?'

'I know where you're going with that,' Smith said, and once again turned away.

'The British are mad at you, sir,' she said hurriedly. 'They're calling you stupid and narrow and—'

'I know, I know – I had a report this morning.' His voice turned testy. 'Anything else?'

It was worth a shot. 'You have the crew members sequestered until they testify, Senator, but can I talk briefly with one of them, Jim Bonney? For background, you know. I won't write anything until you're done with him.'

'Tomorrow,' he said. 'After the day's testimony.'

'When does Bonney go on the stand?'

'Thursday.'

'And when are you calling the Duff Gordons to explain themselves?'

Smith turned on his heel and walked away.

Pinky watched him go, satisfied. If she kept up the pressure, maybe she could make him do it.

NEW YORK CITY

TUESDAY NIGHT

Tess stopped in front of a modest building not far from the Flatiron Building, looking down at the crumpled piece of paper in her hands. Yes, this was the address. Eagerly she stepped up to the front door and pushed one of the two keys into the lock. It wouldn't turn. She felt a second of panic before realizing the obvious. The other key must be for the front door of the building; this one was for her upstairs flat.

She inserted the right key and the door swung open. She took the stairs quickly, saw the right number, and inserted the second key. Again, miraculously, the door swung open. And, for the first time in her life, Tess Collins walked into a place that was all her own.

She spread her arms wide and danced slowly around the modest space. A tiny kitchen, but with an iron stove. A somewhat battered pair of oak chairs, but solid, with legs that would not collapse the minute she sat down. A bed with a cheerful quilt of red and green; a small table with an electric lamp. It was hers; all hers. Whom could she tell? Whom could she share this with? She suddenly wished Pinky were there. She had a feeling that Pinky would understand.

'I will earn it,' she said out loud, a little startled at the sound of her own voice. 'And I will keep it.'

TERRITORIES CONFERENCE ROOM

WASHINGTON, D.C.

WEDNESDAY, APRIL 24

The man was not going to give an inch. A disgusted William Alden Smith watched Bruce Ismay step down from the stand. Twice up there, and still only defensive haughtiness from the cold face of the White Star corporate world.

No, he had not urged the captain to increase the speed of the *Titanic* past the point of safety. Yes, he had heard of the possibility of ice, but their speed was not excessive.

'Would you not regard it as an exercise of proper precaution and care to *lessen* the speed of a ship crossing the Atlantic when she had been warned of the presence of ice ahead?' a puzzled committee member had asked.

'I have no opinion on that,' Ismay had said. 'We employ the very best men we possibly can to take command of these ships, and it is a matter entirely in their discretion.'

And now there he was, back in his chair with arms folded, looking smug. You're not home free yet, Senator Smith thought grimly. I'll let you hightail it back to England only when I'm good and ready.

He looked down at his witness list. Next up was Harold

Lowe, the ship's fifth officer, a man of reputed bravado and colourful language, and probably the seaman most qualified of the lot of them.

'You helped load the lifeboats, is that right?' Smith began.

Lowe nodded vigorously.

'Did you know any of the men who assisted you?'

'No, sir, not by name.' He hesitated, but only for a second. 'But there is a man here, and had he not been here I should not have known that I had ordered Mr. Ismay away from a boat.'

A stir in the room. 'You ordered Mr. Ismay away from a boat?' said Smith with surprise.

'I did, because Mr. Ismay was overanxious and he was getting a trifle excited. He said, "Lower away! Lower away!" I said—'

'Give us what you said.'

Lowe ran fingers through his hair, clearly considering whether he should be discreet. His blunt nature won out. 'I told him, "If you will get the hell out of that I shall be able to do something. You want me to lower away quickly? You will have me drown the whole lot of them."'

Senator Smith allowed himself a moment to enjoy Ismay's flustered demeanor. Quite satisfying, really.

Lowe was at ease now. He told of shouting down at sailors to get the plugs in the collapsible boats before they hit the water, or they'd sink, and watching as the more inept struggled with oars.

'Was there no training before the ship set sail?' asked Smith incredulously.

'There was one drill, but only two boats,' Lowe said. 'We were brand-new to the ship, just the same as everybody else.'

Smith let a silence fall. A collective sigh for what might have been, for what should have been, filled the room.

'So you helped load boats. Tell us what happened when you were in the water,' Smith said finally.

'I got my boat near four others, herded them close – five boats altogether. Then I roped them – figured we'd be seen better by a rescue ship. Then I emptied the passengers out of my boat into the other four.'

'Why did you do that?'

'So I could go back.'

The room went very still. Pinky waited, her pen poised. Senator Smith leaned forward.

'So you could go back to rescue people?'

'Yes, sir. Of course, I had to wait until the yells and shrieks had subsided – for the people to thin out – and then I deemed it safe to go among the wreckage.'

'You waited until the drowning people had quieted down?' Smith's voice had a slight wobble.

'Yes, sir.' Lowe was obviously not a man about to sugarcoat his story. 'It would not have been wise or safe for me to go there before, because the whole lot of us would have been swamped and then nobody would have been saved. When the cries subsided, I rowed off to the wreckage and I picked up four people. Three others were dead.'

'What did you do with them?'

'I thought to myself, I am not here to worry about

bodies; I am here for life, to save life, and not to bother about bodies, and I left them.'

'You could have saved more if you hadn't waited.'

Lowe looked straight at Smith, his voice resolute. 'I made the attempt, sir, as soon as any man could do so, and I am not scared of saying it. If anybody had struggled out of the mass, I was there to pick them up. But it was useless for me to go into the mass.'

'You mean for anybody?'

'It would have been suicide.'

The crowd stayed quiet as the seaman's words sank in. Confused glances were exchanged; Pinky sat still, staring at her notes. No one yet had so vividly put the safe, insulated courtroom observers of this tragedy out there on the water themselves, making them face the question of what was right and what was wrong. Where were the niches and holes in which to hide their proper indignation; no, to hide themselves from a key question: *What would they have done?* Her pen slowly began to move on the page.

Jim was waiting for her on the steps of the Senate Office Building after the hearing recessed for the day. Hands jammed into back pockets, he walked restlessly back and forth, jacketless, seemingly oblivious of the cool evening air of early spring. He looked up as Pinky hailed him.

'I'm told I can talk to you today,' he said. 'But not for a story, right?'

'For background. I'll use it after you testify tomorrow. You see, I have a hunch that you're going to put Lady Duff back on the front pages. Am I right?'

'All I can say is I'm going to truthfully answer the questions I'm asked.'

Together, they began strolling down the hill.

'Were you in the hearing room?' Pinky asked.

Jim nodded.

'What did you think of Lowe's testimony?'

'He's an honest man, and a brave one.'

'Seems to me he took his time going back, wouldn't you say?'

'Are you trying that idea out on me, or do you really believe it?'

That wasn't the reply she'd expected; she hesitated.

'Well?'

'I don't know,' she said.

He looked toward her, his voice tense and serious. 'Think of it, will you? Lowe was scared. We all were – what the bloody hell is wrong with saying it? He did what he felt he had to do, and those smug people exchanging shocked glances in the conference room have no idea what it was like. Sorry for cursing, but there it is.'

'I've heard worse,' Pinky said cheerfully. 'You should spend some time in a newsroom – we're all sailors there.'

'I can't quite picture you spewing out curse words; I'll bet you don't even know the ones I know,' he said with a faint smile.

'Will you come to dinner with me?' she asked impulsively.

'Sure. As long as it isn't at that dingy hotel we're stuck in.'

They found a table in Ebbitt's saloon, far back from the heavy mahogany bar, lit with a single, flickering votive candle. Pinky felt herself sink into the coziness of the booth, relaxing. She wasn't in working mode, although she knew she should be. What was it about Jim that left her feeling unguarded and even a bit softer? Anyway, he was probably thinking only of Tess.

'What are you going to say tomorrow?' she asked finally.

'You've asked me that before,' he said, spearing a piece of potato on his fork. 'My answer is the same. I'll tell them what happened, if they ask.'

'Do you feel differently now about Lady Duff stopping you from going back? After hearing Lowe's testimony?'

He looked startled. 'What do you mean?'

'Well, Tess defends her, saying what she did was no different from anyone else. Says she's being made a scapegoat for everybody's sins.'

'I know.' He said it quietly, almost tenderly. 'We don't feel the same. But I can't tell her everything.'

'I'm sorry I didn't have a message for you yesterday.'

He looked a bit embarrassed at her candor. 'I was hoping, but I wasn't expecting one.'

'I kind of think you were.'

He looked away, saying nothing.

Maybe now she could get to what was bothering her. 'Would you have waited until – how did Lowe put it? – the mass in the water *thinned out*? I'm not defending Lady Duff, but Lowe was pretty cold-blooded, too.'

'Is that what you're going to write?'

Was she? She didn't know, but she wasn't about to say so. She had to file at the telegraph office in a few hours; she could think it through.

Jim leaned forward, folding his hands on the table, his face close to hers. 'That isn't the story,' he said. 'Your story is: *he went back*. Look, we had choices. Yes, I would have gone right back, and maybe I would have been crazy and responsible for killing everyone in my boat. And maybe not. Maybe Lowe wishes he hadn't waited so long to go back with an empty boat that could hold sixty people. But he told his story straight. He's not to trying to smooth out the kinks, like Lightoller saying there was total calm on the ship and no screams in the water. Why clean it up?'

'If it was right for him to go back, then everybody should have rowed back. And they should have done it right away.'

'I'll speak to what I know. The ones who should have gone back were the ones sitting with me in a huge and shamefully empty boat.' He wrapped both hands around his beer, staring into the froth. 'The Duff Gordons are used to getting their way with money. Worked well this time.'

'I just feel—' She stopped. She didn't want the conversation to go this way. Maybe if Jim had rowed back and capsized he would have killed people, not saved them. And maybe there was nothing noble about that, and maybe there was. She wanted firmer ground.

'You're going up against a tough pair, Jim.'

'I have to. She ruled that boat, and she set the tone. It wasn't just not going back. She let things happen.'

'Like what?'

He was struggling with something. 'I can't talk about it.'

'And Cosmo did bribe the sailors to keep quiet about it all?'

'You got that from Sullivan, right? And he probably told you he refused the bribe. The real story? I think the Duff Gordons hinted at much more money than they eventually gave out, and he's angry.' Jim laughed sharply. 'Look, I'll just say what happened. I'm not going to varnish anything. I wish I could, for Tess's sake. I didn't fight Lady Duff hard enough – you think I'm proud of that? And I'm the first to shake Harold Lowe's hand, no matter what gets said about him, because he went back.'

'I think I know why you don't want to testify.'

Jim picked up the mug of beer in front of him and took a long, slow swallow. 'Yeah, I think you do,' he said.

'You know' – one of her shots in the dark – 'this isn't a criminal court. And you only have to answer the questions they ask.'

'They'll ask,' he said.

Chapter 10

TERRITORIES CONFERENCE ROOM
WASHINGTON, D.C.
THURSDAY MORNING, APRIL 25

Another night of little sleep. Pinky, this time crouched down in front of the folding chairs jammed up to the committee's meeting table, could hardly stop yawning. The stories on yesterday's testimony were all over the map. Some reporters were appalled at the 'coldness' of Lowe holding back; others pointed out what Jim had insisted was true: the man was the only person who actually had saved anyone. Staring at the ceiling last night, she had decided that Jim was right. For readers of her story in the *Times* this morning, Lowe was a hero – a real one.

Out of the corner of her eye, she saw two men holding black leather briefcases on their laps, sitting still by the far wall, staring straight ahead. No hustling about the room, shaking hands, conferring – all those restless things congressmen and their aides did. One wore horn-rimmed glasses settled low; the other looked pale as milk. They were too well dressed to be legislators. And right in front of them, twisting uneasily on his chair, was Sullivan. Was he here to back up Jim's story? Not likely. Her gaze traveled to Jim. He was wearing a more formal jacket today, one obviously borrowed, and his wrists jutted out from too-short sleeves as he stepped up to the witness chair. He looked resolute but vulnerable.

She suddenly realised what was going on. But it was too late to warn Jim.

Senator Smith, squinting through the haze of cigarette smoke, banged his gavel. 'We hope today to gather information about what happened in the water and in the lifeboats,' he said. 'Seaman James Bonney is our first witness. A first-time seaman, I understand, who escaped on Lifeboat One. Will you take a seat, Mr. Bonney?'

The questions began. In a steady, almost toneless voice, Jim told of helping to load five different boats before moving to the starboard side, where one collapsible boat hung, caught in a tangle of ropes. Of Officer Murdoch shouting for them to get this boat ready for Lady Duff Gordon. Of rushing forward, helping other sailors clear the ropes to release the emergency boat known as Number One. Yes, he said. Seaman Sullivan was put in charge of the boat.

'Why was it launched with so few people in it?'

'Because Lady Duff Gordon insisted.'

'Are you accusing her of abandoning people on the deck?' Smith asked.

'No, sir. I'm accusing her of thinking only of herself.'

'When the ship sank, did you look for survivors?'

'No.'

'What was the capacity of your boat, and how many were in it?'

'We could have held fifty or more. There were twelve of us, that's all.'

'I believe your boat holds the notoriety of having been launched with the fewest souls in it, am I right?'

'Yes, sir.'

A murmur swept the crowd, a muttering that made the back of Pinky's neck tingle.

Then one of Smith's colleagues spoke up. 'Now let's get to the crux of this. With the most room of anyone, did you not go back to pick up anybody at all?'

Jim's voice was flat. 'Nobody at all,' he said.

'Why not?'

'The others did not want to go back.'

'Did you?'

'Yes. No one agreed.'

'Who was it objected to pulling back?'

'Lady Duff Gordon refused to let anyone pick up an oar. She was afraid to go back for fear of being swamped.'

'Was there, as far as you know, any danger of the boat being swamped if you did go back?'

Jim did not hesitate. 'It would certainly have been possible. But we were in a big boat that wasn't full.'

'How would it have been dangerous, considering that you had a crew of seven in the boat, to go among the people who were screaming for help in the sea?' barked Senator Bolton, another member of the panel. He was clearly still brooding over Lowe's testimony of the day before. 'Did you hear the screams?'

'Of course I did,' Jim shot back. 'We all heard them. I told you, I proposed going back and they would not hear of it.'

'Did you say it to anyone personally?' pressed Smith.

'I called it out to everybody.'

'The man to decide whether the boat should go back was Sullivan, was it not?' Smith glanced over at his next witness, sitting slumped in his chair, eyes darting about.

'Yes,' Jim said with barely concealed contempt. 'He was the man in charge. At least he was supposed to be.'

'And he said no?'

'That's correct.'

'Was his attitude due to the protests of the Duff Gordons?'

'Yes.' This time he looked directly at Sullivan, who looked away.

'Are you sure of that?'

'I only know about my one boat. I should have overridden him.'

'With what authority?'

Jim was silent.

'You say you heard cries? Agonizing cries?'

'Yes.'

'And the Duff Gordons said it was too dangerous to go back to save lives?'

'Yes.'

One of the committee members, a senator with a round ruddy face, leaned forward, his voice dripping sarcasm.

'Then am I to understand that because two of the passengers said it would be dangerous you all kept your mouths shut and made no attempt to rescue anybody?'

'That is right, sir.' Jim straightened his shoulders, taking the blow.

Smith switched focus. 'Were you promised any money by Sir Duff Gordon in the lifeboat?' he asked.

'Yes.'

The room was now buzzing with whispers. The bribe, people were saying; there was a bribe.

'And was that an arrangement with the other members of the crew, to do a certain thing for a certain price? In other words, not to go back?' It was the man with the ruddy face again.

Pinky held her breath. Jim looked very tired.

'It was not proposed that way.'

'What does that mean? He didn't declare it a bribe? Wouldn't that have been a bit strange? Did you think it was a bribe?'

'Yes, I did.'

'I'm wondering what else this so-called bribe was meant to silence. Did anyone in the water try to get into your boat?'

Pinky waited, holding her breath.

'Yes. There were people all around us. More than one tried to climb in.'

'And what happened?'

Silence. Jim's eyes looked bleak.

'Some slipped away.'

'And others?'

Again, a silence. 'It was dark and hard to see,' he said finally.

'Do you think anybody was forcibly pushed away?'

'It could have been.'

The crowd stirred; whispers began.

'That's quite a charge, Mr. Bonney,' said Senator Bolton. 'A very black charge. Are you making a specific accusation?'

'I'm wary of accusing anyone I didn't clearly see, sir. But this is what I believe.'

'Do you have more to say?' Senator Smith asked.

'No, sir.'

'You may step down,' Senator Smith said. He looked out across the room, his heart heavy. Get on with it. Next up was the bony sailor with the pockmarked skin who had supposedly been in charge of Lifeboat One. He sat slumped in his chair, as if bored by the proceedings, even as his eyes darted back and forth across the room.

'Mr. Tom Sullivan, I understand you were the ranking seaman in charge of Lifeboat One. Will you please take the stand?'

Stunned, Pinky watched Jim step down and take his seat. So this was what he had been holding back. An attack was surely coming now. Why hadn't he told the committee that he turned down the bribe? *Because they hadn't asked*. But he had done what he said he would do –

just told the truth plainly, without embellishment. They would chew him up.

'Tom Sullivan, is that your name?'

'Yes, sir.' Sullivan pulled himself up in the witness seat, hands clasped in front of him, clutching his cap. Her source for the original bribery story. His eyes were furious, close to burning a hole in Jim's departing back. But his face took on a mask of gravity as he turned directly to his questioner.

'Let's get your story of what happened on Lifeboat One. You were in charge, right?' Senator Perkins was doing this round of questioning, and he was impatient to be done with it.

'Yes, sir, I sure was. I was master of the situation.'

'How many people were in your boat?'

Sullivan didn't hesitate. 'Oh, fourteen to twenty,' he said.

'We were told by the previous witness that there were twelve occupants, and you could have held up to fifty. Is that correct?'

'Well, we took who we could.'

'We also understand from Mr. Bonney's testimony that you did not return to where the ship sank.'

Sullivan shook his head so vigorously that his collar almost came undone. 'No, sir, we came back after the ship went down and saw nothing. Thank you for the chance to correct the record.'

Smith and the other panel members exchanged looks of surprise.

'You did go back?'

'Of course we did,' Sullivan said indignantly. 'I'm sorry to say this, but Jim Bonney is a shifty sort; he's got an ax to grind, for something.'

'Did you rescue anyone in the water?'

'No, sir, nobody was alive. Didn't hear anybody.' The sorrowful tone was back.

'When did you go back?'

'Soon as we could.' Sullivan waved his hand vaguely.

'Then what did you do?'

'We rowed around.' He glanced quickly at the two men with briefcases, a glance Pinky caught. She stared at the pair.

'Was there any confusion or excitement among your passengers?'

Sullivan seemed totally comfortable now. 'No, sir, I never saw it. It was just the same as if it was an everyday affair.'

An everyday affair? The silence in the room told him he had gone too far. A few murmurings and glances were exchanged. He began picking at his fingers, his eyes once again darting toward the men with briefcases. 'Not totally that, of course. But we were pulling together, you know? It was a sad time.'

'Is there any other incident that you wish to state that would be of interest to the public? Anything about the actions of the passengers, the Duff Gordons?'

'No, sir, not that I know of.'

'Did they refuse to go back?'

'No, sir. They are fine people.'

'Did they offer you a bribe?' Senator Smith cut in.

'No, sir. Mr. Bonney is wrong on that one, too. He has problems. And I have no more to say.'

Perkins leaned back in his chair, his brow furrowed. 'Thank you, Mr. Sullivan. You are dismissed,' he said, glancing at his watch.

'Could I say one thing more, sir?' Sullivan said.

'What would that be?'

'Sometimes people don't think right in bad situations, and then try to cover up their own behavior. If anybody could push people away, it would be Bonney. He's got a bad reputation – he could've pushed people off, you bet. He's the bastard in this room.'

Pinky stared at Sullivan. Loathsome, lying toad, trying to save his own skin by switching stories. She should have published his name. Here he was, playing the humble seaman, just a sturdy man trying to do his job; good show. The Duff Gordons had been more generous this time. She watched as the two men with briefcases slipped out the door and saw one of them give Sullivan a quick nod as he exited.

Who were they? She scrambled after the pair, following them through the exit door, shutting it in time to step in front of one of them. He looked neither startled nor displeased, just indifferent.

'Wait, I need to know – who are you?' she asked.

'That's really no business of yours, Miss Wade,' he said.

So he knew her name. 'I'll bet you're a lawyer. What firm are you with?'

He gave a thin smile. 'Miss Wade, there are many

lawyers in this room. Some, as you know, get elected to Congress. Are you so surprised that a lowly seaman might have representation? I'm afraid you aren't well versed in the law. Good day.' He started to walk away.

'Wait a minute – who's paying you?'

He ignored her and kept walking.

Senator Smith barely looked up as he called the last witness of the morning. One more from Lifeboat One.

'Mr. Albert Purcell, please take the stand.'

A burly, weathered man with large ears and thinning hair settled his bulk into the witness seat. The questioning began, covering the same ground as before – where he was on the ship, what he did.

'After the ship went down, did you hear any cries?'

'Not that I recall.' He sneaked a quick look at Sullivan.

'Did anybody suggest that you should go back in the direction of the people in the water?'

'Not to my knowledge.'

'Nobody said *anything* about going back?'

'No, sir.' Purcell was almost beaming.

'Mr. Bonney said he did. Is that correct?'

'No, sir. He's puffing himself up.'

Senator Harbinson broke in. 'All right, do you remember hearing anything said about presents or about money?'

'Yes, I do, and I will explain how it came about.' Purcell had his details ready, and he was anxious to spill them out. 'Well, you see, Lady Duff Gordon said something like

"There is my beautiful nightdress gone," and I said, "Never mind about that, as long as you have got your life," and I said we had lost everything and then Sir Duff Gordon said later he'd give us a little something to start over. That's all I heard.'

'How long after the *Titanic* went down did you first hear mention of this money?'

'About three-quarters of an hour.'

'Did you consider it a bribe?'

'Oh no, sir. Just a generous offer from generous people.'

'Did it occur to you at all that you ought to go back?'

Purcell responded in lofty fashion. 'No, it was not my place. I was not in charge of the boat; if that had been said, I would certainly have gone back.'

'You were ready and willing?'

'Quite willing.'

'Were you not surprised that somebody else did not suggest it?'

'Yes, I was,' he said, with what he clearly hoped was indignation.

'I don't understand your frame of mind,' Senator Harbinson suddenly snapped. 'You were surprised that no one made the suggestion but you were not surprised that you did not make it?'

'We were half dazed at the time,' Purcell stammered, casting another glance at Sullivan, who was glaring at him.

'Can you offer any explanation at all as to why your boat didn't try to pick up people?'

Purcell hesitated, trapped, then plunged on. 'Yes, well, we would have been swamped if we had gone back; that is my opinion. There were so many people in the water – you could hear that by the cries.'

'Ah, so you heard cries and *didn't* go back? Even to find *nothing*? And, by the way, Mr. Sullivan says you *did* go back under his direction?'

Purcell looked at Sullivan hopelessly; he had stepped into it. 'No, sir. Yes, sir.'

'Did anybody say it was dangerous?'

The coaching he had clearly received reasserted itself. 'No, sir. Nobody said anything like that.'

'Did anyone say you might be swamped?'

'No, sir.'

'Does it not occur to you that you might very well have gone back with a good chance of picking up some stragglers from outside the swarm?'

'Yes, if they were outside, I guess.'

Harbinson was weary. They were all weary. 'It did not occur to you that you might have unloaded your passengers by getting some of the other boats to take some of your passengers, and then gone back with a practically empty boat to pick up some of the poor people in the water?'

'No, sir.'

'Enough of this,' said Senator Smith. All in the room were obviously remembering the forthrightness of Harold Lowe. And Pinky, twisting about, kept hoping that she would see Jim. Sullivan surely had been brought down by this inept fool who couldn't keep his lies straight. Wouldn't everybody see it now?

Jim was standing alone by the front door of the Senate Office Building, drawing hard on a cigarette through pressed lips, staring at the Capitol. Deep furrows had etched their way into his strong-boned face.

'Who—' Pinky began as she joined him.

'Don't ask, because I won't answer. None of it brings back the dead.'

'Look, those two were lying – anyone could see that. You came out ahead.'

'Don't be so sure. You saw those men with the brief-cases? Who are they?'

'I'll find out. If they're lawyers, Purcell should have been briefed better. Relax, Jim. Purcell ruined their story.'

'That woman won't give up easily. You know as well as I do she's got something up her sleeve.'

'Lady Duff?'

'Of course.'

She paused. But she couldn't stop trying to console him. 'What can she do now? The others in your boat know the truth. What is she going to do, silence them all? Somebody will back you up.'

'Who? Besides those dancers and the Duff Gordons, there were only crew members in the boat. And, believe me, they have every one of them in their pocket. They know what they're doing.' He dropped the cigarette to the ground, and immediately lit another. 'What does it matter, anyway? Nobody's going to jail over this. I know it happened in the other boats. I just want the damn thing to be told true. And I want Tess to believe me.'

'I think she will.'

'When it's between me and the woman she thinks is her lifeline?'

'She won't be fooled by a lie.' Why did she speak with such conviction? How did she know what someone in Tess's situation would think? But it was hard to imagine someone not trusting Jim, especially Tess.

'I want to see her, Pinky.'

'I figured I was going to be the go-between,' she said good-naturedly. 'Are you sure?'

'More than you can possibly know.'

There was enough fervor in his words to strike her silent for the moment. There was even more fervor in what he said next.

'The thing is, right now what Sullivan said is what people *want* to believe. It's a clean lie that makes everybody feel better.' He drew deeply on the cigarette and tossed it to the ground, grinding it with his foot. 'You know what I mean? Brave sailors and passengers go back on a rescue mission, but all those screaming people in the water have conveniently died. It's stitched up nice and neat. No wrestling with the choice of one man to wait until most of the people died; no having to believe another sailor who can't muster up a hero for them, not even for himself. Sullivan fills the bill. What people want is a steady type who did the right thing. Whatever that is.'

He turned away. 'I'm sorry, I've got to get out of here.' He stalked away, striding off down the hill. Pinky didn't try to hurry after him. She simply followed him with her eyes.

And from a window in the conference room looking out on the steps, hands clasped behind his back, so did Senator William Alden Smith.

A tall man, that Bonney, striding away, looking quite somber and determined. The man was probably telling the truth, even though there was obviously bad blood between him and Sullivan. Purcell was a joke.

How far did he want to push this? He knew in his heart, no matter what the newspapers said, that there were survivors out there having a hard time living with themselves because they acted out of fear, not courage. Was it worth it to hunt them down and expose them? Look at this man Darling. A good man, from all reports, who did one weak-willed thing, now dead by his own hand. Did he need to drag this arrogant British designer and her husband into the hearings? Weren't they getting whipped about enough in the newspapers?

He stared after Bonney and made his decision.

Twilight was deepening as Pinky climbed on the train and headed back to New York, exhausted from arguing with Van Anda. So maybe it looked like a story about two sailors who hated each other and one idiot. And, yes, her source for the earlier bribery story had turned his story inside out. But Bonney had confirmed it, so it wasn't wrong. He was by far the more believable on the stand, with much to lose. Why would he say that he thought people were pushed off unless it was true? Watch out, you're trying too hard to make Bonney a hero, Van Anda said. Keep the focus on the fact that he and Sullivan were calling each other liars. Are you sure you saw lawyers? Prove it. Follow up tomorrow, and get home and get some sleep. 'The Lowe piece was great,' he threw in before hanging up. She slumped back into her seat, worried. Was she losing perspective? She had to quit thinking about who got hurt and who didn't. Her job was to report the facts, even when her instincts intervened. But it wasn't always easy to choose between the two.

Pinky tucked her bunched-up coat under her head and closed her eyes. Van Anda was right; she'd better get some rest. She had a job to do, and it didn't include worrying about Bonney. She had to get some groceries as soon as she got home, and if she was late tonight the long-suffering Mrs. Dotson would have her hand out again for more money.

Chapter 11

FLATIRON DISTRICT

NEW YORK CITY

THURSDAY MORNING, APRIL 25

No reporters were hovering at the entrance as Lucile and Elinor walked quickly through the front door to the elevator. Lucile punched the up button with relief.

'I can't stay long – I have an appointment with my hairstylist,' Elinor said as they rumbled up to the top floor. 'I don't know why you wanted me here today, anyway.'

'Your hair is more important than my business? Really, Elinor.'

'Your timing is good, I'll say. Right in the middle of Jordan Darling's funeral.'

'Exactly. All the reporters are there. I've been away from here long enough; I can't afford to hide anymore. Thank goodness I didn't have to walk through the usual hordes.

You can leave anytime you want; I'm back on familiar ground now.'

'Madame,' said James in surprise, lifting his head from a worktable filled with a jumble of hats and gloves and jewellery – all necessary accessories for the show. Next to him was Tess, her mouth filled with pins, on her knees fitting a skirt on a model.

'Well, I see you two are keeping busy,' Lucile said with a bright smile. 'James, get rid of that awful green concoction.' She pointed a finger at one of the hats. 'The colour is atrocious. Looks like bile.'

'Yes, Madame. Good to have you back, Madame.'

Tess had managed to remove the pins from her mouth as she stood up. 'It's good to see you,' she said warmly.

'How is your new flat, dear? Didn't Cosmo move quickly?'

'It's wonderful, and I'm very grateful.' Grateful? Thrilled, was more like it. That wonderful, tiny flat on Fifth Avenue – so sparse, so plain, but hers alone. A pot, a couple of cups, and two dishes on the tiny kitchen counter; the first thing she had done was make herself some tea. She was on the payroll now, being paid for her work, and soon she would be paying for that flat. And then she would bring Mother over from England and they would make curtains together and she would begin to be part of a world she could call her own.

'Where is the wedding gown?'

Lucile's voice snapped her back to reality. 'Over here, on the table – I've finished the repairs,' Tess said. Lucile began inspecting the gown, and Tess felt a flutter of fear in her stomach. James was stepping back; two of the models were watching Lucile warily. The seamstress on the nearest sewing machine had stopped work.

Lucile lifted the skirt with two fingers, holding it at arm's length, eyes narrowed. 'Where is the underskirt?' she demanded.

'It was torn and I took it off; this makes the skirt flow better,' Tess said.

'And what have you done to the bodice?'

'It had to be changed – it was torn, too.' She was stumbling, speaking too fast.

First, silence, as Lucile turned the dress over and stared at the bodice.

'*What have you done?*' she finally said. Her hoarse, throaty challenge carried through the shop. 'I have a major show in the offing – and *you* have tampered with my showpiece design, the one that would have been the talk of the town. And now, *now*—' She dropped the dress back onto the table. 'Now it is just the amateur work of a beginner who might be good at stitching up torn garments but who knows *nothing* about the aesthetics of design!'

Tess grabbed the edge of the table to steady herself, afraid she might fall. Her voice was shaky and thin. 'I did what I thought needed to be done to salvage your wonderful gown. There were only a few necessary changes, but I tried to stay true to your vision. Let the model put it on and you'll see.'

Lucile glared at her. 'Don't give me that nonsense. You took a Lucile creation and made it your own.'

'What are you complaining about?' Elinor murmured,

touching Lucile's sleeve. 'You can see the girl salvaged a badly damaged gown – what else could she do? Watch out, the mood here isn't as deferential as usual. Haven't you noticed?'

Lucile shrugged off her sister's hand. 'Here' – she nodded at one of the models and handed her the gown – 'put this thing on so I can see the extent of the damage.' She stalked over to the runway, pointing a finger at James. 'When she's buttoned in, tell her to walk this way,' she directed.

James went running to give the instructions to the model, pausing as he passed Tess. 'You did a good job,' he whispered. 'Whatever she says.'

It was a timid endorsement, but Tess was grateful. She watched Lucile's expression as the model walked toward her, the gorgeous gown swirling and floating around her legs. It was still true to the basics of Lucile's design. But Lucile said nothing, and her stony expression didn't change. Of course, she wouldn't like it; there was no way she could cede that to Tess.

'Why didn't you reverse the side seams, for heaven's sake?'

'I didn't think of it.'

'It no longer qualifies as the centerpiece of my collection, I'm afraid.'

Tess's cheeks burned scarlet. She might have the staff's sympathy, but that would not get her through this.

'You still have quite a bit to learn, you know.'

'I don't deny that.'

'Don't try anything this audacious again.'

Again, that odd, poised feeling of being on the brink of something. Tess held her breath.

Lucile suddenly stood, brushing off her skirt briskly. 'It will have to do. Tess, do something you're capable of doing. Start steaming the nettings on the hats, will you? They are dreadfully wrinkled.'

'Yes, Madame.'

'Only a few days to the show, everybody,' Lucile called out, clapping her hands as she marched into her office. 'Let's get busy!'

'Lucile, can we talk?' Tess said as the two women stepped out onto the sidewalk at the end of the day.

'I am much too tired from fixing the damage around here for idle chatter.' Lucile would not so much as look at her.

'I did my best to help. I'm sorry it wasn't good enough.'

Lucile stared at the waiting car, her jaw held stiffly. 'Be at the shop by eight in the morning,' she said. *'And do not call me by my first name.'* With that, and with a blank-faced Farley holding the door, Lady Duff Gordon stepped in without looking back.

Tess jiggled the key in the door of her apartment, desperate for it to open. It had been a day of not only steaming hat nettings but pressing hems, mopping up spills, discarding baskets of fabric scraps – anything that did not involve picking up a needle, cutting patterns, or adjusting fittings. Nothing beyond what a maid would do. All this, to prove to everyone in Lucile's loft that Madame was still in charge, that she was the designer – as if anyone doubted that. Tess had tried her best, tried to salvage a great design, and her work was wanting. Would she always be wanting?

The key turned. Miraculously, the door opened as it was supposed to, and Tess stepped into her refuge. Turn on a light; close the door. With relief, she leaned against the doorframe. She had worn her servant mask today, and, oh, how hard it was to breathe through. Once, she had looked up from picking fabric scraps off the floor and seen Lucile staring at her with that unreadable expression in her eyes she had seen before. Something different from anger, something she had briefly hoped would make her employer reachable.

Tess walked over to the cupboard, smoothing her hand over the rough-hewn surface of the table as she passed. No word yet from Jim. Let it go, let it go. Surely he would have managed to contact her by now if he had wanted to. She was on her own.

She took a deep breath and looked around. If she wanted this, if this small flat was truly to be a route to a new independence, she had to figure out what it was that Lucile intended for her. Everyone around her molded themselves to whatever shape she demanded in the moment. How could you know who you were, what you could do? Was Lucile's shop a place of promise or just another form of servitude? Was she slipping into the same artful dodging of those who fawned over the great Madame? She felt suddenly bone-weary. She would work hard and well; that was all she could do. Her thoughts wandered back to Jim. Where was he on this dreary night? If she closed her eyes she could imagine herself with him in a horse-drawn carriage, feel his arm holding her close. She wished now that she had sent a message, and wondered why she hadn't.

A pot of water on to boil. A bit of tea, sipped by the window, looking out on the street. She began to calm down. Enough, in fact, to realise that she had no food for her meal. There was a market down the block that she had passed coming home. That was worth one more trip out. Tess finished her tea and picked up her purse, feeling a little better. At least right now this was her haven, and she had the key.

The butcher at the meat counter held up a limp-looking chicken and a leg of mutton. 'Which one?' he said. They were apparently her only choices, and Tess pointed to the mutton, hoping the oven in her flat worked. She wandered over to the vegetable bins and picked up a few potatoes, then some bread. It felt good to be getting her own supplies. Some fruit would be nice, but the apples looked a bit shriveled and she hesitated, her hand hovering over one of them.

'Try an orange. They look better.'

A familiar voice, a shockingly familiar voice. She looked

up into the face of a man standing on the other side of the heaping baskets of fruit. A half-healed scar had left a thin slash of red that ran from his forehead to the tip of his ear, but it had done nothing to diminish his smile. His gray hair was neatly combed, his suit polished and smooth, and he looked much as he had that last night on the *Titanic*. In his hand he held out an orange.

'Mr. Bremerton.' She could barely say his name.

'Hello, Miss Collins.' He glanced down at the mutton in her bag, the smile twitching at the corners of his mouth. 'Looks tasty.'

'What are you doing here? How—'

'I found ways to look you up. Are you doing well?'

Was he really standing opposite her, talking in that relaxed, confident manner? 'I can't believe I'm seeing you,' she said, still somewhat breathless. 'I heard you had survived.'

'Well, I can only hope you're as pleased as I am at seeing you.'

'I am. I am, yes.' She could almost smell the salt air of that last night when the two of them had stood together on deck. Hearing his voice again brought it all back to pulsating life. 'But why are you here? You don't live down here, surely.' She imagined him in a grand home farther up Fifth Avenue – not here, not in this modest neighbourhood of business lofts and small flats like hers.

'I have an office in the Flatiron Building. But now that I've found you, I have a proposal. As good as this mutton looks, would you consider doing me the honor of sharing dinner with me?'

'I would enjoy that very much,' she managed.

'On one condition,' he said gently. 'You must call me Jack.'

'Well—'

'Not yet? I understand.'

What a gentleman he was. She put down the mutton and potatoes, leaving them on top of the apples, and together they walked out, past the startled grocer. Or perhaps she was sleepwalking. Later, Tess was not sure which it was.

The restaurant was called Sherry's, at the corner of Fifth Avenue and Forty-fourth Street, and, to Tess's eye, it was grander than the Waldorf. High, ornate ceilings, sparkling crystal sconces and chandeliers; tables covered with pristine linen cloths; the murmurs of waiters bowing deferentially to diners who looked like full-dressed chandeliers themselves. She made no pretense of not being impressed, and stared about with unconcealed delight.

'We love excess in America, Tess,' Jack said gently. 'And we love copying the British.'

'I can't imagine why. We all want to copy you.' She cradled a delicately bowled glass and then let the first martini of her life slip softly down her throat. It felt strangely dry, leaving a faint taste of herbs that vanished almost immediately on her tongue.

He laughed. 'You do say what you're thinking, don't you?'

'Not always, but I am now.'

'You have much to talk about, I wager. Ah, here are our lobsters.'

The plate set smoothly in front of her held a brilliantly red crustacean, claws arched forward, tiny beaded eyes frozen in mid-boil. She stared at it, wondering what came next.

'Let me show you,' he said gently. Deftly, with a nutcracker, he twisted off the claws, exposing the meat. With a long, slender utensil she did not recognise, he pulled forth an offering and held it up to her. Unhesitatingly, Tess took it. It was delicious. Another sip of the martini and she was telling him about her trials with the mercurial Lucile. She, who tried to weigh every word in this new country, realised that she felt not a qualm about talking to Jack.

'You keep asking about me, but say nothing about yourself,' she said finally.

'I'm your standard American self-made man,' he said with a shrug. 'I sit through my share of operas, but if you want to hear all about Ford's Model T, I'm the man. Brilliant automobile, soon to boast a speedometer and a horn.'

'That sounds interesting,' she said shyly.

'Progress is wonderful,' he said. 'The world is changing, and if you don't change with it you're gone.'

The evening slipped by – thrilling, dazzling. She took tiny sips from her second drink, wary of the dizziness that seemed to make the room glow. She was on a glittery, floating stage, but the best thing was that the man next to her was actually listening, truly listening, when she talked.

And yet not once, not even glancingly, did they talk about the sinking of the *Titanic* and Jack's experience on the *Carpathia.* Only as they rose to go did that strike Tess as strange.

'I would like to see you again,' he said outside her building.

'I would like that, too,' she said.

They stood close, both silent.

'I kept hoping to find you on the *Carpathia,*' she said.

'That matters greatly, that you cared.'

'I couldn't believe you had died. I didn't want to.' She felt a catch in her throat.

'Some might have felt it a convenient development.'

Tess's thoughts flew to Jack's wife. How could that woman not have mourned this man?

'I can't say I remember the time I was out of my head on the *Carpathia.* But if I had known, that last night on the *Titanic,* what I know now, I wouldn't have been so polite. I would have kissed you, Tess. I would have taken you in my arms and kissed you.'

For a moment, there was nothing but the sound of their mingled breathing.

'May I do that now?' he finally asked.

'Yes.'

He pulled her close, searching for her lips with his. There was no need for Tess to say anything, just to go on tiptoe and kiss him back.

Late into the night, Tess lay in bed and stared at the ceiling, remembering the sound of him murmuring her name. Husky, intimate – she could not sleep. She sat up in bed and stared out the window. How could it be that a gentleman like Jack Bremerton was interested in her? He was much older than she was, probably in his forties. So calm and assured. She had never met anyone like him, and he had held her and kissed her. No demands, no fumbling, no skittery fingers. And he wanted to see her again. What could she dare dream about now? Who was he, and who was *she*, given the thoughts she was having?

And there was Jim. She buried her head in the pillow, trying, just for the moment, to block him out of her thoughts, but it wasn't working. He was there; she could sense him by her side. She pushed off the thought angrily; there was no reason to feel torn. She wasn't betrothed, for heaven's sake. There was no reason to feel guilty. Two men, so very different. Jim was more than a village boy, much more, but Jack was a man of the world. Exciting, in a new way. And yet – oh Lord, why hadn't Jim contacted her? Where was he – had he forgotten her? Her thoughts flashed back to the shared moment of offering their halting prayers over the dead mother and baby; of his kindness as with swift, deft fingers he carved toys for the children. She felt again the taste of delight as they skipped together through Central Park. Was she just dazzled by the glamour of Jack's life? If so, where was Jim?

Enough. She pounded the pillow angrily. There would be no sleep tonight.

NEW YORK CITY

FRIDAY MORNING, APRIL 26

The newsboy outside the grocery store ran back and forth, hollering out the news that was bringing him an abundance of nickels and dimes from passersby to stuff into his pocket this sunny morning. Read all about it, the latest bombshell about the Millionaires' Boat from the *Titanic* hearings in Washington. Sailors face off against each other, battling over the truth! Extra, extra!

Tess fumbled for change, taking copies of the *Tribune* and the *Times* to the back of the store. 'WERE DROWNING PEOPLE PUSHED OFF LIFEBOAT ONE? SAILORS EXCHANGE CHARGES,' screamed the *Tribune* headline. Two photographs, one of Jim and the other of the man named Sullivan. And then a subhead: 'WHO IS THE LIAR?' The headline of Pinky's story was quieter: 'CONFLICTING ACCOUNTS BY LIFEBOAT ONE SEAMEN, BACKUP WITNESS STUMBLES.'

She read quickly, hands shaking as she turned pages still sticky with ink. Jim, Jim, are you sure – what did you see? Who are you accusing? She lifted up her head, the sidewalk looking washed with rain, but it was viewed through tears. Not going back could be cold, cowardly, sensible, fearful. All those things. Pushing people away? Cruelty, panic? But it was so dark that night, hard to see anybody, even in her boat, which was jammed with survivors. He hadn't tried to accuse the Duff Gordons. It was so like the man she already instinctively knew. He told what he saw when asked; there was no vilification. And in all of this, who was most vulnerable? He was.

She threw the paper in a bin outside the store and headed for work, trying to remember the sound of Jim's voice. But it had slipped from her somehow. Gone into the air.

Lucile was in the loft, calmly pinning new layers of tulle under the wedding gown, replacing the ones Tess had cut away.

'Good morning,' she said evenly. 'Have you seen the papers?'

'Yes.'

'I was right about your sailor friend. Obviously he *was* the source for the first story, so now he thinks he has us, I suppose. Well, we're not through fighting. Mr. Sullivan's support was helpful. And the other one did his best – not too intelligent a man, perhaps.'

She couldn't stay silent. 'Sullivan was the source for the first bribery story, not Jim. Pinky Wade told me. And I don't believe anything he says.'

'Oh, don't you? Then whom do you believe – this sailor of yours? That there was bribery? An actual murder? What? Are you blaming me for all that?'

'I don't know what happened in your boat.'

Lucile shook out a bolt of tulle, slamming it on the table, cutting through it with a pair of very sharp scissors. 'I'd advise you to figure it out fast. This Bonney creature is trying to destroy us, and don't you dare deny it.'

There was no stopping now. 'He had to testify – he had no choice but to answer their questions.'

'Oh come, Tess.' Lucile stopped, shears in midair. 'His

intent was obvious. Your sailor comes off as somewhat intense and bitter, wouldn't you say? I wouldn't be at all surprised if he turned down our little gift because he planned to angle for more. Blackmail, very obviously. Think what the newspapers would do with that.'

'He's not a blackmailer,' Tess said as calmly as she could.

'Will you stop defending him? We did nothing wrong. Sullivan and Purcell spoke for themselves. And Bonney is making us pay for his own scrupulous conscience.'

'I don't believe he is.'

'I am saying that in the heightened – and heated – circumstances we've all been living in since that infernal ship went down, it's easy to judge in black and white. Look at how the press has treated us.' Her eyes turned mournful. 'Do you believe we're evil people? That we did terrible things? Yes or no?'

'No,' Tess said heavily. 'You are not evil. But sometimes—'

'Thank you, dear. I am deeply relieved.' Lucile's mood changed quickly to bright exuberance. 'I have an idea, a job for you that I'm hoping you'll want to take on. During the show. I want you to be the face of this company. You will be my vendeuse! Who better than you? You know every gown in the show, and you can introduce them all by name. I was going to have you serve the tea and biscuits, but someone else can do that. This will get you an incredible amount of attention.'

Tess barely heard her. 'I know how frightening it all was. What I can't understand is fear so great that people would be pushed away.'

'Of course, that would be murder, my dear. So, what do you say?'

'To what?'

'My offer to make you my vendeuse. Aren't you listening?'

'Oh my, that's generous, but—'

'Then everything is settled. Now, let's put all this behind us and move on.'

Before she could answer, a voice broke in.

'Tess.'

Elinor was in back of them both, leaning against a cutting table, hair piled fetchingly on her head, arms crossed. 'Sorry to interrupt, but it seems like the right time. Shall you and I go pick up the table linens for the show? A little shopping would do us both some good. At least, it would do *me* good. I'm getting sick of hotel rooms and fabric and sewing machines.'

Tess glanced at Lucile. She had put her head down and was smoothing out the length of tulle she had cut, her red nails bright against the creamy gauze. There was no more to say. For the moment.

'All right,' Tess said.

Farley held the car door open as Elinor slipped in, and Tess followed, leaning back into the soft leather seat. A short while ago she had been awed by the magnificence of this smoothly running, polished machine, with its sumptuous upholstery. A short while ago? A lifetime ago.

'Herald Square, Farley,' Elinor instructed before collapsing back into the soft cushions and turning to Tess. 'Good thing I was there,' she said without preamble. 'You and Lucy were heading for a nasty little fracas. You know that, don't you?'

'I've admired her from the first day we met, but not today. I don't know what's true, but I know Jim is not a liar.' The words were surprisingly easy to say. It was like that with Elinor.

'I know, but you need to understand her better.'

'Whenever I think I do, she manages a surprise.'

'I warned Lucy you weren't going to remain meek and eager to sit at the feet of the goddess for very long.' Elinor laughed. 'May I be totally frank with you?'

Tess nodded mutely.

'My sister's world is shaky, and she doesn't even know it. It's not just this *Titanic* thing and all the bad publicity. It's – God, I need a cigarette, and I'm sure I don't have any.' She set to rummaging furiously in her bag, and let out a cry of pleasure – she had found one slightly bent cigarette, compressed tobacco leaking out of one end. She lit it quickly. 'What was I saying?'

'It's more than the *Titanic*.'

'Yes, of course. You see, anyone who goes around in this day and age saying a woman's knees are ugly is out of touch with fashion. Short skirts will come, there's no doubt about it. And Lucy won't stop sneering at them. My poor sister considers herself an irreplaceable brand, and she's so wrong. All that lace and tulle – and actually *naming* her dresses, for heaven's sake.'

'I wondered yesterday if she was afraid.'

'Maybe. You also felt that she treated you like a slave. Correct?'

Tess nodded, not trusting her voice.

'Well, you were right. You salvaged that wedding gown of hers, and you were given shabby treatment. So you're angry. Am I right on that, too?'

'Yes.'

'I thought so. But don't forget, she can teach you a lot about this business. You're talented, and you know you have a future in it if you want. And I think you do want it.'

'I'm not going to deny it – of course, I do.'

'But you're beginning to get restive, right?'

Tess turned away, staring out the window. 'I'm sorry – I told you, I'm having trouble admiring her anymore.' And figuring out what was true, she added silently.

'Oh, for heaven's sake, you were never going to be one of her lapdogs. Please understand. She's struggling, and she won't face what's happening. Look, clients are dropping out; Lucy thinks it's all because of the negative publicity, but I'm not so sure. We had more cancellations yesterday; I'm trying to hold on to Mary Pickford, but she's acting a bit vague. If Lucy's show is a disaster here in New York, it will harm her dreadfully in Paris and London, and she isn't prepared for that.' She reached for Tess's hand. 'Have some compassion, Tess. I know she has been ungrateful and critical of you. But she needs you.'

'How could she possibly need *me*?'

'Well, things get complicated.'

'I feel a great loyalty to her,' Tess said slowly. 'But I fear she's trying to make me into something I'm not. On the ship? She talked about cutting me into pieces, like a bolt of fabric, and putting the design together again in a different way.'

'And that troubles you?'

'It didn't then. It does now.'

Elinor laughed. 'Don't you see, dear? She is your Pygmalion.'

'I don't know what you're talking about.'

'Never mind – it's an old myth of sorts. Now, to another subject – how important is this sailor to you?'

The question caught her by surprise. 'We are friends, or at least I thought we were,' she said, taken aback by her own reserve. It sounded stiff, uncaring, distant. It wasn't enough. 'And I don't want anything bad to happen to him. He's an honorable man.'

'Well, rest easy. Honorable men survive.' Elinor tapped sharply on the glass with a red polished fingernail. 'Farley, drop us at Macy's.' She turned brightly to Tess. 'This is a wonderful store – you'll like it. It's owned by the Straus family, you know.'

Tess looked at her blankly.

'Mr. and Mrs. Isidor Straus, dear. They went down on the *Titanic*.'

When they returned several hours later, the car was filled with boxes of fine linen napkins and tablecloths. For Tess, the experience of wandering the huge store had been amazing. Acres and acres of space filled with clothes, dry goods; lively, laughing people promenading; clerks pulling wonderful garments out of storage rooms, young girls trying on gloves heaped up on counters; women in crisply cut, simple jackets and skirts, walking around, skirts flipping up to show their calves . . .

'See what I mean?' Elinor said at one point, nodding toward a quite nicely turned-out matron trying on hats. 'She's no client of Lucile's. Everything you see in this place is ready-to-wear. This is the future, not floating chiffon.'

In the flurry of unloading their packages, it took Tess a few minutes before she caught sight of Pinky standing in front of Lucile's building, looking as thrown-together as always, the same drooping bag swinging from her shoulders.

'They won't let me up,' Pinky announced cheerfully, without preamble. 'Lady Duff says she isn't talking to reporters anymore.'

'Oh, she's just busy,' Elinor replied airily, pushing open the door with her arms filled. 'Come on up – you can talk to Tess.'

'You're her spokesperson now?' Pinky asked, looking at Tess, eyes widening. Stranger things happened. One minute someone was on one side; the next, on the other. Expediency.

'Of course not,' Tess said quickly.

'No, no, she's just the one who knows what's going on to prepare for the show. You are here to write about that, aren't you?'

They were already in the elevator. She had got this far, Pinky told herself. No use pretending. 'You're her sister, aren't you?' she said to Elinor as the doors closed. 'I don't think we've met. I'm Pinky Wade, and I'm covering the *Titanic* hearings.'

'Ah, I see. Then you're here to make my sister apoplectic. It isn't a good idea at the moment.' The doors opened into the loft and Elinor stepped out, holding them open, and said in genial fashion, 'Tess, just put your bundles on the table, then maybe you could escort Miss Wade downstairs again. Would you?'

Tess obeyed, but the elevator had already descended.

'Well, I guess this is the closest I get to the great designer's secret haven,' Pinky said, peering around at the busy loft.

'Did you know what Jim was going to say in advance?'

'No. But I know it was hard for him.'

'Your story was the best.'

Pinky gave her a quick, grateful glance. 'Glad you think so. Balancing things out isn't easy, especially when I know what I really believe and which way I want a story to tip.'

'Is he all right?' Tess asked. It was a bit of a naked question, but it could be asked; she and Pinky were on the same side.

'I think so. But who wants to be called a liar? Sullivan and Purcell didn't help themselves by contradicting each other. And I'm writing tomorrow about the lawyers in the hearing room. Imagine, they're from the firm that takes care of the Duff Gordons. Coincidence, huh?' Her eyes were still traveling around the room. 'I think the Duff Gordons tried to fix the inquiry testimony. Can't prove it yet, but I think they did.'

The elevator doors opened behind them, and they both stepped in. Pinky was rummaging in her bag. 'Sorry, I didn't get much sleep last night and I'm a mess, more than usual.' She pulled out a comb with some teeth missing and ran it randomly through her hair. 'It's like Jim said – people choose whatever they want to believe and declare it true, I guess. I need proof. Anyway, that's what I'm working on. There's more, and I'll find it.'

'I want you to be wrong,' Tess said slowly. 'But maybe you're not.'

'Tess, you're a real grown-up.'

Tess smiled at this. 'You need a new comb,' she said. 'And I'm glad you are back.'

Pinky looked at the implement distractedly. 'Maybe that's why I never look different.' She tossed it back into her bag; it was time to convey her most important message. 'Jim wants to see you. Very much.'

'Then why didn't he come before he left for Washington? He vanished without a word,' Tess said quickly. The sting of that had not eased.

'But he did try to see you,' Pinky replied. 'He left a note at the hotel. You didn't get it?'

'No, I didn't.' So he had not forgotten her.

'You're not angry with him for testifying?'

'For having the courage to go up there and say what he thought? No. How could I be?'

'You were a pretty good defender of Lady Duff, you know. He thinks you won't want anything to do with him now.'

'I couldn't feel that way,' Tess said. 'I don't want him hurt.'

'I think he's coming off better than the other crew members. I'm positive the Duff Gordons had their big-shot lawyers coaching Sullivan. You're kind of stuck in the middle, aren't you?'

'It isn't like that,' Tess said quickly.

'Will you see him when they let him come back to New York?'

'Yes, of course.' She hoped Pinky, with her sharp senses, hadn't caught her instant of hesitation. For if she had there was no way to tell her the true reason for it. She turned away from the curiosity in Pinky's eyes. 'I have to go back up now.'

'Guess I won't get invited,' Pinky said. Her eyes began to dance. 'Unless I get assigned to cover the fashion show.'

Tess stepped out of the closing elevator, almost bumping into Lucile, who beckoned her into the office.

'I realise from what Elinor reports that I'm going to have to tell you, quite definitely, that I value you and want you to be happy here.' Lucile's hands were folded in front of her, and her voice was matter-of-fact. 'And that if I don't mean it you will leave. Is that right?'

'Yes, that's right,' Tess said, knowing that it was.

'You would give up your future here, and your apartment?'

'I would find another way to make my future, if I had to.'

'Ah, a spark of bravado, Tess? Depending on the circumstances, I suppose. But, I assure you, what I'm saying is true. I do value you, and I'm not out to damage your sailor, even though I think you can do much better.'

Imperious and conciliatory at the same time. They stared at each other, and Tess realised that her knees were still. A good sign.

'With one caveat.'

Tess waited.

'You must promise you will do nothing to damage *me*.'

'Of course,' Tess said.

'Well.' Lucile seemed somehow at a loss how to continue.

'I should get back to work,' Tess said gently, and turned to go.

'By the way, you're too skinny. You aren't in training to be a model, you know.'

Now it was Tess's turn to be at a loss for words. Somewhat awkwardly, she shifted from one foot to the other, her hand on the doorknob. 'I haven't had much of an appetite lately,' she said finally.

Lucile's mood suddenly became exuberantly playful. 'Well, I think we are through a rough patch. So now I want to tell you about a challenge that I think you will love. Maybe it's not possible, but you'll learn a great deal from taking it on. Can you sketch a design, cut, sew, and fit a dress between now and the show?'

'Oh—' Tess caught her breath. 'My goodness, what . . . how . . .'

Lucile laughed. 'Tess, I love seeing your surprise.'

Tess coloured, flustered. Then she grew wary. 'I don't have the talent for that yet. ... I'm not experienced enough. Why—'

'Answer my question. Well, can you?'

'Yes. I can, I think I can. At least' – and all the years of hoping and dreaming were in her answer – 'I want to try.'

'Then that's your job, dear.' Lucile smiled broadly. 'And if it's good – mind you, it has to be good – I will introduce your work at the show. You and I, we need to get on with life, don't you think?'

Together they walked out of the office, stopped almost immediately by the sight of a strange man in a delivery cap waiting for them. Cosmo, his lips pulled tight, stood beside him.

'Who is this man, and who let him up here?' Lucile said as, expressionless and with a quick tip of his cap, he thrust a white envelope into her hand.

'Brace yourself, Lucy.' Cosmo stepped forward. 'And, for God's sake, don't get hysterical. Senator Smith has issued you a subpoena.'

Lucile stared at the envelope. 'How dare he?' she whispered.

'Too much gossip swirling in the air, I suspect. He couldn't resist,' said Cosmo.

Lucile swayed slightly and went pale, then turned toward Tess with an oddly triumphal look. 'Too bad, Tess. You may have to choose sides after all,' she said.

Cosmo took his wife's arm, guiding her into her office. He closed the door on Tess.

'Before you say a word, please note that I am not screaming and crying.'

'Duly noted,' he said with the ghost of a smile.

Lucile brushed the sleeve of her jacket, irritated by a

smudge. This city was so dirty; you couldn't wear anything without some cleaning disaster. She took off the jacket and threw it to the floor.

'Lucile. Sit down.'

'I don't want to talk about that impossible, strutting senator and what he's trying to do to me!'

'Sit down.'

His somber face warned her not to object. Reluctantly, she sat down on the sofa. 'Can't you make this awful thing go away?' she pleaded. 'All I want to do is put on my spring show and get out of this terrible place and home to England.'

'It's not going to go away. I thought we had Smith's assurance that we wouldn't be dragged into this, but you can't trust a politician. They move where the wind blows.'

'When do I have to testify?'

'Next week. He's moving the hearings back to New York for a few days, so people like you and me can't scatter. And, believe me, the place will be packed.' Cosmo was pacing, not looking at her. Keeping his distance.

'I'll answer what I want to answer!'

'You will stick, word for word, with what our lawyers tell you to say. You will not say one extra word, do you hear me?' His voice, hard and even, was that of a schoolmaster.

Lucile was startled at his intensity but rallied quickly. 'Don't underestimate me, Cosmo. I can orchestrate this. I'll dress for the occasion. A very large, black hat with plenty of powder. I can look very pale if I have to. By the time I'm done, the whole country will see how victimised I've been.'

'Good girl.' His smile flickered again, more tiredly this time. 'All Smith will get out of this is anti-British rhetoric. But I have more bad news. There will be an inquiry in Britain as well, and both of us are going to be under subpoena to testify. I've not been able to do anything to stop it. The mood there is that we're an embarrassment to the country. Certainly, my reputation has been destroyed.' His voice turned bitter. 'You think the newspapers here have been bad? My dear, wait until you see what happens there. We are heading into a maelstrom.'

At home? Impossible. Her reputation was unassailable, yet nothing seemed to be holding fast. 'What are we going to do?' she asked.

'I am pulling every string I can. There will be no compromise on putting us both on the stand. Perhaps we can find a way to orchestrate that.'

'Of course, we can. It's tragic, treating us this way.'

'You'll have to do more than rehearse your performance.'

'What do you mean?'

'That sailor will probably be testifying in England, too.'

'The one called Bonney?'

'Yes.'

'That's completely unacceptable.'

'I don't think it's up to you.'

'We'll see about that.'

Cosmo regarded her almost coolly. 'The investigating panel in Washington found him quite believable, I'm told. At least here you won't have to testify with him in the room, waiting to deny your story. England will be worse.

I would suggest that from this point on you do not speak of the sinking or anything of what has happened here to anyone, do you hear me?'

'Why don't you just say it?' she demanded, furious. 'You think I'm the one who got us into this muddle, isn't that right?'

'Can't you answer that yourself? Do you really need me to do so?'

'Don't forget you were on that boat, too.'

'And what is that supposed to mean?'

'My dear husband, you were no hero.' She turned away, taking a deep, steadying breath. 'I will not let them tear me apart in some courtroom. I'll think of something.'

Chapter 12

Almost a week of hard work gone by already. Tess's hand ached. She was holding the pencil too tightly – the sign of an amateur. She leaned closer over the drawing board, softening her strokes. She could sketch in the tucked sleeves she had designed in Cherbourg; that would work. Think of the fabric. Don't think of the subpoena. Don't think of Jim. She looked at the skirt she was drawing. It should be in a stiff but moldable fabric; stay away from chiffon.

She sat back, eyeing her design critically. Hopefully. All these long hours, sketching and resketching, determinedly keeping her mind away from the feeling that everything was crumbling. Lucile would have to testify the day before her show, and the tension in the shop was spiraling upward.

But at the end of each day she would rise from her drawing board, bid the workers good night, and walk out into another world. Jack's world.

There he would be, at her door, tipping his hat, offering his arm to take her to yet another elegant restaurant where the light shimmered and everything was beautiful. Bit by bit, she had pieced together some information about him. Mrs. Brown was right; he was going ahead with a divorce – which, he said, wasn't his first. 'Don't make it a black mark – I'm a slow learner,' he had said good-humoredly, and she had smiled, not quite sure how she felt about that.

Then later, at home, staring at the ceiling: where was Jim? Would he show up for Lucile's testimony? Or was he already heading West, having forgotten her? She had to face the possibility that because of the mislaid note, left unanswered, she might not see him again.

Come morning, she would be back at her drawing board, pushing both men out of her thoughts, concentrating on the most exciting challenge she had ever known.

And now the end of the fourth day. A stab of pain; she rubbed her fingers. She was doing it again, clutching the pencil too tightly.

'She's taking this seriously,' Elinor said to her sister as they watched from Lucile's office.

'She'd better, after what that sailor friend of hers did to me.'

'Don't take it out on her; she's caught between the two of you.'

'Her design isn't half-bad, so far.'

Elinor raised one eyebrow, studying Lucile. 'You know, I actually think you mean it.'

'Why wouldn't I?'

'In another mood, dear sister, you might have given someone this opportunity to see how quickly they would fall on their face. And then come crawling back to the invincible Madame.'

'And what do you think now?'

'I think you want her to succeed.'

Tess glanced up at just that moment and saw the two women looking at her. Lucile acknowledged the eye contact with a brisk nod, but Elinor was smiling.

They think I can do it, Tess thought. And I can.

It was late. Her feet hurt as she stepped out onto the sidewalk; why not hop onto one of the streetcars heading toward home? One was coming her way now, bell clanging, people crowded inside and jammed on the steps, holding on to whatever they could grasp. How did you do this? She hoisted her skirt with one hand, jumped on, and grabbed for a post with the other, almost falling off as the car lurched forward.

'You need some training,' said a girl, giggling, as she hung on to her hat.

A woman holding a bag of apples was running for the streetcar. 'Slow down!' she yelled. Now the woman was hoisting her skirt, grabbing for the post. She tripped on the skirt, and Tess held her breath. But the driver, with an angry shout to hurry up, had slowed enough for the woman, breathless, to pull herself on.

'That was dangerous,' Tess said to the passenger next to her.

'Dangerous? Honey, we do it all the time,' the woman replied.

'She could move faster in a shorter skirt.'

The woman snorted. 'Shorter skirts? Not respectable.'

Tess jumped off the streetcar at her stop, hoping for a soothing cup of hot tea before Jack arrived – something to bridge the two worlds in which she was living. She would not brood over what was going to happen at the inquiry; she could call this a good day. And tomorrow – her heart skipped a beat – tomorrow she would cut the gown.

'Miss Collins?'

A man in a bowler hat was approaching her, the sound of his heels clicking against the pavement. She had been so engrossed in her thoughts that she hadn't seen him.

'Please, an introduction. I'm Howard Wheaton, Mr. Bremerton's secretary.' He tipped his hat, looking uncomfortable as he thrust his arm forward; only then did Tess see the bouquet of flowers. 'He asked me to deliver these to you with his note, and with his apologies for not delivering them in person; he had important business downtown.'

Nobody had ever given her flowers. Tess took the

fragrant bouquet, inhaling the heady fragrance of lilacs and roses.

'The note?'

'Of course.' She flushed as she opened the small envelope tucked into the flowers. 'Sherry's at 10:30?' it read.

'Your response?'

'Please tell Mr. Bremerton I will be there,' she said.

'Thank you; he will be pleased. A car will pick you up.'

She nodded and, somewhat giddily, watched the dutiful Mr. Wheaton walk away.

This time it was a private room, fragrant with the smell of leather-bound books lining the walls. 'I want to spend every evening with you,' Jack said, rising from a chair near the door as he shoved papers back into a briefcase. He had a slightly distracted look, but it vanished as Tess came closer. 'Forgive me for not bringing you the flowers myself. Work intervened, I'm afraid.'

'Mr. Ford's automobile?' she asked.

'I don't want to bore you with business.'

'But I learn things.'

'You're feigning interest, and I adore you for that.' With ease and naturalness, he leaned over and gently kissed her ear.

'Won't a waiter come in?' she asked nervously.

'They have my orders. Not until I ring the bell.'

Jack leaned forward, holding her hand and stroking it. His face looked weary; there was a furrow in his brow she hadn't noticed before that made him look older. But his touch was contained, steady. So sure.

'I have to go to California,' he said.

'Are you coming back?' she asked, her heartbeat quickening.

'Yes, but it might not be for quite a while. I don't like being away from you.' He cupped her chin and turned it toward him. 'You could come with me.'

Tess drew in her breath, shocked. 'That's impossible.'

'Are you sure?'

In the silence that followed, she could hear a clock on the wall ticking. Then his hand tightened on hers. It dawned on her, the realisation, yes – there was a possibility of a different answer. She didn't want him to go away. She hesitated.

He smiled, leaning back. 'I know, Tess, you aren't that kind of girl. But wouldn't it be a lark? I could show you a wonderful life out there.'

'I'm sure, but – I have work here.'

'All right, forget that idea. I'm an impulsive man, I suppose. Or so any number of people have told me. But this is different. I knew you were extraordinary from the moment you tiptoed into the *Titanic*'s gym. I wanted to lift you down from that silly camel, but you wouldn't let me. It was all I could do not to kiss you.' He laughed. 'I knew right then that you were the one to change my wandering ways.'

Was he teasing? 'I need to go home soon, it's very late,' she said, hoping she didn't sound priggish. Looking around the room – the books, the flickering candlelight, the privacy – she realised that he was pulling her closer, but it didn't feel inappropriate.

And then they were together on a velvet sofa, all pretense to interest in dinner gone. He began smoothing her long dark hair, twining it around his fingers, rubbing it against his cheek, looking baffled when he tried to insert the comb that held it up in place.

'I'll do that. I can't leave this restaurant not looking respectable.'

'My preference? Your long hair would clothe you – nothing else.'

She closed her eyes. A man had just said that to her – a man like no other, a man whom she didn't have to immediately slap and denounce, a man whom she could or could not give permission to say such things. She had that choice, and it was delicious. What was it about this man? His assuredness. There was safety here – is that what it was? No worries, a haven. She closed her eyes and let him kiss her.

So little sleep. Her back ached as she bent over the cutting table the next morning, a pair of scissors poised in her hand. The muslin version of her dress had worked. The slant of the bodice basting needed to be adjusted, but it looked good. Still, she hesitated. Lying flat before her on the table was the beautifully moldable cream silk she had chosen – a fabric that, cut correctly, would be both soft and substantial. One of the most luxurious bolts of fabric from Lucile's generous stock. She could not make a mistake.

'Would you like one of the cutters to do this part?' James said gently.

Tess looked up and saw that a handful of Lucile's workers – seamstresses, cutters, trimmers – had gathered around the table to watch. Several of them smiled tentatively.

She glanced in the direction of Lucile's office, wondering where she was. She had hurried in and out earlier, murmuring something about a meeting with her lawyers, obviously distracted. Everything was happening at once. She was on her own here, the way it had been when she repaired Lucile's wedding gown, and that made her apprehensive.

'Thank you, but I think I can do this,' she said. She willed her hand to be still. 'Here we go.'

Tess cut into the fabric with a firm motion, allowing the scissors to glide along the pattern lines with only a few stops for adjustments. The fabric was separating beautifully, cleanly. Her confidence grew as she cut the sleeves. She had to trust that she had left enough material for the elaborate tucking she envisioned.

As she cut the last piece, the silence around the table erupted into clapping. 'Great job,' James said, beaming. 'Takes nerve, the first time you cut fabric like this.'

It did, it did. It was like being on top of a mountain, standing here, still holding the scissors, as the seamstress she had chosen began carefully basting the gown.

'Tess—' James beckoned her over to the other side of

the table. 'Look at this.' He held up a small curiously made metal contraption.

'What is it?'

'It's a hookless fastener. Watch.' He pulled at a flat piece of metal, exposing what looked like interlocking teeth, then pulled it back up, magically closing the space with the teeth alternately connected. 'The salesman said you can sew the cloth edges into things like money belts and life vests. What do you think?'

Tess turned the fastener around in her hand, charmed by the ease with which it worked. Would it add bulk to a gown? Hard to tell. It might work, though. She ran her fingers over the tiny rectangular teeth, fascinated.

James's eyes danced. 'Knew you'd be interested,' he said.

It was hours later when Lucile burst from the elevator, marching in with a flower consultant who was busy scratching notes as she threw out instructions. 'The flowers must look beautiful under blue lights; bring in *nothing* that turns green or sallow, do you understand?' she said. 'I won't tolerate it. Do not forget the urns; they must be five feet high, no shorter, and – yes?' She glanced impatiently at Tess's expectant face.

'My gown is cut and basted – would you like to see it?' Tess asked.

'Lovely,' Lucile said with a hasty wave of the hand. 'I'll look later. You've worked hard, dear. Take tomorrow off.' And, with that, she and the consultant disappeared into her office.

It was oddly deflating, as if she had somehow been

dismissed. Tess straightened her shoulders and beckoned to the model who had just wiggled into the carefully basted dress. 'Walk toward me,' she said.

She couldn't help holding her breath. Yes, the gown moved just as she had envisioned it would – the creamy silk breaking into varying hues, as subtle as a wave breaking on the sand. The sleeves needed extra tucking, but that wasn't a problem; the material was there. Yet something bothered her.

'How do you feel, walking in this dress?' she asked the model.

Obviously surprised, the model stammered an answer. 'I like it – I don't feel caught up in gauze and lace.' She immediately coloured, clearly horrified at her criticism of Lucile's style.

'That's all right,' Tess said gently. 'I know what you mean.'

'Just one thing, if you're asking.'

'Yes?'

'It's a dress for daytime, just right. But I'd hate to catch it in a train door.'

Tess stared at her creation, remembering her ride on the streetcar. She reached over to the table and picked up the scissors. No need to think it through; she knew what she wanted. Within minutes, it was done – eight inches of precious fabric cut from the hem. She'd take ten if she dared.

'It's going to be ready for the show – I can hardly believe it,' she said to James.

'We never doubted it,' he replied. 'Long day, Tess. Time to go home.'

The wind currents outside the Flatiron Building swirled around her as she walked past, sending her skirts billowing. It amused her to see the men loitering nearby in hopes of getting a peek at an ankle or two. A policeman stood at the corner, ordering the oglers to move along, since nobody could do anything about the winds. They wouldn't need him once women got brave enough to shorten their dresses.

A man was standing on her stoop. Jack? She moved closer, and saw that he held a cigarette in one hand and was restlessly combing back his gold-flecked hair with the other.

No, not Jack.

He saw her and smiled, and she caught her breath. Oh, she had missed that smile.

'Tess.'

'Hello, Jim.'

'Well, it's done.'

'Yes, I know.'

'I did what I had to do. I tried to tell you in advance, but I guess you knew by then what was up and decided you didn't want to see me.' His eyes were guarded but steady: so deeply blue. 'Anyway, now I'm here to ask what it cost me.'

'Pinky told me you sent me a note, but I never got it,' Tess said.

'You didn't?' He looked stunned.

'No,' she said. 'I don't know why I didn't – I thought you just forgot me. Or—'

A light was dawning in his eyes. 'Or I had talked to Pinky for her story without telling you?'

'Yes.'

'All I wanted to do was give you a ride around the park in one of those fancy carriages,' he said gently. 'And tell you I was going to Washington but coming back.'

'I would have liked that,' she said.

He gave her a rueful smile. 'I kept hoping you would show up – those horses knew me pretty well by the time I left. My guess is the Duff Gordons intercepted my note. But at least I know you didn't stand me up.'

'I owe you more – that wouldn't happen,' she said quickly.

'Would you have understood? That I had to testify?'

She needed no time to form an answer. 'You said what you honestly believed, and that's more than the others did.' She reached out her hand. 'It hasn't cost you my friendship, if that's what you mean.'

The look of relief on his face cut through to her heart. She did not want to move, even as he reached out and their fingers touched. Not even when, standing there, he slowly drew her hand to his face, kissing it with undisguised tenderness. Gently, she disengaged, her mind in turmoil.

'Can we walk awhile? Maybe through another park in your nice but less fancy new neighbourhood?' His eyes were alight now, not quite dancing but warm with relief.

'Of course,' she said. Her hand had felt so good, held inside the curve of his fingers. She hadn't anticipated that.

Jim had a long stride, but so did she, when she put her mind to it. He was talking quickly, giving her his impressions of Washington, talking in the rapid way of someone who has been storing up tidbits to share. He stopped as they entered a park and leaned down to pick up a rolling chestnut, then, laughing, tossed it toward a racing squirrel. They had to talk soon.

'I've stayed with Lucile,' she said.

'I know. And I don't blame you.'

Her face flushed and she looked away.

'Stop accusing yourself, Tess.'

'I'm torn—'

'You think you're the only one? Torn between choices? We all were.'

'Jim, the committee has called her to testify.'

'I guess I'm not surprised. Is she making you choose sides?'

'Why did it have to go this way?' she burst out, her eyes filling with tears.

Jim tossed another chestnut without looking at her. 'If you need to pull away from me to keep your job, I'll understand,' he said. 'I can take anything, as long as I know you're my friend.'

'I am,' she said fervently. 'I am, I always will be.'

They walked in comfortable silence until Jim stopped and turned her toward him.

'I've got good news,' he said. 'Really good news.' He suddenly seemed almost shy.

'What is it?'

'Mrs. Brown, your ally in the lifeboat?'

Tess nodded, waiting.

'She saw me whittling away at the hearing in Washington, and started praising my work, very over the top. I thought she was a bit daft.'

'She's not daft at all,' Tess said quickly.

'I'm trying to be modest, okay?' He grinned and tossed another chestnut, sending the industrious squirrel in fast pursuit. 'Anyway, she liked what she saw, and commissioned me to do a piece especially for her.' He glanced sideways at Tess, teasingly. 'A bigger version, to tell the truth, of the one I carved for you. She wanted the whole ship – why, I don't know.'

'You mean a model of the *Titanic*?' Tess wasn't sure how she felt about that.

'Yes.'

'That's wonderful, Jim. But – doesn't it give you nightmares, revisiting the ship?'

'No,' he said slowly. 'It's a bit healing, actually. Anyway, she came up with something even better.' He cleared his throat and faced her squarely. 'My dear Miss Collins' – he made an elaborate bow – 'you are looking at somebody described as a master craftsman by an excitable lady who can make anything happen. Best of all, for me, a job.'

'That's fantastic,' she said, laughing. 'Absolutely fantastic.'

'So – and do remember you are looking at a *future* "master craftsman" – this whittler from London now has a job in a woodworking shop – a great place, good money.' He was talking faster now. 'The place is brilliant. They've got the best carving knives I've ever seen, and I'll be doing some specialty work for them – relief carving, on mirrors and the like. To pull out from the wood a face or a picture – I love that. What—' He stopped dead and slapped his forehead. 'What am I thinking of? It's nearby. Want to come and see it?'

An instant of hesitation; then Tess nodded, caught up in his excitement and pride. He quickened his pace, and she almost had to run to keep up with him now. 'Guess what? Lucile is letting me design a dress for her show,' she said breathlessly. 'I'm working with wonderful material and it's exciting—'

He stopped suddenly, turned, and lifted her by the waist, swinging her around. 'That's great news. Look at us – we're both finding what we want! God, it *is* exciting, isn't it?'

'Yes,' she said, laughing, still breathless, not wanting him to let go. How could she feel this so intensely – what about Jack?

He lowered her gently, taking her hand again as they resumed walking. The memory of the first time they had touched hands on the *Carpathia* flashed, the intimacy shared without words.

'Does the woodworking shop mean you're staying here? Not heading West?' she asked.

'I'm here for now. Maybe later, who knows? I'm in a union shop, so I can do union work here. It's good to be flexible, especially when you've got reasons not to leave.' He flashed her a quick grin, then looked around, as if only now noticing where they were. 'I've heard of this place,' he said. 'They call it Union Square. Lots of speeches and demonstrations. A good place in a good country.' He barely broke stride. Finally, a few yards farther on, he stopped and pointed. 'There it is,' he said.

Tess saw a somewhat shabby building tucked between two boarding houses. Jim grabbed her hand, opened the door to the shop, and stopped as they stepped inside, inhaling deeply. 'Smell the sweet wood?' he said. 'I love that smell.'

Tess nodded. It was such an aromatic, earthy smell – comforting, really. No tinge of wetness or coldness; no hint of sea or salt. The floor was covered with shaved scraps of wood, some tissue-thin, some crunched together like a woman's curls. A soft, powdery substance coated a long, battered oak table that held a jumble of tools, the likes of which she had not seen before.

'You can do anything with these tools,' Jim said, picking one up. He nodded toward a smooth slab of wood. 'It's the frame for a mirror,' he said. 'I'm working on it now.' He nodded toward an elaborately detailed Baroque mirror hanging next to the table. 'That's my model.'

'Where is the *Titanic*?'

'In the back room.' He took her hand again and together they walked to the back of the shop, Jim nodding and joking with a few of the woodworkers. He clearly already felt comfortable here.

'There it is. I've only begun, really. Got a lot of work to do on it yet.'

Almost fearfully, Tess stared at the ship. The four smokestacks, carved bold, gave her a shiver. How grand and enthralling they had been.

'Go ahead, Tess. Touch it. It's all right.'

With one finger she followed the curve of one of the finished lifeboats. Tiny and still, but a perfect replica. The slender ropes tied tightly, not swirling and slipping across the deck. The delicately molded steps leading to the lookout's station, where no binoculars waited . . . She touched the stern, the last part of the *Titanic* any of them had seen.

What did I learn? she wondered. What did it teach me?

'I've got a lot more work to do to get it right,' Jim said, standing at her shoulder.

'Jim, it's wonderful.' She couldn't take her eyes off the model. 'Where were we standing when we met?'

He pointed to a place near one of the lifeboats. For a moment, they both looked in silence, saying nothing. Then Jim spoke quietly.

'I once said to you I didn't think we were so different, and I saw in your eyes that you didn't agree. I hope that's changed.'

Straightforward and honest. Regardless of the tumult in her heart, she must be, too. But how? What could she say?

He laid his hands gently on her shoulders and turned her around to face him. 'I need to see your eyes,' he said with such tenderness, she could say nothing else. 'I'm going to kiss you, Tess Collins. Something I've wanted to do since our walk through the park.'

She couldn't help herself. His arms around her, his lips on hers, the powerful, sensual feel of him – for a long, slow moment, she met his hunger with her own, winding her arms around his neck, touching his soft, unruly hair. He whispered into her ear, then met her lips again. What was she doing? She pulled away.

'No, no. Jim, I'm too confused.'

'I'm sorry – was this too fast?'

'No, that's not it.'

'Tess, there's so much I want to say.' He was talking rapidly again. 'All I've been able to think about for days is the idea of building a new life in this country with you.' He held up his hands, palms out. 'These are my tools, my passport to better things, just like yours are. Tess, we have our futures right here.' He touched her chin, looking into her eyes with an expression so hopeful, it was painful. 'Can you give at least some consideration to it being the two of us together?'

And there it was, like a warming light, and so much in her wanted to respond, to say yes. But another part of her held back, looking in another direction. How could she know – how could she be sure of anything right now? 'I think all this is wonderful, and you're wonderful, and I have a bond with you that I'll share with no other in my life,' she managed. And then stopped.

It took a long moment, but the colour slowly left Jim's face. 'Are you saying no?' he said.

'I'm saying I'm not sure.'

He stood very still, looking as if he had been slapped in the face. 'It sounds like no to me. Is it because I testified?'

'No, no, I admire you – I meant that.'

'I would never compromise you, Tess. Maybe I was assuming too much, too fast? I'm sorry, I can wait.'

She tried to think of what to say.

'Or – is there someone else?'

She nodded slowly.

A pause. 'Did I miss a signal?' His voice shook slightly. 'I never knew. Have I been wrong about that?'

'There wasn't anyone before, please know that. But—'

'But there is now.'

'Yes,' she whispered.

He stepped back, looking so stunned that she had to stop herself from reaching for his hand. She couldn't have reached him anyway. Heartsick, she saw the light in his eyes fade. He was retreating from her – how could she have expected anything different? His hands remained at his sides.

'Forgive me for taking too much for granted.'

'I'm very confused, and I don't want to hurt you,' she said. Stupid, meaningless words that meant nothing. She had done precisely that.

'I don't think that's in your control anymore.'

'I still feel it.'

'That won't do either of us any good,' he said. 'Look, I presumed too much.'

'No, it's that so much happened so fast. Oh, Jim—'

'It's all right,' he said mechanically. 'But I should go now.' He shoved his hands into his pockets, stepping through the doorway. 'Look, I'll walk you home. It'll be dark soon, and you shouldn't walk alone.'

'No, it's all right if you need to go. I can find my way.'

He looked away, silent for a moment. A breeze had sprung up, moving softly through the trees, ruffling his hair. When he spoke, it was in a tone simultaneously flat and curious. 'I might as well ask, I guess. You really think I'm just a village boy?'

'How—'

'How did I know? Your Lady Duff spread it around on the *Carpathia*.' He shrugged. 'It doesn't matter anymore. I wouldn't want you to be ashamed of me. Makes for an awkward setup.'

'I'm not, and I never could be,' she managed.

'Nice to hear, I guess.'

'Please, Jim. We have something important between us, a friendship – let's not destroy it.'

This time he looked at her in total disbelief. 'Are you really asking for that? Just – snap my fingers and change how I feel about you?'

'No, no, that was stupid.'

'I think I need to walk somewhere. I wish you well,' he said. He turned his back to her, his shoulders bent under a mountain of hurt, and strode away.

Look around, she thought. Please. But he didn't. She turned and walked slowly in the opposite direction, stepping over the wood chips, smelling the sweetness of this place. She had just lost something huge, leaving a hollowed-out space that felt as if it could swallow her up. If she had only had more time to think it through. And what did that mean? The only thing she knew for sure right now was that she could no longer hold these two men in separate compartments in her heart.

Jack was waiting outside her building in a dark-blue Buick, the engine running impatiently, its silver headlamps glowing. How long had he been waiting? Tess walked slowly, both relieved to see him and yearning for time alone. She wasn't ready; she needed to go into her flat, close her door, and catch her breath.

He stepped from the car, leaned forward and kissed her

cheek, eyes watchful. 'Maybe you don't want to explain anything,' he said. 'But I need to know where I am.'

So courteous. Jack always treated her as someone with dignity; already she felt calmed.

'You saw me with the man from Lifeboat One who wanted to go back,' she said.

'He must be a very brave man.'

'He is.' Again her eyes were filling up.

'And he loves you – am I right?'

She nodded.

'Why are you crying, Tess?' His voice was so gentle. Not anxious, not angry, not probing.

'I'm not. It all happened too fast.'

'Perhaps you could explain.'

'I refused him.' Such a cloaked, old-fashioned word.

Jack's shoulders, visibly tensed, began to relax. 'Are you sure?' he said. 'I saw the way you looked at him. I won't stand in the way of something you want, but I have to know.'

'I'm sure.' Listening to her own voice, so thin. Nothing coming out of her mouth sounded clear-cut and certain.

'You may just want to be.'

She covered her face with her hands. 'How are you so wise?' she asked.

He sighed. 'Experience. Too much, actually.' He paused, then went on. 'Uncertainty isn't a bad thing. I wish I could slow everything down, but I can't. May I hold you?'

She needed to know more, to take time. But in his arms everything seemed to disappear. It felt so good to float above the ground, to put aside her worries.

'Am I invited?' he murmured, touching the pulse in her neck with his lips.

'Yes.'

'There is something I want to propose,' he said. 'Marry me.'

Tess froze.

'I know it's fast, but I've looked long enough and made enough of my share of mistakes to know when it's right.'

'But you're still married,' she said.

'The divorce documents were ready for our final signatures when I stepped onto the *Titanic*. You are a cautious one, Tess.' His smile was warm and kind. 'If I allowed myself to be timid, I wouldn't be who I am today.'

'I'm not timid, I'm just – just surprised.'

He raised an eyebrow. 'So where is the brave and adventurous girl I met on the *Titanic*?'

'I don't want to be married, not yet,' she burst out. She could see her mother's face, hear her cautionary words. 'I know what happens. I've told you, I want to work, I want—'

Jack laughed. 'I'm not asking you to choose,' he said. 'I'm one of the few men you'll know who can give you the life I know you want to lead. You can have it all. Do you doubt that?'

She shook her head.

'Then what's the problem?'

It was too easy, that was the problem. She pulled him closer, unable to say the words.

'I have to think about it,' she whispered.

Chapter 13

Pinky squinted through a soup of fog and rain as she waited outside the imposing offices of Dunhill, Brougham and Picksley on Fifty-seventh Street. Stakeouts were the most boring part of her job, but this one shouldn't last much longer.

The massive front door of the establishment suddenly swung open. Out stepped three men.

I knew it, Pinky thought triumphantly.

Sir Cosmo was dressed, as usual, in an impeccably perfect suit, his mustache as manicured as ever. He was speaking hurriedly to the pair – one wearing the same horn-rimmed glasses she remembered from the courtroom. They shook hands as she watched, and Cosmo walked away.

Pinky approached the two men. The one in the glasses stiffened as he saw her.

'Hello there,' she said cheerfully. 'I know about your

plan, fellas. I guess the only thing I don't know yet is how much the Duff Gordons are paying you.'

Tess heard the rain drumming on her bedroom window and buried her head back under the covers, wishing for sleep without the wild pitch of dreams that had consumed her all night. No use. She sat up in bed, thankful now for being given a day off. She needed it. But Jack's voice, his persuasiveness, remained in her head as she finally rose and put the kettle on to boil. She could hear shouting from the next apartment, a man and a woman fighting. Last night, when she crept into her own bed past midnight, she had heard their bedsprings squeaking urgently through the wall. She might as well have been back home. She didn't want to live a life like that, all anger in the day and sex in the dark, and many babies and no money.

What if there was plenty of money? What was wrong with marriage then?

She poured her tea and sat down to sip the fragrant brew. Jack could teach her about this new country, navigate her through the trials ahead; he would be there to protect her and make good things happen. He lived on top of his world, not fighting for a place within it. She could relax for the first time in her life. And if it had all happened in too breathtakingly short a time, that couldn't be helped. Don't think of Jim. Simplify. He was right; in a way, they were alike – poised on the brink of new things, thirsty and ready. But neither was each other's navigator. And wasn't that what she wanted now?

Slowly, she dressed. She would take a walk uptown, maybe to Central Park. Anything, somewhere to be around people; such a dreary day. She wished she would hear from her mother, but nothing yet. It did bring home the realisation that in this vast new country, there was no one in whom she could confide.

Tess pulled on her gloves and took her umbrella and set out, slamming the door loudly, which silenced her quarreling neighbours. She shivered in her thin coat and pulled it closer as she stopped at the grocery for the newspaper. She couldn't break her habit now of scanning the stories, bracing for the sight of Lady Duff Gordon's name in some newly shocking context.

Her eye stopped and fixed on a small two-paragraph story. There was a memorial service today for Isidor Straus – the co-owner of that amazing store in Herald Square – at Carnegie Hall. A special farewell for a man of distinction, the paper said, whose wife chose to stay on the ship with him, rather than leave him to die alone.

She closed the paper. That's where she would go today. She would pay homage to someone she didn't know, whose fate had been tied to her own. He and she existed in a common fraternity now, dead or alive, one none of the people on the *Titanic* would choose, but there it was. It made – what an odd, bleak thought – for a sense of belonging to something.

It was a long walk, but it soothed her spirit. By the time she reached Forty-second Street, the rain had stopped and the sun was breaking through. A garden of red-and-white striped umbrellas suddenly came into view. Women in spring hats and men in Sunday suits were clustered around flower stands and vendors selling sausage and peppers, while groups of children sat on the street, watching a puppet show. Of course, it was a street festival, complete with a band, the violinist wearing a red cap with a drooping tassel that bounced against his cheek as he played. A woman in a yellow apron was spooning out an ice-cold confection in different flavours and colours. Curious, Tess came closer.

'Gelati,' the woman said, smiling, seeing her interest. 'Better than ice cream.'

Tess smiled back and opened her purse. She took a bite from the small cup the woman handed her; the smooth, light chocolate was delicious. So she would pretend she was Italian for a little while, shedding all thoughts of deadlines and doubt and hurt.

At Carnegie Hall, the crowds clustered on the sidewalk turned quiet and somber. She joined them, asking a man, 'When do we go in?'

'Do you have an invitation?' he said.

'No, I didn't know I needed one.'

'Heavens, madame, everyone knew that.' But he said it kindly. 'Never mind; here comes the mayor.'

A large black carriage drawn by horses was pulling up to the curb, and two policemen began pushing the crowd back. Tess watched as a portly man dressed all in black stepped down from the carriage, then turned and helped a middle-aged woman descend. She took his arm, and the two of them walked past the crowd and into the hall. More carriages and automobiles were pulling up, all in a long, black line. The crowd was silent, except for the sound of a woman crying.

After the last guest entered the hall, a guard left the outer doors wide open, a kindness, people whispered, to allow them to hear the prayers and eulogies. No one tried to enter.

A soft chanting came from the hall. 'They're reciting Kaddish,' the man next to her said, obviously assuming that she wouldn't be familiar with the Jewish prayers.

But she was. A memory of what she had heard out on the sea in that flimsy lifeboat was spilling forth. Someone, in another boat, had been reciting this mournful prayer, his voice caught and held in the still, freezing air. She lowered her head, surprised at the solace it gave her now.

'Tess?'

She looked up. Pinky stood there holding her canvas bag close to her chest, wearing a limp hat that still dripped with drops of rain.

'You're covering this?' Tess said. Her voice might sound cold, but she couldn't help it. Pinky always came with noise and tension, and right now she was thrusting herself into Tess's one calm moment in many days.

'Not on assignment. I just thought I'd come by. I knew him.'

Tess felt a twinge of shame. 'I feel a little like I know him, too,' she said.

They stood together silently, listening to the rhythm of the Hebrew prayers. When the service ended, the mayor and other dignitaries climbed back into their automobiles and carriages and drove away.

Pinky broke the silence. 'So you have to boil silkworms to make silk?' she said off-handedly.

'What?' Tess said, startled.

'You know. Silk. I'm reading up on design and stuff. Got Van Anda to assign me to Lady Duff's big fashion show. That's tough on the silkworms, don't you think?'

'I suppose we could cut everything out of linen and wool,' Tess said with a smile, reaching for her handkerchief. 'But think of all those shorn, shivering sheep. Give me that hat of yours – I'm going to try and blot up the water.'

'Do I look too sad?' Pinky said, handing it over. 'I have to say, you do.'

Tess stopped walking, concentrating on her blotting task before she answered. 'I am a bit,' she said before handing back the hat.

'Because of what you told Jim. Yesterday.'

'Do you always know what's happening?' Tess said with a flash of irritated surprise.

'No, not everything. Who's the other man? And I'm not going to apologise for being intrusive – I'm just asking, and you don't have to answer.'

'No, I don't. And I won't. Sorry, Pinky.'

Pinky shrugged. Nothing ventured, nothing gained. 'How is it going at Lady Duff's studio?'

'Are you asking me is Lucile all distraught and frantic about having to testify in two days?'

'I'd be surprised if she were. I figure she's looking

forward to putting on a grand performance. New York is happily waiting.'

'Then what are you asking?'

'How about how things are for you, or am I just digging for gossip?'

Tess smiled, relenting. 'She's letting me design a dress, and if it's good enough she'll put it in her show. It's done, except for a tuck in the sleeves. I'll show it to Lucile tomorrow, and truly, I'm proud of it. I think she will like it.' Much more than that, she *prayed* that Lucile would like it.

'Silk?'

'Yes.'

'Too bad – I wanted to write about cruelty to silkworms.'

They both laughed, and continued walking, but Tess found herself slipping back into a melancholy mood. She was about to make some excuse so that she could break away and be alone again when Pinky spoke.

'My father isn't doing too well. The woman who takes care of him during the day said he's too cranky for her; I'm crossing my fingers she won't quit.'

'I'm sorry, I hope not.' It was easy to forget that Pinky's brash spirit hid real troubles.

'I figured I would pick up some tomatoes for him at the street market after old Mr. Straus's memorial.' Pinky took off her hat, changed her mind, and crammed it on her head again. 'Thanks for getting some of the water out of this thing.'

'If it starts raining again, I have an umbrella.' The

words were out so quickly, she couldn't pull them back. Now Pinky would expect her to keep walking.

'That's good, thanks.' And then, as if she had just thought of it: 'Why don't you come home with me? I'll make us some lunch. You might like meeting my father; he's basically a good person, just thinks that the whole world should revolve around him. But then that's the way it always was, I guess. I've got cheese and salami, fresh.'

So Pinky wanted to talk. What was there to say? She wanted to talk, too.

The stairwell smelled faintly of urine, and Tess tried to hold her breath as long as she could as they climbed up to the fourth floor.

'We take turns scrubbing the floors, my neighbours and me. Usually it smells fine, but I'm the one who didn't do it yesterday. Sorry about today.'

'I've smelled worse,' Tess said lightly. And she had. She just didn't like to admit it.

Prescott Wade was propped up on several pillows, staring out the window with an open book in his lap, when they entered his bedroom. He was a smaller figure than Tess had envisioned, more frail. But his thin, bony fingers grasped her hand firmly when Pinky introduced them.

'Pinky talks about you,' he said. 'You're the girl working for the big designer, right? Only in America, that kind of thing?'

'I'm trying.' She liked his brusqueness.

'Good, don't settle. Sarah here, she's a good reporter. But she wants to be Nellie Bly.' His eyes traveled toward Pinky. 'She can't do it with me around. I guess I clipped her wings.' His eyes closed and he turned his head to the wall.

Pinky gave his shoulder a swift pat and beckoned Tess to follow her out of the bedroom. She began hacking into a head of lettuce, frowning slightly. 'He's not himself, but then he never is anymore.'

'Do you think of yourself as Nellie Bly?'

Pinky paused, her knife hovering above the vanquished lettuce. 'I would like to travel around the world the way she did. Meeting people, riding camels, shooting rapids—' Her eyes turned dreamy. 'I could do it, and I could do it with just clean underwear, same as she did. No luggage.'

'Why?'

'Why did you want to come to America? Because I want to have adventures and see the world, that's why. But, to tell you the truth, I'd settle for more money.'

'Can you get that?' Tess asked curiously. In her experience, it simply didn't happen.

'Women don't get raises at newspapers. Just lots of praise, if you're lucky, but no money. Here, slice the bread.' She shoved a loaf of bread and a butcher knife toward Tess.

'What's wrong with your father?' Somehow, as she sliced bread and Pinky made the salad, the question didn't seem intrusive.

'He's had several heart attacks, and each time he gets weaker.' Pinky kept her head down as she cut into a tomato.

'I'm sorry.'

When Pinky looked up, her eyes were unusually bright. 'He's not always easy, but he's a pretty good father. I give him morphine for the pain. Do you like your salami thick or thin?'

'I like it whichever way you choose to slice it.'

'Thin it is.'

The next few moments passed in relative silence as the lunch was laid out on a table covered with oilcloth. That task done, Pinky put her hands on the back of a chair and looked straight at Tess.

'Sit down. I have something to tell you,' she said.

'About what?'

'About Jim. He's in trouble.'

Tess lowered herself into a chair, not taking her eyes off Pinky.

'The people who want him out of the way have been digging around in his past, and they've discovered an old indictment from the coal-strike demonstrations.'

'What?' Tess almost knocked the bread tray off the table.

'I'm told the police were arresting everybody in sight, clubbing a lot of heads, things like that. When the mine workers fought back, a cop got slugged. Jim was one of the crowd, and a union organiser to boot. Don't be too shocked; the charges were dismissed a few days later.'

Her hands began to tremble. 'So why is Jim in trouble?'

'Because someone managed to reactivate the indictment against him.'

'Someone? Who?'

Pinky didn't answer directly. 'Did you know he's been subpoenaed for the British hearings?'

'No, he didn't tell me that yesterday.'

'I guess he had more important things on his mind.'

Tess winced. 'Please, Pinky. Don't.'

'I'm sorry, Tess. But you know how you hurt him.'

Tess nodded.

'Okay. Anyway, that means he'll have to go back. He'll be arrested the minute he steps on English soil, and that "scandalous" development will get full play in the British newspapers, shooting down the credibility of his testimony here. Voilà, he'll no longer be a threat to the Duff Gordons, because who wants to believe a criminal? After the hearings are over, Lady Duff skips off to the next fashion show, the charge will be dropped again, very quietly. Neat package, actually.'

'How do you know all this?'

'I've got sources. I'm a reporter, remember?' Pinky's grin wasn't quite as easy as usual. Neither of them had touched the food.

'So, Lucile is out to discredit Jim any way she can.'

'Sure. Nobody stands to profit the way she does. And it turns out it *was* her lawyers coaching those crew members when Jim testified. Big law firm here. I checked them out.'

Tess blinked, trying to absorb the news. First, disbelief – then anger – and now, deep inside, fury. Yes, Lucile was capable of this. It was outrageous, imperious – everything. 'Does Jim know?' she managed.

'He found out last night; he's surprised, but kind of stalwart. You know, the British thing about the stiff upper lip.'

'Are you writing a story?'

Pinky paused before replying. 'I'm waiting. The minute I write it, it does exactly what she wants it to do. I'd rather wait and see what tricks she'll try to pull testifying here.'

'You are sure about this?'

'I'm positive, or I wouldn't be telling you. Eat something.' Pinky shoved a slice of salami between two slices of bread and handed it to Tess. 'There's another possible outcome.'

'What is it?' Tess took the sandwich and bit into it; she couldn't taste a thing, not with the hard knot of anger engulfing her.

'If somebody with better lawyers on the job than Lady Duff – not an easy find, mind you – manages to quash the indictment before it gets publicised. Stomp it back into the past where it belongs. Guess who's working on that?' This time her grin was authentic.

'All right, who?'

'The terrific, smart, rich Mrs. Brown. She's furious. She's got big plans for Jim, and she doesn't want to lose him. How's the sandwich?'

'I can't taste it.' Tess pushed it away and stood. She paced, unable to stay still.

'You're pretty upset.'

'Did you think I wouldn't be? Playing such a dirty trick on Jim, trying to ruin him? I'm furious that she would hurt him.'

Pinky pushed back from the table, too. 'Somebody already has,' she said quietly.

They fell into a momentary silence.

'I'm sorry,' Pinky said again. 'I guess I like to think you don't deserve him.'

Tess was too shaken to mount a defense. 'I don't,' she said.

'So what are you going to do?'

'I'm going to quit. I will not stay with that woman – I can't stay there one more day, not now.' The shock of disbelief shredded away; she had no doubts. It wasn't enough to pay off those seamen for their testimony – no, Lucile was too controlling to settle for that. She wanted all criticism silenced. 'I can't work for her anymore. I'd never trust her again.'

'You can move in here,' Pinky said. 'I mean it, you know. You can start making dresses – I even have a sewing machine – and when you make some money you can get your own place.'

'How would I find clients?'

'No problem,' Pinky said buoyantly. 'I'll send everybody I write about to you, and maybe even Van Anda's wife; she could use some fancier clothes. Tess, it's a great idea. You don't need Lucile!'

Tess felt her smile falter. Pinky was so brashly American, all exuberance and confidence. She knew how to defy the rules; maybe there was something to learn from that. There had to be, because she was stepping into a void.

But there was Jack.

Her feet ached from the long walk home. Jack was waiting for her. She took the flowers he held out to her without seeing them. 'She's done something terrible to Jim,' she blurted.

He looked at the flowers, which she had unthinkingly dropped to the sidewalk. 'All right, tell me,' he said.

And she did, letting it all spill out, caring not a whit how it sounded, as he listened in silence.

'You care quite a lot about this man's welfare,' he finally said.

'Of course, I do,' she said. 'How can Lucile do this? She's trying to ruin his life, just as everything is opening up for him. Part of me can't believe it, and another part thinks, For goodness' sake, how naïve can you be, to be so surprised? I—'

'But what is your role in all this?' he asked with something of an edge to his voice. 'What are you going to do, Tess?'

'I'm going to quit, of course,' she said, surprised at his question.

'You would walk out before the show? Abandon the chance to show the gown you're so proud of?' He said it in such a gentle yet probing way.

'Does that make me sad? Yes. But I don't have a choice.'

'There's always a choice, Tess. That's what makes life so complicated.'

'Well, this one is mine.'

Jack put out his arms and pulled her close. 'Perhaps that means you're closer now to making a more important choice,' he murmured.

She said nothing, just closed her eyes and waited for the comfort that came with his embrace. Tonight it was elusive, even when she finally noticed the flowers.

Pinky sat in the kitchen for a long time after Tess left. She picked at the salad, rolled a piece of salami between her fingers. Well, she had done what she set out to do. She had set something in motion, and she would just have to see what came next.

'Sarah.'

Oh, for God's sake, she had forgotten her father's lunch. She made a sandwich hastily, put it on a plate, and walked into his room. He wasn't fooled.

'Stale bread,' he said.

'I was thinking.'

'About that young man you've talked about?'

Pinky sank heavily onto the bed. 'I wish you weren't so observant.'

'So what's the problem?'

She hesitated, wondering why she should bother, knowing he was quite capable of falling asleep in the midst of what she wanted to say. 'He's hurting because of Tess.'

'So she dumped him for someone else.'

'How did you know?'

'I didn't. Damn it, Sarah, it's always the same story. Your generation didn't invent it, you know.' His thin fingers brought the sandwich up to his mouth, then dropped it back on the plate. 'I'm tired, think I'll go back to sleep.'

'Sure.' She stood, ready to leave. She just wanted out of this bedroom, out of this apartment, out of everything.

His hand reached for hers and squeezed, again with surprising strength. 'I'm not so drugged up I don't know how you feel, kid.'

With a rush of gratitude, Pinky squeezed back.

Chapter 14

The morning light shone weakly through a window in need of washing, but even bright sunshine wouldn't have lifted Tess's spirits. She sat on the bed, brushing her hair, pulling through the tangles. One by one. There was no need to hurry. And there was no need to rehearse what she was going to say. She adjusted her hat, weaving the hat pin carefully through the straw, then walked out into her future, whatever it was going to be.

The doors of Lucile's private elevator opened, inviting her into its exclusive domain. How laughable it was, the idea that being allowed inside a cranky, slow elevator was a mark of privilege. She lifted her skirt slightly, ignored the elevator, and took the stairs.

'Tess, where have you been? Come here!'

Lucile's voice rang through the loft, turning every head toward Tess as she entered. Billows of silk and wool puffed up from the humming sewing machines, catching the light now streaming through the windows – a wonderful, shimmering sight. A catch in her throat – how she loved this place. She didn't allow herself to linger. Only a few wondered why, as she walked through the loft to the runway set up for the show, she did not immediately take off her hat.

'My goodness, dear, I'm been dying to see you. Why are you so late? Never mind, just look!' Lucile pointed at a model, who, as if on cue, began to stroll down the runway toward Tess. She was wearing Tess's finished gown. The richly hued cream silk looked even better than it had two days ago. With a shorter skirt, it bounced, catching the light, tossing it back into the room, catching it again. It was as she had imagined. Her dress. She had done this.

'It's absolutely *marvelous*!' Lucile said, clasping her hands. 'I fixed that little tuck in the sleeve for you this morning, is that all right?' She didn't wait for an answer. 'Perhaps it's a bit shorter than it could be, but my clients can order it any length they want. Tess, you've done a fabulous job. It will absolutely be in the show.'

Tess kept staring at her gown, even as Lucile's praise grew more elaborate. The dress didn't work, not fully. She stared critically at the bodice, and decided that not only should she have angled the darts more; a square-cut neckline would have been better. It had almost worked.

'It isn't as good as it should be,' she said.

'Spoken like a true designer, dear. Of course it isn't perfect, but it's got a fresh feel to it, and I'm happy. Don't be so hard on yourself. Why do you look so dour?'

'May we talk in your office?'

Impatiently, Lucile shook her head. 'No time – we have much to do. What is it you want?'

It wasn't an easy thing to open one's mouth and shatter the lively, bustling mood. 'I'm sorry it had to happen this way, but I am quitting,' Tess said quietly.

'What? You are *what*?' Lucile almost shrieked the words.

Tess felt as if she had lifted a knife and plunged it through a crowd. Why would her leaving matter? But heads were turning, eyes wide. A hush fueled by quick whispers flew through the loft.

Tess pointed at her dress. She couldn't trust herself to pick it up.

'Letting me make this was a bribe, pure and simple. You were buying my loyalty.'

'What are you talking about?' Lucile said.

'You knew money would be too blatant. Money was for those sailors, so they would lie about Jim Bonney at the hearings. But a bribe it was.'

Lucile's face turned gray. She clutched at her heart, and James came running out of the office to hold her up.

'I didn't need a bribe. I would have stayed because I wanted to. But not now, not for anything.'

'What are you talking about?'

'Oh, Lucile, please stop pretending. You're plotting to paint Jim Bonney as a common criminal in England – that's what I'm talking about. To actually get him arrested on a false charge. Why? Was he that much of a threat to you?'

'I couldn't care less about that sailor.'

'What happened in your boat?'

Lucile stared at her, features frozen. She turned away.

'You're hysterical. I do not know what you're talking about.'

'It's easy to deny, I guess. But I can't believe how easily you would try to ruin a man.' Tess's voice was cracking now.

Lucile stood braced against a cutting table, her eyes dark as brackish water. 'I have nothing to do with any absurd scheme to send your sailor to jail. Do you understand?'

Of course she would deny it, that was her nature. This woman in front of her, her mentor, the woman who had so casually plucked her from a life of service and opened up the world to her, was perfectly ready to bluff this one through. She no more cared what happened to Jim than she cared what happened to the people who could have – who *should* have – been in her lifeboat. All this, all this around her – the fabrics, the clothes, the dreams – everything was built on selfishness. The only thing built on anything admirable was Jim's behavior after the ship sank.

'I would respect you more if you admitted the truth. But it doesn't matter; I can't work for you anymore.'

'That's just simply not possible, Tess. I want you here, and I know nothing about any plot to destroy that sailor.'

'I don't believe you.'

Lucile thrust out her chin, her lips pulled thin. 'Then you are breaking your promise to *me*.'

'Goodbye.' Tess turned to leave.

'Just what do you think you're going to do, Tess? Make beds and clean toilets again?' Lucile said defiantly.

'I don't know, but I'll find out.'

'What about your dress? Don't you want it in the show?' It was the last arrow in her quiver.

Tess turned back, aware that all eyes were on her, caught by this unprecedented act of self-immolation. 'I don't care,' she said slowly. 'Call it your own, if you wish. Or throw it away.'

'Perhaps I'll get some pillowcases out of it – is that what you want?' Lucile was playing to her audience now, desperately.

'That would be fine.' Tess turned toward the paralyzed workers in the room and smiled. 'Thank you all, you were wonderful to me,' she said, and then marched out of the loft, leaving only silence in her wake.

SENATE OFFICE BUILDING
WASHINGTON, D.C.

William Alden Smith greeted the visitor to his Washington office in the Senate Office Building with weary courtesy.

'My goodness, Senator, you look very down in the mouth,' his visitor said as she walked into the room, filling it with her girth and her hearty voice.

'Hello, Mrs. Brown,' he said. If she was here to once again push her case for going on the stand, he would have to discourage her firmly this time.

'Not having much fun, are you?'

'Of course not, this is a serious matter.'

'You've not had a great run in the British papers, I see.'

'Being called "a born fool" because of my lack of nautical expertise is a weary experience,' he snapped.

Mrs. Brown laughed. 'Oh, come now, Senator. When you asked Officer Lowe if he knew what an iceberg was made of—'

'Yes, yes, I know.' Did she have to repeat it?

'And he said, with a straight face, "Ice," can't you smile a bit at yourself?'

'I am more concerned with serious issues. Do you realise the man who told us there were no binoculars on the ship is being ostracised by all the surviving officers? Nobody will talk to poor Fleet, which is outrageous. He won't come out of his room at the boarding house, not even to eat. I'm worried about him.'

'Quite properly, of course. But you're doing a good job,' Mrs. Brown said, settling herself cheerfully into a chair, not appearing a bit in awe of his quite imposing office. 'It's a thankless one, and you haven't pretended to knowledge of ships or the sea. I like an honest man.'

Mollified, Smith allowed himself a smile. 'I do have trouble remembering which end is the bow and which is the stern,' he admitted. 'But when my investigation is complete there will be a strong, comprehensive body of information for the public to digest.'

'With no one admitting to anything, of course. Isn't that the way of the world?'

'Indeed it is.'

She wiped her forehead with a wrinkled handkerchief. 'My, it's hot in here, I would think politicians wouldn't like the heat too much,' she said absentmindedly. 'You're wondering why I'm here, right? Well I'm not here to persuade you to put me on the stand, if that's worrying you. But I sure could use some help.'

'What about?' he asked, caught off guard.

'That obnoxious couple, the Duff Gordons. Not a very nice pair, I'd say. I think they're out to crush that sailor who testified about their behavior on the lifeboat. You know who I mean, right?'

Smith remembered the sight of Jim Bonney's long legs striding away from the Senate Office Building. 'Yes, I do,' he said.

'Well, I found out from the *Times* reporter, Pinky Wade, that he's about to be caught in a nice little trap they've set up.' She swiftly filled Smith in on the details, then sat back, folding her hands over her ample stomach. 'Can you pull some strings? Get somebody paying attention to what they're trying to do?'

'I don't have much leverage with British officials,' Smith said dryly. 'They seem to think I'm some kind of comic figure.'

'I know that – Lord's sake, the same is true for me. Don't let it get you down. But you have contacts over there; I know you do. A couple of old classmates, I hear? In the House of Commons?'

He wondered how she happened to know this, and peered at her more closely. She must be more keenly intelligent than she appeared.

'All it would take is for somebody to check the records and block any attempt to reactivate a dead charge. Just a little fresh air on what's going on, you know?'

'I will make some inquiries,' he said carefully. 'All I can do is raise interest among the right people and see if they're willing to follow up.'

'Good enough.' She beamed. 'Bonney is a very talented man, you know. An artist. He'll do well here, if he can shake the *Titanic* off his back.'

'I believe that may be true for many of us,' Smith said, feeling his weariness descend again.

'Well, Senator, my feeling is, none of us ever will get free of it all the way.'

'Indeed,' he said with a sigh. 'We go back to New York this afternoon to hear more testimony tomorrow.'

'So I hear. With Lady Duff Gordon as a star witness. Do you think we will learn anything more of the truth in Lifeboat One?'

'I will at least have this beleagured woman on the record, whatever she says.'

'A modest goal, Senator.'

'Mrs. Brown, you may be surprised.'

Lucile threw open the door of the hotel suite just as Cosmo, standing in front of the sideboard, was pouring a glass of bourbon from a crystal flask.

'I'll take one of those,' she said, tossing her handbag onto the sofa. 'I've had a terrible day. That ungrateful girl has quit on me, accusing me of all sorts of things. I never should have brought her here, I can see that now.'

Cosmo poured a second glass and turned, holding it out to her. His gaze was calm and steady. 'For you, dear. You are going to need it.'

'What does that mean?' she said, walking forward and taking the glass.

'I've had the report on what happened today. I thought Tess might make a little noise, but she acted quite rashly. Too bad.'

'What are you saying?' She was holding the glass now, staring at him.

'Can we pass on the indignant part of the scene? You wouldn't have wanted to know, and I'm quite weary of hysterics.'

'Wanted to know *what*?'

'You already know, I think.'

For a moment, there was silence.

'Cosmo, what did you do to me?' Her voice had an authentic quaver.

'I have done nothing *to* you. I have done something *for* you. That sailor will no longer be a threat. I do hope you still understand the difference.' He drained his glass with a quick toss.

'Tess denounced me and quit. I don't quite see how that was beneficial to me.'

'For God's sake, you can do without her. If my plan goes through properly, the British press will have reason to treat us much more kindly. We can't stop what Bonney might say, but we can change how reporters react to him. Think of it as a chess maneuver, Lucy.'

'And he goes to jail?'

'Briefly. Just long enough for public opinion to exonerate us for being victims of a deceitful rabble-rouser.'

'But I have lost Tess.'

'Your substitute daughter, of course. For the one you actually lost.'

In the silence that followed, the mantel clock seemed to tick louder than usual.

'You were not happy about the pregnancy, as I recall.'

'I would have adjusted.'

'Nonsense. A child would have drastically complicated our lives.'

'Let's see. What was it? Respectability and money for you and – let's see, what was there for me? I've forgotten.'

'Don't sneer at me.'

'I'll tell you what I got. The woman I loved. Or so I thought.'

'This is such a tiresome story,' she said, taking off her jacket, turning her face away. 'As for this sailor, you must find another way, Cosmo. I can't tolerate this. Several more clients canceled this afternoon, and I think it's because Tess's tirade is making its way around town. I don't know who will come now.'

'That's a price you may have to pay to stave off a worse disaster back home.'

'Is that all the sympathy I get from you?'

Cosmo slowly poured himself a second shot of bourbon and stood holding it, staring at the glass. 'I'm afraid there's more. I will be with you for your testimony, Lucy. But I'm going back to London tomorrow night.'

She felt her first jolt of fear. 'You're leaving me here alone? Not staying for my show? Whatever is so important that it takes you away at this crucial time?'

'I'll stand by you for the inquiries, here and at home. But that's all I can promise.'

'My God, Cosmo, what are you saying?'

'I believe things have changed for us – quite significantly, I'm afraid,' he said. 'I've enjoyed over the years being the quiet supporter who could make things work for you. But not anymore. It isn't just this caterwauling American press tearing my reputation apart. It's the fact that you see me far more as a servant than as a husband. Just one more obedient follower doing the bidding of the great Lucile.' He looked at her fully for the first time in a long while. 'I've made the mistake of letting you get away with it for too long.'

Lucile swayed, the bourbon sloshing to the rim of her glass, spilling onto the carpet.

'Hold yourself up, dear. I'm not going to grab you.' Once again, he drained his glass. 'You will have to fend for yourself here, I'm afraid. As I said, I will stay by your side through the inquiries. After that, I don't know.'

'You would leave me? *Abandon* me?'

In the long silence that followed, she looked as if she might truly faint.

'I said, I don't know.'

'Then I will be thinking of alternatives myself.'

He smiled faintly. 'That's my Lucy. I like your instinct to fight back, always have.'

'Then you surely aren't serious?'

'Yes, I am. Never more serious about anything in my life.' He nodded toward Lucile's bedroom door. 'Elinor is in your room, waiting for you.'

She turned, white-faced, and walked unsteadily through the parlor to the bedroom door. It opened as she reached out to turn the handle. Elinor, her eyes pitying, stood there, holding out her arms.

The day's light was fading when Pinky heard a sharp knock on the apartment door. Probably a neighbour complaining about the smell of her burned brisket again. Why did she keep overcooking the bloody roast? Too much on her mind, that was why. Braced, she opened the door and found herself staring at Jim Bonney.

'Got some soap and water and a mop?' he said.

'I'm sorry about the smell, I'm just so lazy—'

'Just get me the bucket of soap and water and throw in some bleach.' He patted her on the shoulder, reached behind her, and pulled out a mop leaning against the wall.

'I keep it there because I'm always just about to clean the hall.' Stop apologizing, she told herself as she hurried into the kitchen for Fels-Naptha and water. Within a few minutes, Jim was scrubbing the stairs with ferocious energy.

'You shouldn't be doing this,' she protested.

'What do you think I did on that ship? I'm better at it than you are, I'd say.'

'Not better, just faster.' She bit her lip. There she was, firing off again.

'Suit yourself. Smell anything?'

He was at the bottom of the stairs, leaning on the mop and grinning up at her.

She sniffed. 'No,' she said delightedly. 'Well, just the bleach.'

'Then my job is done.'

She reached out for the bucket and mop and stood aside for him to come in. 'Now you have to stay for dinner,' she said. 'That's my thank-you.'

This time it was Jim who sniffed the air. 'Burned meat, right? Smells delicious. I accept.'

Now, close up, she saw how worn his face looked. This was no social call, much as she wished it was. 'Come join me in the kitchen,' she said.

He sat down heavily, rubbing hands turned red with laundry soap. 'You haven't written anything about this indictment?'

She put a pot of water on to boil and began peeling potatoes. 'I want to see if Mrs. Brown can turn it around. I told Tess.'

'You did? What did she say?'

'She quit. Denounced Lady Duff and walked out.'

Jim went still. 'She quit?'

Pinky glanced at him, long enough to see the astonishment in his eyes. 'She did it for you, nobody else. She has nothing to gain, and that's the truth.'

He dropped his head, then lifted it quickly. 'She shouldn't have done that. I don't need empty gestures.'

'Gestures?' Pinky turned fully to him, astonished. 'That's no *gesture,* that's a genuine *protest,* and you should know it better than anyone.'

'I'm grateful. But Tess is giving up what she loves; I don't want her to do that. And it isn't going to change anything. That's done, over with.'

'I'm sorry, but you don't sound as if you believe a word you're saying.'

'I have to make it true,' he said quietly.

'Just get this straight. She sacrificed hugely for you today.'

'She's in love with someone else. That's the fact of it.'

Why was she working so hard at this? It was her big mouth again. 'Maybe you think that, but you don't know for sure.'

He lifted his head. 'What an optimist,' he said with the shadow of a grin.

'I fake it pretty well. Are you braced for Lady Duff's testimony tomorrow?'

'She'll say what she wants to believe.'

'With plenty of theater thrown in.'

He laughed, then looked around the kitchen. 'Look, can I help? Put together a plate for your father? Better get that brisket out of the oven.'

'Oh, yes, I'm forgetting it again.' She opened the oven door and pulled out the roasting pan, her face flushing from the heat. He wasn't asking her to be his advocate with Tess. No hints about carrying messages. Had he really given up? She didn't believe it.

Dinner this time was in a restaurant with walls that glowed like a fine glass of Burgundy. Tess could only pick at her food – richly marbled roast beef, currants whipped into a soft cheese soufflé – unable to muster the energy to eat, not even such fare as was before her. She listened distractedly to Jack, barely hearing him.

He threw down his napkin. 'You've got only one thing on your mind right now,' he said, and then fell silent.

Tess barely heard him. 'I kept defending her. What was wrong with me? I should have realised that everything had to be done her way. I did what I had said I would never do again. I kept my head down, tried to please—' She put her fork down; it was no use. Again, she could hear her father's voice. Yes, she had been a foolish girl, but not by doing what he warned against. She had been foolish *not* to speak up, *not* to step forward.

'You are here with me now. You've left Lucile. Isn't that enough?'

With effort, she shifted attention. 'No, not while Jim is in trouble.'

'He isn't caught in their trap yet. Who's working on it?'

'Mrs. Brown, from the ship; she spotted his talent in carving and is starting him in business here.'

'Ah yes, Mrs. Brown. The indomitable, unsinkable Margaret.' He smiled. 'We've had some business dealings over the years. Quite a formidible woman, and she knows how to pull strings. So you've quit in protest. Now what?'

She could hear the clock ticking behind her. 'I don't know. I know what you're asking me, but I just don't know yet.'

'A sensible response. In many ways, I'm a stranger to you.' He sat back in his chair, gazing at her thoughtfully. 'I'm asking too much, I'm afraid.'

She straightened up in her chair. 'Then tell me who you are.'

'The product of a fairly predictable life with more privileges than most, but I earned them myself. A slow learner, which probably explains two divorces.' A silence fell between them. 'Not enough?' Ruefully, he touched his sideburns. 'Turning gray,' he said. 'I'm sensitive about that. Does that help?'

'A little.'

'Well, you don't seem to have as much hesitation over your bond to that sailor. And how long have you known *him*?'

'That's different,' she said, startled.

His face clouded. 'Maybe you love him, Tess. Maybe that's what's holding you back.'

He looked so profoundly sad, she couldn't sit still. Silently, she pushed the table aside and moved close, her arms encircling him. He had a right to know where he stood.

'Please give me time,' she whispered. He cradled her head with one hand, and they both held on.

Chapter 15

'I'm ready.' Lucile stood in the bedroom doorway, dressed all in black, surveying her face in the boudoir mirror. 'Do I need more powder?'

'You're fine,' Elinor replied. 'Cosmo said to make sure you review those briefing papers before we go downstairs.'

'I don't need them,' Lucile said with a faint echo of her usual haughty manner. 'And why isn't Cosmo here to tell me that himself? He's a coward, that's what he is—'

'Stop it, Lucy, he's not a coward. This is going to ruin him, and you know it. They're already making "doing a Duff-Gordon" slang for bribery back home.' Elinor's face was almost as pale as her sister's.

Lucile said nothing at first, pulling a white lace handkerchief from her glove and dabbing her eyes. 'We've both been maligned, and I'll not let them get away with it. And Cosmo won't leave me; it would only deepen the scandal.' She looked directly at her sister. 'I'm right, aren't I?'

Elinor forced a smile. 'I hope so.'

Again, a silence.

'We need to go downstairs soon.'

Lucile sighed. 'Is the white handkerchief against the black dramatic enough? Or should I wear a white lace collar, too?'

'Save the collar for London.'

'I can handle this just fine, Elinor, stop looking at me that way.'

Elinor, for once, was neither jaunty nor flippant. 'Of course. And I will do my best to pick up the pieces.'

The East Room was filling rapidly. Pinky stood near the back of the room, scanning faces so intently that she didn't see Jim making his way toward her through the crowd until he touched her shoulder. His cheeks were high with colour and he was smiling.

'What are you doing here?' she said, drawing him to a corner. 'You'll be swarmed by reporters, if they see you.'

'I had to take that chance. I have news,' he said. 'That indictment? Withdrawn this morning. Don't know why, don't know how, but it's dead.'

Pinky slapped her pencil against her notebook triumphantly. 'I knew it! I knew Mrs. Brown would find a way to set this right. How did she do it?'

'She didn't. She told me this morning neither she nor Senator Smith could get any help from the British government.'

'So what happened?'

'I don't know. Neither does she. A mystery – how about that? But now I don't have to go back to England and prove I'm not a criminal. That might not be what most people think is good news, but it sure is mine. I probably won't even be subpoenaed now for the inquiry, since I've got a job here.'

A man, mopping his brow vigorously in the intensifying heat of the crowded room, shouldered past them, mumbling something about the impossibility of finding a seat. Angry shouts were coming from the doorway; once again, people who wanted in were having trouble pushing into the room.

'Thanks for the brisket,' he said soberly. 'And for being on my side.'

And then he was gone, leaving her to stand there wondering what had happened to her journalistic objectivity. Because he was right.

No, he wasn't gone. He had stopped still as a woman approached him, and now they were facing each other, inches apart. It was Tess, and Pinky drew in her breath. What was *she* doing here, after quitting yesterday? Were they both crazy?

Jim appeared so quickly that Tess had no chance to prepare herself. He looked different somehow. He was dressed in new clothes, a crisp shirt and sweater, but that wasn't it. No, there was more – a different kind of energy to him, a focus. She felt suddenly awkward.

'Hello, Tess.' His smile was bright but carefully impersonal, his manner calm. He didn't look flustered at all. 'I hear you quit your job with Lady Duff.'

Tess nodded, not trusting her voice.

'You didn't need to do that, not for me. It was your big opportunity, and I don't want that to be lost to you.'

'She wanted to damage you, and I had to fight back.'

'So when she went right ahead—'

'I had to quit. You mean more to me than the job,' she said simply.

His steady gaze faltered. Behind them, the grandfather clock in the Waldorf's lobby began to strike the hour, heavily and ponderously. She counted. It took him eight strokes before he responded.

'I don't understand. Not given what changed between us.'

'It was the only thing I could do. My only power.' She laced her fingers together, pressing them tightly in front of her.

He looked at her, both baffled and cautious. 'Explain, please. Why, for me?'

She wavered. If she could only reach down inside herself and pull out the right words. If she could yank them forth, cup her hands around them, offer them – what were they? She thought of Jack. His steadiness, his confidence. And then the moment passed, lost somewhere in the seconds marked by the ticking clock.

He shrugged. 'I guess you don't know why. Punishing yourself like that for a village boy was probably a bad move.'

She turned her head away. 'Jim, please.'

'I'm sorry, Tess. That was petty of me. It just came out, I guess.'

'You're angry.'

'Because you tossed me over?' He shrugged and shoved his hands in his pockets with a touch of swagger. 'Yes, I guess I am. But I don't want you hurt.'

'Jim, I'm so sorry, I want us—'

The sad, steady look he gave her silenced her. They both stood for a moment, neither able now to find any words, let alone the right ones. Then Jim nodded toward the rapidly filling rows of chairs. 'Better grab yourself a seat before they're all gone. I assume you're not here to offer Lady Duff your moral support?'

'No.' She had found her voice. 'I saw you.'

This time he was the one who hesitated before speaking. 'Tess, the indictment was withdrawn this morning. I'm clear to stay.'

'Oh, my goodness, what wonderful news,' she gasped. Her hands flew to her mouth. 'I am so relieved, so glad. Who did it? Was it Mrs. Brown?'

'No, it wasn't. I don't know how it happened, but it did.' He smiled, differently this time. There was a glint of something in his eyes, but he blinked it away, then turned to make his way through the crowd and out the door.

By ten o'clock, the East Room and lobby were jammed with people packed together more tightly than ever. Tess tried to make her way out of the crowd, planning to listen from the doorway, but she couldn't move. She sank into the only seat left, near Pinky, as Senator Smith banged his gavel once again.

'Our first witness this morning will be Lady Lucile Duff Gordon,' he announced. 'Please make way for the witness to move forward.'

And, in almost eerie obedience, the crowd parted.

Lucile walked slowly through the opening space to the front of the room, a tiny figure all in black, wearing a large black hat with a veil covering her eyes. In one hand she clutched a snowy white handkerchief. The room went almost completely still as she settled into the witness chair.

Senator Smith glanced at his fellow committee members a bit uneasily. This was no frightened, illiterate crewman. And all Britain would be ready to pounce if he didn't handle it right.

'Lady Duff Gordon, tell us about how you and your husband came to be in Lifeboat One. Let's start there,' he said.

'Of course, Senator,' she said with calm hauteur. 'I had quite made up my mind that we would be drowned, and then suddenly we saw this little boat in front of us – a tiny thing – and I said to my husband, "Ought we not to be doing something?" My husband asked if we might get into that boat, and the officer said in a very polite way indeed, "Oh, certainly, do; I will be very pleased. And then we were helped in."'

Tess glanced at Pinky, who raised an eyebrow. What sort of singsong manner was this?

The questions continued, becoming less general; Lucile went on answering in a strong, haughty voice, painting an almost ludicrous picture of politeness and gentility in Lifeboat One, dabbing periodically at her eyes with the handkerchief.

'Now I must ask you, after the *Titanic* sank did you hear the cries of the people who were drowning?'

'No, after the *Titanic* sank, I never heard a cry.'

'You did not hear any cries at all?' Smith asked, incredulous.

She looked at him, matching his own tone of incredulity. 'Wouldn't I know, Senator? My impression was there was absolute silence.'

It was said with such serene certitude that the room exuded hushed awe. A good performance deserved appreciation. Everyone knew it wasn't true, but this small woman on the stand was, by the strength of her will, determined to make it true.

'Did you hear anybody shout out in the boat that you ought to go back, with the object of saving people?'

'No.'

'You knew there were people in the water, did you not?'

'No, I don't think I was thinking anything about it.'

'Did you say it would be dangerous to go back, that you might get swamped?'

'Heavens, no.'

Senator Smith held up a copy of the *Sunday American* with Lucile's interview. 'You speak in this interview of hearing agonizing pleadings for help. Which is it, madam?'

She never hesitated. 'That so-called interview is a total invention,' she said. 'A disgusting journalistic invention.'

Tess could hardly sit still. Was she really saying all this?

'And what about the rumors that your husband paid off the crew members so they would not go back to help the dying?'

'He can speak for himself, of course. But all he offered was a little help for them to get started again.' Her voice was becoming more brisk and impatient.

'Your testimony quite drastically differs from that of the seaman Jim Bonney.'

'Well, of course it does. He is a menace, as far as I am concerned. And, if I may say so, a liar.'

Tess found herself rising to her feet, staring at Lucile, oblivious of the eyes now turning in her direction.

'I assumed that's what you thought,' another committee member murmured. 'But we need you on the record. What do you have to say to his charge that people were pushed away from Lifeboat One? That some were close enough to be pulled into your almost empty boat?'

'Total nonsense.'

Tess could stand no more. She began pushing her way out of the room, not caring who watched or who knew her identity. But she felt Lucile's eyes following her. It struck her that one always knew when Lucile was watching.

Lucile turned to Smith, her voice wobbling slightly. 'How much more of this, Senator? I really am a busy woman.'

'Madam, we are dealing with life and death here,' Smith retorted. 'Your lack of patience is disturbing.'

'I'm sorry I do not meet your expectations. May I go now?'

The panel was silent; the room was silent.

'You are dismissed,' Smith finally said. 'But' – he raised a hand as the crowd began to stir – 'after a short break, we have another witness this morning.' He paused for added effect, then said, 'Mrs. Jordan Darling, who was also on Lifeboat One.'

Lucile's hat slipped, her startled eyes suddenly visible. She gripped the edges of her chair, stumbling slightly as she rose. A lively murmur immediately swept the room. The widow, yes, the widow of the man who disguised himself as a woman and then, publicly exposed, committed suicide. Can you believe it? Why would she want to face the public after her husband's cowardly behavior?

Pinky was already squeezing her way through the crowd, trying to reach Tess. But Elinor reached her first.

'I must talk to you this afternoon,' she said. 'Truly, it's urgent.'

'About *what*?' Tess replied angrily. 'About your sister's lies?'

'I've not lied to you, Tess. I'm saying talk to me. Please.'

Tess took a deep breath, replying just as Pinky, breathless, reached her side. 'I'll decide after I hear what Jean Darling has to say.'

Senator Smith was quite pleased with himself as he surveyed the crowded room. Lady Duff Gordon had made a mistake if she thought her arrogance would win the day in an American inquiry. No one could accuse him of having hog-tied a member of the British upper class; the silly woman did it to herself. *Entitlement,* that was the right word. He would be glad to be done with the lot of them.

'Our next witness is not here under subpoena,' he began. 'She has specifically asked for this opportunity to put on the record a few thoughts on the frailty of human character in the face of tragedy.' He stared out across the quiet room, relishing the reaction to his modest note of suspense.

'Will Mrs. Jordan Darling please take the stand?'

Tess swiveled in her seat, watching the graceful, lithe figure of Jean Darling as she threaded her way through the clutter of chairs to the front of the room. She wore a gray jacket and skirt, with a string of tiny pearls at her throat. She held her head high. The lights from above glittered off her impeccably arranged hair, which was now almost pure white. A flash of memory took Tess back to the moment when she saw the Darlings dance, all poise and lightness, onto the *Titanic.* A delicious, airy moment filled with ripples of delighted laughter and applause. Gone forever.

'It is not necessary for you to offer testimony,' Senator Smith began. Would she break down? You never knew with women, and the more genteel they were, the less predictable. 'I want to emphasise that your appearance here is purely voluntary, at your request. I want that noted for the record. Is that correct?'

'Yes, Senator.'

'We are all aware of your husband's unfortunate demise, and I wish to offer my condolences.'

'Thank you.'

'Can you tell us why you wished to come here today?'

Jean Darling appeared quite calm as she gazed out at the room. Her demeanor was serene – that of a woman who had asked to do this and was not going to indulge in qualms now. Even if it meant being burned again in the ferocious gaze of the newspapers or subjected to more jeers and derision.

'I am in awe of the stories of bravery I've heard during these hearings,' she began. 'The man who took off his life belt and put it on his wife's maid? I know my husband would have wanted to be that man.' She paused, the crispness of her usual ladylike tone softening. 'But I must tell you, only part of me regrets that he wasn't. Another part would still snatch a cloth from a table and throw it around his shoulders, anything to save his life. Even though' – her voice was shaking now – 'I as much as killed him with that gesture. I will be haunted all my life by three things: the fact that I did not let my husband die the way he would have preferred, and the fact that it did not occur to me to join him. The third, and worst, is that perhaps the lives of two children could have been saved by our both standing back.'

Tess closed her eyes, brought back again to the shrieking cacophony of breaking glass, grand pianos tipping into the sea, beds, chamber pots, luggage, people clawing up the deck as the ship sank. Acts of bravery, accusations, stupid behavior – it was all in this room.

'You don't have to do this, Mrs. Darling,' Senator Smith interrupted gently.

'Yes, I do. I won't be long, Senator.' She opened her small handbag and drew forth a white linen handkerchief.

'I thought at first that speaking out would help clear my conscience, but that won't ever happen. I've given that idea up,' she said, clutching the handkerchief tightly. 'What I believe now is that accepting the reality of my decision is what is important. I can't forgive my actions, or the actions of another. The rashness of a moment changed my life and my husband's, and there were probably other quick decisions that changed the lives of other people on that ship. When my husband died, I wanted to place blame. I wanted to *avoid* blame. Not anymore. I want to acknowledge that my character was not strong enough to be brave, and if any others secretly feel the same please know you are not alone. I only hope that, if tested again, I would be up to the task.'

The room was preternaturally still. Tess could hear the breathing of people sitting in the row of chairs nearest to her. If they didn't want to understand, it didn't matter. Jean Darling had pointed plain and clear to the sad heart of it all. She had done it, alone.

'Is there more you want to say, Mrs. Darling?'

She straightened her back. 'I thought not, when I asked to come, Senator. But I have changed my mind.'

The room stirred.

'What would you like to tell us?'

'It is in reference to Lady Duff Gordon's testimony.' She drew a ragged breath. 'There were opportunities to be brave in that lifeboat that were not taken. We had room, we had plenty of room. But we were all driven by fear. No, that's wrong.'

'What do you mean, Mrs. Darling?'

'There was one brave man, and anybody in that boat who denies it is still driven by fear.'

So at least some pieces of this sad puzzle were going to fit together, Senator Smith told himself. 'And who was that?' he asked.

'Jim Bonney. And *that* is reality. I'm finished, Senator.'

'Just one moment.' Senator Bolton's raspy voice cut in, sending a ripple of surprise through the room. 'You are not an official witness, madam, and you can refuse to answer. But, given the charges and countercharges about what happened on Lifeboat One, I wonder if you can fill in some of the gaps. Were people trying to get in your boat? Was anyone pushed off? What did you see, exactly?'

Mrs. Darling sat back, a startled look on her face. But when she spoke her voice was composed. 'People were calling to us from the water. I saw one man grab the side of the lifeboat to pull himself in.'

'What happened then?'

'I heard a scream, a woman's scream. I saw a man stand up, holding an oar above his head. Mr. Bonney swore and stood up, wrestling with the man who raised the oar, and got it away from him.'

'Why was it raised?'

'To knock that poor soul off the boat.'

A tingling sensation spread across Tess's head and neck, as hot as fire, even as her hands turned to ice. Hardly a breath was drawn in the crowded room. This was the truth of what happened in Lifeboat One.

Senator Smith stirred uneasily. This was more than he had bargained for. If he asked now who that person was who raised the oar, he would lose control of these hearings. It would, quite possibly, be seen as the final straw by the British, who were already convinced that he was on a witch hunt.

'Do you have more to say?'

A long silence. 'No,' Mrs. Darling said. 'It's over.'

'Thank you, you may step down.' Senator Smith looked out over the array of quiet, stunned faces before him. 'Please allow Mrs. Darling to leave before we clear the room.'

Pinky joined Tess, and together they walked out with the almost silent crowd.

'Look,' Pinky said, nodding in the direction of a woman standing, unrecognised, by the open door.

It was Lucile. She had removed her lipstick. Her face was still, lips fading into pale skin, and the black hat had been discarded in favor of a scarf. Without her usual colour, she looked like a bird that had been stripped of its plumage – so much so that no one seemed to recognise her. She was suddenly, surprisingly, impossibly small.

Not a word was exchanged as they walked by.

Outside, Tess said quietly to Pinky, 'I have to leave now. I have to go pack my things.'

The walk home was peaceful. She felt the warmth of the late-afternoon sun on her neck and took off her hat to lift her face to its rays, taken fleetingly back to the moment that she and Jim stood over the bodies of the mother and baby on the *Carpathia*. I turn my face to the rising sun; O Lord, have mercy.

All the losses. Left with a lifetime of shame and dishonor, Jean Darling had mustered the courage to acknowledge her mistakes, a voluntary action that would be foreign to Lucile. She would never break out of the silky cocoon she had woven for herself. She would most likely rather march grandly over a cliff.

A hoarse shout to look where she was going as a driver clattered by. Tess stepped quickly back from the curb.

It was over, this particular dream. But the Duff Gordons had been stopped from ruining Jim's life, and that was all that mattered. So she walked now on the streets of New York, once again just a servant girl from Cherbourg without a job. That mattered, too. But not as much. And why did she feel a strange serenity about it all?

'My goodness, Tess, you *are* in a fog. You were ready to walk right by me,' a voice said with light amusement.

'Elinor,' Tess said in surprise. Lucile's sister stood on the street corner, her always present parasol – a green one, this time – shading her eyes from both the sun and the glances of passersby.

Elinor gestured toward a waiting car, which Tess hadn't noticed.

'Have you decided to talk to me?'

'I know you'll want me out of the flat very soon, and if you could give me a week more I would appreciate it. I will repay you for your kindness.'

'Oh, for God's sake, Tess, get in the car.'

'Why? What do you want from me?'

Elinor thrust a copy of the *New York World* toward Tess, her light manner evaporated. 'This afternoon's paper, a little late with the story, but it will be read with some relish around town. If you will just read the headline, please?'

Tess took the paper and held it with both hands, a faint wind rippling the pages. She squinted and read, 'Lady Duff Gordon's "Loyal" Secretary Abandons Ship.'

'Not the front page, mind you. But just wait until tomorrow. I can imagine the headlines now: "Secretary Walks Out During Lady Duff Gordon Testimony." Things like that. Did you plan it? No, I thought not.'

'Here's the headline, Elinor: "Brave Sailor Vindicated of Vicious Duff Gordon Charges." Do you really want to play this game?'

Elinor sighed. 'They're all nails in Lucile's coffin, my dear. Especially, if you recall, since the spring show is tomorrow. Please talk to me.'

Tess folded the paper and stepped into the car, with Elinor following. A fleeting thought occurred: for the first time in her life, she had been referred to as a 'secretary.' Not as a maid.

Elinor rapped on the window that separated the passengers from the driver. 'Just drive around, Farley,' she commanded. 'Anywhere. Show us some of the sights of New York.' She settled back into her seat, turned to Tess, and wasted no time.

'Cosmo is leaving her. Heading back for London. And over half the reservations for her show have been canceled. She's slipping, Tess.'

'Cosmo is leaving?' Tess couldn't believe it.

'She ordered him around one time too many, I'm afraid. That last fight over the sailor cracked things open.'

Tess just stared, puzzled.

'Oh, of course, you don't know about that. God, I need a cigarette. Do you mind?'

Tess shook her head, waiting.

A match flared, and Elinor's meticulously manicured fingers touched it to the end of her cigarette. She inhaled deeply. 'That's better,' she said, sighing.

'Will you explain, please?'

'You put on quite a show, denouncing her. But Lucile wasn't the one trying to get your sailor friend arrested. It was all Cosmo's idea.'

'Without her knowledge – is that what you're saying? How could that be?'

'Oh, my dear, you really don't know how things work in our world, do you? Cosmo is in charge, always has been. There have been a few unfortunate financial setbacks for Lucile's competitors over the years – nothing that could be tied to him, of course, but he has been devoted to paving the way for her. That's what he was doing this time.'

Tess covered her mouth with one hand, staring straight ahead. 'I was wrong?'

'Don't overreact,' Elinor said airily. 'Remember, Lucy doesn't want to know the mechanics of how Cosmo gets things done, which isn't quite the same as being totally innocent. You understand that, don't you?'

'Yes, I do. And after what she had to say today, don't even *think* of asking me to go back.'

Elinor seemed to crumple, the air and lightness disappearing. 'I know, I know. She is so stubborn and wrong, and if she loses her business *and* Cosmo, I fear for her. Everything that's been building up has finally culminated. A rich man can open up the world for you, but he can also close it down. Lucile forgot that, I'm afraid.'

Tess could not hold back what was probably a useless, naïve question. 'She's done such arrogant things. But you are her sister. Do you still love her?'

'Love?' Elinor inhaled, then exhaled a slow spiral of smoke before answering. 'I'm not sure what that means. People talk a lot about love, and most of it is rubbish. My sister and I are bonded, and always will be. We're a pair, and we understand each other. If life doesn't offer happy endings, we know how to manufacture them.'

'What do you mean?'

'I've rewritten my life more than once, you know. And Lucy does the same thing, only with fabric. Romantic, ephemeral clothes that create fantasy – what a lovely way to float through life. But one has to be quick to change direction in order to make it work. She isn't quick.' Elinor paused, then added quietly, 'Do I love her? Yes.'

The two women sat in silence as Farley swung around a corner and drove past Union Square. Tess stared out the window, recognizing the path where she and Jim had walked when she told him about Jack. Just one more hole in her heart that wouldn't heal.

'What do you want me to do?'

'Just show up for the show. Let the reporters know that the "secretary" changed her mind and stayed loyal.'

'I'm not going back, Elinor. I can't. I may owe Lucile an apology for accusing her of trying to get Jim arrested, but I can't work for her anymore.'

'Just for the one day. Please. Don't forget, your sailor got out of that trap.'

'How did you know that?'

'Tess, I make a point of knowing *everything*.'

Jean Darling's words swam through Tess's head, not quite absorbed yet, looking for a place. Not forgiving, not excusing. This wasn't about forgiving; it was about accepting what couldn't be changed. Offering a helping hand from the lifeboat, perhaps, futile as it might be for both of them.

Did she want Lucile to fail? Yes. She deserved it. No. It would ruin her life and those of the people who worked for her. One last gesture; maybe it would teach Lucile something. She would move forward from that.

'She'll probably throw me out,' she said.

Elinor smiled. 'Maybe – thanks for taking the risk. But my bet is you'll save her from full humiliation. By the way, I'm paying the rent on your flat until you're able to do it yourself.'

'Is that supposed to be a bribe? You saved it for last.' She realised once again that she still liked Elinor.

'I don't do bribes, dear. A waste of time.'

Pinky sat on the edge of her father's bed, stirring a cup of tepid soup, waiting for him to wake up so she could coax a little food into him. Bad days, good days. This – according to the always complaining Mrs. Dotson – had been a bad day. She wished he would be up for talking tonight. She needed to talk to someone. Lady Duff's testimony was ludicrous, but it was Jean Darling who made it a smashingly good story. And how did that indictment get dropped? Maybe Jim didn't care, but she did. And what happened when Jim and Tess confronted each other? She dipped a finger delicately into the bowl of soup and tasted it. Chicken broth with carrots, his favorite, but it was getting cold. Why did she feel so weary?

'So here you sit, moping over cold soup.'

She jumped. Prescott Wade was awake, a remnant of his familiar grin on his face.

'I'll heat it up,' she said,

'Don't bother, I'm not hungry anyway.'

'You have to eat.'

'So what happened today?'

She told him about the hearing – about Lucile, about Jim. He was actually listening, unlike those many evenings when he drifted away and she ended up talking to herself. She hated that feeling of being in an echo chamber.

'Whoever got that indictment quashed knew what they were doing,' he said, breaking into her recounting. 'Maybe somebody worried about what Tess would do. Lucile's sister, the Hollywood gal?'

'Elinor? I don't think so. She's in a different kind of world.'

'Who did Tess dump the sailor for?'

She started. He must have heard Jim telling her what happened. 'I don't know.'

'Has to be someone connected with the hearings or the dress shop. She hasn't been here long enough to meet anyone else.'

She sighed, and put the bowl of cold soup down on the table next to her father's bed. 'I don't know why I care,' she said.

'Work and your feelings are getting all mixed up, aren't they, kid?'

She nodded numbly.

'Well, it's not a crime to lose objectivity, even in our business. Who matters more to you, Sarah? Jim or Tess? It sounds complicated, and you may have to choose.'

His voice was stronger than she expected – and so was her answer. 'They're both my friends,' she said.

He knew when to stop talking. The two of them sat in silence until Pinky groped for a handkerchief in her skirt pocket and blew her nose with vigor.

'You're shaking the bed,' he said, and chuckled.

She flashed him a grin and tucked the handkerchief back into her pocket. 'I'll go fix us both a decent dinner,' she said, getting up.

'You know what I think?' he said as she started to leave the room. 'I think I see your future, Sarah. It's a good one. A happy one.'

'What do you see?'

'You're going to put on your hat and travel the world. You're going to dance across the moon. I'll bet on it.' His face crinkled into a smile.

'I don't want you gone,' she whispered.

'I know, kid. I love you, too.' His smile broadened. 'By the way, I have a hunch about who killed that indictment.'

'You do?' Startled, Pinky almost dropped the bowl of soup. 'Who?'

'You're a good reporter. You figure it out.'

Chapter 16

Tess paced the floor of her flat, counting the steps back and forth. Anything to pass the time. Lucile's show would begin with high tea at two in the afternoon, a little early for teatime, but in America it apparently didn't matter. She would show up just before the show began, and who knew how Lucile would react? Was she crazy to have agreed to this?

She stopped pacing and briefly closed her eyes, thinking of what was now going on in that magical loft. The lighting was being adjusted, the curtains arranged, the programs – she had seen the design, and it was quite striking – were being arranged at the door. The music stands – for Lucile's favorite string quartet – were being set up next to the catwalk. All of this, now, today, farther away from her than ever before.

Slowly she looked around her small room, memorizing its contours. Goodbye to all this, and don't waste time feeling sorry for yourself – ups and downs and all that. And there would be work; she would design and stitch and do what she did best. She would be afraid, but she could do it. She sat down on that thought and stared out the window, willing herself to look beyond the obvious: to see what was hidden in the trees, behind the buildings; the small markers of what came next, discreetly etched. Look for them.

'Move, move, everybody move!' Lucile clapped her hands, surveying the frenetic activity in her loft, now magically transformed to the House of Lucile, caught up in the last-minute frenzy of preparation, giddy with pleasure.

'The gowns are *spectacular,*' Elinor murmured as her eye took in the scene.

'Indeed, they are. The mannequins, of course, are American – not quite up to British standards but reasonably sophisticated all the same,' Lucile said. 'If they only had the discipline to walk for two hours each morning with books balanced on their heads, they would have decent posture, but no, Americans like to slouch.' She rolled her eyes, then clapped her hands. At her order, each model obediently strolled the runway, taking a practice turn for Lucile's inspection. Good, lips were rouged properly, hair arranged the way she wanted – then she frowned.

'What happened to the boutonniere I wanted on that girdle?' she demanded of one of the mannequins.

'The flowers were soiled, Madame,' the girl answered nervously. 'I took them off.'

Lucile impaled her on an icy stare. 'Then why didn't you speak up so new flowers could be made? I fear you have no brains in your head. Just feathers.'

Elinor tapped her sister on the arm. 'Not worth a scene,' she said. 'You don't want a mannequin crying.'

Lucile turned away with a dismissive exclamation, stalking over to the tea tray and picking up each cup for inspection. 'These are not clean,' she announced loudly.

'They are, Madame. I think you're seeing a slight discolouration,' said James quickly. 'But we'll have them rewashed immediately.'

Lucile returned to her sister, pulling her to a corner of the room. 'Is Mary Pickford coming?' she asked in a low voice.

'She promised, for what that's worth,' Elinor replied. 'She might want something modern—'

'*Why,* for heaven's sake? What is wrong with these actresses? Don't they understand that they look sensual and beautiful in my gowns? Hollywood is so vulgar. Really, Elinor, I don't know how you can live and work there.'

Elinor smiled a bit tightly. 'It pays, dear sister. And a vulgar movie star who doesn't bother reading the newspapers is just what you need today.'

Lucile deflated instantly, as limp and flat as a punctured balloon.

'I know, I know – I'm just being cruel.' Even Elinor couldn't bring up the absence of Cosmo's comforting, supportive presence.

'Is it going to be a disaster?' Lucile asked.

'Not with a little bit of luck.' There was no use telling Lucile of the dozens of last-minute invitations hand-delivered last night to second-tier members of New York society. Lucile would scorn many of them, but that was a problem for later. All she needed to do was fill the damn room.

Lucile lifted her chin high. 'I will see it through with dignity.'

Elinor patted her arm. 'Said with a minimum of drama, dear. I'll be here, whatever happens. Remember, no tears. You can't risk swollen eyes today. Not pretty.'

The sun was high when Tess left her room and walked out to the street to make her way to 160 Fifth Avenue. She would walk slowly and wait within a few yards of Lucile's studio until the clients had arrived. Recognition was not a problem; she was just a name in the papers, no more than that.

'Tess? What are you doing here?'

She turned to see Pinky's astonished face. 'Showing up one last time,' she said as calmly as she could.

Pinky's eyes widened. 'After quitting? You're backing out of that?'

'No.' How to explain? 'I'm not going to stomp on her. She has too much at stake today.'

Pinky looked genuinely baffled. 'This is a cruel woman who was ready to ruin Jim. And you're going to support her today?'

'She wasn't the one doing that; it was Cosmo. I'm not here to defend her.' Tess wanted Pinky to understand. 'I'm paying back a debt, in the only way I can. She brought me here.'

'Pretty expensive passage, I'd say.'

Tess tried to smile. 'I agree. But remember what Jean Darling said? Pinky, don't always be a reporter.'

'I'm not, that's part of my trouble,' Pinky said with a sudden wistful smile. 'Tess, I've got news, too. The *World* offered me a job. More money.'

'That's wonderful. Aren't you happy?'

'Not really. It's a rag. Well, at least compared to the *Times*.'

'But—'

'I know. I don't have much choice.'

'Are you sure?'

Pinky was too surprised to answer. They stood together in silence, watching as the first black town car rolled up in front of the House of Lucile. It was half past one o'clock.

'How many? Maybe I've miscounted.' Tess hoped she had.

'Ten cars, fifteen women. Plus a few reporters I know, all ready to write about the death of the House of Lucile. How many was she expecting?'

'Over fifty. Please don't rub your hands in glee.'

'Look, I hate her pretensions, but I saw how defeated she looked yesterday. I'm not completely hardened, you know.'

'Who is that?' Tess pointed at a woman emerging from one of the automobiles. 'She's beautiful.'

Pinky followed her gaze to a carefully dressed woman wrapped in a feathery silk coat. 'That's Jack Bremerton's *first* ex-wife – big scandal when he divorced her,' she said. The statuesque Mrs. Bremerton stood, immobile and queenly, waiting for the doorman to open the door of the building.

Pinky turned and saw the bright flush spreading across Tess's face as she stared at the woman. 'Tess?'

Slowly, Tess transferred her gaze back to Pinky. 'Sorry, I wasn't paying attention,' she said.

More cars were drawing to the curb. A sudden flurry of aides tumbled from them, bowing and murmuring obsequiously, holding out their hands to assist the brightly lipsticked women emerging like gauzy puffs of colour from their limousines.

'The stars have arrived,' Pinky said, pulling out her notebook. 'I've got to get over there. See you inside.'

'Who is it?'

'First one is Pickford. Second one is Duncan, the one with the scarf.'

'I didn't think they would come.'

Pinky gave her a slightly exasperated look. 'With all these reporters here, why wouldn't they show up? What actress wouldn't?' And she was gone, hurrying toward the door as the silver heels of a tiny Mary Pickford disappeared inside.

Tess prepared to enter herself as three more cars drew up and stopped. Several women emerged from each car, straightening hats and tugging at their wraps, then stood somewhat awkwardly on the sidewalk as if awaiting orders.

Just then Elinor emerged from the building, nodded briskly, and ushered them in, whispering instructions. She glanced up, saw Tess, and nodded in the direction of the women.

'Shopgirls hired to fill the room. Are you coming?' she asked with a smile.

Tess nodded, marveling at Elinor's resourcefulness. She would do anything to get her sister through this. And if agreeing to show up was some sort of trap for Tess, it was too late to back out now.

The loft was transformed. Even though she had been part of the preparations, Tess felt swept away by the elegant results. The chiffon-draped stage was lit from beneath by hidden spotlights that cast a glow as soft as candlelight. It was all dazzling and magical, just as she had known it would be. To the side, partly hidden, Lucile's musicians were playing something beautiful. She wished she knew what it was. There was so much to learn.

James and a couple of aides were quietly removing the two back rows of chairs, the noise masked by the music. Servants in black dresses and crisp, white linen aprons were serving tea, while reporters, including Pinky, stood along the walls, relegated to the sidelines.

Lucile, dressed in a plum-coloured Grecian tunic, her brilliant red hair piled high and a queenly smile on her face, was greeting each guest with just the right combination of warmth and hauteur. Watching her, Tess realised that she was seeing the full magical creation of 'Madame Lucile' for the first time.

James spied her, his eyes widening in shock. It occurred

to Tess that he might think she was here to cause a disruption. And she might, without intending to, if Lucile, the ever-mercurial Lucile, spotted her and ordered her to leave. She could only hope Elinor was right – that the one thing Lucile craved today was to avoid humiliation.

The musicians paused as Lucile mounted the stage, a spotlight on her determinedly calm face. 'My dear friends, you are about to see an *extraordinary* collection; I would venture that it is the best of my career. I am sure you will all agree.' She nodded slightly to a secretary holding the all-important order book. Tess knew the message: the secretary was to watch reactions to each gown. After the show, she would quietly approach clients whose interest seemed most likely to translate into a purchase. Very discreetly, of course.

Elinor, sitting near the front, glanced back at Tess, raising a questioning eyebrow. But Tess couldn't get her legs to move.

'And now—' Lucile lifted her arm, palm up, facing the catwalk. 'The first piece in the 1912 spring collection of the House of Lucile! I call this gown, my dear friends, the Sighing Sound of Lips Unsatisfied. Listen to the whispers of the chiffon as it moves, and you will know why it is so named.'

A murmur spread among the reporters, punctuated by a titter, but Lucile's guests clapped politely as a mannequin swathed in powder blue strolled out of the shadows, turned slowly to reveal the gown, and then vanished from the stage.

'Next is this lovely tea gown, quite appropriately named a Frenzied Song of Amorous Things,' Lucile announced as another mannequin in a shimmery mixture of tulle and brocade took to the catwalk.

The titters from the reporters were louder this time. Tess winced inwardly. No number of suggestions had deterred Lucile from continuing to name her dresses.

'Could be that dressing gown of hers that went down with the ship,' chuckled one reporter, a bit too loudly.

The tiny but regal Mary Pickford lifted a small gloved hand to her lips, as if to suppress a titter herself. Lucile's lips were pulled tight now, her expression still.

Tess could leave her alone up there no longer. Without a thought of what she would do when she got there, she approached the stage.

Lucile glanced swiftly in her direction, her face pale as clear ice. Tess braced for a scene, an order to leave. She was probably walking into a disaster.

But there was no surprise in Lucile's eyes. None. Tess's suspicion was true; this was a programmed drama. Elinor had hatched it with her sister's full knowledge, knowing that nobody got away with surprising Lucile. It was a waste to be indignant, Tess told herself. Lucile could get through this now, appearing to be vindicated, and it didn't matter if it wasn't true; it just had to appear to be true – until the show was over.

'My dear friends, I want to introduce to you a promising new young talent whom I have been mentoring,' she said, turning toward her seated guests. 'And here she is, Tess Collins!'

Again, scattered applause. Close up, Tess could see the lines curving deep across Lucile's brow and the dark shadows under her eyes. Even if she was a pawn here, she could still give Lucile this one last thing. She smiled out at the audience.

Lucile hardly paused. 'And just in time, too,' she said with a flick of more than triumph. 'The next gown you will see, ladies and gentlemen' – her gaze flickered as she glanced at the reporters – 'is the creation of Miss Collins. A quite elegant confection in silk – without a name, unfortunately.'

The spotlight swung to the catwalk entrance, allowing Tess's surprise to go unnoticed. Elinor had persuaded Lucile to keep her gown in the show? Lucile surely would have tossed it in a bin. And yet here it was.

The mannequin moved forward, not as languorously as before, the lights dancing off the fabric, deepening its texture. As the model turned, the shortened skirt flipped up, revealing a quick display of skin above her boots. A murmur went through the room, but no titters.

'Miss Collins, tell us about it,' Lucile said suddenly. 'This is your creation.'

Tess looked out at the crowd, hesitating, wondering what she could possibly stammer out. 'This is a dress designed to move naturally, that is uninhibiting,' she began. 'But I wanted it to be practical and modern, so a woman could get out of carriages and motor cars quickly, walk fast on sidewalks; run without tripping over her skirt. Everything is changing, and women's clothes have to change, too.' She paused. A few heads nodded slightly, and she felt encouraged. 'Within a few years, for example, we won't be fussing with dozens of buttons on our gowns; we'll have new kinds of closures, and that's just one thing. But right now, even though it may seem daring, we can shorten our skirts. We don't need to be sedate anymore.' Was she actually saying these things? The mannequin had completed her turns and was moving backstage. Tess watched her go, her critical eye in full operation. Maybe the bodice worked, after all. But it was so plain, nobody would want it. The applause was lively. She saw in Lucile's face a flash of surprise: the audience actually liked that boringly simple gown.

'My young student and I will now alternate the introductions,' she suddenly announced. She bowed to Tess, seemingly enjoying her startled look. And probably also the fact that the rude tittering had stopped.

Pinky stirred restively in her seat as the show progressed. She couldn't think of a less likely event for her to be covering, apart from the fact that she was here to follow the drama of it all. Sitting for a couple of hours staring at dresses filled with furbelows and ribbons was not her idea of a good time, although Tess's contribution looked easy and comfortable. She looked around at the women in the room. Hard to believe they could be so fascinated by clothes, of all dreary things. Their faces looked waxen, carefully powdered; their lips various shades of cherry pink. They sat erect, probably held up by corsets.

Her eyes continued to travel around the room, her gaze stopping finally on the tall Mrs. Bremerton, who somehow managed to look totally fascinated and totally miserable at the same time. Getting the combination right must take a lot of practice. Why had Tess looked so upset at the sight of her? Idly, Pinky doodled with her pencil on a copy of the program, then stopped, pencil poised in the air.

Of course. That's who the other man was. It fit. Tess had asked about him, talked about him – and then, not a word. What an idiot she was! Her father had guessed it immediately; he hadn't lost his sharpness for reporting. For her, it had to hit her in the face. So what did she do with this one? She shifted her gaze to Tess, almost wishing she hadn't figured it out.

The show was almost over. The model wearing the wedding gown – the pièce de résistance of Lucile's design work – swept down the catwalk with full drama, the dress sparkling as its intricate beading danced in the light. A burst of appreciative applause filled the room as Lucile signaled the lights to rise. The quartet, on cue, switched to a livelier tune. The guests began to stir, smoothing down their dresses, chatting in low tones with one another, smiling at Madame Lucile, some with genuine admiration.

With Elinor hovering, Mary Pickford chose one of Lucile's gowns, dictating the changes she wanted in a lightly musical voice. 'No tulle under the skirt, please,' she instructed. 'And would you shorten it – oh, maybe seven or eight inches? I like shorter skirts.' She did not order Tess's dress, but really, that was too much to expect.

After the audience members sipped tea and ate tiny

lemon biscuits, effusively thanking Lucile as they drifted toward the door, Tess realised that there had been only two more orders for gowns – one from, of all people, the cool ex-Mrs. Bremerton.

'There will be more orders later,' Elinor said at her elbow. 'My bet is, someone will order your dress.' She sighed. 'Still, things are changing. It's in the air, really, and I wish Lucile would heed it. Or at least stop giving her dresses these ridiculous names.'

'Why didn't you tell me Lucile was in on this little ruse?'

'That you were coming? My dear, with her volatility, I wouldn't dare leave that to chance. And if I had told you, you wouldn't have come. Anyway, it's just as well; she knows it was a performance.'

'And I was one of the players.' What did it matter anymore? She could walk away from the deception. But she felt compelled to offer something else. 'I don't think I've fully understood before today how much talent she has. Her gowns are gorgeous, truly beautiful, but, more than that, their structure is so artful.'

'It's true,' Elinor replied quietly. 'But her time is gone.'

Slowly Tess walked toward Lucile. Madame was standing straight as a rod of iron at the entrance, chatting brightly in her throaty voice, saying goodbye to the last of her guests, waving the reporters out with a well-manicured hand. For just a moment, after all were gone, she stared after them, her face unreadable.

'Lucile?'

Lucile started, then turned around. 'Ah, Tess, now I'll learn your true motives for showing up today.' Her bright smile was back in place. 'Wasn't this fun? That silly Isadora Duncan, always complaining about gaining weight. But did you notice she didn't hesitate to ask for hot chocolate instead of tea? Really, these actresses. And did you see that poker-faced Mrs. Bremerton? She obviously came out just fine from her divorce; that's apparent from her pick. There is just so much to do now. We—'

'Lucile, please.'

A pause. 'Ah, as I suspected. You haven't changed your mind, have you? This was – how best to put it? An *acted* show of support.'

'I hear you expected that.' Tess felt very calm. 'But in another way I'm not acting at all. You didn't know about the scheme to arrest Jim, and I'm sorry I denounced you.'

'I don't forgive you, Tess.'

'I'm not asking for forgiveness, Lucile.'

'You are being outrageously—'

'Rude? Impudent? Arrogant?'

'Beyond your station.'

She looked so fierce and, yes, fragile. 'I don't work for you anymore,' Tess said gently.

'Then why are you here?' Lucile demanded.

'I came back to help you through this day. I want no part of ruining you or your business.'

'Well, that's appropriate, I'd say.'

'You really are a masterly designer, Lucile. And this is a superb collection.'

'I'm glad you realise that.'

'I'm sure it will sell.'

'Well, it will, of course.' Lucile's voice was slightly thin.

Suddenly she reached out a hand and rested it on Tess's arm. 'Stay with me,' she said quickly. 'I'll train you, if you want to stay in this country. Or you can come back to England with me. I'll take very good care of you, give you every opportunity. That's a promise.'

Slowly but firmly, Tess shook her head. Lucile's nature wouldn't change. It would always be to praise and criticise and goad and condemn, ensnaring everyone into a constant dance of trying to please, running harder, doing anything to please Madame. Not only could she *see* the web; she could *feel* it, and she'd not let its sticky pleasures catch her again.

'We would end up hating each other,' she said.

For a long moment, Lucile said nothing. 'Well, that's a decision made,' she finally managed. Nothing soggy now. Crisp, crisp as a cracker. 'Perhaps you're right.'

She patted her hair and began to turn away, then stopped, as if making a decision. She turned, pointing to her office. 'Please come into my office – I have something to tell you privately.'

There was nothing private about that glass-encased box, although it might seem to be so to a woman who lived always in the public eye. Without comment, Tess followed Lucile.

The door closed. A pungent, slightly acrid smell filled the room, even though the wilted flowers had all been removed. Lucile's desk was a chaotic jumble. Unused invitations, a spilled box of face powder, scissors, even a wad of used chewing gum – one of Lucile's vices, according to Cosmo – wrapped in paper. Lucile seemed to notice none of it. She folded her arms together, turning partially away from Tess, not looking at her as she spoke. 'You called me regal once. Remember?'

'Yes, I remember.'

'I'm not, of course. I came from a family as impoverished in its way as yours. I scrabbled up the ladder, dear, breaking a fair number of rules along the way. But I came from nothing to something. I like the taste of success, however unattractive in a woman. Do you understand?'

'Yes.'

'Of course, you do. When I met you, you were ready to fight your way up that ladder. I saw me in you.' She turned to face Tess squarely. 'I lost a child at birth, long ago. She would have been about your age. Am I to lose her again?'

'Are you talking about *me*?' Tess managed, astonished.

'Of course.'

Tess tried to regain her voice, but the silence was awkward; she saw that in Lucile's eyes. 'I'm sorry you lost your child,' she finally said. 'I had no idea—'

'I can see that. Well, I thought I would try. But you must know that risking humiliation is not something I do lightly.' Lucile began picking at a small tray of tea cakes balanced precariously, amid all the jumble, on the edge of the desk. 'I suppose you have reason to be glad you aren't my daughter. I would have been a terrible mother.'

'Lucile, I am truly sorry.'

'Never mind, I can see by your reaction that it's done.' And yet she made no move to leave the office. She began picking off bits of frosting from a cake, absentmindedly dropping them back on the tray.

'I'm not one who likes to revisit traumatic events, as you know,' she said, not quite in control of her voice. 'But there is something else to clear up.'

'What is that?'

She straightened her shoulders resolutely. 'What happened in the lifeboat.'

Tess caught her breath and waited.

'I did the exact right thing in ordering those men not to go back, and I stand by that. I don't care what people have to say about an empty boat – one takes care of oneself first.' She paused. 'There is something, I suppose, to what Jean Darling was saying. About avoiding blame. About the impossibility of forgiving oneself.' She waved her hand distractedly. 'That kind of hand-wringing isn't for me, but I might as well tell you, somebody did grab at my leg in the lifeboat. Quite a shocking, frightening thing, really.'

'What did you do?' The close air in the room was making Tess faintly ill.

'Will you let me finish? You might want to. I told you, someone grabbed me. I couldn't see who was pawing me.' It was almost as if she were talking only to herself now. 'I thought it was some clumsy seaman. So I pushed him away, as hard as I could. And then I heard a splash.'

Silence. It was several seconds before Tess could respond. 'What happened next?' she finally said.

'I called for assistance, of course. He grabbed at me again, and one of the men pushed him away.'

'With an oar?'

'Yes.'

'My God, Lucile.'

'I don't know who did it, if that's your next question. It was dark.'

The convenience of night. 'You must have some idea.'

'If you're asking if it was Cosmo, I could hardly believe *that*. And you'll be happy to know it wasn't your sailor, because he got up and fought the man who was trying to help me. Almost capsized us. I've told you all I know.'

'Why didn't you say all this when you testified?'

'Are you serious? I would be accused of murder.' Lucile began pacing. 'I wasn't the only one,' she said. 'You stand there, looking so shocked; why did I tell you this? There were other ... splashes, but I could see nothing. We wanted to survive – what is wrong with that? What are you going to do now? Tell the world?'

'Oh, Lucile.' She wanted to cry and scream at the same time.

Lucile's voice was rising, her words coming faster. 'Why are those of us who survived to blame? Did we cause that calamity? Do you remember what it was like to watch that ship go down? My God, I couldn't believe it. Tipped onto its bow like a toy, a toy of nature, a sight like none anyone has seen, and we're supposed to come out of it unscathed? Go back to civility, men tipping their hats to women, saying "after you" when getting into the lifeboats – what a joke! If there is a God, surely he was amused – how stupid are we to sail the ocean on something built out of toothpicks? *We* were the toys! What is going on in this world?'

And with that cry she stopped pacing. 'I find it hard to believe that I was the only one pushing him away, but maybe I was.'

'You weren't trying to kill the man.'

'Of course not. I simply didn't want to be touched. At least, that's what I tell myself.' Her back was to Tess now. That proud, rigid spine, straight – inflexible.

'There was no time to think,' Tess managed.

'Yes, yes, but you notice, of course, that I never told anybody. My character wasn't any stronger than Jean's.'

'So why *are* you telling me?'

'Oh, just to clear the air, I suppose. Things always have been a bit murky between you and me.'

'Complicated,' Tess said softly.

Lucile turned at that and gave her a quick, hard smile. 'My dear, *all* my relationships are complicated. Good luck to you.'

Tess was suddenly blinking back tears. 'You brought me here,' she said. 'You gave me a chance. You pointed the way, and I thank you for that.'

'Oh, for goodness' sake, don't get weepy. Really, that's enough. Goodbye, Tess.'

'Lucile—'

But Lucile turned to the door, opened it, and walked away, leaving Tess in midsentence.

'James!' she cried out, clapping her hands angrily. 'Where are you? Get somebody to clean up that tea table, will you? And let's get these curtains down tonight. Isn't anybody going to do any work around here except me?'

Tess left the office, walking slowly toward the elevator and Elinor, who was waiting at the door.

'So she told you what happened,' Elinor said calmly. 'She did say this morning she wanted the chance to do that.'

'Maybe she's blaming herself for something she couldn't have done on her own. She couldn't have had the power to push that man off the boat.'

'She told me it was Tom Sullivan who wielded the oar.'

'On Cosmo's order? Or hers?'

'We'll never know. My guess? That sneaky oaf did it on his own. See how we piece our stories together? To redeem ourselves, I suppose.'

'Why did she want me to know?'

'She decided after listening to Jean Darling's testimony. Said it was something she had to do. I know she didn't ask you to keep this private, but I hope you will.'

Tess could only nod. Another choice.

'By the way, Lucile asked me to give you this.' Elinor held out a small velvet bag and put it in Tess's hand. 'She called it a memento. Something about keeping you safe and soothing the heart. She said you would know what she meant.'

Tess slowly undid the strings, her eyes stinging. The moonstone earrings.

'Please don't say you can't take them – please don't do that to her.'

Tess slowly nodded again. 'Thank her for me,' she said.

'I hope you know she's dreadfully sad about losing you.'

'There was much more I wanted to say.'

'So did she, I suspect.' Elinor sighed for a second time. 'But what is done is done. You read the future right, if that's any consolation. My sister can't change. Do you have any plans? What are you going to do?'

'I don't know.'

'Well, good luck. You know you're in a small category of people – you survived Lucile.' Elinor said this almost tenderly, taking the harshness out of her words. 'Stay in touch, and if you ever need any help look me up. That is, if you ever get out to California.' She paused. 'I'll speak to a few people about finding you a job. I hear the one who calls herself Coco Chanel is hiring. Moving beyond hats quite quickly. You obviously have a future in – what is that expression Lucile hates? I remember – the "rag trade."'

Tess smiled. 'I'm still very good at buttons, though they'll soon be out of date.'

'Follow up – it's a start, anyway. Oh, before I forget—' She pulled an envelope from her bag. 'This came for you yesterday.'

Tess's heart leapt when she looked at the handwriting, each letter so carefully, painstakingly drawn. So her messages home got through. She pictured her mother squinting under the light of a candle as she wrote. Home, a connection to home. She tucked the letter into her pocket to read later, when she was alone.

She stepped into the elevator, catching a last glimpse of Lucile pacing the aisles of the shop, her hair slightly askew, giving orders right and left as the elevator doors closed.

Just as she had begun to understand, it was over. Her thoughts flashed back to the grand woman who had walked the deck of the *Titanic* as if she owned the world. Madame Lucile. Walking beside her, hearing the silky rush of awed whispers left in her wake. Do you know who that is? The most famous, the best, couturiere in the world. To wear her clothes was to be at the pinnacle. And it had all dissolved – all a fantasy.

Tess closed her eyes, opening them only as the doors drew apart on the ground floor. No one hovered – no yelling reporters, no clients. She stepped out of the elevator, feeling herself leaving one dream and entering another. The only reality of the moment was her mother's letter.

Chapter 17

Pinky stood on the sidewalk, looking uncharacteristically diffident as Tess stepped out of the building. All the society guests had vanished, but there were still clusters of hired shopgirls waiting for the town cars, bubbling with giggles about the posh event to which they had been invited at the last minute, with payment, no less.

'You stayed,' Tess said with a rush of gratitude.

'Oh, I thought maybe I'd wait for you. Didn't think you were going to hang around up there. Want to come to my place for dinner?'

Maybe it was the kindness of the offer, maybe she would have let go anyway, but the tears came.

Pinky looked a little alarmed, but that didn't stop her from awkwardly patting Tess on the back. 'I can't say I understand what you were trying to do, but you gave better than she deserved,' she said.

'I had to give back something. I owe her a great deal.'

'Was it hard to walk out again? Were you tempted to stay?'

Tess shook her head. 'No. I'm not making those compromises anymore.'

'You don't have to tell me; I can see how she eats everybody up. But your dress looked nice.'

Tess managed a shaky smile; any fashion comment from Pinky had to be a novelty.

'I'm wondering why you got all flustered when you saw Mrs. Bremerton,' Pinky ventured. 'Something was happening, and I think I know what.' Maybe that was too blunt, but there it was, out in the open. Things were always better out in the open. Most of the time, anyway.

'You're a good observer,' Tess said.

For an awkward moment, neither of them spoke.

'I don't know what you're doing tomorrow, but would you like to come to the suffragist parade? It starts in Washington Square, under the arch. Have you seen it yet? It's a beautiful arch.' Changing the subject was not Pinky's strength, and she was stumbling over her words now in a rush. 'Remember I told you about the white horse? It's beautiful, and the woman riding it has this incredible long hair, so it will be very dramatic; photographers like that. I'm hoping for the front page. Especially if the women raising money for a memorial to the men of the *Titanic* show up. They're furious because the suffragists are saying the *Titanic* women shouldn't have been so quick to let the men die instead of themselves. Quite a juicy little story.'

'Pinky, it was chaotic,' Tess said wearily, not wanting to relive it all once more.

'Well, equality cuts all ways. Everything gets political, that's all I know. So there will be jeers and jokes, but it's a good thing when women pull together.'

'Thank you, I'll think about it,' Tess said. Suddenly she envied Pinky. It was easy for her, seeing everything so simply; it must be comfortable to be so confident of choices.

'Why Bremerton instead of Jim?' Pinky said unexpectedly.

'It's not like that. They're very different.'

'What does that mean?'

'Are you asking as a reporter or as a friend?'

Pinky had already decided, somewhere around the time that fancy wedding dress upstairs floated past her stupefied vision. 'A friend,' she said.

'Jack is—' She groped for the right words. 'He's a magical man from a magical world.'

Pinky looked honestly puzzled. 'Where do you go with that?'

'That's what I'm trying to decide.'

'Well, he's rich and must be in love with you, so I guess you think you'd be crazy to pass him up. I suppose you want to get married. I thought about that once, and there was this man ...' Pinky's voice turned wistful. 'But I couldn't do it. I don't want marriage – I'd feel like a mouse in a trap.'

'It doesn't have to be like that.'

'Usually it does.' Pinky wasn't sure how to tell Tess what she couldn't bear to lose: the thrill of walking into a room, knowing that, as a reporter, she carried an identity that commanded attention, if not respect, knowing the job shielded her from being dismissed or ignored, knowing it gave her access to such a wide variety of worlds, even though sometimes they scared her. 'I couldn't give up my job for anything,' she said. 'You have, and that's brave.'

'What are you saying?'

'You gave up your job for Jim.' And this time Pinky had the sense to say no more. She had seen the look on both their faces yesterday.

The two women stood in silence for a long moment.

'I've got a big chicken ready to go in the oven,' Pinky finally said shyly.

'Thank you. But not tonight. I have things I have to do.' Impulsively, Tess hugged her.

'Maybe I'll see you tomorrow?' Pinky asked.

'Maybe.'

'If you come, it'll mean something.'

'Oh? What would it mean?'

'Just an instinct. Bye, Tess.' Pinky turned and walked slowly up the block in the direction of her office, wondering if she was right or wrong. And maybe it wasn't true that she would give up anything that threatened her job. That didn't make her safer. Maybe the only thing that mattered was giving up the idea that there was a place to hide. She inhaled deeply; maybe it was time for her to take a risk. Tess had.

Van Anda eyed Pinky as she made her way across the newsroom to his desk. Even with plenty of practice, he couldn't quite read her mood. She had lost a little of her bounce lately, and he knew the signs – she was getting bored with the *Titanic* beat. But hell, she was still churning out great stories.

'So, what've you got for me from the fashion show?' he said with a grin, but she didn't seem to be in a joking mood.

'They had to pack the room with women salesclerks to make it look respectably full,' she said. 'Not a good day for the House of Lucile.'

'How much can you give me? And get something in there about the clothes, for God's sake. Women want that.'

'There was a nice yellow dress. Silk.'

'You have an eye for fashion, I see.'

It was their usual comfortable back-and-forth. But Pinky couldn't leave it at that, not today. 'Carr, the *World* offered me a job.'

Van Anda straightened fast, his chair creaking under him. 'Job? What sort of job? They don't use women.'

She stared him in the eye. 'Yes, I know. Just good reporters.'

Van Anda cursed silently; he had flubbed that one. 'They can't have offered you much. You're not considering this, are you? You'd be crazy to leave the *Times*.'

There it was, her opportunity. All the way back from Lady Duff's loft, she had been rehearsing what she would say. She could do anything – dive into any story, ask any outrageous question, pursue a lead or a source with total persistence – and she didn't give up until she got what she wanted. She was proud of what she did, and proud of how she did it. She was all of this. And she had the respect of other reporters and her editor. So what was tying her tongue?

'Look, maybe you need a break from disaster stories. I can put you on a team investigating the mayor's cronies – some good stuff there. We—'

'I want a raise.'

'What?'

'I want more money. I deserve it.'

'You get good money, for this business.'

'The typesetters get fifty cents an hour, and I get less.' She smiled at his expression. 'Didn't think I knew that, did you?'

Van Anda groaned, leaning forward. 'Pinky, you're a smart woman. But things are tight in this business right now.'

'They're always tight.'

'I wish I could help you on this.' She had to be bluffing – she would never leave the *Times*. No sane reporter would leave the classiest paper in the city.

But her courage was growing. 'I want a raise. I want a dollar an hour.'

'You've got to be kidding.' Van Anda was stalling now. Lose one of his best reporters? Not a good idea. 'Why don't we talk a few months from now, and I'll see what I can do.'

Pinky tried to swallow past the dryness in her throat. Here she was, walking the plank, sawing it off behind her. 'No, sir, I need a raise *now*.'

Van Anda leaned back in his chair, staring at her. 'You would actually go work for that rag?'

She thought of her father, of her constant money dance with Mrs. Dotson. 'Yes.'

'Go write your story; let me think about this.'

'I would rather settle it now. Get that off my mind, which will let me write a better story.'

Here she stood, demanding to be paid almost the same as his other reporters and, truth be told, she was worth it. That much money for a woman? It wasn't done. But times were changing. Lord, who knew what was next with women like this. She wasn't backing down, or smiling, or trying to win him over. She was setting the bar. Amazing.

'What are they offering you?'

'A dollar an hour.'

'Jesus, where do they get the money?'

'Beats me.'

'Okay, kid. Seventy-five cents an hour. Best I can do.'

'One dollar.'

They stared at each other. If there was ever a time when she mustn't break eye contact, it was now.

Van Anda threw his pencil down on the desk. 'Okay, one dollar. You better be worth it.'

She grinned wide, but her legs were trembling. 'You already know I am, Carr.'

'Yep. Do me a favor, will you? Keep this under your hat or all the men will want more money, too.' He was scratching his ear, looking a bit shocked at himself; they would joke about it later, maybe tomorrow.

Pinky sailed back to her desk, humming. She had done it;

she had good news to bring home to her father. Forget the chicken. Tonight it would be fresh corn and a flank steak. Today, she felt she could see the future. It was all right. And she would, as her father said she would, somehow, herself, someday, dance on the moon. Or, at least, see Africa.

The solid click of the lock on her apartment door was an incredible relief. Alone, Tess sank into a chair and pulled her mother's letter from her pocket. Just the sight of the familiar handwriting gave her a sudden longing for home, so much so that the first words on the page were shocking:

> *My dear daughter, you've survived a terrible tragedy, but above all, don't think about coming home.*

She read on, her hands holding the paper so tightly, it almost tore:

> *You have done a brave thing, and I want you to find your place in that new world of New York, whatever it might be. We both know that if you were here you'd be cleaning parlors and mending dresses for the rest of your life. I lie in bed at night staring at the ceiling and trying to imagine what it must be like. I can almost imagine it being me.*

There was more, mainly news about her father and her brothers and sisters, and about the neighbours and the price of cheese and meat and the bad year for potatoes. She read eagerly, starved for the plainness of her past life. And then at the end:

I've told you to look for opportunity, dear Tess. Keep your head up, not down. Don't settle for safety. Push forward – you are not foolish to try.

Tess folded the letter smooth, staring at it on the table in front of her.

You are not foolish to try.

Try for what? Jack would open the whole world for her. Not only that, he could help her open up the world for her mother. To think of it, to think of her mother freed of the grinding labors of her life, of having some ease and comfort, was overwhelming.

What an extraordinary thing to have a man like that love her. It made her feel valued in a way she had never known, as if she danced inside a fairy tale. She had dreamed about him, and had then found herself gently enfolded into his version of the world. But perhaps the same had been true of the second Mrs. Bremerton. And the first.

She could allow herself to think of Jim, too. To remember the energy and excitement of life bursting from him, surrounding her, making her laugh and dream and think – that's what he represented. Not security, just hope.

There was no more time to avoid the only question that mattered. Why was she thinking of choosing a man who could make her whole? How could she do that when she didn't yet know who she was in this new world?

She stood and walked over to the dresser, where she had placed Jim's lifeboat, picking it up, tracing its lines and curves with her finger, wondering suddenly if it would float. She carried it to the washbasin, drew water, and placed it gently inside. It rocked a bit on its slightly rounded bottom, then moved forward, bumping against the side of the basin. How skillfully it had been carved. She thought of Jim's deft fingers, his excitement when he took her to the carpentry shop. She waited. Why did this matter? It didn't, of course. But it did float. And she found herself yearning to hope.

The sky was fully dark when she knocked on the door of Jack Bremerton's office. She waited, it seemed for a long time, before she heard the rattle of the chain inside as it was unhooked.

The man named Mr. Wheaton – Jack's secretary – opened the door, his eyes widening. 'He isn't expecting you.'

'I know, but I have to talk to him.'

'Oh, dear.' He hesitated, as if debating whether to let her in. 'Well, he's not here at the moment, but please come in. He's with Mr. Ford at dinner. Is something wrong?' He was watching her carefully.

'I do need to talk to him, Mr. Wheaton.'

'Of course. Would you like a sherry?' He moved to a sideboard, picked up a crystal decanter, and poured a glass of the wine-red liquid, giving a quick little bow as he handed it to her. 'You mean a great deal to him, you know. I do hope nothing is wrong.'

Tess sipped the sherry, wishing Jack would appear. She didn't want to talk with Wheaton, not now.

'I'm happy to hear the seaman who rowed Lifeboat One escaped the trap set by the Duff Gordons,' he said.

'It was a great relief,' she replied in surprise. She wondered how he knew.

Wheaton turned and placed the decanter on the sideboard. He seemed to make a sudden decision. He looked at her, his features sharpening. 'You know who arranged that, I presume?'

It took a second or two before she realised what he was telling her. 'It was Jack?'

'Yes.'

'Oh, my goodness.' He had done that for her. He had saved Jim from shame and trouble. He had done that, taking a burden of worry from her shoulders. The fact that he was powerful enough to do it so quickly was amazing. What an act of tremendous charity.

'He doesn't want you to know.'

'Why?' she asked. She wished he would come in the door right now, this minute, so that she could thank him to his face immediately.

'He didn't want it to influence you. He didn't want you to marry him because you were – grateful. It wouldn't be enough.'

'No, it wouldn't.'

'I'm guessing by your manner why you're here. I realise Jack is impulsive and all this has happened quickly. But I must say, if you have concerns he is a fine, upstanding man.'

'I know that – I truly have never doubted it,' she said.

Together they heard the click of the lock on the front door.

'Goodbye, Miss Collins.' Wheaton smiled faintly and disappeared through another door, closing it gently behind him.

And now Jack was standing in front of her. He blinked, startled, then seemed to know, without a word being spoken, why she was there.

'Let me hold you first,' he said.

'I can't, I just have to say it.'

'No, I will. You aren't going to marry me.'

'You are an amazing, quite wonderful man. But no, I can't.'

'Why not?'

'I don't feel what I want to feel.' It hurt to say it; his eyes widened.

He strode to the sideboard and poured himself a glass of sherry. His voice, though still relaxed, had an edge. 'Tess, I love you. I will make you happy, you can do anything. There's plenty of money. I told you, if you want a design shop, I will give you one. What do you want? I'll get it for you. I want to spoil you.'

Tess's thoughts flew to Cosmo and Lucile. 'I don't want to be spoiled.'

'It's perfect, you and me. Where is your courage?'

'I'm trying to exhibit some now.'

'Go ahead, then. I'm listening.'

There was no way to express her doubts gently. 'I feel borne along on your enthusiasm and certainty, but it isn't real enough for me.'

Jack seemed back in total control of himself. 'Tess, do you think I'm under any illusions about the source of your attraction to me? May I say it bluntly, dear? It's all right to want money and security; women have their reasons for marrying older, established men. It's the way the world works.' He flashed one of his calm, wry smiles. 'We each have our bargaining chips.'

'I wonder if we both are acting on what we *want* to be real. You've had two wives already.' She thought of the first Mrs. Bremerton, standing at Lucile's doorway, as hard and contained as a marble statue.

He blinked. 'That's cruel of you. I can't undo my past mistakes.'

She swallowed. 'You might eventually want a fourth one.'

'So *that's* what this is all about.'

'The fear of that might make me become someone different. But that's not why, Jack. It's much more.'

'What *matters*? What matters besides us? I adore you. What more do you want?'

What more, indeed? She would have comfort beyond her dreams. But not to be able to give back in similar measure – to love him equally – would leave an emptiness that couldn't be filled. And then, eventually, she wouldn't try. She would take; she wouldn't give. She would be left with a tepid heart.

'To be wholly myself first,' she whispered.

'If we all waited for that, we'd do nothing.'

'I want to try.'

His eyes wavered. He rubbed a hand through his hair as he drained the glass, then stood and stared at the wall. 'Well, at least you're telling me to my face. I tend not to do that in my life. So there's my character flaw, dear. I'm a coward. But good at chess.'

'Jack, you saved Jim, and I thank you for that from the bottom of my heart. It was a selfless act.'

'That damn Wheaton!'

'I'm glad I know.'

'Well, it wasn't selfless. I just wanted you, with unencumbered emotions. It was the easiest way to guarantee it. And I suspect Jim has something to do with your change of heart.'

'Yes, he does. But he doesn't know it.'

'Well, perhaps you should let him know.'

'I'm afraid it's too late for that.'

His reply was almost kind. 'Perhaps not.'

'In a way, it doesn't matter.' She could tell that he didn't understand, so she switched the subject. 'Why did you do something so enormously generous?'

'Because I like having the power to get what I want – that's what it's about. I enjoy winning. It was just one more thing I could do.'

'I don't believe it's only that.'

He sighed. 'All right, Tess. I don't like people like the Duff Gordons who casually ruin other people's lives, and I'm happy to thwart them. And I don't like companies like White Star. Lord knows, I've made a lot of money off their kind, but that doesn't mean I believe their delusions. When they get in trouble, they'll offer up anybody to save themselves. Here's the joke – companies like White Star end up believing their own boasts. World's grandest ship, indestructible – that kind of thing. That's when they get in trouble. And they don't see it. So they do it again and again. And people like me find ways to profit.'

'That sounds – very American.'

'It is. Look,' he added slowly, 'you're afraid I'll get restless and move on; that's what my wives said. You could change that.'

'Not by myself.'

'Maybe that's what I wanted most. Your faith in me. It's obviously not there.' He looked at her sadly, tenderly. 'You are so fresh and young, my dear. Perhaps I would kill that with my own cynical take on life.'

There was nothing more to say. They stood apart, strangely relieved, without grief. 'I wish you well,' she said. 'Jack, I'm trying to be the person I believe I am, because if I don't do that, if I play a role, any role, I'll end up making us both unhappy.'

'Like the famous Lucile?'

'Perhaps.'

He let out an almost derisive snort. 'She certainly proved a powerful role model.'

Tess turned to go. She had done it, snipped her second lifeline in this new country. Yet there was no uncertainty, no anguish, just that same pervasive sadness that had taken her out of Lucile's loft and brought her here.

'What made up your mind?'

'My mother, in part. Mostly my own common sense.'

He paused, absorbing her words. 'And I don't fit into that.' He raised a hand when she started to reply. 'I guess that proves I can't start making more out of my life by shaping yours.' He moved forward, giving her a gentle, brief embrace. 'Goodbye, Tess.'

She hugged him back. 'Goodbye, Jack.' She opened the door, then squeezed the knob tightly as she closed it behind her.

The morning was cloudy, with a soft wind blowing, bending the fragile tulips that grew in clusters along the edge of the flower beds at Union Square. Tess, her loose hair blowing in the wind, gazed across the park to the short, nondescript building that held Jim's woodworking shop. She had no reason to think she would see him, and certainly no intention of approaching him, but somehow she had found herself here, waiting for something to come clear. Perhaps she was just here to say a silent goodbye. She would soon know.

And then she saw him. His lanky figure, slightly hunched forward, his gait loose and springy – a young man hurrying toward his future. She couldn't make out his features under his cap, but she knew that man, those hands. I know how he feels, she told herself. Everything is open; everything is possible. How can I interfere with that?

As he reached the shop, he turned in her direction. She lifted her arm and waved slowly.

For a few seconds he stood still, poised on the step.

Then he lifted his hand and waved back; waved for a long, sweet moment. Then he turned, disappearing into the shop.

So it was, indeed, goodbye.

She made her way toward Washington Square Park, inhaling the sweet smells of spring in the air. Her step was steady. Everything was ahead.

The park was a sea of patriotic colour, with flags of red, white, and blue waving amid an array of women dressed in dazzling white. Tess walked through the crowd, amazed at the energy and excitement. Women were pushing wicker prams with swaddled, bored-looking babies in them, while others laughed and shouted to one another, some of them singing songs she had never heard. They all wore hats – silk bonnets, straw boaters – and banners across their chests proclaiming VOTES FOR WOMEN. One group was raising a large sign, a sheet inked with the words WE DEMAND EQUALITY. How many were here? Pinky's story had said this morning they expected twenty thousand people, women from the home, the theater, women's clubs; even Quakers would be on the march.

She looked around, craning her neck to see above the crowd, and spotted a graceful stone arch. This must be what Pinky had been talking about. Getting to it was taking some elbowing. 'You going to the tallyho parade, lady?' shouted a man cheerfully as she tried to squeeze by him. 'All the way up Fifth Avenue? You ladies have the strength for that?'

It was a carnival. Breathtaking. All this activity for the vote? Young girls in pinafores were running around with canvas newsbags selling suffrage magazines or twirling parasols with WE WANT THE VOTE scrawled across their cotton surfaces. Young men stood on the sidelines, poking one another and laughing.

Tess's eye was caught by one small knot of women, looking quite grim, waving a banner that read YOU DISHONOR OUR BRAVE MEN. A woman in a gray serge coat was shouting at a stout suffragist in white. As Tess moved closer, she saw that the woman in white was Mrs. Brown.

'How could you betray us by supporting these people?' yelled the woman in gray. 'You were with us on that ship! What was wrong with saving women and children first?' Her voice spiraled into the wail that was so familiar to Tess; remembering it made her shiver.

'Honey, it cuts both ways,' Mrs. Brown replied in a firm voice. 'We had good men and some rotten ones. Same for women – don't get your bloomers in such a frenzy.'

That only provoked more shouting. Another woman in white thrust her face full at the woman in gray. 'Accepting male chivalry just weakens us,' she said urgently. 'Don't you understand?'

Mrs. Brown spotted Tess and gave her a hug. 'Well, dearie, now you're seeing how we do things in America,' she said. 'I kind of wish my suffrage friends had left this particular argument for equality off the books. It's cutting down on the numbers today.' With a wave, she began to drift back into the crowd.

'Tess! Tess!'

Pinky had spotted her, and was jumping up and down to get her attention. 'You came!' She elbowed through the crowd and grabbed Tess's hand. 'Isn't this incredible?' she said. 'Everybody is here – mothers and housewives, milliners, librarians, social workers, laundry workers. Tess, everybody is for it; we're going to get the vote!'

'I've never seen so many different kinds of women in one place,' Tess said. She briefly wondered how they had all been able to get permission to leave their jobs for the march.

'We've got Chinese women here. Their feet are bound when they're babies and they can barely hobble around, so they will ride in a carriage. But *they* can vote in their country – what do you think of that?' Pinky pointed in the direction of a carriage covered in flowers. 'Our oldest suffragist is ninety-four; she'll ride in that. And we've got thousands of men joining us. Isn't that something?'

Tess nodded, not trying to talk above the din.

'We're organizing now. Come over here – I want to show you the white horse. I get my chance to ride it before we start; it'll be a good picture for the *Times*.'

'Who rides it in the parade?'

'A woman lawyer, believe it or not.'

Pinky was greeted exuberantly as she joined the crowd around the horse. 'Your turn, Pinky!' someone shouted.

Tess reached out to stroke the animal's nose. It was a beautiful mare, tall and strong, with intelligent eyes, as dazzlingly white as the dresses on the women gathering for the march. Its gaze seemed to rest on her, offering pride. She liked that.

'Up you go!'

Pinky, helped by two other women, swung herself up into the saddle. She felt filled with excitement, and it wasn't just because of her chance to play this little part in history. Last night she had feared that Tess was about to vanish, but something had changed even as they talked. She had felt it then; she knew it now.

She clutched the saddle horn, feeling strong and powerful. She could see everything from up here. 'This is wonderful!' she shouted, scanning the crowds fanning out throughout the square.

'Be sure to hold on,' Tess said.

'Hold on? I want to gallop around the park!' She glanced down at Tess. 'Come on, you've got to get up here.' She slid her way down the flank of the horse and jumped to the ground. She grabbed Tess and put the reins in her hands. 'Climb on!'

'Why not?' Tess said, laughing. And up she went, swinging her leg over the back of the magnificent animal, pulling herself tall.

The view was breathtaking. Her gaze swept out across the splendid, exciting square. Yes, she could see the horizon, the view so much more sweeping than she had expected. She saw now what Jim had seen, what had been there all the time. So much to do and know, and yes, she could do this.

And then she saw something else. A familiar figure, cap pushed back, walking toward her. She saw him moving closer, saw those clear, blue eyes. She heard a laugh – whose? Her own. And it was all right. She could be right or wrong, but her vow to herself was clear now. She would be strong and not always too careful, not settle for a smaller life, and face what was true.

What was true? Perhaps it was here, staring her in the face.

'May I help you down?' Jim said. He was standing beneath her now, his hands on the bridle, looking up, his eyes alight.

Palms up, arms stretched out, she reached toward him.

'Yes,' she said.

Author's Note

Much of the testimony in this book is taken directly from the transcripts of the U.S. Senate hearings in the aftermath of the sinking of the *Titanic.*

The basic bones of the story are true: Lady Duff Gordon, a world-famous designer, escaped with her husband and secretary in a lifeboat that, according to various reports, could have held between forty and fifty people instead of only twelve. She adamantly opposed going back for survivors. Cosmo Duff Gordon did offer the crewmen money – whether as a bribe to obey his wife's demands or as an act of gratitude, no one really knows.

Cosmo and Lucile were vilified in the press on both sides of the Atlantic. Although in my story Lucile testifies in the United States, she and Cosmo actually escaped that ordeal. However, they drew heavy attacks when they were forced to testify in England.

The public scorn and ridicule took a toll.

In the aftermath of the hearings, the House of Lucile – yes, she did give romantic names to her gowns – began its long decline, and Sir Cosmo and Lady Duff Gordon eventually separated.

Senator William Alden Smith delivered his final, emotional report on the U.S. *Titanic* hearings in a crowded Senate chamber on May 18, 1912. At the heart of the disaster, he said, was a reckless 'indifference to danger' at several key points.

He listed them: The *Titanic* was moving too fast through an iceberg field. The crew was inexperienced. There were no binoculars on board. Wireless communication was inadequate. There had been no lifeboat drills, and there were not enough lifeboats for all the people on the *Titanic.*

He successfully urged Congress to pass legislation that would mandate sufficient lifeboats on all ships.

And the great Margaret Brown – later remembered as the 'unsinkable Molly Brown' – was a true oar-wielding heroine of the *Titanic.*

All else is fiction, with the exception of a puzzle at the heart of this tragedy for which there is no single answer: why did only one lifeboat make an attempt to save those dying in the water? It is on that question that my story is built.

And finally, Millvina Dean, the last survivor of the *Titanic,* died at the age of ninety-seven on May 31, 2009. This was exactly ninety-seven years to the day after the *Titanic* was launched from Belfast.

Kate Alcott